## Also from F. Killian:

### A Boke of Swordes
a short story collection

### Bone Orchard Gospel
a roleplaying game

# A Boke of Swordes

For Howard
Who cannot read.

# A
# Boke
# of
# Swordes

## F. Killian

# Contents

# Brother War

ow do I tell thee
Of the crash of waves
And the crack of swords
And the blood upon the surf?

Two forces large
Two forces fair
Two brothers grown apart
Who met with axe and lance and song
To split the other's heart

So long they fought
That afore they met
Their quarrel they forgot

'Twas glory then
That forced good men
To march in spring's cold rains

And wet the mail
Of hard men and hale
By færie eastern sea

To each their cause
wast right and true
Not once wert they giv'n pause

Three hundred knights
Ten thousand men
Ten thousand three ahorse
All fools and blind with lordly love
And set on damnéd course

'I beg thee come,

And wet thy blade
'Less thu yieldest to me'
So cried the brother in blood red
When he his kinsman sees

'O Brother dear,'
Answered the Blue,
'Myne hungry blade thu'll fear'

Both men laugh'd loud
For both were fools proud
And thus the banners flew

And horses crash'd
As lightning lash'd
And cold Hel ope'd her gates

Two metal waves
Met on the sand
And fill'd new Golmwyr graves

On came Blue's host
Wanes kiss'd their helms
Good Sir Trystam led the van
His elden sword alight in gold
In death he failed each man

Bloody Gulen
For the foe fought
With heavy hammer blows
And on his stony black tomb-hill
A sturdy rowan grows

Youth, elder slain
Men and boys cold
Echoing cries of pain

Red brother strives
Taking many lives
His axe cuts ir'n and steel

Blue is press'd back
Wading in waves black
Their steeds wild and fear-wet

'Thu hast lost, foe'
Laugh'd Red Draspar
At his kin's desp'rate show

Then flew a shaft,
A spear's hard wood
And threw from horse Draspar
His red capes pool'd as curses flew
At his kin-foe Kaspar

With Draspar down'd
Blue tried to drown
His brother in the sea
Their steel storm'd as fury built high
Death the only decree

With cold great might
Red gave the fight
The most a man could give

A crash, a crack,
Both men did attack
And brought their guards to bear

The forces met
Two hearthguards dead-set
To slit the other's veins

And in each crowd
Stood Red and Blue
Their mottos shouted proud

Eight men Red slew
Then ten men more
And clove a path towards peace
His brother match'd that bloody road
his brother for to cease

The surf waist-high
When brothers met
Their heavy blades in hand
Lightning from their steel leapt and crack'd
As grave-wine choke'd the sand

'Comest thu kin
And slow thy arm
Afore thu tire again

'Thy age ist great
And a breast of hate
Cracks hearts and bones it burns'

Red burn'd at this
His brother's hiss
Of ill will and lost love

'Age ist wisdom,
Had not by fools
Who suck still at our mother's thumb

'Abandonest thu
All hope of fame
But infamy embrace
For the victor writes the whole truth –
None wilt recall thy face'

Red's blade of white
Blue's blade of gold
Bit and tore as foes grasp'd
In cold surf and hot blood and hate
Skin rain-stung as by asps

As they two struggl'd
Their forces follow'd
Each man's fate by steel juggl'd

Blue's men fought well,
Would not yield to Hel,
Yet there wert more of Red

The vanguard flagg'd
Men's blood fervour sagg'd
And they hope'd for an end

The brothers two
'Midst the sea-squall
Until Red slew brave Blue

But Red too hurt
His shield arm split
Bones shown from breast to wrist
Ne'er 'gain to strike a noble shape
His fate by doom was kiss'd

With Kaspar Slain
His men soon fled
And those not swift enough
Wert cut and bled by cruel Red swords
The sands with gore made rough

The victors then
Trav'l'd towards home
Though Draspar'd not see't 'gain

For on the path
His heart fled of wrath
And he to his wounds fell

Was it sorrow
Or poison'd bone marrow
What quell'd Mimir's kin?

Not e'en poets
Can tell this truth
Our dooms art all secrets

Oréanders
Where once he sat
Welcome'd home his cold corse
Tears fill'd the city like rain
This triumph was for worse

He there was burn'd,
Unlike his foe
Left in the sand to rot
Noble words wert said o'er the corse,
All kind as they were taught

But few kept love
For their master
Who for pride had don'd glove

Sons gone for good
Slain 'spite chain hoods
To serve two men's great pride

And with them dead
The Blue and the Red
All things were as before

Their sons made war,
Bit their tongues,
Lives of pain they all swore

Though they for sooth
Knew that they too
Destroy'd their own poor sons
To follow the hubris of kin
'Til they're 'neath grave-duns

The wives whisper
To their daughters
Of foolishness of men
And what was lost for want of gain
On beach and cliff and fen

Dynasties pass
Dynasties die
Yet here nothing changes

The beach and bones
And the sad ghost-tones
Rest for all time here by

I walk past graves
On cliffs above waves
Of Red men some name great

And down below
Lie endless bones
Of Blue men they laid low

It matters not
Whose blood I bear
For the pain and choler
Lives within all who claim this past –
Food for the grey scholar

Those with no tie
Wilt gladly tell
Of blood and knight-glory
Whilst we sword-kin bear the sin-weight,
Our folly but a story

The brother war
Like so many
Did all involved sore mar

Yet sometimes I,
A son-and-some, try
To picture the beach clean

To see in mind
What may have in kind
Been a place of treaty

But naught but cold
Black waves and wind
Fill the void – hide eld gold

Someday I too
Wilt field a force
To crush and maim and kill
To break kin's hearts and rend all love
To enforce our sires' will

All great songs sing
Of terrible things and war
What minstrels call fame
A shame I call, ne'er giv'n rest

# The Henge Knight

ark! All men ken the tales of Arthur's knights. Brave, grim men whose swords line the moon-table of Avalon. These tales have been told for age-on-age – since before ages were e'en right reckoned. And yet still they are told, in these days where steel and coin rule more than iron, for they cut deep into our hearts and awaken the fire our race has left to die. In these tales are Arthur's fyrd-lords made immortal. What is true may change from gleoman to gleoman, but the names and the fierce hearts remain ever the same.

It is Geol – that time in year's cold ending where the fierce Hunting God drives his mad chariot through the dark holts of the world, spirit hounds baying as they scent the prey their antlered master sets them on – when our tale begins. All the mighty hill-city of Camelot is shut tight against the cold, and the horrors they cannae hope to stand against. Shutters are nailed shut to defeat whipping winds. Hearths burn brightly beside high-stacked faggots of dry wood. Larders and stores are well-stocked with numbing ales and wines. Clubs and notched blades rest protectively 'side every locked door. And atop the tall hill squats that famed dark-doored fortress called Camelot.

Modrenacht it was. Mother's Night. From the high castle-mound echoed down the spell-songs of the woman-priests who presided. All who heard these haunting disír-drones kept courage, for they knew the guiding light of womanhood favoured their fey-loved High King. The corpses of hateful men were hung from the keep's walls, bloody claws having wrent their flesh whilst they yet drew breath. Inside, beyond the happy cries of hungry ravens, the pagan ladies of the Dragonsson's court flushed with pride and drink, kenning that that night they had their pick of all the strong champions of that doomed nation.

That king-place was of mighty stone, left by Roman princes as a looming spectre over the Britons – a ghost of an older empire. When its high walls had been claimed by Arthur he had set to restoring it – making it a cele-bration of right rather than a reminder of sorrow. But Westermen in those days did not yet have great skill in stone, and many workmen had died to bring fractured stone atop fractured stone, leaving still great gaps in the walls and holes in ceilings for rain to flow in roaring curtains through. The work continued, but slowly, and many wings of the old Latin palace stood inde-

10

fensible and unlivable. In those wings where Arthur lived with Gwenhyfar and his knights and other wives were fixings made with wood, with which his people were great craftsmen. So in that winter feasthall were the paneled walls bedecked with carven wyrms and painted battles – sigils burned on high-backed chairs and wondrous shutters of curious design. With those shutters closed, the only light upon the celebrations were the flickering fire-tongues of a hundred torches and a thousand candles. They painted black crevasses in the laughing faces of the folk of Camelot and made a haunting vision of that joyous night.

As the court ladies cavorted, choosing their bedmates and their wine, a merry gathering sat about the stage near the high seat. There, near the blood where the Christian men had been cut, gut, and sacrificed, sat that very King, and with him his greatest wife and his four nephews - those who were not also his son.

The High King rested lazily, one long leg stretched to the floor whilst he supported his weight on the stairs on one elbow and hoisted a silver cup with his free hand. He was young, yet far from a boy, with a broad chest and honey-brown hair which hung in waves past his shoulder. His trim beard showed red in the light, and his happy grey eyes fell ever on fair Gwenhyfar. He was yet a man of optimism, and suspected neither his wife nor friend-thanes of villainy, though he himself was guilty of the king-villainy all crowns bring.

And Gwenhyfar. Handsome Gwenhyfar. She was reed-thin, but with wide hips and an alluring swell to her chest. Her skin was smooth and milky-white, and her hair a tawny so dark as to appear almost black in the poor light. She loved Arthur dearly, and Camelot beside, yet even now felt the pain of new loves growing. This night her thoughts were on another man – a knight here at feast – and how she could never betray her lord for him. She did not search the hall for the treasures of Mother's Night, for fear she should fall prey to this unhappy joy, and instead sat behind her husband – so he could not see her teary blue eyes – her legs resting about his shoulders and her fingers twined in his hair. Whenever one of Arthur's laughing kin should look to her she would smile wanly and glance aside.

Of those nephews there were four, who grinned and drank and chided their ring-kin. Gareth was named the youngest, who was perhaps too noble. Next was Gaheris, who few would mark save for the matricide he was doomed to carry. Agravain was near-eldest, and murder-mad for love of his duty. Yet most marked of the Orkney princes – both in this tale and in the hearts of those what knew him – was the eldest heir: Gawain.

The others beside Gawain were but children, and he was barely a man. When this cold tale begins Gareth had not yet held a sword, and Gaheris had never been to war. Gawain had seen but twelve summers when he came to squire at Arthur's court. He had come in a time of great strife, when Arthur warred with the Northmen in their wyrm-ships, and in that chaotic time had Gawain been made a man. Even still, nearly ten years gone on this rainy Mother's Night, the Orkney heir wore on his arm a bracer woven with the beard of the first man he slew, those white-blonde hairs a dark reflection of his own thick, black locks. His brow was low and his beard newly shorn; his face a marble image with twin star eyes. His wide lips were often given to song, and when he found himself beguiled his shining smile betrayed his dangerous mien. Larger was he than his king, yet no less beautiful, and the two were known to be fast friends, despite the hatred and love he bore their mother Morgause.

Here too, not far removed, stands Myrddin, that strange and wicked warlock what held the King's fascination. He stood with fingers deep in his robe and his high black hood pulled to its greatest height. He watched for those whose wyrds most crossed the weft of Avalon, and this night his eye fell on Gawain. And beloved Gawain felt that mystic gaze and denied it, with a shiver as at a momentary draught.

Spirits 'neath that storied roof were high indeed, when unexpectedly there came a great pounding at the keep's heavy doors. So great was this announcement that it drowned the hall's pagan pipes and all present looked in surprise to the gate. Presently the doors were thrust open and sheets of grey rain drenched the hall's far end. And from this watery curtain rode a fearsome figure, his terrible steed unbothered by the fortress's many steep steps and narrow bridges which doubtless it had journeyed on to the heart of this king-hill.

No greater man had any there seen, for in height and breadth there could be no equal. At first many thought him troll or ogre, and swords and dirks hastily were retrieved. Yet he sat atop his mount with more grace and ease than ever some giant-kin could perform. He was handsome as well, though he was strange and eery, and there were a few women in that court who fantasied that they should take him as their Mother's Night choice. Yet clearly this was no mortal man for, though his skin seemed clear and pale, he glowed a ghostly green, as if a drowning-spirit in the fenns. His attire as well was all in green, e'en the furred hood which hid his brow and rested wide upon his shoulders. Greeny hair hung low from his cloak and lay, like concealing chamber-shrouds, over his thick arms. A beard of the same hung over his chest entire, and rested amongst the mane of his horse, whose hair was also green acrost, though darker on the coat. He wore no armour and carried no shield, and his horse wore only a finely sewn cloth and a noble's saddle. In one mighty fist he held a branch of holly, its red berries winking with excitement, and in the other he held a monstrous axe.

The iron in the visitor's hand was ugly - wicked sharp and dearly beaten. Its head was nearly four feet from aft to fore, and hung as far from top to beard's bottom. The pitted iron showed green in the light - for what other colour would it show - and beaten gold wrapped its long haft. Gold as well danced in runes along the cruel edge - witch-spells to curse and fell. Where gold did not fall on its long handle - as long at least as any a mortal man - green iron bound it, so only the briefest hint of the lively wood beneath was shown. Where bark did show were more runes set - this time in vert - and about this shaft were wrapped also many ribbons of that same cursed co-lour, all bound to the axehead. And, though this dealer of death doubtless weighed a stone or two or maybe more, he held it as lightly as the sprig in his other fist. It was no new nor heavy thing for this aberration to take a life.

Casting his cold eyes about the silent gathering, he spoke in a deep and resonant timbre, "Tellest thu me, who amongst thee ith greatest here? Whose crown holdeth thine hearts?"

All present stood silent as his bass voice echoed, entranced as they were by the cursèd hue which draped him. Some thought him handsome, many thought him strange, and all found him terrible. They waited, unmoving, for their High King to lead them. To answer this unworldly challenge with iron, wit, or verve.

Arthur stood, his strong heart not as quelled as others, and the Princes Orkney stood beside. "Ye are welcome," quoth the King, that estimable lord of graciousness and ambition. "I am Arthur, the Dragonsson, and ye are come to Camelot's hall. Surely ye know of it, and of me, yet I ken naught of ye. By what are ye called and why are ye come?"

The knight sneered with venom. "I have no need of welcome, and mean no time here to spend. Of Camelot I indeed do know, and I ken it to be-eth the hame of mighty men. No iron nor horse-foe mayeth slay these men. These dealers of injury. No war taketh from them their breaths. I seek to prove this boast.

"This branch I bear ith of peace, and under such I come. I have mighty arms and rich armours at myne own hame, and yet I have left them. For myne interest is not to war, though war-worth I seek to prove. Doth any here dare to game this knight?" His burning eyes swept the gathering 'neath his raisèd holly bough.

"An odd game indeed brings ye here with such a weapon and challeng-ing our swordsmanship and valour," bellowed back Arthur King. "Know ye that ye shalt find no shortage of hard answers should ye raise edge against us."

"I have telled thee truly, I seek no battle," growled the uninvited guest.

13

"If such were myne will not one amongst would stand to it. Thu are children all in myn eye. Nay, I come at this joyous carnal feast to have a new year's game - a jest of Geol. Tell me! Be-eth there any in this hall what dares try against me? I propose a strike for a strike; as I am dealt I shall deal in return. Yet should this brave man best me he shall have this mighty arm - this grim great edge which weighs myne fist. Indeed, he mayeth use the axe e'en to deal that same first blow. I shall not flinch and shall wait for the worst. Brave men! Hardy men! One amongst thee claimeth this axe forever and so too rend myne flesh. On this floor shalt I kneel unmoving, providing my foe allow that I may, I say once more, return the same. Yet," and here he smiled a grisly smile, "one year I shall allow the man to favour his skin afore I claim it. Come at me, thanes!"

All those gathered stood astounded, and none moved save the wizard Myrddin, who stroked his stripey beard - in humour or in rumination. The fearsome foe looked over all, his red eyes burning at the High King and at his princely guard. When none answered his call he cleared loud his throat and stretched wide his arms, his mountainous spine popping and cracking with fearsome sound.

"Mayhaps this ith not Arthur's hall? For Arthur and his sword-mates art world-known, yet there ith naught fierce nor fell here. No boasts nor proud songs. Art thu not proud? Not greater than other men? There is that round board 'round which thu sit, though its creaking soundeth louder than thy tongues at myne challenge"

This proved too great an insult for Arthur, that dread-lord of menfolk. With naked blade and red-flushed face he advanced on that villain, though dwarfed in its shadow was he. "Ye art mad, fair fool! To come here and make so brash a speech. To taunt so fell a fyrd. Yet should ye truly seek the weight of death gladly shalt I deal it ye. None here are afeared of thy cockrel cries. Grant me thy crooked cleaver and I shall show ye the blessing of the hand of Avalon."

In three swift strides Ythyr's son strode to the green knight's side and held forth his noble arm. Into that open paw was that viscous weapon placed. With his hand now free, the agitator stroked his wild beard afore doffing his furred coat and dismounting his red-eyed steed. He stood high above that noblest liege and looked down on him with grim humour. Held high the lord that fearsome edge, and considered grimly the strike which might be made.

Yet, as bold Arthur made to fell that fell fiend, a hand reached forth and rested 'pon his arm. He looked and found 'twas Gwenhyfar, who had stepped forth from the shield of Orkney's sons. He met her sea-grey eyes and saw in them a sadness he did not yet ken and could not yet fathom.

14

"Let another man try this game, husband." She felt in that moment all the love of Arthur she feared to lose, and her tongue weighed upon his spirit heavy. And heavy as well suddenly seemed the greenish axe, and its head scraped upon the floor.

A new hand gripped the haft, and a strong-jawed man begged his lord allow him the honour. 'Twas Gawain, lord-presumed of northward Orkney, and he fixed his determined gaze on his foe. He glanced then to his liege and smiled humbly. "Of all thy lords - all thy knights - I shall be missed least. Were I not also thy nephew I would already have been forgot. If I triumph I make both our names greater. And if I should perish?" He shrugged and a handful of admirers laughed, despite their fear. "What of it? And if ye think my offer ungood, I beg ye not let it colour thy thought of me."

Leaving the eye of his queen, Arthur King met the eye of Gawain, then those of other trusted knights in the hall. Amongst them was Lanslod Lak, the greatest of Men, and he who ripped Gwenhyfar's chest asunder. Yet his own chest also was in pain, for his loved lord's lady would not take him, and his ardour for the King would not let his passion betray him unless it built to an unkennable pressure, which it had not yet done. Lanslod could not bear the possibility of Arthur's crippling, and so nodded grimly. Seeing this, the other admiring knights nodded also and soon so too did that mighty sire. The thane of Lak looked longingly on the royal bride and she, with tears, looked to the rain.

Gawain stepped lightly to the sovereign's side and strongly gripped the fatal tool. The Britons' High King did not at once release the blade, but warned with care his nephew, "Take care, Cousin. This visit reeks of spellcraft, and I have no doubt that whatever blow ye deal shall be dealt again. Be not too zealous, though do me proud." Then Arthur took his leave, returning towards his throne, one strong arm wrapped greedily about his wife.

And so stood stalwart Gawain before that man-mountain of verdant hue, the axe in his great arms. The giant smiled and spake, "Let us again speak the terms agreed, afore we begin our play. Firstly though, I ask thy name - the label of myne axe's new lord. If thu canst tell it truly I shalt trust thee in all things, though it be an easy ask."

Gawain nodded as he met that tow'ring gaze. "Gawain am I hight, of Orkney born. Loth King sired myne brothers and I, and Arthur's sister bore his sons. As for our game - if game it may truly be called - it is agreed that I shalt make as mighty a strike I may, and ye, if able, shouldst do the same in twelvemonth's time."

The beast grinned. "Promise-est thu me to seek me out when a year is passed, Gawain."

"And where would I call on ye?" Orkney's eldest had a star in his eye, for he expected ne'er to be forced to come calling; the King's warning he had already forgot.

"I shalt tell thee once I have taken myne blow, for if it should render me unable to return the notch such knowledge would serve none."

"That suits me just as well. Though I do swear to seek ye if needs be."

"Then let the thing be done."

"Gladly," replied Gawain, and hoisted high the axe.

Seeing his doom upraised, the faerie thane knelt, his head bowed. With one great fist he swept aside his lank hair, revealing the clear skin of his nape. Gawain waited for his prey to lie still, marvelling at the beauty in this thick neck. But soon, the giant sat still, and with no further hesitation did Loth's son let fall the blade. It struck cleanly through. Broke skin. Shattered bone. Split fat and clove sinew. The great head tumbled free, hair still gripped in its owner's right hand, and the axe lodged itself in the stones at their feet.

A torrent of bright blood flowed from the wound and Gawain and others stepped back to rescue their boots, yet the corpse did not move a hair - did neither topple nor shiver. Like a stone it sat. Until it stood.

With mighty poise the green knight took to his feet, pulling its skull from before the toes of the horrified crowd by its leash of locks and hoisting it high above. Clambering atop its steed with no noted hindrance, it held out its ghastly pate towards Gawain and Arthur both and its wicked mouth spoke, even as the stump of his execution bled all down his torso and along the flanks of the unblinking horse.

"Steelest thyself, Gawain!" Seest thu that thu art set in one year's time to take this same wound as new year's gift! Thu hast promised and these knights are witness. Many know me as the Knight of the Green Henge, and to ask after it thu shalt find directions well supplied. And so comest thu! Or prove thyself coward." He laughed loud then and, with a kick of his crying horse, fled back the way he had come. Fire lept from the stones where the hooves met, sending wails of terror from many throats, and the heavy doors slammed shut behind him, leaving silence in his wake.

No man there knew from whence that knight had come, and not e'en the woman-priests knew of that green henge. Yet spirits were lifted once more by the laughter of Gawain. At first it was from fear, though soon it was at the absurdity, and by the time Arthur joined it was with pride at a mighty deed.

Shortly the celebrations resumed, and women soon took their chosen men to bed. By midnight's coming the mood in the hall had entirely forgotten the eldritch thane which had disrupted their carnal festival.

16

Arthur had taken a seat once more - this time upon his rich, oaken throne, and flirted coyly with the women who came to beg his bed - yet he had already been chosen by Gwenhyfar. And Gwenhyfar, that sorrow-wed consort, sat at his arm, her hands wrapped tightly about his bracer. He looked in time to her melancholy gaze and saw that it rested upon Gawain, who crowed and cavorted as admirers fought over his favour.

"Worry not, Stone-of-myne-Sword. Gawain is a true thane. A mighty man. A favour from the gods of the Earth. Rain-to-myne-Field, all is well at Year's End." And he kissed her, but she could taste his worry.

Turned he then to the named Orkney lad and beckoned, "Come! Bring here that terrible axe and hang it there above the table, so as we feast we may look on it and remember thy deed. Its cutting days are done, and now let it be Sir Gawain's first trophy above the moon!"

And so the axe was hung with other trophies of other thanes, all about the red-draped walls which enclosed that famous board. Swords and heads of beasts and broken banners and færie gifts and the wicked Geol-axe. And for the remainder of that night the terrible game was unhappily forgotten. Joy and flaming passion ruled Mother's Night.

W hen Year's End is passed and New Year is birthed all await cheerfully the blooming of the many-hued flowers, following swiftly on the footsteps of the expiring snows. Mud cakes the sturdy boots and trailing dresses of man and maiden alike as children cower or clap with glee at the shudder-clap of storms as rain sweeps away the memory of the old year. Rich, wet smells assault the senses. Hounds become anxious to fly over forgotten fields and cause ruckus with young masters as virile lovers feel their blood rise as they too are infected with new life. Vibrant springtimes travel all-too-swiftly into heated summers, ripe for toil, war, travel, and gaiety. The hotter season clings on, until folk are unsure if it has overstayed its welcome or if they wish it would never leave. And, just as they have decided that they should like to keep it as their constant guest, cold winds whip through the shutters and tear it all away. Yet there is naught to grieve for, for with chill Autumn comes not merely the reminder of another year gone, but also the blossom-ing of many strange colours in the canopy, and the thrivant return of fanciful mushrooms and vibrant mouldes on the forest floors. Here too come the rains. And it is those rains, as they gradually turn icy, which drag the year back towards Gaol, and Modrenacht, and white Year's End.

And, as it was still as true then as it is now, a year passed and the fated time approached once more. It was still a few weeks yet until Gawain's debt would be due, but he had begun to feel a restlessness in his soul and naught seemed able to calm it. The gods were silent to his prayers and hunting brought only damp to his bones. Wine soured his heart and women brought fire which swiftly fled and left him emptier than before. Sparring and riding reminded him only of how lonely he and his arms-brothers were in their violent calling, and songs stumbled when he meant to compose them and fled when he meant to sing them. Morose and melancholy was he, and gazed he often at the trophy-axe above the order's table, fearing to take the blow he'd dealt.

Snow had not yet come to the tawny-brown forests of Camelot, but its scent was in the air as Gawain stood atop an ancient wall and wondered after the mysteries of death. He had just resolved to attempt a nap - something he did oft of late, though sleep rarely came to him - when he heard soft footsteps on the stone behind him. Turning, he found Gwenhyfar, her red hair gently flaming in the wind and her cold eyes fixed and unyielding. He smiled and she came to stand beside him, gazing out at the westering sun.

"Fear ye thy journey? And its end?" Her voice, as ever, was as sad as her mien. Even those unpossessing of the foresight to ken her sins knew her to bear a trail of tragedie darker than the cloth of any gown.

Gawain, like many a young man, did not like his faults shown to the light of day. He did not like being made to feel weak. Even though all men - even strong ones - have holes in their armour. Orkney did not look to his queen, just as she did not look to him, but gazed out at the fading light of the sky. "I am a thane of Arthur's table. It would be foolish for me to fear the fulfilling of a promise made. And no son of Loth shalt be made a fool." This last was often proven wrong.

"Aye. Ye serve Arthur." Her endlessly deep eyes – twin ghostly meres – glanced to him, then away, as flighty as a doe. "Remember always that no heart may serve fully two loyalties. Ever there is a greater love between the two, and to serve them both can only pain."

"I serve no man but Arthur. And my father, of course, yet he also is Arthur's man." He laughed fully - too fully for the quiet battlement, startling a family of doves. "And certainly do I hold no bonds to the Henge Knight save the promise of my neck." His skin paled even as he spoke of his fate, but he swallowed and willed a blush back into his handsome face.

"You have never loved a woman, nor a man." There seemed no guide to the changing winds of Gwenhyfer's words. "Hold thy tongue and let me speak. I am a queen, and will have my say.

"I mean not fornication, admiration, nor envy, but love. 'Tis a different thing. Something other. The passion of love far outweighs any passion ye have yet felt. When ye draw thy cock and fuck some doe-eyed maid ye feel the building, crashing, unconquerable wave of thy release. In admiration of

18

the young gallavanter's beauty ye feel the rosy furnace-fire light thy cheeks and thy mind fills with fanciful visions of dream-days which will never come. When ye envy those ye see as better ye feel the thrill of jealousy - the drive given by thy hatred of being less.

"Yet love. Love is another thing. A better thing. A more terrible thing. Your seed burns hotter in a sturdier sword when ye rut in love. Thy dream-days often come true when ye share lives in love. A great pride fills ye to know that others envy ye more than ye they when ye show thy love. Love is a mighty thing.

"Yet love... Love can also be terrible. There is no greater pain than having your love forgotten, no greater shame than failing to live up to love, no greater anguish than seeing thy love dashed upon the rocks of the shore and left raw and meaty for the gulls of envious lessers. To lose love is to fall lower than all the dungeons of all the most terrible lords of Hel."

The queen stood as tall and regal as ever she had, her grey dress – lined in blue and gemmed in red – gently billowing in the cool breeze. Yet she seemed smaller somehow, and Gawain felt somehow ashamed to see her suffer. Though he knew not – could not know – what suffering held her.

Arthur's wife sighed and looked down. Down to the banks of the great wall where a shepard managed his wards, happily driving them home. "I have heard some say that love may run in many ways. That there are those strong in love who may share it with many. But I have seen naught to make me believe it. Each heart is bound for one breast and one breast alone." Her voice fell then to a breathy whisper, nearly inaudible. "It can only be thus."

Still without looking to Gawain, she turned away. Pausing briefly, she spake, "I hope ye keep thy handsome head," and left towards a shadowed arch into the fortress. Under that arch Gawain could see a figure waiting, with an embroidered spear sewn upon his breast. The queen passed him by, unnoticing, and he followed close on her heels. Gawain, like many, thought Arthur lucky to have a friend like Lanslod Lak to protect the honour of his favoured consort.

At last the day had come. That fated leave-taking that would see Gawain begin the road towards his head's unhoming. The young thane's brief, strange meeting with Gwenhyfer had staid with him as the leaves fled their boughs and cold rains led white flurries into the lands of the Dragon King. Why had she spoken so of passion, love, and loyalty? Was she a seeress, as were so many women of that age? Gawain was made all the more unsettled by the affair.

He saw very little of Queen Gwenhyfar after that, busy as she was with the duties a woman of such standing has. Even on this, the day he was to set forth from Camelot, she did not show her face. When Spring came she would travel on a golden swan-prowed ship to the lands of the Franks to visit for a time the kin of Lanslod Lak, but Gawain would not be present to greet her when she returned, affected as he would be by the result of his questing.

Yet it is an unkind fate for a knight to set forth on a geas with an unquiet heart, and so Gawain went that day to the chambers where his aunt Morgaine staid, hoping to find wise counsel. Morgaine was the wife to King Urien, and mother to King Yvaine (there were many kings in those days), but she misliked both and spent many months in the house of Arthur. There were rumours of her promiscuity - promiscuity King Urien despised - and there were those who said she desired the bed of her brother, Camelot's sire, and so despised the dreamlike Gwenhyrfar for her position in his eye. Once, it was said, she loved a man named Accolon who arthur slew, by way of her own trickery; neither ever spoke of Sir Accolon, but it was true that when Arthur and Accolon quested together only Arthur returned. But for all the rumours of men or women she bedded or wooed, it was known that she was sometimes frequent consort to the mystic, Myrddin. And this was thought good by many, for she was known to be a sorceress herself and it was some-times said that magic, if spilled, could poison the blood of common men - so it was better if wizards fornicated with wizards. It is likely by her many spells that she kept her beauty. A thriving, dark beauty that stirred the lust of all - even her kin such as Gawain – even as her age passed half a century. She was a priest of secrecy, symbolism, and sex. She was much respected and much feared.

As Gawain came to his aunt's chambers, admitted by a love-(or lust?) struck young guardthane at the door. The enchantress reclined on a long, low couch, running her milky-white fingers over the textured lines of an illuminated tome, done in a style uncommon in those pagan lands. She was arrayed in a gown of heavy green silks, which fell alluringly acrost the form of her wide hips and strong shoulders, even as it concealed nearly every inch of soft flesh. Thick thread of black and precious gold laid flowers upon the folds of the dress. The green of the cloth matched the dark colour of her eyes, which blinked, large and wide, from above her patrician nose and wide, pale lips. Lustrous black hair fell - unbound and wavy, yet untangled and mesmerizingly reflective - acrost her breastbone and down her back. Golden rings and silver piercings adorned her hands and fair face and subtle tattoos ringed her throat and hid in the corners of her eyes.

The young knight knelt in deference, his eyes cast down – as much in

20

respect as in shame at the thoughts her presence brought him. "Sister-kin, I come to seek advice. I beg ye advise me afore I go forth to forfeit my life."

Morgaine clicked her tongue admonishingly and shifted, gently closing the leather covers of the book. She shifted with the grace of a cat, stretching her supple spine as she slid bare feet into soft mink slippers. "A man who says he must die, will. Sit, cousin. Join me." She motioned languidly to a position on the couch beside her. Thick, black curtains shielded much of the light of the sun, and the thin ray that was allowed through spread seductive warmth on the bench. The witch-woman smiled, her lips drawn, as her nephew joined her and she threw one arm – surprisingly strong – about his shoulder. "Look on me. We are family. Not foes." As he did, his cheeks flushed, she leaned forwards to a low, oaken table where she poured two silvered chalices of pungent, black wine with one hand. Offering one, she kissed her red-faced nephew lingeringly on the lips before taking her own. She sipped slowly as she eyed him to begin.

Gawain stammered, then stopped. He knew that strong folk spoke firmly. And if he could not resist his own blood how could he resist the Henge Knight? "I must face the green visitor from Modrenacht last. Must find him afore that night comes once more. Yet I fear. For if I receive the same blow I dealt I surely shall be slain." His voice was low - too low, yet it could not be helped.

"That axe is heavy and sharp, son." Her hand rested now on his thigh as her other swirled her wine cup. "And of course ye shall die should ye take it full-force. Ye should have known to be wary of færie visitors, yet also should ye be wary of the fate of a man who denies his honour. Ye have fucked thyself with thy promise, yet be certain ye fuck thyself no further.

"There are ghosts aplenty in the lands around, and brigands, ogres, and ghouls. Keep in thy breast the memory of Arthur's love and fall not to any temptation. Let no one tell ye what ye want, but take what thy soul needs.

"Claim the objects of thy heart, Gawain," her claw squeezed harder on his thigh, drawing his desperate gaze to hers. "Damn all others. If ye do not take, they shall. Take. Take. Take all ye can carry. And fuck the wants of those who would control ye."

Gawain's mouth was dry, his lips parted and tongue raised. With his hand not full of wine he gripped his aunt's thigh, though not as hard. "What would ye have me do?"

She sneered then and released him, making space between them that seemed an ell, though it was only an inch. "Ye listen like a babe. As bad as ingrate Yvaine." Her scorn was as painful and as magnetic as her invitations. "I shall enchant ye a token. A belt perhaps, to steel thy skin? For surely ye are not able enough to defend thyself from sorcery on thy own. What curse

21

is this that makes of the blood of Igraine such idiots? Come, and I shalt fit ye with such a spell that no armour shall ye have need of."

They stood together, but Gwain pulled her to face him. "Nay, lady. I shalt not accept thy pity-relic." His anger at the insult had washed away his desire like a wave ravishing a fisherman's hovel in a storm. Naught remained. "I will not admit to weakness I do not possess and wear cantrips to declare my impotence. Gawain is a man and Gawain is –" He halted mid-speech when he saw a figure hidden in the curtains.

There, secreted in the weighty folds of the window-shrouds, stood Myrddin. The wizard's eyes burned with fire and amusement as he smiled at the startled knight. He was arrayed all in pitch, with his onyx hood pulled low. It would be no wonder he had not been seen, in that shadowy robe, were it not for the shimmering rings and coils of gold which hung on his hands and beard.

"I will not take thy gift," Orkney's son declared, and threw himself from the chamber, stumbling into the hall.

G an he then to the steward's hall for to be fitted and kitted for his journey. Rage and self-loathing had dispelled from him the fear of recent weeks, and he marched tall, blood hot, to face his fate.

Arrayed on a red cloth were the great gifts which his king had allowed him to bear upon his task-road. Proudly he stepped forth, and allowed the pages to dress him.

A coat he donned, of fine, red fabric from the east, beyond the grip of Christ, its swirls and lines mesmerizing to see. Red as well was the heavy cape he bore - born of that same far country - and all along its inside was sewn finest ermine. Heavy boots to bear the road, and black mail from hood to toe he wore, each ring etched with the name of Arthur. His gorget was hammered with tales of giant-slaying. A coat of plates was fastened and tied acrost his broad chest, and sleeves fit with gilded dragons lay upon his arms and hung upon his legs. Mitts of mail he was given and gauntlets buckled in steel. Golden spurs clattered as he walked, and his sharp sword - called Maiden's Fame - swung from a black belt studded in silver and set with precious emeralds.

Dressed thusly he went then to the hall where kept the woman-priests, and they prayed loud and laid curses on those who would harm him. They cut his cheek so he tasted blood, and fed him fiery spirits that burned raw his throat. On his forehead they painted runes, and each one planted a salty kiss upon his palms.

22

From there came he to the table-room, where many waited to greet him. The Queen smiled and the knights clapped his back and the King kissed him fondly and his admirers clutched him as if he would be devoured. All laughed and cheered and begged him to return. But everyone – Gawain not least – knew he may never return.

In the lower courtyard his mighty steed, red-furred Gringolet, was saddled with a gilded seat, and wondrous blankets and capes of yet more gold and yet more red. Gawain visited him here and raised the fearsome helm hung on the horn of the saddle. Runed and deep-browed it was, and set with tusks and horns. It gleamed in the sun and dazzled those who followed his progress. He kissed its brow, runed in the same places as his own, and donned it, a heavy, red cloth cap beneath. A golden crown was worked about the cap of dark iron, and on it maidens hung branches of holly.

So too was brought him his round shield, stout and rowan (to dispel harmful magics). Red it was, and gilt upon it a mystic sigil – a pentacle in the manner of the famed and distant wizard-king Solomon; that endless sign, each line and point bound to another so its enchantment carries on forever. It is called the Endless Knot by some, and it is a defense against all wickedness. Eight points it has, for eight is a thing of power. And bound about with circles and aided by etched spells it is. It is a powerful symbol for a powerful man. Gawain's arm hums with power as he hoists it. Yet many men carry magical shields, and shields may fail, so he does not see it as akin to the shameful gift offered him by Morgaine.

The fearsome færie axe also was brought, and he dared not look upon it. Gringolet danced as it was harnessed to him. "Return that trophy to the wall," laugh his brothers, "and yourself to the table, if ye remember!"

A squire handed him his stout war lance and, with one final salute to meet the growing huzzahs, Orkney's heir hied his steed on and Gringolet bounded towards the west. Sparks flew on the paving stones of Camelot's streets as he passed, and many who saw cred in excitement and fear.

At the castle's mighty gate sill stood Arthur, and beside him his friend Lanslod Lak. "It is a shame for him to be lost," spake the King.

"Ye warned him well. Yet he is young and brash," spake his friend.

"As are we, friend. Many mistakes we ourselves have made and still shall make." He does not expect the true gravity of his words.

"He shall be butchered and beheaded by that elf," answered Lanslod Lak, his heart tight with regret at the love he bore Arthur's wife.

Both men cried hot tears.

T hrough Lloegyr, the kingdom of Camelot, rode noble Gawain, his cloak of red-spun wool flapping in the stormy air. Soon he began to hunger, yet no game he found. Loneliness took him, and he tented in ditches, dells, and forest copses, wet with rain and with none but Gringolet for company. Lamented he often not having taken more lovers to bed, more friends to play, more teachers to lecture. For now he was starved, isolated, and miserable. What had begun with a resplendent sendoff had now surely become a grim death-march.

He came in time to northern Wales, near Anglesey, then rode on. Acrost oppressive windy beaches and flooding fords he struggled, ever growing more regretful of his life. From there rose rocky highlands and at last his way advanced to the land of Wirral, where villains and angry men made home.

His whole journey long he asked any he would meet – though there were few – if they knew of the Knight of the Green Henge. Yet it seems his foe had lied, for none knew of him, and none could say to have seen a mighty giant of green skin. But in Wirral he was told that a man asked not after the Henge Knight, but after a knight who would seek that fey figure; it seemed this stranger asked after Gawain.

And so, following the words of those who answered him, gallant Gawain sought the mysterious stranger in Wirral and found, in a wooded dell, the wizard Myrddin.

The magician had a small campsite there, and about it were deer and brock and birds and even a wild cat, all standing too close and too still to be natural.

Arthur's magicker, dressed in black robe and mantle sewn with silver stars, invited his guest to sit, and offered fresh bacon and sweet apples. He seemed strangely at home here in the woods, despite his glittering rings and dangling pendants, merely sitting on a felled log and managing the meat over the fire.

Gawain dismounted and glanced to the sorcerer's simple green tent, filled only with a blanket and a small travelling sack. The smell of the food overwhelmed his starved senses and made his knees shake and stomach churn and twist. And so they ate. And spoke of common things as they licked grease from their fingers and shared a laugh over Myrddin's meagre skin of black wine. They did not speak of the quest as they ate, nor Myrddin's purpose in Wirral.

Yet when the stomach of Orkney was full – a thing he had thought would never come again – he eyed his host and asked, "Why have ye come hither? Doubtless thy way was by magics. For how else could I have been outpaced? But I must ken thy purpose. I have always feared ye, as sane men must, but ye do Arthur well and I too would value aid."

Myrddin contentedly sucked his fingers, probing with his tongue for last morsels of grease which had caught under his rings. "Must a man have a purpose to visit Wirral? O aye. I suppose one must. 'Tis a horrid place." He winked then, first with one piercing eye, then the other. When he continued it was seemingly unrelated. "Arthur says he would like to have a melee in the spring. Mayhaps when Lady Gwenhyfar returns from Frankia. It may be a bloody affair."

"The melee or the visit to Frankia?"

"Did ye know that there are places on this Earth where it never rains?" The wizard observed the thane with rapt attention.

"I had heard someone claim such," answered Gawain, already frustrated by Myrddin's odd manners. "Yet I am on a quest. And glad of thy company, for I have been most lonely. Yet I wish for more than food and sup from ye. Tell me something I ken not, wizard! Show me thy might! They say ye may put Solomon to shame, yet all I have ever known ye to do is watch me lecherously from the shadows. Be that thy magic? The magic of discomfort?"

When the magician smiled he showed his moon-white teeth. "I must truly be getting on." He brushed his hands on his cloak and stood.

"Nay!" In anger, Gawain gripped at the sorcerer's shoulder, but found only empty air.

"Find thy true self in thy heart. Trust no other to tell ye thy truth. Lithe only to thy own council. Ye are more a man when ye make decisions for thyself." Gawain turned to see Myrddin behind him amongst the trees, a few paces away. The witch smiled once more. "Now I tell ye to remain chaste on this journey and to deny all hospitality. Wear always thy mail kit. And never refer to another by their name."

Then swiftly – too swiftly, it seemed – the magus sprung forwards and clutched at Gawain's throat, his thumb and forefinger slipping under gorget and mail and leaving a burning, stinging red line there. In a blink the mystic was gone.

Gawain swore and rubbed at his neck and settled down to rest. The pack Myrddin had left was filled with nuts and preserved meats.

As he entered the highlands, Gawain often found himself taking to foot to lead his horse over uneven ground or to clamber up cliffs, only to meet Gringolet later along the path; his companion was as loyal and clever a horse as ever a man had. Heavy mists fell on the northlands, and many waterways blocked his path.

Yet the finding of fords was not the greatest of the knight's woes at these crossings, for at each there were terrible foes, and more between. But Gawain was mighty and well-sworded and fought bravely to defeat every horrid creature that opposed him. And in each case he was the victor. And when he tired most of fighting the fell and foul he sometimes found strange wonders, the likes of which he would never tell another of, for fear of being disbelieved.

At more than one rocky stream he crossed sword with fang as fierce wyrms slithered from beneath the stones. Rising from 'neath the waters or in dark caves, they reared and hissed and spat hot breath. Those with claws rent at the sigiled shield. Those that spoke cursed him and taunted him with secrets and lies. Those with wings beat them so he must strive to reach them as if marching into a gale, his black hair behind him. But ever he left their scaly corpses broken and bloody, and never did he pause to search for their crooked treasures.

Wolves hounded his way, and many nights he could not stop to sleep for fear they would be upon him. Two times they did attack, yet both times they were driven off with fire and steel, and once he took the head of a great grey beast amongst them. Once more they came near his camp, but he kept the head of their captain on his saddle and they shied away in fear.

In the crags Gawain combated wood-trolls, trundling from dark holes with slavering jaws and gnashing teeth, fat fingers eager for man-flesh. Under the ever-present blanket of heavy mist Arthur's thane wrent their grey flesh and severed their wagging black tongues. When they made to unhorse him or thrust them from a cliffside – throwing their heavy bodies at him and at the brave Gringolet – he met them with fast footwork, good horsemanship, and more biting steel. They too followed him at night, their yellow eyes and gibbering speech peppering the dark, but the mighty worthy was never bested nor sorely wounded by their assaults.

Territorial bulls drove him with their great horns from their grazing lands and bears sometimes came for him as he made passage too close to their caves, their bellows echoing on stone. Once, a boar and its kin caught him afoot and chased him through a wood, squealing, until he clambered up a tree and waited out the night for them to lose interest. He did not harm those innocent animals – not malicious like the wolves – save if he should be wanting of meat; and even then, a sword is a poor tool for hunting. Once Myrddin's gifts ran dry he once more knew great hunger.

Ogres – great, ugly man-things – hurled curses and stones from the heights. Came to duel him with cudgel and towering seax. And each mighty beast he cleaved. Each cruel skull he split. It is said that from that time on – so great was his slaughter of their wicked folk – that Gawain became in the tales of ogres as those beasts are in our own.

War is a wearisome task, this Gawain knew. And his arm ached from the many salyings he had done. But the weather – O woe – the weather was the worst. Often on the arduous journey, assaulted by sleet and gale and downpour, Gawain wondered if he even had the strength o meet his quest's end. He thought perhaps that he would deny the green giant his death by dying asleep in a ditch. Rain came relentlessly, and frozen more oft than not. For fear of foes he slept in armour, and the chill froze his joints. Long past he had lost blanket and bedroll, and slept only on naked rocks. It was in this Hel of ice and hunger and dreamless nights that he stumbled into the days of Geol, alone and without warmth of any kind.

On the second day of Geol, nigh-crippled by his trials, Gawain tumbled from the broad back of Gringolet. Lying unmoving in the cold mud, Gawain began to cry. And as he cried he muttered pleas to any god or spirit that would listen. "Please. Please do not let me die alone and in the cold."

Later that day he came, defeated, though no foe could best him, to two great hills, and between them a forest of hundreds of oaks. About every tree were blankets of sickly moss, and on brittle hawthorn branches sat grey birds which sang piteously. Even the birds shuddered at the cold. The ground was wet and the forest soon became swamp. Yet on he ventured, his weary head hung low.

All the day long he muttered his prayers on numbed lips, and wondered after warmth.

And mayhaps his prayers were heard, for as dusk threatened the sky he came upon a hold in the darkling holt. About its feet lay a dark moat, and the castle itself sat upon a mound of grass and soil and hedge. Many wide trees were about it, disguising more devious ditches, but all was lit by the welcoming light of scores of torches.

In that tempting warmth-light Gawain saw the mightiest hame ever held by king or lord – though it may have been the fault of his long endeavours, yearning for respite. Gasping at salvation, Gawain hied Gringolet on to the edge of the fence which ringed that mighty manse – a trench at the mighty steed's feet.

"Ho! Keeper! Ho!" cried Gawain in his handsome voice, cracked by hardship. The high stone wall, lapped by the dark water of the inner moat, seemed to reach beyond the bounds of the sky, so tall it was. The knight marvelled at the ancient fortifications – the well-wrought crenelations and heavy barbican. Surely this Roman seat would stand until the end of time. Grim towers, like fists raised to curse the gods, bonded the walls together – walls carved in every stone with knotted dragons and weathered runes. Fresh pennons hung in bright colours from every peak, hardly darkened by the rain. "Keeper! I seek solace! Heed me!" And soon enough a face appeared.

A small face it was, in a high window above the great gate. Yet it seemed friendly to Gawain for his long time in the wilderness. "Who calls?"

"'Tis Gawain, of Orkney born and of Orkney prince! Thane of Arthur and quester after glory! I beg thy master welcome me so I needs not spend Gaol in the cold."

"I shall inquire. Wait there, good knight!" And the face was gone, only to return shortly. "Welcome ye are given!"

And so the sturdy gate was forced wide and servants came to lay bridges over moats, open fences, and welcome their noble guest. In reverence the servants knelt as he passed, and Gawain proudly raised his weary head.

Once in the bailey on the hill, Gawain dismounted, handing his reins to two stout, winsome men, who smiled at him with admiration and interest. His helm, his blade, and his broad arm-board he relinquished to eager pages, trusting in the stolid laws of hospitality to keep him safe. The great wicked axe he also gladly surrendered to their care, hoping for a time to be freed of its reminder of his doom. His face he washed from a bowl of icy rose-water, its sides golden and encrusted in rubies.

And he was led by yet another handsome lad to a carven hall, warmed by a roaring hearth and filled on every wall with trophies of the hunt. And as he sat and warmed his fingers, the lord of the hall came and spake in a booming voice, "Ye are welcome to dwell here as ye wish. All within these walls is thine even as it is mine!"

Stunned at the charity, the knight bowed his head. "Gramercy. If ever I may repay this debt I shall." And he stood to face his host.

The host was wide-thewed, bearded, and noble-boned, and as he took Gawain into a rough embrace, Orkney was enchanted by his heady musk. Gawain thought he had rarely seen a man so fit and hale. With auburn beard and a fearsome-strong jaw, the lord stood with confidence. His silken hair flowed like a waterfall over his sturdy shoulders.

"Come, sir knight, and I will show ye thy chambers." And Arthur's agent was led gently by the hand. And as they went his host reminded him that all here was his, and any men he needed by any task would be at his call.

In those chambers named was a great oaken bed, carved all around with scenes of fey wonder and knobbed and gilt in gold. Heavy woolen quilts guarded against the cold and carpets from far lands were tacked to the walls and draped on the floors.

And as well in that room, where the exhausted gallant was left were four strong men, naked but for the vines inked on their arms. They spoke to him in joyous, friendly voices as they undressed him. Gooseflesh rose on his weathered skin as his byrnie and rough tunic were taken from him by gentle hands. Soft robes of silk, light as spiderwebs, were lain on his sore shoulders, and the pleasure almost pained him after so long afield. He seemed in raiment and in wonder a new-made prince of spring.

These strange and sensuous servants of the castle-lord knew not from whence their handsome visitor had come, but thought that surely there must be scant few men of better worth in all the world. This they told him in awed, breathy whispers.

A cheery fire roared in the hearth in this room, as in the chamber before, and a stout chair was set before it. And afore Gawain could once more sit, his attendants wrapped him in a thick, hooded cloak, embroidered in gold-thread and ermine-furred within and along the edges. And then the men left him, their services available at the tolling of a bell, and the knight sat snugly – yet still with regal bearing – and warmed his weary limbs.

In time he began to doze, and as he woke he found a table set in his chambers, with silver spoons and steaming bowls. He slipped his bare feet into slippers he found near and went there to sup.

To him were served many delicious seasoned soups, a variety of fishes, bread which choked his senses with its heady aroma, meats, gravies, and condiments of many sorts. All this he devoured with gusto, eating until he felt ill and then eating more. Often he told the attendant men, some now garbed in woolen skirts, of his delight at so divine a feast. Wine poured in merry waterfalls, and the servants laughed to hear tales of his adventures – now seeming to him so far away and so much less terrible.

As the meal finished, and darkness took the sky, Gawain rose and cleaned his face. From elsewhere in the stronghold came the tones of wailed chants – priests or faithful crying out in supplication. "Ye are to meet the lord once more. And as well the lady," whispered one of the attendants, and the thane of Arthur gladly took his hand.

He was taken then to the lord's hearth, and that gracious host asked his name and home and court. Gawain and Orkeny and Arthur's were the answers given. "I had not weened I welcomed so great a gallant when my gates I opened!" remarked the giant, and preparations were made to make the halls all-the-more festive. The knight clearly felt the admiration of all the men who looked on him, and glowed to be thought well of.

Some time the two sat and spoke of manly things, until at last – the hour dark – the forest baron offered to introduce the knight to his lady fair. And so they made way into the stony halls, arm-in-arm, and followed the keening songs of womanly worship until they came to an open arch. Through this arch were many candles, and robed women taken in ecstasy, their throats warbling with love and fear for the gods who ride the woods and write the ways of wizarding.

The chamber was filled with comely damsels, and Gawain stood in the entry in awe and appreciation. Even hidden in heavy robes and cloaks of flowing hair their beauty surpassed his most ardent dreamings. Each was pale of face, dark of hair, and bright of eye, and each fell silent as they looked upon him.

Stood then the most comely of all, and Gawain felt a stirring in his loins. More tempting even than Gwenhyfar or Aunt Morgaine he found her, and in her eye was lust. Yet by her pale fingers she led another whom he had not at first seen and, though this other had in her eye the same flesh-hungry gleam, he was loathe to gaze upon her. For she was ugly, crumpled, and crooked with age. Yellow and sick-thin her skin was, and this skin was bared for all. For the crone – squat and frog-legged – stood naked and unashamed, though her flesh was not wholly bare, for it was painted and inked. She smiled wide, but seemed as a predator as the lady beside her seemed a prize.

"Who is this?" asked Gawain, and his host spake, "My wife," and pointed to the handsome girl. He would say naught of the withered wench. Indeed, seemed not to see her.

But the fair one – wife to the host – came forwards and took Gawain by the hands and welcomed him, and gave him a warm embrace and deep kiss that Gawain returned, though he was shamed. "Come," she said, in sultry tones, and she led him by the arm away. Yet they were not alone, for the lord followed behind and the crone whispered things into his ears that he could not remark, but filled him with yet more shame and fear.

He was led from the chamber of wailing faithfuls to yet another cheery hearthroom, and here he was led to a couch where he sat with the old woman. The castle-mistress took her own high-backed chair, and her husband stood beside with one great hand gently on her shoulder. "We are so pleased to have ye, noble knight," she spake with a warm lilt. "All that we own is thine," reiterated her lord.

"Glad am I as well," spake Gawain and felt the shadow of the crone cold by his side; she who none would speak of.

And late into the night the three made joy and sang and riddled and danced and smiled. The lord offered up his fine hood as prize for any who was the cause of most joy over Geol, and Gawain nigh forgot his quest and ill-feelings. The wicked watcher at his arm left in time, but only to travel to the far, shadowed corner of the chamber, there to watch the frivolity with black eyes. Deep in wine, Gawain found even the mysterious old woman welcome company.

In time morning came and Gawain, not recalling having gone to rest, awoke in his sumptuous bed. Dressing in a gown of soft, red velvet with green jack and mink slippers, he made his way blearily through the halls towards where he heard sounds of merriment, his head ringing with the memory of a night of drink.

His morning stumbling brought him to a bright feast-hall, lined on the east with wide, high windows to catch the coming sun. It was a week to Modranacht, and all seated – ladies and huntsmen and squires and the lord – were dressed in happy colours. Song flowed like wine at the table and wine carried sonorously to every lip.

The place's lord sat at the table's head, and at his left the black-eyed crone, clothed now – all in black, sewn with silver sigils confused to Gawain's eye. Yet the lady sat not near her lord, and instead sat half along one long end of the table, facing east. And beside her was the only barren seat. And so the Heir of Orkney met her fiery gaze and sat close beside her.

"Welcome, Gawain!" cried the hill-fort's master. "Share with us our sumptuous feast, and too our every pleasure. All that ist mine ist thine!" His grin was wide and white and his eyes sparkled like stars.

And so Gawain feasted. And the game and pies and ale and puddings – all and more were amongst the richest ever he'd eaten. "How came thy husband by so wondrous a kitchen?" he asked the lord's lady.

She smiled as she cleaned pig-grease from her full lips with a pale finger, then licked them for good measure. "My lord has had many ill lucks, and so it is only fair that he should be rewarded in measure."

"What ill lucks could assail such a man?" asked Gawain of Loth in great surprise. But the woman only smiled and laughed and kissed his handsome cheek.

And so the feast carried on. Indeed, it seemed never fit to end. And ever richer plates were brought and strong wines as minstrels began to sing and men of the lord's house to boast. The lord himself had many stories to tell and many attentions to give, but was seated far from Gawain and barely gave him an eye. At first this injured him. He felt abandoned and unloved - moreso than a new guest should. But the wine narrowed his gaze and lifted his heart, and the lady laid oft her strong hand on his thigh.

The two spoke most often to each other rahter than to others, and leaned closer as wine made all words those of secrets and compassion. They wiped each other's faces of food and kissed each other's rings. Ran fingers through each other's soft hair and grabbed lustily beneath the table.

A time later – none could tell how long – the two took leave of the hall, unbothered by servants with fresh platters, and fell into each other in a storm of longing. Her breath was hot and his sweet, and both had strong claws. He bared her breast and she his, and as he dug his fingers into her buttocks and suckled her tit she held his blade and bit ragged wounds on his neck.

Too drunk, however, were they to consumate, and in time they fell apart in their own purple seas of drink. But a promise made she as they both left, and it seemed to the knight to rhyme with her husband's words. Said she, "as has been done to he shalt be done to thee." And Gawain smiled in his soft sheets even as he clutched his unhappy stomach.

M̲ore days of revelry followed – how many Gawain could not say, for wine made the coming and going of the sun too great a task to master. A few times more he saw that lusty lady, though never again in that week of debauchery did they have time alone. The crone he soon forgot, and if she remained he, like the others, took no notice. The axe he kept e'en further from his waking mind.

Finally, on a day where the festival seemed close to losing its fervour – the partiers hoarse and sore and larders running bare – the castle's lord called for the knight in his chambers. As he walked the carpet-hung walls Gawain felt his skin turn to ice, wondering what had been told his host.

Orkney's prince found the hall's master in a fur-stoled robe, warming his hands by a great hearth and his breast with mulled cider. "Ah! Brother!" he called in bright friendship, grasping the traveller soundly and kissing his cheeks. "Such pleasure it has been to have thy light here as the year wanes. Our celebrations would not have been the same had ye never found us." And with that warm greeting Gawain's fears were dispelled.

"Gramercy," thanked the thane. "Yet I cannae take all credit for the fair festing of so fey a feof. I hope someday to see ye at Arthur's hall, where we can treat ye as well as I have been treated. But if there is any way now I can thank ye for the warmth I've welcomed say it, and it shalt be done."

The giant dismissed the offer with a wave of his hand, drowning Gawain's nose in his heady musk. "I do not do this for reward, but for pleasure. When I seek reward I make it well known.

"But tell me true, what takes so noble a knight so far and in such foul months from the comfort of the High King's hame? Surely it must be a matter of great import."

"In sooth, sir, 'tis truth," answered Gawain. "'Tis not by choice I walk this wasted land. I seek the object of a geas, though where it lies it seems no man can tell me. And O!" Here the man was sobered. Reminded of his honour and his death. "I would surrender all the fields of Logues if they were offered only to find this fate by year's end!"

"Tell me, what is this quest?" asked the master. And he was told. And Gawain asked him if he knew of the Green Henge or its fearful guardian.

The great man laughed then, much to Gawain's surprise. "Fear ye not, sir knight, but stay here in faith and fire for a time longer."

"But Modranacht is but three days hence," answered Orkney with furrowed brow.

"I know the way to that fated place – not a league from mine own door! Stay and share some more and on that day I shall show it ye."

Gawain at this news was joyous, though perhaps it was improper for him to be so. In his mind the weight of the search was lifted, and he needed not worry until time came to offer his head. He would please himself with the time he had, and go to the gods in high spirits and well fed. Drunk too, if he could have it.

Soon the lord made a great bellow, pleased at his guest's good mood, and called to his chambers a gaggle of young things, for which the two of them with to play. And so with carnal and fraternal love was let fly the day.

When at last their lust was spent – soft, nubile bodies all about – the grinning host spread his wide arm about the knight's bare shoulders and offered him more wine. "One think I will ask, since you offered thanks before."

"Anything, dear friend," spake the thane, naked and without shame.

Taking a serious cast upon his face, the castle's man replied, "Ye have travelled long and weary been. Much rest ye yet must need. So stay ye here and take my bed, and sleep there sumptuously."

"So great a gift! But I have no thought to share a night 'side ye."

"Nay, nay, for I sleep little in these days, and mean early and often to away. A couch I'll take, or other bed, and hunt during the sun. Yet ye will rest, and decompress, and my wife will make assured. One wife I have and one wife I shall leave, to comfort ye as fit. And should ye need a meal or walk? She shalt make sure of it. Remember well, that what is mine is thine."

And Orkney's Son, both hot and wary, grinned and sweated in his wine. "Your wishes I will obey."

"Yet this is not all," and Gawain's caution was full returned. "For I am a betting man, and sharing fair as well. So each day on my hunt I shall share my wins with ye. And whatever comes to ye herein, ye shall give to me."

"All things I am to share?" was asked.

"Is it not only fair?"

And Gawain could naught but full agree, yet in his lust despair.

And so was the compact made, and yet more celebration had. And afore they both to bed awayed, a tender kiss the two men shared.

In the morn, well before Gawain would wake, the hunting lord was off, and with him many men, hounds, laughing ladies, hawks, and one crooked old crone. The beasts of the forest fled in fear and arrows flew and blood was let. It was joyous in the savage hunting-way that is not seen today. And Gawain slept late in the luxurious bed of the lord.

It was well past the rising of the sun when the subtle creak of the chamber's hinges woke him. Anticipating no harm, but cautious and curious, he kept closed his sparkling eyes. The perfumed notes that reached him told him it was his host's wife, and his breath caught as he felt her weight rest upon the bed. In the fire of drink he had wanted her – needed her – but with the sun above and a clear head (though with a dull ache) he wished for her to think him slumbering.

Yet she did not leave, and so after some long time he oped his eyes to find her lain ther beside him, dark hair spread acrost his chest and pale skin beckoning. With her full red lips she kissed him deeply, and he could do naught to resist.

"Good morning, Sir Gawain," she cooed, her greedy fingers playing on his stomach. "Such a careless sleeper ye are. Now ye are my prisoner, and if we do not come to terms I shall be made to bind ye to this bed. And be assured, my bonds are quite strong."

"What terms, gentle lady? For I imagine I may find them easy to fulfill. And if not, I do not imagine I shall suffer much as prisoner of your will." His heart warned caution, but his own will burned brightly in his breast.

"O, ye shan't suffer too much." She laughed gayly.

"But I fear, lady dear, that I am not dressed for the occasion. Let me rise and array myself for parlay."

"Nay, for sooth, fair sir," she pressed herself firmly on him as she spoke, the gossamer arm of her gown lying acrost his chest. "I find ye dressed much as I would like. But I will not fully deny ye the chance to rise. Yet rise here, where I can govern ye better." And he felt her hand about his hilt.

He made to protest, but she shushed him with a kiss even as she sat astride him. He moved her hand from its rest and shielded his prize from her grasp.

"Sir knight," she pouted. "My husband is gone hunting. So too are gone the men, the maids – even my servants are in field or abed. The door is

34

closed and locked with firm bolt. Am I, lady of the house, not permitted the pleasure of the greatest delight this place now offers?

"Ye are welcome to my body – to drink of it thy fill. My need drives me to serve ye, and take what joy I will."

And with that Gawain's unsteady walls were toppled, and he laid with her and she with him. And they craved and gave fierce kisses and rough love. And when at last she left him, spent and drained, he smiled and thought little of what a jealous man would do should he discover what a man like Gawain had done to his wife.

He rang a bell and the house's handsome servants came and commented on his healthy glow. They dressed him and brushed his hair and led him by the hand to the feast.

And at the feast he sat with her and the two laughed and sang and drank. And all who were there would say they acted the best of friends.

That eve, when the lord returned, he called all the house to observe, and arrayed for Gawain the great gains of the hunt.

"How does this please Orkney's Pride? Ever have ye seen such fine venison? Such great antlers? Give me the thanks ye think I deserve."

And Gawain gave great praise, and filled his host's chest with satisfaction.

"I give it all to ye, Gawain. As I promised, it is thine." He clapped one great hand on Gawain's back. "Now what have ye for me?"

The lady was not to be seen, but the crone was. She watched as Gawain turned his pale face away. "Alas, for all I have gained ye already possess. I can give ye nothing new."

"Then give me something familiar!"

And Gawain, thinking himself clever, kissed the man full on his lips. When those two were disconnected the lord, with light in his eye, asked from what source he gained such a gift, but Gawain would not tell.

They laughed then, and drank, and went to sup in hall. And on that way the knight was glad of a friend like the lord.

T hat night by hearthlight the two men's vows were renewed. Wine and song bled from the gathered feasters, and eyes shone bright with glee.

In the morn once more the lord did depart, and Gawain slept late as well, his head muddied with drink.

And when the lady came Gawain gave even less resistance than before.

When the two were finished they drank rose water and lunched on scones and made off to share their afternoon in the garden. So true their bond already seemed that both trusted the other to lust for them still, even if they should take gentle time together in the cool air. And whilst they flirted in the yards an impish glees took hold of her, and she fled – laughing – from Gawain.

"Come find me, Love, and if ye can I'll give ye any kiss ye desire."

Gawain laughed as well, and scampered after the cuckold's bride. All throughout the high hedges and flowing trees of the garden he heard the airy tinkling of her laughter, yet ever she was four steps ahead. Five.

He was beginning to grow frustrated with her skill at the game, when at last he caught sight of a black-slippered foot disappearing around a hedge Proclaiming victory, he burst lustily around the corner and grabbed the silver-mooned mantle of the magician Myrddin.

As if stung, the knight recoiled.

"Am I not the prize ye sought?" asked the wizard, his smirk glimmering with teeth of silver and gold, deep in his lips.

"Ye know ye are not," the thane glowered. "What business have ye here? Ye have fared long from our master's court."

"Arthur is no master to me, as a virgin is no master to the unicorn. I wend as I please, and watch warily the ways of woe-sodden fools."

Gawain liked not to be called a fool, but less to argue with wizards. He scowled, yet made peace. "When last we met ye were not so rude. What want ye with me?"

"When last we met ye were not so brash," laughed the wizard. "But, deprived or dick-proud, ye remain a cursed man. I meant only to ascertain how well ye heed my warnings."

"Then ascertain, for I have things that need doing."

"Were it needed, I am certain those things could do themselves, and mayhaps in greater ways." The smiling sorcerer upheld one ringed digit to stay the blustering knight. "Tell me, do ye remain chaste?"

"Ye know I do not."

"And have ye denied all hospitality, or taken each gift?"

"Taken all, and gladly," growled Gawain. "'Twas ye thyself what told me take no orders from any man, and thee a man I ween."

"And no mail; ye wear as well I see," spake Myrddin. "So since ye seem so set to defy my warnings, I'm certain ye ken the names of thy hosts?"

But to Gawain's astonishment he found that he did not. Not even the woman with whom he had trysted.

"Indeed, much of what I have said may have been in poor wit, but I warn ye be wary, O heartful man. A wizard may only ward so well." And Myrddin touched his own throat, even as the line he'd burned on the thane's throat lit up with sharp pain. "The time of testing comes soon, Gawain, and I fear thy eye is turned too far astray."

And with that the wizard was gone and the pain as well, and willful Gawain was free once more to play.

That eve, to the cries of horn and hound, the lord once more appeared, this time with the rich carvings from a mighty boar. And he was praised by maids and thanes and serving folk. His men told of his valour, and of how his shining sword had dealt the killing blow.

Alongside the meat he brought the head of the boar, and no larger swine any there had seen. He had it brought, and to Gawain called, "And so is this swine thine, as was agreed, and ye must share as well!"

And Gawain once more kissed him full and long upon his lips, his strong hand upon the nape of his host's wide neck. Yet still he would not tell how he came upon that gift, nor did he give truly all he had received.

Another great feast was had and revelry of great strength. And the whole night long the lord laughed with him and proudly beat his back as friends do and his wife made desirous, unchaste gazes at them both. Loth's son was lief to be amongst such friends, and to be the subject of such desire, but Myrddin's visit had unnerved him, and so he begged leave to be upon his quest with the sun.

But the lord would hear none of it, and commanded the thane to stay one day more, and then he would take him to his fate.

The huntsmen left well before the dawn, barely rested and still sore drunk. But Gawain slept on in the lord's bed. And slept fitfully.

He dreamt anxious dreams. Green dreams. And in those dreams the lady wife's skin was green and when they fucked he bled from his throat. And when he saw her face he saw the face of the crone who none seemed to note.

Kisses woke him. Gentle on his ear. "'Tis morning, Sir Knight, and ye are late to rise."

And rise then he did. And nearly forgot his dreams for want of her.

When they were both spent, lying in the effluence of their lovemaking, she spoke long and fairly of how she admired him. She produced then a ruby ring of gold – the only thing she had worn into the thane's chamber.

"Take this, Prince, and wear it near thy breast. Remember by it the joy we have shared." And he took the ring and later bound it by a cord about his neck. "But this... What is this? So ugly a thing on so fine a flesh." Her finger traced Myrddin's gift.

"The mark of a magician."

At this she recoiled, but hid her aversion swiftly with a coy smile. "Wizards are not to be trusted."

"Some say the same of women."

She called him rude for his rebuke. A swine. He tried to laugh with her but she left instead.

With a sigh and a shrug, Orkney's champion robed himself gaily and went to join the serving men who loved him so well. They all called him gallant, and begged for tales and shows of valour.

When the lord returned he found Gawain engaged with three lithe maidens in a mountain of furs arrayed before the fire. A red-haired lass gasped, then laughed in surprise and the knight stood, unashamed in his nakedness. For he was naked save the lady's ring upon a throat-cord. "Friend, ye are returned! And here on the last day of my tenure."

"And it seems ye have had a mighty fine evening," laughed the giant.

"Such a wondrous welcome within these walls I've had. I would not squander it. For tonight I am thine in any task ye ask. But tomorrow I away with good guides sent by ye."

"Indeed," said the lord, his voice uncommonly grim. "A squire I shall send ye in a few hours time, after he has had his own early Mother's Night.

"But here," and he tossed a fine fox skin to his guest. "My greatest gain. All I ask last of ye is to do as ye promised and give thy gains to me."

And Gawain laughed and kissed him close, but said naught of who gave him such pleasure (and more). But the lord this time seemed less amused, and left with word that Gawain should catch what rest he could, glancing briefly to the ring above Gawain's heart.

But that long night the knight did not rest, but tossed and turned as howling winds carry mountains of snow onto the lands around. The witch-mark on his neck burns.

All-too-soon the morning-birds begin to call, and with each twitter, cheep, and warble he remembers the warmth and wanting of the nameless lady fair. He feared now the lord the manse - though he knew not why - and wished swiftly to be on his way.

Long before the first bells were to ring and the first ray of sun to shine he rose and summoned to him one of the tattooed serving men who had served him so well in his time there. "Bring byrnie and beast saddle. Wake the page. I mean to be garbed, arrayed, and away afore the house awakes."

The servant hurried to do as was said and soon he returned to lace the noble in warm clothes and strap him in shimmering plate and drape him in black rings. Last of all, he himself threw on a velvet coat, lined in mink and roped in gold. On its back and been sewn Solomon's Star.

When to Gringolet he came he found his steed also well-attired and groomed. The omen-axe dst hesvy nearby, abandoned as he revelled. The noble steed pranced with joy to see his master. Swiftly was he mounted and his shield granted. His squire-guide held the rains as they made to leave.

The bridge was brought down and the broad gates unbarred and opened. In silence the squire led him on.

The journey took them past crooked, barren tress and along icy cliffs, all clouded in mist under a grey sky. Burbling brooks bound their path. In time, as the sun rose, they stopped atop a snowy hill, their breath steaming.

Gawain's guide did not glance to him, but stared with stony eyes ahead. "Do not go."

But Gawain knew now there was no escaping his fate. His stomach felt empty, though he had breakfasted well. Myrddin's witch-scar burned. He felt the weight of the færie axe upon his back. "I must."

Now the boy looked to him briefly and with great sadness, then pointed. "Enter there that forested dell, and stay to the cliffy side. Once at the basin's bottom look to the left, and there shall be the henge."

The knight thanked the man and held his lance upright. Rode he then down that wicked way, but the squire fled afore his descent had e'en begun.

Down the wending, wooded way he went – down into the dark where crooked boulders and gnarled trees choked the sun. Once at the floor of the gap he turned to his left, and there saw a mighty hill, somehow still green, stood in a solitary, grey beam of sky, and on it a grim jumble of ancient standing stones. Trotting Gringolet to the base, he thought to bind his lead to a tree, but thought again and let it hang.

"When I am dead, ye should have the freedom to flee."

Coming then to the hill he saw that it was hollow. Hollow and dark. Centuries of soil and bough had wrapped the henge and made a cavern to house its heart, and grass had grown green atop it. The menhirs he saw above were but the top of the mighty pillars. He thought mayhaps something moved beneath.

Now, Gawain was brave, but even brave men can feel fear. And he felt a deep fear of that hill-hole. And so, helmed and mailed with a lance on one shoulder and the mark of his doom upon his back, he climbed the mound. He stood atop until he heard a horrible sound.

It was a howl to shatter his bones. A roar to rend him. A troll-croak straight from Hel. Pale-faced, he swayed and leaned against a carven stone.

"I am come, Sir Knight! Come claim thy stroke!"

But no reply came save the same horrid shriek. At last, cold with fear-sweat, he resolved that he must needs enter the hollow hill. And so, with great care, he began to descend. After all, if he feared his death, why should he fear it more below the earth than above it?

Many generations of tangled rootwork encased the stones, and more than once he caught his heavy boot in a narrow space and nearly twisted or broke the bone. But there was a light below, as if from a candle, and he strove ever downwards. His spear he soon had to abandon, but he stubbornly clung to the rest of his gear. He was kitted for war, as if he had not resolved to lay his bare nape before the witch-knight's blade.

At last he found a place where he could rest his feet on stony soil, though the height of the hollow made him hunch. Ever towards that yellow-white flicker-flare he gan, his sword undrawn but ready. He had not heard the call since he began his climb, but he liked the silence less. Above, clumps of green sward or occasional flakes of falling snow tumbled down into the dark maze.

Finally he turned a corner and found the light came not from a candle, torch, nor lamp, but from the luminescent surface of a white pool. The ceiling here was high – nigh as high as the whole height of the hill – and all about were the bases of the pillars. The moon-shimmer of the mere bewitched Arthur's bondsman.

But his trance was ended when the horrid sound came again before, out from behind a standing stone, stepped the green knight.

The knight was dressed as before, and drug an axe as large and wicked as the one he'd held before along the stony ground, sparking as it went. He skirted the edge of the pool and stood three ells from Prince Gawain, hefting his quelling-tool over one mighty shoulder. The damned thane's shoulders ached when he saw his axe's twin - he'd had no need to take the marker of fate from its plaque above Arthur's moon-table.

"I have come," said Gawain dully, as if in a dream.

"Gawain!" grinned the fiend. "May all the gods keep thee! By myne will, Sir, I welcome thee to myne place. It seems thu art a trusty soul, for in proper time thou comest to fulfill a promise made! Now that one twelve-month is passed I mean this Modranacht to repay thee the debt thou didst win.

"But come, be-est thu not so grim. 'Tis only us two who share all within this place. We may all do and say as we will! If still a man thou art, doffest now thy helm and preparest thou for a sweep alike the one which swept my head away. Unless thou meanst to argue?"

"I will make no argument," spoke the knight in the same droll voice, as his head he unhelmed. He gave a faint, sad smile then and before he knelt

40

said, "Make certain ye do it well in one stroke – I shan't allow another without first I being granted the same."

Dread coated the stalwart's neck as he presented it to the headsman. The useless axe he had carried on his journey – now fled of all dread – was discarded behind. He listened with weary heart to the rush of air as the giant's lusty limbs lifted the fresh axe high, poised to end his life. And he flinched not even once as the halberd fell. But the edge never landed.

"We must speak, Gawain. Thy due will still be done, but thou must ken the tests thou hast failed." And when Gawain glanced up he saw the green face of the lord of the manse. "Stand, sir, and let us speak as men." The fierce host leaned then with one awesome arm on the axe with which he aimed to end poor Arthur's friend.

Gawain stood, still wet with fear, but angry also at this illusion revealed. "Ye lied to me, giant! I thought ye my salvation, and a friend besides."

"I did not lie. Thou never asked myne name. And as for friend, I wish to think such as well." The grim man's lips looked as if they wished to smile, his eyes as if to weep. "But thou hast done ill by me. And I ken thy daliance with my wife."

The last of Gawain's blood left his face then, and his mouth filled with spit. "It was wrong of me to take her."

The greater man grew wroth at this, and ground his teeth, then softened and released a mighty sigh. "Thou didst not take her, any more than thou take the love of the Dragon's Son. And there was naught wrong in thy act, for did I not often say that 'what is mine is thine?'"

Shamed and confused, he replied, "Ye did."

Shaking his head, the giant continued, "I wilt not begrudge thee for not sharing a bed with me; no man nor woman born should e'er be forced to lay where they would not. Thou shared thy passion in ways thou wished. But when I asked, thou hid from me in shame. Trust, Sir Gawain. Trust is a test thou failest."

"I... I did not know..." said Gawain. He looked down to his muddy black boots. "How could I?"

"How much clearer can I be than to tell thee all that I mean? E'en myne wife told thee. But thou trusted not."

"I had thought... I did not wish thy love for her to be lessened."

"Do not lie! To me nor to thyself. Thou hid the truth for fear myne love would diminish, aye, but the love thou feared lessening was for thee, not she. A man may love fiercely in many ways, if that be the build of his heart.

"Love freely and love in trust. The only harm a lover brings is by retreating and by thinking without fact. My woman – nor any – is no villain,

41

and I no ravening wolf. Friendship comes in many forms, yet all are built on trust."

Gawain thought back to the Lady Gwenhyfar, when he had met her on the wall of Camelot. How certain she had been that love could only run two ways. What sadness had set her heart so? And what self-serving greed had blinded him to his host's generosity? Made him covet the man's wife for his own alone?

"There seems no apology I can make which can explain my lapse." The thane looked up from his open palms. "But tell me, by what name are ye known? Who is this friend I have lost? And what has caused so monstrous a skin to hold ye?"

The Henge Knight took off his own helm and shook out his mighty mane. "Bertilak be the name thy friend bears, for thou hast not lost me – only hurt me. And as for myne colour-curse? 'Tis the work of wicked Morgaine, who in witch's weft wanders myne hall."

"Morgaine?" Gawain's shock overtook his fear. "In the form of the crone whom all dismiss?"

"Dismiss out of fear. For she be a sorcerer of great and ill repute, versed by Myrddin the Malefactor himself. Baneful bed-mates they, and punishers of pride." The green one's face was sour with disgust.

"But Morgaine... She is my aunt!" Orkney's pride was unbelieving of the truth.

"Aye, thy aunt and half-sister to Arthur! Her mother the Duchess of Tintagel, on whom doughty Ythyr King later begot the famous King of Camelot. She sent me in this guise to do harm unto the Dragon's house – to put such horror in the heart of Gwenhyfar that hurt should fell her, and leave her husband free to be seduced once more.

"Yet that noble wifman was unstirred, and almost myne axe was destined for her beloved, which Morgaine would not have wished. But that crown-lord was kept alive by thy intervention. And in this thy wicked kin saw a new chance – to test the type of man her nephew would be. And here thou art, and her test thou failed."

"But," Gawain was indignant now, as incensed by Morgaine's machinations as by his own failings, "she has, more than any other, taught me selfishness, secrecy, and greed. She is not like others of her sex, but full of covetousness and guile."

"Then mayhaps she meant thee dead." It was the giant now who sounded resigned. "But whatever her aim, the curse must now run its course. Ne'er would I have thought myself aught but blithe to defeat the witch, but thou art a man I loved."

"And thee I loved as well," spoke Gawain with shuddering voice and watery eyes.

Then he knelt, and Bertolak donned his dark helm, horned with black and laquered green. The axe was raised and flesh was cut, and a mightier stroke was never in those lands seen again. Blood spilled on ancient soil.

But that was not the end of Gawain. For he clambered out from that henge-hole and made his way to Gringolet. About his throat he bore a thick green scarf, stained dark in places with fresh blood. In his hand he held the axe.

Rode he long, wild, western ways back to the court of the King. As he climbed the hill of Camelot, he bore a joyous red hood won in some contest of which he seldom told. And there he was greeted and gifted and entered in song. But he was a more sombre man now – though kinder and more trusty according to many.

For all his life thereafter he was nevermore seen without the shawl about his throat which, with age, grew ever blacker and more frayed. Some whispered that it was to hide the mark Myrddin left, which had turned aside the blade and slain baneful, baned Bertolak. Others whispered that it held on his head, for the giant's axe had indeed undomed him, but the magician's magic had maintained him. In this latter camp some rumoured that at night he unwound the neck-binding and placed his head upon a stand to guard him whilst he slept. Others said that if ever it were to come loose the beheading would be complete and Orkeny's Eldest would be given to the grave; these would have you believe that it was in this way that Medrawt, his brother, quelled the champion in the dying days of Avalon, but I have heard that he instead died of a mortal wound from Lanslod Lak as he defended the trust of Arthur, though Arthur already had despaired of life.

And of Myrddin? Did he save the boy to spite Morgaine? Or to aid her? Gawain was nevermore a friend to his aunt, but she seemed hardly to take note.

No matter the truth of it, it remains that Sir Gawain continued on and did many more great deeds, and bedded many more lovers. But ever he wore Bertolak's gift, and nevermore a lie he told. It is a special sadness that the likes of Loth's son shall never be seen again.

# The Hill of Cold Silver

nd if ye can retrieve it and bring it here I'll offer a hundred silver – a year's tithes."

Sir Childe nodded. "The price is well enough, though it makes me wonder if there be not greater danger in the hill than ye let on. What was the tome's name again?"

"*Emendations on the Congress with God* by the hand of Hali the Younger. It is very old, and doubtless very fragile. Be careful not to finger it much, nor let it be exposed to rain. When the scholar wrote it he was already quite old and his pen had become –" but the twittering priest was interrupted by the knight's heavy glove on his gesturing – pleading – right hand.

"We shall find thy text, Father, and return by next noon for the coin." Turning, he mounted his noble steed and looked down once more. "Keep safe, dream well, and pray for us to your god, whichever that may be, that our quest succeeds."

As the two knights rode off in a cloud of pale road-dust, away from the crumbling plaster and stone of the priest's temple, the elder of the pair looked to Sir Childe. "An unhappy name for a book. Where I hail from such would be questioned or quarantined, or else would be old enough to have been writ by Greeks."

"I know not the Greeks," spake Sir Childe, turning his grizzled jaw towards his companion, "but a barrow seems quarantine enough, do ye not ween? No man I ken seeks library in tomb-hills. No man save our friend the village priest, that is."

"Ye speak true," grumbled the Crossways Knight, golden crucifixes on his white cape sparkling in the late sun. "And in truth it matters little to me what heresies spread in these lands; my God lives in heavens of other worlds, to which someday I may return. Whatever offenses Hali wrote are offenses to no Lord of mine."

Sir Childe knew of many gods, yet followed none. Aye, he knew some prayers, could name a handful of common godlings, and wore a jangling pilgrim's garden of charms, tokens, and medals, but he had never heard the call of any church. He admired the Crossways Knight however for his devotion; though the man had not been 'neath the heavens of his God for many years he still bore a deep love for him which overshadowed aught else, and

Childe knew mickle of love – and of loss as well.

The two rode for the rest of the evening, through pallid heather and dry-caked mud. Above, the stars of the Hyades and Aldebaran shone, marking the road to the great lake also called Hali, even in the day. In time the twin moons rose, and somewhere beyond them Childe knew that the spired heights of Carcosa rose, full of the reveries of the King's court. A court once full of men, but now filled more with magi. Rumours spread of the King's new faith, and his forgotten love of sword and counsel. Even the Cross-ways Knight, who had been to court, spoke in hushed tones of the strange company kept; he spoke also of his own former friend who settled there – a man of great might with some hidden magics who had followed Childe's companion to these lands after many years apart. The Crossways Knight had only ill to say of that mysterious parliament, and thusly of its monarch, but Childe was a loyal man – a royal man – and would not damn the court for fear of damning the King.

The twin suns finally began to set, the sky turning a violent tawny as its lord sank into his nocturnal tomb, and the rolling fields of heather gave way to rising, crooked bluffs. A chill air blew between the bone-white sandstone cliffs, howling softly and playing at the horses' ears. And on the two went, between those towering stone hills on unroads untraveled by men in all the ages of history. 'Twas said the place was haunted by the spectres of long-dead philosophs, and this Childe did not doubt. The clitter-clatter of shale, knocked loose by the capering of little gods on the scrub-painted hilltops – invisible to all but the corner of the eye and the heart of the imagination – made an occasional chorus to their silent ride. The avenues between the mesas were wide, and the early night illuminated them brightly, but despite this it proved simple to lose one's way and often they were made to wheel their mounts about and choose a new path.

It was after the dozenth wrong path that Sir Childe – who had been pray-ing softly to whatever would listen to guide them on their way – called them to a halt. The cooling wind, now made bold by the death of the silver suns, whipped and cracked at his great, yellow capes as he dismounted. He fum-bled at his breast with his thick leather gauntlets until he found the charm he sought and drew it to his lips. The Crossways Knight looked away with disapproval yet said naught. The pewter medallion was rough in form, but depicted on it the squating shape of Montus, the God of Unfound ways. As his kissed its cold face he begged for a sign to lead on towards the barrow which held their antediluvian prey. He promised silver, gems, and maps of unmapped alleys for an answer, and as surety he bit his lip so his kiss sat bloody on the trinket. He then looked up and took once more to horse.

"Ween ye that shall do more than thy other prayers?" asked the yellow knight's companion with barely-concealed disdain.

"I know not what to ween," he replied, "but I hope that it shall find us the way."

"And what if we are to find the barrow? Shall we assault it with fire and sword? Do the dead fear such?"

"We may have no need of steel. Or we may. The ways of the world and its mirrors are often unknown to me. I have heard that sometimes the ancient dead wish only to sleep, or to speak."

"To speak curses!" the white knight spat. "I have been inside burial mounds to face evil afore, though all times previous it has been beside my brother's bastard, who now serves as my enemy's steward in other lands." He grew quiet for a short while before glaring once more before them. "Yet in all my times 'neath corpse-earth I have yet to find aught but fiends and kin of Cain. Sorcerers, succubi, spectres, and lichmen – all hungry for blood and misery. Nay, Childe, we walk only into damnation. By God! I had hoped my descents were done. Take heed, fellow, and let it not speak should it try, for it may weave dark spells with its black tongue; cut it swift and cast what charms thy gods may grant ye that it may not rise anew."

"They are not my gods," spake Sir Childe, feeling the cool breeze on his face. "Not in the way that thyne is thyne. Where thy god is lord and teacher both, these are but fellow travelers I sometimes meet along the way, and whether they aid or nay is a matter of friendship or pity, not duty."

"For a knight ye are mighty free with thy allegiances." Yet he argued no further.

Whether it was chance, the approving eye of Montus, or some other sense that led them towards their sought-after path even Sir Childe could not say, but by the light of their red torches they did soon glimpse the path of black stones which the priest had told would lead them to their prize. Each was but the size of a child's fist, but flat and perfectly round. They led, each a half-pace from the last, in a meandering line deep between a cleft in two high hills which neither had noted afore.

"Deviltry and witchcraft," swore the Crossways Knight, and Sir Childe would not disagree.

Slowly and with a growing weight in their hearts they followed the path of black stone into the night. Above, the tops of the hills grew closer and closer until even the bright stars of the Hyades shed no light on their journey. Stones occasionally clattered above them 'neath the footfalls of mischievous sprites, and the flickering lights in their hands painted the austere lines of the stony passage as vast, undulating, hungry waves of death. Both knights spoke prayers as loud as they dared – which was not so loud at all – to ward off ill. Perhaps the foreigner believed some protection was granted, but the yellow-caped cavalier had few such illusions; here the hills and their gods ruled, not the gods of man.

In time the passage began to widen once more even as the black stones grew more numerous. By the time they were under the light of the twin moons once more the entire ground was tiled in black – a shadowy bath-house floor which rang under the shod hooves of their mounts. The horses grew shy as they breathed the air there, and Childe did not reproach them; it was sharp and cold like steel in winter. The land before them stretched towards the horizon, flashing silver and gold under the moons as clouds moved at incredible speed under no wind. And in the distance, wreathed in a white-blue aura, lay a wide white hill.

"This is no godly place," whispered the Crossways Knight, and his low voice echoed forever acrost the expanse.

Sir Childe turned back and looked to the hills from which they had come. Only the two which framed the path remained, standing tall and grim in an endless plain of black rock. In the crevasse from which they had ridden yellow lilies sprouted and waved invitingly, tempting them to return to the rational world. But they had made a promise, and the priest had promised them coin. And for a knight dispossessed – as they both were – silver was as certain a need as food, rest, and love (which they also both lacked, save love of God or King).

And so they hied swiftly 'crost that dreaming flat, their hearts beating and their horses' eyes red and rolling with fear – though they would not run, for they knew there was no escape on any side. As they neared the hill they saw that on it was a sward of snowy white, long and wild. This grass also grew up between the loathsome stones at their feet, and pushed some aside to reveal pale, wet earth. Beneath this carpet could be glimpsed chiseled corner pillars of white marble, erected by some strange mason in the ages before ages. Coming to a halt, they saw that the pillars and the walls which bound them – together forming the base of the hill – were set all about with tortured and beautiful faces. These masks were not carved nor mounted upon the stone, but were glimpsed in the undulating patterns of the flat pearlescent facade of the masonry.

"E tu che se' costi, anima viva, pàrtiti du cotesti che son morti," breathed the elder knight. Sir Childe looked to see the blanch of fear in his compan-ion's cheeks. Feeling the question in the yellow rider's eye, the foreigner answered, "A bit from an old poet."

"One of the Greeks?"

"Another tribe." He swallowed hard and ran his good hand over his stubbled jaw. "There are other ways to fill our purses. Need we venture further inside this Hell?"

"We have given our word."

"I have come to learn that there are times when a word does not bind as else it might." Yet he pulled on his reins and followed Childe in a route about the mound, in search of a gate.

And indeed a door there was on the further side. Old and stained it was, of some solid wood, cracked and turned ochre by some perfidious fungus. An iron rim was set about its border, rusted and black, and an iron ring was set on its face. And beside this ring, in the centre of the door, was a curious sigil which occupied much of the space – almost invisible for it was set in yellow paint nearly the shade of the moulde. It had three arms, crooked and splayed, arranged about a ringed centre. At the sight of this portal the Crossways Knight gasped and clutched at his chest. It was many long breaths before he could summon words.

"That same sign marked the barrow where I lost my nephew, and the horrors it brought were not worth what else was gained. All misery in my new life was brought by servants of that rune. We have no reason to risk our souls against the power of this evil." And he made a sign acrost his chest.

"But does not thy god entreat ye to confront evil whereever ye should see it? What mighty paladin are ye if ye blanch at paint on stone?" Childe knew his companion would reproach his goading, yet he had little desire to enter the hill alone. "I have seen your silvered sword raised high 'gainst many a fearsome foe, and seldom have I known ye to shy from the punishment of sorcery."

"There is more than sorcery in this place," he answered, and was quiet.

Dismounting, the two swordsmen led their steeds closer to the hill. The beasts whickered as they were brought near, yet did not resist. A pair of iron rings were set in the wall near the door, and to this were the mounts tethered. They donned their baldrics and the Crossways Knight, unable to hold aught in his mangled left mitt, slung his shield over his shoulder; on it was borne a bear pierced by many arrows. Approaching then the portal, the two stood uncertainly but with solid footing. At last Sir Childe stepped forth and laid one gauntlet on the iron ring which adorned the portal. Behind him he heard the whisper of steel as his companion drew his silvered blade.

The door-iron seemed to warm his hand, even through his mail, yet his bones felt as ice. In these conflicting temperatures he had the clear and unsettling sensation of his soft skin sloughing off his finger-bones and pooling like wax at his feet. He stifled a cry – only mostly succeeding – and looked to his arm, which lay unchanged. Grinding his handsome teeth, he steadied himself and pulled at the door, which opened easily – silently – and with the thick scent of roses too long from their stem but not yet dead. Beyond could be glimpsed white floor tiles, heavy and full of masks as the marble of the outer hill. The moons gave no light down this passage.

Returning to his steed, the yellow knight unhooked his sturdy lantern from his saddle and lit it. The crippled knight who accompanied him peered futilely into the gap, and Sir Childe shone his light on the darkness. What was revealed was a long, white hall, descending into the earth and set on each side with pillars carved in endless spirals and death-sigils. As the oil-bright met the reflective stone it skittered away and made new shadows in the domains of the grim pillars and these shadows danced and clawed in pagan mockery of their pursuer.

"If thy mouth opens only to speak on how ye mislike this place ye may tell it its job is done," spake Childe with grim mirth.

"Never before have I felt so clearly God's wisdom that I shall not walk from this place," answered the elder.

"Ye may wait with the horses."

The silver-sword glowered but stepped forth into the uneasy barrow, shoulders squared and blade ready. He spake a prayer and Childe ran his fingers acrost his charms before he followed.

At first their feet echoed endlessly in the hollow hill, but once they had gone far enough that their light source no longer touched the entrance they heard the heavy door slam, and the sounds it birthed drowned out all sensation, all thought, all sentience. The world they had left behind was truly and forever gone. There was only the timeless unknowing of absence.

Wallowing in an empty and endless space of despair and non-being, Sir Childe let fall his lantern and began to run. As the darkness grew, so too did his footfalls, their steady drum lending to the music of the sanity-rending portal's closure. The part of him that was still him ran in fierce defiance – intent to defeat the demons of this place – with runed blade in hand. But the part of him which dreamt to the cadence of the echoing passage ran with the fear of the unknown and with the need for love and for validation. Somewhere behind him the Crossways Knight cried out, but his companion could not hear him and would not have turned back if he did – not when the need was ahead, the fear behind, and his steel hungry for enemy flesh.

And there the floor fell. Like his thoughts, his vigilance, and his love, the tiles of the floor began to drift apart. For an eyeblink the soldier in him clung tenaciously to earth, leaping deftly from one marble slab to the next as they drifted further and further apart and further down. But his footfalls were loud and the door-boom louder and the dreamer - the fool – which lived in his head and played chaos with his heart stepped – or slipped – off and he tumbled, headlong, into the sensationless abyss below.

It was quiet now, and he fell with no speed and no light. Somewhere, too, fell the Crossways Knight, his silvery capes churning in the nothingness. But, though they were close enough to touch, they did not – could not – know they were so close. An age they drifted without the mind-break tantrum of the wyrd-drum, and in that absence Sir Childe let himself be lost, and wander the idyll-garden of the man he once was.

Before he knew what love of King could be, and knew better love of lady. When gods could be trusted and admired, and his sword was heavy and bloodshed a burden. What world was this where comfort dwelled? What land where it was pleasure to be ignorant? How long had he ridden the homeless road? How long the killer's currents? If there were ever a door back to Before he must surely take it. But there was no such door – could never be – and tears burned his cheeks to be reminded of what was lost.

"...door..."

The voice drifted through forgetfulness, and Childe knew it well. His father.

"...land..."

Nay, Master Homart who tutored him well.

"...damned..."

His mother, whom he had never known.

"...door..."

Mireal.

"...thy arms to pull," came clear the voice of the Crossways Knight. His silver-bright blade flashed as it pointed ahead into the oppressive naught to where a ledge of white stone hovered, domed by a lintel of screaming faces.

Again Childe was entreated with his arms to pull, and he found that he could traverse the absence with broad strokes, as of a swimmer. His companion, sheathing his weapon, clutched at the yellow worthy's sturdy boot, for with his dead arm he could not effectively ford the cruel dream-sea. They flew that way, the cynic and the cripple, through the crushing un-night.

It was not so long – a moment and no more, though at first the gap had seemed great – before they found themselves on their knees on solid stone. Behind them eternity yawned. On their knees they shook and wretched until their memories were empty or imprisoned once more. And when they lifted their heads, eyes wet with regret and with discomfit, it was onto a wide chamber of marble pillars beyond the gate. The lantern had been lost, yet a dull golden light seemed to flicker about them, and by this eery glow were they gifted sight.

"Ye shall lose me here," whispered the Crossways Knight. "God is calling me home."

"There are no doors home in this trap, merely mirrors showing what we have passed on our road."

And as one they rose, drew once more their shimmering steel, and stepped forth.

In that chamber of columns the darkness thrived, and empires of shadow grew and multiplied in the wake of their strange illumination. Like torchlight, or a sun under water, it moved, and the marble floor looked both shifting and solid beneath their hard boots. At the edges of Sir Childe's eyes the shadows walked as men, and stepped acrost alleys of naught. His blood beat hot and his unnerved mind wandered back to better – forever gone – times.

He thought of the gardens of his home – the debt-denied estates of Lanaulon. Above, the silver suns. All about, tall hedges – shaped in his memory as the pillars of the subterranean hall and not in any shape they truly held in life. The noble columns of his own childhood home – ancient in design though not in construction – watched over the paradise of lost happiness. His father's laugh drifted through the menagerie like leaves in autumn and red and golden seed-dust gave a soporific texture to the air. He felt the warm weight of Mireal's hand in his, yet when he turned he could not see her. Somewhere a great bell tolled, a sound like steel on stone. His tongue tasted of wine and he could smell the rich notes parading from the kitchens. A summer which never was could never be again. He squeezed tightly at the ghost in his yearning grip, but it was limp, like a dead thing.

In the garden a man walked between the pillared greenery. Yet he was not like any man. He was tall and lithe, with skin of shining argent, and when he turned his head Childe saw that the eyes set in his sharp features were milky like those of a blind man. The thing was gone in an instant and he whispered assurances to Mireal. She was safe. Nothing could hurt her nor tear him from her. The world would no longer turn and 'neath the goggled eyes of the moons they should be wed. Another near-man strode through their path, and he smiled with sword-sharp fangs.

Steel rang and Mireal's long-gone hand pulled for freedom, but Childe would not let her go. Not this time. Even as the creature strode closer on unnatural stilt-legs he thrust the spirit protectively behind him.

"Ye shall not have her!" he bellowed. But it wanted him. It reached with two hungry claws, whistling low in its throat, yet he could not defend himself, for his fighting-fist was clutching his past. "Have me then," he spake low, "if it means her I must never forget."

The deep-cold nails of its cruel talons brushed his cheek and he glimpsed in the sheen of its precious skin the burnished lustre of Mireal's seaborn skin, the bright and blue flash of her eye. And all was gone.

With the sound of the suns above being cloven and rent by a blade of searing-hot metal the beast was skewered. The terrible unreality of that beloved garden once more gave way to the flickering gloam of the white hall. The Crossways Knight stood sweating, his silvered blade stuck nearly to the hilt in the chest of the dream-hunter and mud-silver blood running in his black beard. In the dark, more silvermen flashed, flickered, strode, smiled, and disappeared. The emptiness was sick with the fiends.

"I weened ye already hellbound by the light in thy eyes," panted Childe's accursed saviour. "But now ye are returned and I counsel ye to lift the blade ye have dropped and wield it aside me lest we fall to their seeking claws.

Bleary-eyed and still three-quarters dreaming, Childe of Lanaulon fumbled for his fallen blade. "Were ye also beset with dreams?"

"Only of the doom God brings me." And together they stood in the dark. Swords upraised. Hair slick with sweat. Runes and silver shining in the witchlight as their enemies advanced.

Through the anxious blackness came a lightful host, and in each hungry face was a mirrorlike sheen. The men swung and their brands became the well-levres of their foes' browning blood. With vigour unknown in common man they pumped their arms, flooding the floor with putrescent gore. Yet no sound ever did their foes make, and ever on they came, sometimes stealthily dragging the corpses of their fallen brethren back into their lightless shield, to be burned or entombed or returned to life. Childe had hoped that when he died he would meet the eyes of another of his folk, yet it seemed that here lay his doom 'gainst unworldly fiends.

Their breath came in hitches and the tendons in their shoulders burned with the weight of their swords, yet on they fought. Slashing-bright edges clove sharp-bright skulls and the champions' eyes were made kaleidoscopes of violence. Blind with blood and blind with terror, Childe could see no escape for he and his noble companion. Imagine no future. Yet is no future so terrible when one lives forever in fear of the past? Nay, not so terrible at all, thought the yellow rider, and his thrusts began to slow.

It was then the chime sounded. High and tin – a clarion of clarity in the gloom. Again it rang, and even the silvermen seemed to pause in some primitive awe. Claw and blade both lowered, and the two knights blinked in unbelief as the creatures parted to make an aisle for their passage, many still bearing the wounds of their conflict.

"Do my eyes see aright?" gawped the Crossways Knight. "Do the demons make way?"

"They do," spoke Sir Childe, his voice far from glad.

"A trick it must be."

"And if it is? We have no recourse but to walk their gauntlet."

And so the two, weary arms still anxiously holding their steely armaments at the ready, advanced down the corridor of unreal flesh. The silvermen watched them with glittering eyes and needle-rich maws, but made no move save the metal blood which fled their grievous cuts. As they progressed slowly onwards, ever onwards, the lines of dream-things seemed not to lessen. Indeed, the ranks seemed even to grow thicker as they were pulled inexorably down that endless hall. Strange pillars of ivory and eyes loomed into the darkness, and silent cries choked the eerie air.

"It is worse now. Much worse."

Sir Childe looked to his companion, whose face was slick with sweat (as doubtless was his own), "What is?"

"The knowledge that my journey with ye nears its end."

"Belief often tempts the gods to action."

The Crossways Knight shook his head and made a crossways sign with his sword. "The One God has a plan, and no man can change that, no matter how hard they may strive. If ye are to make it from this whole, ye are to do it alone."

The yellow knight thought to answer, but decided against it; a man's doom is his own burden. He looked ahead, and knew that both their dooms, should they be preordained, lay directly ahead.

Lit by a brilliant unlight, there stood an impossibly tall portal at the end of the smiling path. Childe's eyes stung to behold it, but could not be parted from it. It seemed to yawn, empty and growing, as its call echoed in his bones.

"God dared not enter," whispered one of the silvermen, and the Crossways Knight was startled to hear one speak, though his companion was not – Childe had seen many strange things in the world, and all the more since the King had taken council with warlocks. They uttered no further warnings but, as one, the ghastly guardians raised their left hands and pointed clawed, bony fingers towards the opening.

The elder knight stood, still gawping at the guardian what spoke, his head tilted as if listening for some far-off sound, until Sir Childe urged him onwards with a firm hand. Onwards towards oblivion. Towards death. Towards congress with God. The yellow knight's carpet of charms jangled under his heavy cape as his dark boots pulled him past the doorstep.

And into the naught.

Pure.

Empty.

Naught.

Their footsteps echoed silently as they ventured further beyond the realms of man's power.

Childe felt a pressure in his chest as if his heart yearned to escape. But in the same breath his organ felt lighter than wool-strands on water. His eyes glazed as he found himself fumbling to focus, and far away he heard clear and familiar voices.

"Driant?" choked his companion. "Brother?"

*It is not him,* Childe tried to say, though his lips were sewn shut. *And that is not my father. My wife. That is not undone Lanaulon I hear.* Hot tears burned through the sweat and blood on his cheeks.

"All can be forgiven," cried the Crossways Knight, and Sir Childe watched the blurred shape of him begin to move swiftly away. All can be undone."

*Goodbye, friend.* But the outworlder would never hear him.

All about were walls of naught encircling endless plains of non-being, and amidst it all trudged Sir Childe. The air was something akin to cold, and the battle-sweat on his skin turned to ice, worming under his paper skin to chill his bones. His limbs were heavy and his mail weighed on his broad shoulders. Lowering his coif, he let his lank hair fall in waves, matted with exertion. His blade was heavier than a writ of guilt, yet he held tight to it, imagining (and half-convincing himself) that its solid grip was instead the lost hand of his beloved, which made his heart heaviest of all.

Loud echoed his steps in the void, and he went on, uncomprehending, for an endless time, his eyes drawn ever to the past. It was only after he had already taken a score of steps on dark stone that he noted his surroundings had changed.

Gone were the endless fields of naught and here was a cold expanse of stone. Braziers of green fire burned along the walls, but even so the hall stretched impossibly high and wide – beyond all seeing. Much of the great floor was empty, but some ways ahead a dark shape, flickering with green, rose. The way was long, but Childe was beyond weariness.

His sore hands gripped the sweat-black leather of his sword hilt and his empty mind burned through the sockets of his eyes. At last he was in sight of the shape and saw it to be a gathering of shelves, deep with books and lit by greeny torches in black brackets. From the centre of the lonesome library rose a small ziggurat, and atop it a casket of silver and glass.

"The Congress with God," murmured the knight, unwilling at first to imagine his goal in reach. Lowering his blade, he walked swiftly to the nearest shelf and claimed an otherworldly torch upon reaching it.

The shelves smelt of dust and dry moulde and the air tasted of copper. At first he merely walked the aisles, eagerly watching for the desired tome, but many of the texts had no titles on their spines – or no spines at all – and soon he sheathed his blade so he could dig frantically through the collection, sometimes burying his arm to the shoulder in ancient vellum and parchment as he sought Hali's fabled text. No wind penetrated the stillness of the hall, just as no thoughts of danger penetrated the stillness of his thoughts – frozen only on the pursuit of his goal. So strange had his journey been, and so terrible his ordeals, that he was unable to allow himself aught else to consider.

The crinkle and crack of yellowed writings filled his ears even as the must reddened his eyes and wet his nose. He sneezed, obliterating the runed sheet betwixt his fingers and shuddering his flame. He felt another rising and threw his hand up to protect the other artifacts from his showering gunge. Pulling his wet fingers from his face, he stepped back a moment to observe the shelves. They had not seemed so many on his approach , but they were, and they were deceptively deep. "I shall be years searching," he thought in dismay. "And all for naught but silver." In that moment he hated all coin. In his despair his thoughts traveled dreadfully to the fact that he knew not the path home – home to his horse and the open road, for his true home was now merely a fantasy.

"Seeker..." The voice was as the written letters of a sad poem on a summer's day. "Seeker..."

Childe needed but an instant to realize that the unhearable whisper resounding from above. Above at the height of the ziggurat. From the silver and glass of the mysterious bier. He thought to ignore it, but the insistent call came again and again, boring into his fragile skull with the scent of Lanaulon and the taste of crashing steel.

"What do you wish of me?" His voice was loud, yet it quavered. One hand rested on his swordhilt, yet was too weak to draw it.

"Ye seek..."

"Aye, I do," cried Childe in consternation.

"Seek..." it repeated.

And as that word flowed down the steps of the ziggurat Childe heard its pull. Felt it in his feet. Raising his torch in one white-knuckled fist – its greeny light casting a ghastly hue – and his other tight about the scabbard of his heavy blade, the yellow knight began to climb. For once his journey was neither far nor painful, nor even strange save for the silvery half-voice which beckoned him on. Time had barely passed when he stood above the ancient corpse-case.

And through the milky window atop its face he glimpsed the cadaverous inhabitant within. Its skin was grey and lined, splotched sometimes with black and everywhere folded over itself and wrinkled. Black claws rested at its side and silver bracelets, rings, brooches, and crowns hung on it and struck through it, making a mail of riches. Silvery eyes gazed through the pane, and moved as Childe moved. Upon its chest was a blackleather folio fitted with ill-cut pages.

"Seeker..." it moaned through lips which never moved.

He lay his hand upon the casket and it was cold to the touch, stinging his skin even through his gauntlet. With his other he leant his greeny torch against the burial stand. His eyes met those of the thing and his breath stopped briefly in his throat.

"Ye are the guardian of this book."

"Aye..."

"Is it..." Childe glanced to the rough-skin cover, then back. "Hali's Emendations?"

"On the Congress with God..."

With great difficulty the yellow knight drew his blade, only to rest it heavily on the corpse-lid. "I will slay ye if needs be. I will have the book."

The torch in his hand shuddered and jumped in the muted laughter of the wraith. "Not I... 'Tis ye what must be fought..."

Childe had no intention of fighting himself, but feared the sorcery of the tomb. "What means ye?"

"So full... Of love..." The lightless eyes smiled with sadness. "Love of life... Of woman... Of steel..." It hurt somehow to hear each accusation. Each more than the last, though he knew not why he should be ashamed of such. "But most of all... Of King." Childe's heart felt as if an iron stake had been hammered into it to split it asunder. "They fill ye... Heavy... Like stones... Drown ye in the world-river...

"Banish ye all love..."

"Nay!" he shouted into the echoing, empty chamber. "I shall decry no love. Surrender ye the tome!" And he raised his sword pommel high to break the glass.

"No home... Life on roads... Blood... Fear... Life forsakes ye..."

The yellow knight shivered with unconquerable dread.

"Dead... Lost... Past... Betrayed by her weak flesh... Woman forsakes ye...

"Mireal!" gasped the charm-laden lordling. His arm ached to shatter the tomb but could not be lowered.

"Blood... Once more... Blood... Guilt... Fear... Death... Steel forsakes ye..."

The heavy-bladed brand lit afire and the angry red flame licked down the hilt and coursed over the champion's hands in waves. He cried out in agony and surprise, shaking with the effort to free himself from this curse-spell.

"Duty... Fealty... Doom... Ignorance... Thaumaturgy... King forsakes ye..."

With a prayer leaking from the last of his lungs and an effort like breaking one's own back with one's own hands, Childe released his shoulders and dropped the fiery weapon with a shatter-crash on the panes of the corpse-coffer.

The blanket of flame fled from its metal wick and cascaded over the silent lord of silver as he uncried defamations and warnings which drove like needles into Childe's mind. But, staunchly yet still gasping for breath, the knight reached with burned arms into the inferno. In one charred glove he gripped his gilt edge and in the other Hali's pages. He looked one final time into the sightless, rolling orbs of his tormentor, then descended to the library below.

Beneath his arm the book boiled to be read – even to be opened. The myriad charms clattered and scrambled to be shy of the thing, and those what touched it were discarded by their parents in the godhalls. It was a living thing, breathing with ink and biting with blasphemies. Sir Childe, in his desperation, could allow himself only to see a simple book.

Once he reached the floor he removed the tome from its rest 'neath his arm and examined it as the silver lord's pyre raged above him. Unheard, several pendants fell to the stone and were forgotten. "All this for a book," he thought, running one numbed finger over the surface of the cover. Uneven letters stamped in the leather proclaimed its name: *Emendations on the Congress with God*. Harmed by the curiosity of the cursebook, the knight rested the volume in the crook of his arm and gently – gently – opened to the first page.

He read but a few words before he slammed shut the treatise, his eyes fountains of heartbreak making rivers on his cheeks and his heart straining to split itself once more in twain. He could bear to read no more. He could not bear to have more that he held dear torn from him by truth. Yet he could not leave that moment with a heart unbroken, and he mourned loudly for the love he knew he had lost.

Sir Childe was not surprised to find the priest and a handful of armed men – dressed in rusted, hand-me-down mail and with spears nearby as blunt as their clubs – waiting for him outside the pass. He left the sandstone cliffs behind atop his steed – glad to be rid of the ghost-ridden expanse which housed the hill and from which the yellow knight could not recall how he had escaped – and led the Crossways Knight's own mournful mount. He saw the cleric sitting high and proud on an old, broken work-horse – both expended but too valuable to dispose of. His white scarves flew in the wind of the dawn gloaming and his heavy wool cassock hung on his thin frame like a coat of wet fur.

"Sir Knight!" called the clergyman, waving with one skeleton arm, re-vealed to the elbow as the sleeve fell to its own weight. "Ye return, as I knew ye would. Where is... ah." The victorious quester had neared enough for the priest to see the calculating recognition on the horseman's wan face. "I suppose it was too much to hope ye both should return. Yet 'twas a death in service of a noble cause, I assure ye."

"The cause is silver and no other. And as for my fellow, I know not that he is dead." His look challenged the priest to ask more, yet he did not.

"And silver I have, Master Horse." One grim hand clutched the faded, once-noble hilt of the workhorse's saddle. "Yet mayhaps ye may be wanting more?"

"More silver? I assume ye mean for more work." Childe observed the armed peasants, and they met his glare with the prideful gruffness one fel-low in a conspiracy gives to another. "What work is this?"

"Goodly work! Godly work!" proclaimed the knight's patron. "The land suffocates as sleep slips unnoticed into its soul. The King on his gilded throne learns lullabies from somnambulists as rot beds our villages. Sor-cery has supplanted sword and screed in our kingdom's seat and men are too afraid to dispel it! Our village has seen enough of the negligence of the King and has joined with the brotherhood of a new age. Surely the book has tempted ye – shown ye the truth of things. To have one such as ye – so noble a knight – at our side (or even, at our head) would surely draw more impassioned countrymen to our cause! Follow thy heart, Sir Childe, and rise up in service to a new age!"

"Ye would ask me to betray my King? Lead peasant armies on Carcosa and its generals?" There was a tightness in the weary warrior's chest and in his sword arm . "Nay, that I shall never do."

The fyrdmen bristled, but their leader spoke swiftly from atop his bent-backed steed. "But think ye of the people of this land! How they suffer!"

"They would suffer more without a king."

"That is not true!" bellowed the godsman, though he quickly quieted, glaring at Childe with caution and deviltry.

"It is by love of the King that these lands are protected. Maintained."

"But they are maintained no longer!"

"A knight must love his king, and so I do. I shall do naught against him. Now I will have my silver and be off."

The purse clinked in the theologian's white hand. "Thy blade hungers. I ken men like ye well. Ye pretend to noble airs, but hunger for hot blood like winter wolves. Let us lead ye to thy prey."

"I love my steel, aye, and yearn to feel its bite more than I would wish. But if ye war with Carcosa it will be thy flesh I rend. And if ye withhold my purse it shall also be ye I cut." The footmen bristled once more and tightened the grips on their spears. "I am tired, but I am also the veteran of many bloody geases and shall not be cut down by thy like." He rested Hali's text on the horn of his saddle and drew his blade - sparkling in the sunrise. His other hand he held forwards.

The priest blanched, turning somehow even more pale, before tossing the pouch. Childe caught it easily, burnt hand or no, and turned wordlessly to leave.

"Master Yellow," he staid his mount yet did not look back towards his former employer. "The book!"

Lanaulon's heir had entirely forgotten the tome. Looking down, he could see its unassuming face in the newborn suns. He could take it. Defy these fools. Read of all the sins of human assumption.

But nay.

He loved life too much to lose more convictions, though he no longer knew what the book had taught him to forget. His aching fingers let the ancient text drop to the soil, pages spilling from the binding - sorrowful paper tears - and rode off to the sounds of the priest's curses.

He was proud of what he had done before that challenger. Mayhaps the cleric was right and the King's time was done. Mayhaps the cantrip-council in Carcosa did spell doom and blood. But he had confirmed all the loves he knew - could ever know.

Of life.

Of steel.

Of King.

He did not hear as the ghost he once loved cried out for him in agony and was forgot.

# The Burned Man

ome poor bastard had been poaching the King's deer. Only one or two, but it was still a crime against the Crown. No matter that there had been no true king for a century or more and the Shirrif held dominion over the Royal Forests. A crime was a crime. And the Foresters Royal were the men tasked with punishing the criminals.

Donals Ameerish - often called Donals t'Gelt by those who begrudged him his tribal ancestors - was the most feared of the foresters of the city of Hihalem and was proud of his job. He knew times were hard and that the guilds made it difficult for some to earn their keep within Hihalem's ancient stone walls, but that was no reason to turn felon - and it was certainly no concern of his; when a man kills the King's deer he learns to lament it.

This particular poacher was an older man named Amnur Mosham with a house outside the walls. He had once been employed in the Shirrif's vinyards down Wendwater way, but had begun to slow in his old age and been retired. Normally his son would be responsible then for the family, but the son was a yeoman for the shire and was away with the fyrd. Tough luck.

Mosham's poverty was apparent in the state of his home - barely more than a shack - which lay amongst a ramshackle hoarding-village between the city walls and the Royal Forest. It was not far to walk, but even less far to ride. So Forester Donals and his retinue rode, he in a brilliant green doublet and hose and they in whites and browns.

"What d'ye mean to do 'im?" asked Cemric, Donals's brown-locked cousin. His eyes shone with the thrill of barely constrained legal authority.

"Teach 'im t'King's justice." Ameerish gave a wide, toothy smile. It sat handsomely on his strong jaw, framed by thick black locks, but was offset by his pointed and crooked nose, dark brow, and cruel black eyes. The gathered men merely chuckled low - they knew enough to tell a dark mood in their master. Few felt pity for the forester's prey.

It was not long afore their steeds' tramping hooves found the dirt of the track leading to Amnur Mosham's hame. Outside, a comely common lass hung clothes to dry whilst a towheaded young boy played in the grass with a straw dolly. As the dark men dismounted the boy looked up, and for a moment his blue eyes met the forester's.

"Wifman!" Donals called. "We come fer Amnur Mosham. Be ye kin?"

The woman's face filled with fear and she abandoned the last of her laundry in a woven birch basket. "Me husband's father he. What ill's he done t'Forest?"

"'Tis his mind an' none o' yers," spoke Fogran, another forester with the troop.

At this the woman called her son to her and motioned with one hand towards the wattled house behind her. "He is old, and harms none other. Spare him some."

"I'll spare what I feel is earned," growled Donals t'Gelt as he forced open the wooden door to Mosham's house.

*I can change it. He doesn't need to die.*

Some poor bastard had been poaching the king's deer. Only one or two, but it was still a crime against the crown.

This particular poacher was an outsider – some knight seen riding the Royal Forest with livery and horn and banner as if he had the right. But this red rider was no knight of Hihalem, and if he carried writ of the Shirrif he had yet to show it. Forester Donals suspected he did not have such, for he had been seen delivering the stolen venison to a house in the hoarding-village to the west of Hihalem. Some altruistic hedge knight come to earn his name in song. His luck he chose to rob the wood Donals Ameerish mastered.

"What d'ye mean to do 'im?" asked cousin Cemric. His eyes shone with a lust for slaughter.

"Teach him t'King's justice." Ameerish gave a wide, toothy grin and the gathered men chuckled loud, anticipating the armiger's demise.

The Royal Forest was an idyllic woodland, largely free of the mark of men. But Donals t'Gelt cared little for beauty and, as he rode his sturdy mount 'tween noble oak, pale birch, and mystic ash he felt naught but a growing frustration. Whoever this knight was, he had covered his tracks well. Around midday Fogran found the scattered coals of a small fire and a trail of hoof-prints, but even that was swiftly lost as they approached the thick of the wood. By evening Ameerish had lost not only all traces of their quarry, but his last shred of patience as well.

Calling his cousin to him, he spake, "Cuz, gather yer boys. We shan't find this foe by ear, eye, or nose it seems, so let us find him by heart. It follows he cares some for the folk he fed – Mosham I ween the name. Let us see what can be gained by a visit." By the end, the irate kingsman's voice had

61

become a coarse growl, and his kin's eye glimmered to see a new villainy afore them.

With whoops and calls, the forester company thundered back towards Hihalem, intent on making an example of the poacher's assumed friend.

*Nay! This isn't supposed to happen!*

They had not ridden far along the forest paths, but the villain was suspected of camping somewhere near the walls. the forester and his two peers – Cemric and Fogran – dressed in heavy cloaks, dark leathers, and mail and bore shining swords with weathered blades. The men that followed wore but leather hoods and padded jacks and bore cudgels and knives. It was indisputably too many men for one brigand, but what if he travelled in company? and it never hurts to show the strength of the Crown.

"What d'ye mean to do 'im?" asked cousin Cemric. His eyes shone with a lust for slaughter.

"Teach 'im t'King's justice." Ameerish gave a wide, toothy grin and the gathered men chuckled loud, anticipating the armiger's demise.

All-of-a-sudden there was a crack – a twig broken under a horse's hoof – ahead and to the left. The King's men bristled and presently a smartly arrayed knight on a sturdy horse rode out from behind an obscuring stone.

"I knew I would find ye here, foeman," spake the knight. "Thy laughter is much too loud, methinks, and thy crimes too dire. Dismount, I say, and prove with thy body that I have mistaken my enemy."

With a snarl, Cemric t'Gelt rode forwards, broadsword swinging wide, but the brigand wheeled swiftly and – in a lightning-swift slash – cut a bloody gash in the forester's arm, severing iron links and muscle both. Donals's cousin cried out and dropped his weapon, riding a bit away and howling as he gripped his maimed limb.

"Cur! Blighted bitch-son!" cried Fogran, his blade in hand, but Ameerish staid him.

"I telled thee once, Ameerish. I face ye alone."

"I ken not what sin ye seek to punish me for, yet I relent." As he began to dismount Fogran gripped his shoulder and hissed for him to let them all be upon the fool. That Donals was mad. "I have done many since. Yet all 'ave been for t'Crown. And t'Crown protects." And Donals was naught if not proud. And vengeful.

The knight as well was dismounting, a contented smile on his young face. Behind him, the wounded lawman screeched and swore. Taking his shield from his saddle, the knight swung his sword deftly in anticipation.

Once afoot, the dark-eyed forester drew his long blade as well, gripping it with two hands like a club. "Come at me then! But know that whether I live or die ye now have struck a man of law."

"Yet ye shalt be dead and I shalt be satisfied." And with that the younger man lunged, shield forwards and blade high.

Donals raised his hilt high and parried, sliding his steel off his foe's and swivelling the blade about to strike at the boy's head. But the boy was swift and dived forwards, too close for the blade to hit. The blazoned shield hit the forester in the ribs and knocked him backwards, but he recovered quickly and blocked two more frantic slashes – from below, then from above. His opponent grinned in manic rage, his crystal eyes teary with exertion. Donals swept his cape to catch the sword as the boy made to try another swift strike and, left-handed, cracked his hard pommel against the other's mailed skull.

Reeling, the boy stumbled, and in that moment Donals struck. The first cut the knight parried above his head – barely – but it loosened his grip on his sword. The king's man kicked at his opponent's knee, knocking him to the ground and freeing him of his blade, then ran him through on the point of his own wicked weapon. For a brief second the face of the poacher froze in utter shock at being defeated, but then he vomitted his lifeblood and spasmed his death-dance.

Forester Donals turned, wiping his blade on his rough cape. "Friend Fogran, bandage my poor cousin, then be ready to ride. I ween the man this man fed royal game was named Mosham, and I mean to have from him the names of any other conspirators in this game."

*Again! This time it will be different.*

Cemric continued to yowl as the party rode back towards Hihalem. He would have to see a chirurgeon on their return – could lose a hand. The maiming of his blood filled Donals Ameerish with fiery fury. It was not long afore their steeds' tramping hooves found the dirt of the track leading to Amnur Mosham's hame. Outside, a comely lass hung clothes to dry whilst a tow-headed young boy played in the grass with a straw dolly. As the dark men dismounted the boy looked up, and for a moment his blue eyes met the forester's.

"Wifman!" Donals cried, yet he declared no more, for he was interrupted by the whistle-thud of a crossbow bolt finding flesh.

The wounded kinsman to Donals's left, still upon his horse, choked and girgled as hot red blood fled between the fingers he held to his punctured throat. In a tumult, t'Gelt's party reeled and shouted, drawing weapons and attempting to shield their vulnerable faces. Another man fell before Forester Donals's eye found their assailant.

High ahorse sat the brigand-knight. The very same whose heart he had pierced not an hour gone. His coat was clean and unblemished, and he had the flush of life in his cheeks.

"Donals Ameerish! Ye defeated me once, but I will not see justice undelivered. Leave thy men and duel me ahorse." The deathless foeman slung his bow in a saddle-sheathe and drew his blade and board.

The forester had no patience for ghosts and no intention to waste more muscle on a phantom, and so ordered two thugs to take him. They heard whispered the word *witch*, yet they went. And were slain in hand.

"Only ye shalt I face, t'Gelt. My breath-home is shielded from other swords." His red blade was thrust high above his head. "Prove my cause is unjust, or die and prove me true!"

With a bellow, the forester charged forwards, his remaining companions behind. The boy recoiled, his steed tramping nervously. Did he truly believe t'Gelt would face him fairly? He turned and spurred his steed away.

"Sieze the Mosham man! Hold the house!" commanded the lawman, motioning three of his men to remain behind.

"Nay!" cried his prey in fury over his shoulder as he rode. "Ye must face only me!" And he turned about in order to charge the oncoming kingsmen.

But the dark-haired forester was closer than the boy weened, and sharp steel severed his head above the shoulders. The horse bucked and shook its mane before settling. The corpse sat, bobbing, upon its back for a moment longer before slumping to the soil.

Donals sent one man for the knacker to take the corpse and rode back, muttering, to where Fogran stood outside the Mosham hovel, one hand holding the hemp leash which bound the criminal Amnur's wrists.

The gaffer was wide-eyed with terror and confusion, and a dark wet spot ran down one leg. There was no sign of the woman nor child – not that Donals much cared. He wiped and sheathed his glutted murder-tooth. "Take 'im to the tower cells. We'll ask 'im on poachers and witches when he's rotted a while." Fogran grinned with black teeth and led the man, blubbering, away.

With anger and sadness the forester dismounted and went to where the corpse of his cousin lay. He did not touch him – that was knacker's work – but ground his teeth and promised to raise a mug to speed his path on. What deviltry brought this doom on this day to such a loyal servant of t'King? E'en a knighthood would not have protected a man from this. There was no fairness in it.

But the trouble was not over. For nary an hour had passed from Am-

64

nur Mosham being confined behind an iron gate beneath the square Friar's Tower when the tower's copper alarum-bells began to ring. Forester Donals was not far when they sounded – in fact only acrost the street in the rathaus preparing to drain a goblet of wine with the bailiff as a reward for such a harrowing day. But when the bells rang he left the red undrunk, snatched his black scabbard and belt from the bench beside him, and hurried down the sturdy steps to Hihalem's dusty street.

Buckling his baldric, he shouted to guards scrambling towards the gaolhouse. Barking orders they had already begun to follow. Two guards lay dead by the sturdy fore-gate, and two more on the stair. Three men ran upstairs and the forester led four more below. A wounded gaoler stumbled out a warning, but too late to be of any use.

Ahead, about the curve of the passage, a figure in red turned and met Donals's gaze with an icy-blue stare. The poacher-knight once more stood before him. Both men already had swords in hand.

It was too narrow for more than a man alone to comfortably fence, and so Ameerish left the guardsmen behind with a lunge and an animal bellow. How many times must he kill this man? His sword swung down and flashed loudly on the miscreant's parry.

"I'd thought to have more time," growled the boy, pushing his opponent away and up, scattering his retinue behind. *Ting-ting* echoed the grappling steel in the stony walk.

A larger man, t'Gelt forced the boy back down – closer to a landing where his men could corner him. He struck with elbow and pommel. Kicked at the red knight's legs as he thrust forwards and down, forwards and down. But the poacher parried each thrust, cut, and stroke.

Until the stairs ended.

The boy stumbled as he found the flat ground, then cried out as his foe's point pushed past his defenses. Blood welled and flooded down the boy's face, but he pushed back with his sword hilt high, knocking t'Gelt on the chin.

"This is not over! This tale does not end in a cellar!" shouted the boy, and lept upon the forester.

Ameerish kept his leathered forearms before his face, and his byrnie guarded his upper arms and chest, but the unexpected weight of the felon's black boots knocked him to the ground and shortly he heard the sounds of the foolish men above being soundly slashed and routed.

"Dogs!" shouted the forester as he struggled to his feet, his own skull bleeding from pommel and stair. "Follow 'im! By Moon or Meadow I shall have his skin, and no horse will outrun my vow!"

*It had to be done. Yet it was not enough.*

**D**onals sent one man for the knacker to take the corpse and rode back, mutering, to where Fogran stood outside the Mosham hovel, one hand holding the hemp leash which bound the criminal Amnur's wrists. Somewhere to the south, a pillar of smoke rose and stung the forester's nose. Fire so close to the forest was a bad idea. He'd have to punish those men too.

The gaffer was wide-eyed with terror and confusion, and a dark wet spot ran down one leg. There was no sign of the woman nor child – not that Donals much cared. He wiped and sheathed his glutted murder-tooth.

He meant to order the man removed to the Friar's Tower, but before his jaw moved he noticed a man riding swiftly from the south – on what looked suspiciously like *his* horse. As the rider neared he saw that it *was* his horse – a stallion he had bought should he ever fancy to ride the lists. He recognized the man too – a man who worked an acre near his hide.

"Elgin! Do you turn thief now? And be so brash to ride thy prize to his master?" He could not decide whether he was more angry or confounded, but tried to sound amused.

"Master! friend forester! Tragedy!" The man's face could be seen now to be streaked with ash, his tunic singed and torn. "A fire! My brother flies fast to the rathaus. O Master Ameerish I am –"

"Out with it! What burns?" A heavy, black weight was filling t'Gelt's gut. "Why do ye ride my horse to me?"

"The fire. 'Twas thy hame." Ameerish cried out in shock and horror and kicked his mount, but the farmer staid him with a shout and a heavy eye. "Naught remains. The house is ash. The villain used oil."

"Amalette! Gwenelle! I must care for my wife – my daughter. Even Demals – he is yet too young." But he did not spur his horse again, for the messenger's tear-streaked face told all.

Donals's jaw was so tight he could barely unclench his teeth and his eyes were red and wide with violent sorrow. His fingers gripped his sword's hilt in its saddle-sheathe so tightly his bones threatened to break his skin. "Who used oil? Who did this? What foe flamed my fam?"

The farmer shook his head. "I know not for certain, but others say they saw a... Pardon, 'tis strange. A knight in red with hair like straw. He fled before the smoke was seen. Through a window most-like; the door was barred."

A gasping sob escaped the lawman's throat and his eye travelled back in the direction of the witch-man he had slain. The fiend still walked. He turned his horse to face Fogran and his prisoner, just as the other forester

66

made to mount. Donals's face was fury.

"Slit the gaffer. Our party hunts us as we hunt him. Let him feel pain." As the old man gurgled his last and fell to Fogran's knife, Donals t'Gelt turned to face the wood from whence the killer of his kin had come. He shouted, his voice cracking, "Devil! Foeman of all life! I curse ye and swear now to end ye. By Cemric. By Amalette. By Gwenelle and Demals. By all ye have illed. I shall bury ye."

*The Fire was a mistake! It mustn't happen again.*

Donals sent one man for the knacker to take the corpse and rode back, muttering, to where Fogran stood outside the Mosham hovel, one hand holding the hemp leash which bound the criminal Amnur's wrists.

The gaffer was wide-eyed with terror and confusion, and a dark wet spot ran down one leg. There was no sign of the woman nor child - not that Donals much cared. He wiped and sheathed his glutted murder-tooth.

He meant to order the man removed to the Friar's Tower, but before his jaw moved he noticed a man riding swiftly from the south - on what looked suspiciously like *his* horse. As the rider neared he saw that it was his horse - a stallion he had bought should he ever fancy to ride the lists. He recognized the man too - a man who worked an acre near his hide.

"Elgin! Do ye turn thief now? And be so brash to ride thy prize to his master?" He could not decide whether he was more angry or confounded, but tried to sound amused.

"Apologies, friend forester, but thy wife lent me the steed for dint of calling ye to home." The man's face was red with exertion, his tunic wet with sweat and soil. "An arsonist was caught near thy hame. Thy house is whole. He burned himself. My brother flies fast to the rathaus but I fear the vandal may not live to see a cell."

Donals furrowed his brow, but thanked the man. He motioned Fogran to take the cottar to the tower cells, then followed Elgin back towards home.

Arriving before his mighty, oak-walled cottage, his wife Amalette came to greet him, their children watching curiously from the door. He dismounted swiftly and embraced his spouse, kissing her deeply with his scarred hands gripping her cheeks. She was red-haired and tough-skinned, her arms weathered from the labour she aided their neighbors in. She was stern yet filled with joy. And Donals loved her. For all his faults as a man - and he knew there were many - he loved her deeply.

She assured him the family was safe and held his hand tightly before letting him follow Elgin to a red-roofed shed where the arsonist lay dying.

The forester swore and made the sign of the evil eye when he saw the man curled upon the straw; even with the burns and the blood he recognized the sorcerer-knight who had slain his cousin – and twice been slain himself. He delivered a solid kick to the boy's stomach and his foe vomited black. Elgin stood silent in the doorway.

"Please... I... I sorry... 'S wrong..." The felon could barely speak through his scarred lips.

"Quiet, cur! No words will save ye." But he did not kick again.

One crippled claw reached out from the mess of a man on the floor. Grasped at Donals's boot. "Mitake... Mitake... Too cuel... Ne'er should I... Ne'er." Then one icy eye slid up to the forester's face, the other a whitish jelly in the morasse of his wounds. He sucked at the saliva, viscera, and bile leaking from his lips and stretched them until they cracked. "He did this me. Thy foe. Me. But ano'er. Sto' 'im. Or 'e'll do it again. An' again. The Tower... Slay him. Yet spare Amnur... Pease..." All that came after were croaks and moans before the young man expired on the floor of the shed, lying in a bed of blood.

"What he say?" asked Elgin, but Donals did not reply, only turned and once more mounted his still-ready steed.

"Wifman," he called to Amalette, "gather men to guard the hame. I have business at the Friar's Tower." And swiftly he awayed.

As soon as he passed into Hihalem and under the stony Cumbler's Bridge which marked passage into the market square he knew all was not right. No one strayed into the street and shutters were sealed all about. Trotting further in, just past the corner of the ostler's, he saw a corpse – a guardsman freshly dead – lying face down in the street, blood and beer pooling under him and displaced dust and gravel marking signs of a struggle. Only then did the bells begin to ring.

Forester Donals swore and spurred his steed towards the squat, square tower. He swore again as he dismounted, seeing more dead men before the entrance and within. More guardsmen would be coming now with the peel of the bells, but Ameerish felt he had no time to spare. Drawing his shining steel, he charged through the open gate, then rushed down the stair towards the dungeon, passing bodies as he went.

Ahead, about the curve of the passage, a figure in red turned and met Donals's gaze with and icy-blue stare. The poacher-knight once more stood before him. He bore a fresh, wicked scar over one eye, perhaps from his fight with the burned man. Both men already had swords in hand. Ameerish lunged down the narrow stairwell with an animal bellow. How many times must he see this man die? His sword swung down and flashed loudly on the miscreant's parry, which moved almost faster than the strike.

"Quick ye are. Yet not quick enough," snarled the boy, pushing his opponent away and up. *Ting-a-ting* echoed the grappling steel in the stony walk as the forester found himself vying desperately for his life.

Finally t'Gelt - a larger man - was able to force the boy back down, yet still it seemed his every move was countered - anticipated. Neither of the two battles before with this warlock had he seemed so ready. He thrust with his elbow and was knocked in the crown by the red knight's pommel. Weakly, he made to parry, but the boy battered his blade down. Triumphantly, the victor stood above Ameerish.

"Now ye pay fer crimes undone. Suffer, Donals t'Gelt, and drown ye in the rivers of Hell!" But as he raised his shimmering edge he paused, and both men heard swords clashing above.

A voice echoed down the grey, torchlit way, "Sir Ranald! Sir Ranald! Too many men come to the bells' voice! Ye must try once more!" But the voice... The voice was also Ranald's! How could there be two? Already there was one dead Ranald in t'Gelt's barn.

The knight shrieked in frustration and fury, but Donals had already unsteadily gained his feet. Sir Ranald made one last wild swing, which the forester only partially parried, and fled up the steps. Clutching his wounded ribs, the lawman gave chase.

Stumbling into the open door to the street, he saw fresh bodies in the dust, though not all dead. A party of guardsmen shouted as they pursued a fleeing foe down a nearby alley.

"Ranald!" he roared as he launched himself after. Swiftly he caught up to his prey and the boy only barely managed to turn in time to parry the heavy strike. But Donals's weight carried him forwards and pushed the villain to the soil.

With a start he saw that the scar over his foe's eye was gone and that moment of hesitation gave Ranald the chance to regain his feet and barrel headlong into the forester's bleeding chest.

The wind knocked from him, Donals still managed to swing his left fist, cracking the murderous bannerman on the joint of his shoulder and sending him reeling against the outer wall of the Friar's Tower. The boy swung wide with his blade, but the older man gripped his wrist and slashed at his face. Sir Ranald pulled away, but not fast enough to entirely avoid the steel point of the sword.

Caught once more in shock as he saw blood well up the fresh cut over his foe's eye, Donals t'Gelt loosened his grip enough for the boy to pull away, snarling and spitting. Behind, more guardsmen were finally arriving and hurrying down the alley past the disturbed ranger, but the knight was gone. Both of him.

Cleaning up after the disaster at the Friar's Tower was a significant ordeal, and the knacker had to enlist the help of the local gongers – no one else was suited to the task. But that was none of the forester's concern. His concern was apprehending Sir Ranald.

Fogran made an appearance shortly after Donals managed to remove himself from the killing field and seek care for his injured side. He was leaving the chirurgeon, freshly bandaged, for the Cold Quarters for an ale when his peer caught up with him in the street. He told the glowering forester – who had not been present for the massacre but had, instead, been engaged with a whore acrost town since shortly after depositing the prisoner in the dungeon – about what had happened and who the eyes of the city should be on the watch for.

"Not our business no mer," spat Fogran, his drool black. "It in't forest work and so in't fer foresters."

Donals nodded agreement, but did not truly mean it. For Sir Ranald had hurt his pride, his city, and his kin. And he had still done the poaching. He would not allow the warlock to walk free. Leaving his fellow behind, he made his way towards the rathaus to speak with Garson, the local herald-of-arms.

For many years had Ameerish known Garson Herald, though he did not necessarily consider the man a friend. The frail clerk was much too dry in manner for the forester and, frankly, quite boring. Yet he may be of some help in finding the rogue poacher.

After an awkward greeting and an offering of watery ale (which Donals accepted – ale is ale), the lawman laid down his request.

"I seek a criminal. An arms-bearer and a queller of men. I want fer ye to tell me from where he hails. Mayhaps that lord may help vengeance be fed." He did not mention the other Ranalds. The one in the barn who had warned the forester, the one in the tower who had burned the first, and the one who had warned the second.

"Be this the witch-man?" croaked the balding official, his bristling eyebrows waggling with interest. "He who emptied the Friar's Tower of men and filled the street with blood?"

"Aye, the same." Donals had little mind for gossip.

He described then the heraldry the man had borne upon his chest. The golden moon above the crossed grain flails with seven stars arrayed about. All on a field of blue encircled in a black ring, jagged like a fire's flickerings.

"It does nae sound familiar," mused the clerk, but he promised to peruse his records.

But his records found no mentions of arms of such make. And whilst this did not help in the means of finding a nearby lord who could punish

70

his wayward sword, it did mean some help from outside could be expected; lords did not take kindly to those wearing arms they had not earned. It was referred to as 'breach of rank' and was often more deplorable to the armiger-lords than witch-craft. So, at Donals's request, Garson wrote letters to all keep-holding folk in the lands around with warrants for the arrest of the criminal Ranald the Fell-Handed.

Yet he was not apprehended in any other land, nor in the city of Hihalem. The mysterious challenger was never seen in those lands again, and Amnur Mosham rotted and died in the Friar's Tower. And t'Gelt went without his revenge.

*Fie! Why would I betray myself? I need another distraction.*

Y et he was not apprehended in other lands, but rather at the edges of Hihalem itself. That very same night the villain was found by two of the bailiff's men. He was knocked cold with a lump on his head the size of a sword pommel and lying near a signpost just outside the gates to the city, his wrists tied. Who had done this none could say, but he was imprisoned in a cell awaiting a swift judgement.

The lord of Hihalem at the time was a bullish man named Cenric, and he was wroth over the deaths dealt on his bondsmen. On the subject of breach of rank he could not be bothered to wait the time it would take to confirm Garson Herald's findings with nearby regents, but he accepted easily Donals Ameerish's accusations of witchery.

All the long hours Ranald waited in the cell he said naught until he was collected for his punishment. As he passed the cell of the unfortunate Amnur Mosham he said to him, "I am coming, kithman. Ye needs fear naught and no man."

He was taken to the scaffold on the Street of Bones, between the knacker's and the temple. There he was led up the thirteen steps and bound tightly to a post of sturdy pine. His charges were read and the bailiff asked, "Any last words, witch? And warn ye, should it be a spell ye'll face worse than flame."

Smugly, with the glaze of a true believer in his eye, he spoke firmly, "My work is as yet undone. The Tower's victim shall still see freedom!" A leathern gag was then fitted between his teeth to prevent the muttering of curses and the straw at his feet was set alight.

The burned man screamed, as most men do when put to the torch, and Donals t'Gelt was pleased to hear it. Yet still he imagined that his troubles were not yet done. And he was right.

Late in the night, long after the knacker had nailed the poacher's corse to Hihalem's gate as a warning to those who sinned, and long after dark, a rider came to the forester's home and woke him with heavy fists on the sturdy door. He told that there had been another assault on the Friar's Tower, and that this time Amnur Mosham had been freed. Donals had never donned his kit so swiftly, and he rode like Hel herself was at his heels for the city gate, sword-hungry and bow in hand.

The night was bright by moon and star and, as he neared the pack of hustling men-at-arms flooding from the city gate beneath the witch's blackened frame his sharp eyes noted two figures fleeing hard to the north. No others were ahorse, and so with a cry he hied his steed on towards his foe.

One was tall and garbed in a long surcoat with a drawn blade shimmering silver beneath the black smears of blood. The other wore a simple, worn tunic and stumbled as he ran. As Donals neared the armed one turned, revealing clearly the face of Ranald and its wicked scar.

"I've burned ye once, falseman, and I'll do it again and again til ye stop rising!" The revenge-mad forester already had an arrow nocked and did not slow his steed.

Ranald of Many Lives pushed Mosham onwards and turned, sword gripped in two hands. "A thousand times I'll rise, to see thy ills –" but he interrupted himself with an anguished shriek as a white-shafted arrow sped past him and thudded home into flesh. His aim had been for the witch, but the look of defeat on his foe's face was nearly as good to t'Gelt.

Donals was not near enough to see if Mosham lived for a breath more or died as soon as the arrow pierced his heart, but the knight shrieked with inhuman anguish and swore a long string of curses. The forester smirked and drew his long blade, leaning as he rode so as to take the foeman's head. But Ranald ducked at the last second and rolled off the road, abandoning the limp corpse of his self-appointed charge. Before Ameerish could wheel his horse, the felon was fleeing through the bracken, not bothering to look back.

With a cry, the kingsman gave chase, but the ground was rough. Too rough for a horse to travel swiftly. And though the lawmen searched all through the night, they could not find the trail of the witch.

*So close! This time he'll live. I promise.*

The night was bright by moon and star and, as he neared the pack of hustling men-at-arms flooding from the city gate beneath the witch's blackened frame his sharp eyes noted two figures fleeing hard to the north. Yet, as he reached to hie his horse he noticed another pair, hurrying with heads low towards the Royal Forest.

Those fleeing to the wood were dressed nearly identically to those fleeing north, though the dun-cloaked one ran slower, and the red-caped one kept his sword sheathed. Donals paused. Surely this was some ruse. There were seemingly many Ranalds, but he thought there was only one Mosham, and he was old and crooked. With a cry he hied his steed towards the westerly pair, who strove not to be seen.

The red along the road looked back, then halted, shouting taunts at Donals. The red he pursued glanced over his shoulder then tried to hurry faster.

But not fast enough.

Mosham was a half-step behind the wizard-knight and felt the bite of forester steel down his spine while he struggled to keep up. Ranald turned and shrieked in terror and fury, and his twin to the north echoed him, equally as anguished – either he also saw Mosham fall, or felt it in some way in his crooked witch-heart. Behind, the men of the watch had divided themselves, half hurrying to t'Gelt and half to those fleeing along the road.

Yet nearly as soon as he had bellowed, Ranald leapt behind a standing oak with tangled roots. Soon he was running on rough land Donals feared his horse could not traverse. He drew his bow and fired thrice, but only the second shot found its mark, and that did not damage his foe enough to halt him.

Donals swore and, shouting for a man to handle his horse, leapt from the saddle to pursue his quarry. This ended now. Ameerish would make certain of it.

*Fie! Once more. One final time.*

Fury and pride drove Forester Donals into the wood, chasing after Ranald. Ever just beyond sight, the warlock danced through the undergrowth with speed and determination to match – or overshadow – his own. At last, he lost his quarry entirely.

Limbs burning and quiver half-empty, the kingsman took a moment to take stock of his situation. It was late – or early – and he was far from Hihalem. He wasn't worried about becoming lost in the wood – it was his job to wander its bounds – and trusted himself to gather or kill what food he needed. It wasn't a crime if he did it. Leastwise not one he'd punish himself for. He resolved to take a brief rest and continue his pursuit tomorrow. More men would likely be on their tail by then – only the southern stretch of the forest was haunted.

He slept fitfully in a soft bed of rotten leaves – anxious to enact his violence on the foe. And when he woke he scavenged what he could and began once more to examine the land about for tracks. He thought he had found some and, as he followed, he found and slew a roe calf with a sure arrow to the eye.

But in time the trail grew cold once again and, despairing, he realized that he could not clearly see the sun through the canopy. He was sure in time he'd find his bearing, but he was just beginning to doubt he would see the villainous poacher again. He called out to Moon, the spirit of vengeance and unexpected fortune, begging for the chance to revenge his cousin's death. Yet there was no response.

Not until his wandering was interrupted nearly two hours later by a sandy voice from behind and below him.

Turning, he found an odd creature crouching in the undergrowth. His head struggling to reach the height of an ell. The thing was warped and bent. Its skin was the red of clay, and it stood upon stunted, too-short legs. Too-long arms clutched a fire-hardened spear and two bulbous eyes crowned a crooked nose. A wispy white beard adorned his chin and a tall felt cap adorned his crown.

"Yer look lost, manling."

T'Gelt had never seen a kobold before, but he had heard tales aplenty from his Granam as she sat weaving by the wide, western window of his childhood home. He knew them to be clever, tricksy, and wild. Granam had warned him ne'er to trust them, and always to bear gifts. Fumbling with his belt, the forester produced a pewter Bridge charm.

The thing eyed the pendant bemusedly. "Is it fer me, manling?" Donals nodded. "Keep yer trust charm, manling. Little will make me trust yer more than yer trust meself."

Ameerish nodded and pocketed the charm. Of course it followed that mistrust would travel both ways. "Aye. I am lost, Master Kobold. But I seek no place but rather a person. A foe in red who stinks of sorcery."

"I've not known sorcery to stink," said the creature with a smirk. "Yet I 'ave seen a red, red man, who muttered of murder and second chances."

"Ranald," growled Donals.

"I dinnae ask his name. Nor shall I ask yers. But a manling in deep woods is rare and worrisome."

"What said he? Ye say he muttered."

"A magic to undo time. Methinks ye have made a mighty foe of a wicked man." The creature leant on his spear, its pommel buried in the soil.

"But who is he?" The question was more for himself than the wood-wight, but he snarled it at the small man as if 'twere his fault. "There are three of him. All squabling, conspiring, and killing together."

"Seems to me they are all the same man. Mayhaps in seeing his mistake he means to warn 'imself once more. Undo the failure ye 'ave set on 'im."

Donals was silent for a time. Smouldering and grinding his teeth. Wishing there were no witch he was forced to hunt. The kobold merely blinked at him.

"Ye say ye saw him?"

"He was headed west, and no manling home lies that way."

"Can ye point the way?" The kingsman meant to treat with the trickster as little as he must.

"Will ye believe me ef I say?" The creature's eyes were bright. "It matters not, for if I were to lie and send yer to death I'd send yer the same way the man truly went."

"Then send me to death."

And so the twisted little man told of the Black Menhir which borders Lake Tolan, and the paths that wend that way. It was a strange and wicked pillar of sorcery which calls to the wronged and foolish with the light of Moon and the whisperings of the god men call A Wise Fool. It was a perilous path, through the Haunted Pass which cuts through the Geltish Range – mountains cursed with hungry packs of devilish woe-pigs. But Donals was comitted, and so thanked the creature before leaving to pursue his doom. The kobold watched him leave in silence, then shook his head at the passions of men.

With visions of blood and vengeance, all frustration was lost to the master forester. And with a path laid out by one of the Woodly Folk he travelled with almost a spring in his step. And, almost as if a spell had been lifted, he shortly began to notice signs of his quarry's passing once he began to follow the path he had been given.

Through the sun-spackled wood he sped, ever behind the murderous magicker. And within a day he came to the wood's edge. Beyond he could see the rising peaks of the wide Geltish Range, and the deep cleft of the Haunted Pass. But no ghost had ever hindered Donals Ameerish. It would only be a day through, and beyond that Lake Tolan and the Black Menhir.

He made a fire in the eaves of the forest and slept lightly, dreaming of red, wizard blood staining his steel.

The fog hung low in the morning when he rose, and the sky was crimson. It would stay crimson until well after the sunset. The grim autumn sky fit the forester's mood well, and he slit his palms to spill blood on the soil as thanks to the spirit called Ingress, who gave blessings to murderers. He hoped to sway the fylgia from Ranald's side to his own.

And through that rocky dell he went, as monstrous squeels echoed down from the heights. He had never seen the monstrous woe-pigs, but he knew them to be as real as ghosts. But, like ghosts, they had no reason to stall him. Past old bones and eery whispers he travelled at great speed, the whole way following the deep boot-prints of his prey. His cousin would soon be avenged.

Much he could have told of the road he walked, but his was a quest of blood and fury, not boots and wind. As the red sky waned his venture neared its end and he saw the crooked point of the Black Menhir, and soon too heard the lap of the lake's waters.

It was an old stone. Older than men, some say. Its sides were rough-chiseled and black as coal. Strange runes or pictorals may once have covered it, but now its sides, both crooked and smooth, were bare. The pillar stood on a hill of dark grass, wet with mud. But it did not stand alone, for atop it a figure could be seen, gazing up at it as if at a god. Or at a doom.

"Ranald!" bellowed the kingsman, and the figure half-turned in surprise – a silhouette against the bloody sky. The figure froze, then frantically moved out of sight behind the standing stone, struggling with his belt. "The time has come to face justice!" Donals began to struggle swiftly up the swampy hill. Humid, cold air fled off the dark lake beyond and chilled his skin, tickling his bones.

Cresting the rise, t'Gelt glimpsed the corner of Ranald's red cape flapping in the wind from behind the ancient pillar. The ranger's sturdy blade was already drawn and he lunged forwards, grasping at the cloth. His fingers closed around it and pulled, and the other man yelped as he twisted and wrenched, eventually freeing himself from the weatherworn mantle.

As Donals came around the stone he met Ranald's wild-eyed gaze, looking for all the world like a man who had heard the knock of the bailiff's men on his door. "Yer wicked ways have found their end, outlaw. No lord claims ye, so let Lord Steel take a new bondsman!"

The cry of sword 'pon sword rang and was dulled in the shore-wet air. There was a desperation in Ranald's eye, and a hatred deeper than any kingsman had seen before. It was not fear, and was not the hatred merely of being caught, but a hatred which defined the man.

Beside them, the stone was cold. Watchful.

Donals t'Gelt deflected another furious overhead strike, binding the poacher's blade and pushing him onto his back foot before attempting to slice into his shoulder. His knuckles smarted from where he had knocked them against his foe's hilt. Rain was falling in a thin mist now, but dark tears stood out on the grime of the outlaw's face.

"Ye had no right! No leave to take a man's life!"

The forester laughed, "Yet ye do?"

This infuriated Ranald even further – if that were possible – and he unleashed a spinning flurry of blows. "What I do I do for justice! The East Wind knows the canker ye are!"

"Canker!" He laughed again, and lightning struck the surface of the lake, with thunder but a breath after.

Ranald was gasping for breath now, his offensive tiring. "It comes," he muttered, and lightning arced again, nearer. The stone flashed blue in the light of the storm.

The stone.

This man was no witch, but a vengeful sod who had stumbled upon eld dream magics. Again and again he had come here, to the shores of Lake Tolan, and travelled back to conspire and contend with himself, all to spoil t'Gelt!

Donals wrenched his blade, forcing his foe further from the plinth. The poacher-knight's eyes were wide.

"Nay! 'Tis close! Only one more. Please!" he entreated the sky as lightning flashed all around. "One final time let me walk the past and punish this foe! This man-murderer!"

"There will be no more spells or past-walking for ye, cur. Let this be yer final death!" And with an upward thrust, the kingsman sent the younger man's blade sloughing into the mud as his own sunk into his ribs. Pulling out his sword as Ranald burped up brackish blood, he brought it down again and split the man's tow-headed crown.

The man's open throat gurgled as he collapsed. And at that very moment the lightning struck the Black Menhir and illumined it in bluish flame. In that ghastly light Donals looked down on the ruined body of his foe – the flails and stars on his coat split and sundered by the gash that swiftly filled with rain and blood.

Who was this boy? Why had he cared so much about the old man? Ameerish looked up at the stony pillar behind him, now dark once more, and shivered. He felt both that the trouble was done – it must be – yet also that he had not seen the last of the time-walking outlaw knight. Yet how could both be true? He resolved to put it from his mind, as best he might.

He left the corpse on that cursed hill, 'neath that cursed stone, and made the journey home in three days. Briefly he wondered if this had been a mistake – if the menhir had been the source of the magic and if it might bring Ranald back – but he was too tired from his wrathful quest to pursue the idea. His wife greeted him in tears on his return, and his children laughed as he hoisted them on his high shoulders. The other Ranald he had left behind had been burned in his absence.

The knacker and the priest had been busy with all the corpses from the attack on the Friar's Tower, but beyond that life seemed to return to normal. And Donals Ameerish - ultimately a simple man, gladly entertained - nigh forgot the furor which had taken his cousin's life and ignited such anger (and fear) in his breast. It was not until the autumn that his bitter, worried thoughts returned to the time-walking poacher knight.

For the men who had gone away to the fyrd in the spring had returned, and their families had come out to greet them. Amongst that crowd the forester noted Gaffer Mosham's daughter and silent, tow-headed son. But those two were not to meet their man returned, for he had died in the lands called the Princelings and only his corse returned.

The woman cried and the boy's icy eyes looked on the body - black and rotting on its litter - with horror, panic, and confusion. But one of the men - a knight Donals knew by the name of Ronthil Whatt - attempted to reassure them with tales of his bravery and valour.

"And look," said Sir Ronthil, motioning to the dead man's chest. "Fer his service yer da was made a knight. And fer the love he earned of our captain it was made familial. Means it passes along. Yer a knight now, boy." Whatt ruffled the boy's blonde hair with a sad smile.

Something about the scene made spiders crawl up t'Gelt's spine, and as the body was brought by he gripped Sir Ronthil's arm and asked the dead man's name.

"Same as 'is boy," answered his friend, "Ranald."

And with icy veins forester Donals saw the arms printed on dead Sir Ranald's red surcoat. The golden moon above the crossed grain flails with seven stars arrayed about, all on a field of blue encircled in a black ring, jagged like a fire's flickerings.

Behind, in the wake of the procession, young Sir Ranald, blonde-haired and blue-eyed, met Donals's gaze, and the kingsman felt a chill he could not contain, and a hatred he knew all too well.

# The Hurt

R7542-Z4.332

Right on the line. I signed my name for the last time and I became AR7542-Z4.332. I lost the name I had been born with and which I had used when I wrestled, boxed, played football [hard and rough and good]. They said those who fought got all the respect, and that it was what every good citizen should do. I'd joined up to fight our enemies, but I wasn't ready [then] for what it meant. A life off-world, far from family, friends, and everything I had ever known [playing sports and late night vidshows and concerts]. A hard life, training on a desolate world. It was going to hurt.

It started [the hurt] on the morning after I signed my name.

I kissed Mamma goodbye and gave Pop a hug [he was a hard type, and liked that I was entering the service] before I got on the bus. The magnobus whizzed along on fast magnetic tracks, high above the bustle of the city. We would be to the station soon. There were other boys there [and girls] excited for their first day. We joked and bragged and wondered what our hard life would be like. I said that I had shot a deer once with a bow. One of the girls liked that. It was just past noon when the magnobus settled onto its platform in the off-world station and we filed out into the bright sun, scorching after the shielded windows of the magnobus [blue and speckled].

We were all hungry and a boy pointed to a cafeteria where they sold sandwiches. We started to head that way as a man next to the shuttle started yelling. The girl who liked my bow story gave me a strange look. I smiled but she did not. Someone grabbed my arm. It hurt when he grabbed my arm, but he pulled me away from my new friends and the cafeteria [BBQ and mustard, sparkling sodas, salty chips]. Didn't you hear your name, said the man with the hard grip. No. AR7542-Z4.332, that is your name. I did not remember what that meant and he hit me. Do not forget. Now board the shuttle. But I have not eaten, I said. He did not like that and he said that I would not get food on the shuttle either. He shoved me roughly onto the steel loading ramp [Xed in sharp steel with holes through it to look down on the city] and I fell. My shins were bleeding, but the officer beside the shuttle kept yelling and I had to get up and go onboard.

The seats were hard [steel buckets with thin leather-synthetic worn from hundreds of young butts just like mine]. A coarse black belt was drawn over each of my shoulders and clipped between my legs. It rubbed my neck on both sides. And there were no arm rests. The cabin was cramped and sweaty [hot, hungry recruits in too-heavy civilian clothes] and there were no windows. It's a long way to the base, said the officer who had yelled when everyone was onboard, so try to sleep. If it hadn't been so long I would not have been able to sleep, but it was very long, and I slept in short, restless patches [nightmares]. There was a tube for water and a tube for pee [humiliating].

A long time later we got to the base. We signed Xs after our names [numbers] and were led to a cafeteria. It was cold and angular [all steel] and the food had no smell. They told us to eat as much as we wanted. The food was bad. My knees still stung, even though they had stopped bleeding a long time ago. After food we were taken to our bunks and told to change. There was no privacy and we had to strip and put on our jumpsuits togeth-er [boys and girls – some laughed]. The material scratched but it was thin [which was nice]. Outside it was hot and dry [red sky, two blue moons] and the machines to cool the base didn't seem to do much [on purpose?]. Officer told us to stand up straight, follow orders, don't be stupid, be heroes some day. One boy was a joker [broke his leg].

Training days were hard [every day was training day, Sundays started later]. Running laps, jumping, climbing walls. We learned wrestling and shooting guns. Officer showed how guns could overheat and burn skin down to bones. I tried to be careful, but one day I screwed up and burned my hand [bone shining white in the red sun – sand-dust got in the wound]. It hurt like Hell and my fingers didn't want to work. I went to the medic [pointed the way, no guide] and he said, better in a day, and put cold gel on it before sticking my hand in a little thing like an oven. I couldn't take it out until it was healed [seal around my wrist]. My hand was numb until the next day – until it was healed and I had to go back to training.

On wrestling days lots of boys and girls got hurt. I had to wrestle the joker kid a lot. He was bigger than me, and didn't like to lose. One time I beat him but when the officer wasn't looking he broke my arm. I had to spend a day with the medic, a machine knitting the bone and muscle back together. That one only hurt at first.

I learned the way to the medic fast. We all did. No one died [not al-lowed] but sometimes people got hurt bad. One friend of mine, she broke her back climbing a rock as part of a course. Won't walk again, grumbled the doctor, and we all felt bad. She had to be transferred to archives to work with computers. I didn't want to break my back, but I also didn't want to get in trouble [wanted to be a hero], so I tried hard. And trying hard gets you hurt [believe me].

Sometimes in order to do better than other recruits, you have to push yourself. It hurts the first few times you tear a tendon, lifting something or throwing something, but you get used to it. In live-fire exercises I learned how to take shots from enemy weapons in order to achieve objectives. The officers liked me when I did that, and those don't even take a full day to heal. AR7542-Z4.332, they would say, you have what it takes. And I do. I know that the enemy won't give up and neither can we. Sometimes a broken finger helps you think [focus on what you need to do]. It's not as hard to pursue a fleeing target when a broken rib heals so quick.

Some recruits snuck out and did things that aren't allowed [drugs, sex, illegal music and vids], but I didn't need that. I didn't have time anyway, with all the time I spent with the medics. I was going to be a hero someday [face on vidscreens] and heroes don't do bad things. The joker did lots of bad things, but the officers taught him. He was in the medic almost as much as I was. He complained about the hurt, but he was wrong [it's not that bad].

Eventually I graduated [like everyone – the service needs soldiers]. I was sent to fight the enemy and I volunteered for the front. Normally they don't let people volunteer for where they go, but normally people don't volunteer for the front. I got a heavy pack and heavy armour that scraped my skin and a big, hot gun. I drove magno-skiffs [two guns, twenty soldiers in the back, heavy steel plating, no shields] and we were in a lot of tough spots. One time we were hit bad and I lost my arm. It took almost three weeks to grow that back. Joker got a sharp piece of steel in his spine above his tailbone. He's basically dead now [can't fight] but they let him work dispatch. There must have been a lot of hurt.

I won medals for bravery and for kills [I would shoot the enemy until my hands were too hurt to work the gun] but nothing that any other good citizen wouldn't do. Sometimes I would make a mistake on purpose [but I would pretend it wasn't] and get shot. Not for the commendations. I don't know why. But it only takes an hour or two to fix a shot from a gun. They offered me promotions, but I stopped taking them after it would mean I couldn't fight on the front. Couldn't be a hero. Killing enemies and saving planets and getting shot, beaten and broken [for the service].

Ten years in the service. I think more of me is new than is old. It doesn't leave scars though. Clean and pretty, just like the day on the bus. I can remember every one though, and they aren't that bad. Not like when I cut my shins getting on the first shuttle. That had been much worse than all the broken hips and cracked skulls I've gotten. Now it doesn't hurt anymore. At all really. Sometimes it is boring [shoot, shoot, crash, medic, run, shoot, medic, cut, medic, fall, medic]. Sometimes I miss the first time I burned my hand on the gun, could see the bone [sand-dust got in it]. AR7542-Z4.332, they say on vidscreens, is a hero. I'm like a mascot, but it doesn't mean the same thing to me. I've been cut and stabbed and mangled everywhere I can be and there is nothing new. I suppose all there is is shoot, shoot, crash and medics and loud cheering. I don't drink, because that makes it worse [makes the hurt less].

I got a mail though [interesting]. It was from joker, said he may walk again [shoot again]. New technology can fix anything. I've never been shot in the spine before.

# The Scent of Witch-Iron

he Great Days are over. The silver sun shines on drab plains and windy shores as the land falls into disrepair. It seems that - despite the best efforts of moral men and earnest craftsmen - tools chip and splinter, foundations sink, and wells run dry.

And no help comes from the King. He sits in his city of yellow spires and converses with his cult of wizard-advisors, oblivious to the rot on the world. Hedonists and insularists, the cloaked and hooded avatars of descent who wander Carcosa's halls encant the rhymes of the end. Their green-robed grandmaster, the sorcerer Gargond, whispers to the monarch's wizened ears of Other Roads - ways beyond the salty sea and the darkening Lake of Hali and even beyond the distant Hyades. The King is as decrepit and past repair as the kingdom.

Acrost the land farmers are unable to til their fallow fields, cattlemen to milk their dry charges, textilers to weave on crooked looms. Even nobles find themselves dispossessed; taxes raised too high for them to ever be fulfilled, upset and aimless peasants set to revolution, wars lasting long beyond the bounds of the commanders' coffers. The world is weary and many are made wanderers by the fading light.

Sir Childe, a knight in a yellow cape of whom I'm certain even you have heard, makes his way along the dusty road. No steed nor fellow follows him, and his thick blackleather gauntlets shield his eyes from sand and salt. His stomach churns for want of a fresh meal, and his scalp itches for want of clean water to wash. What does he seek? His life lost meaning to him long past. Perhaps even before the world moved towards slumber. Coin calls him and steel keeps his bed. Somehow he struggles on.

Ahead, on a small knoll, sits a small hamlet. A cluster of stone homes, their thatch-roofs set over ancient, knotty ruins. Ill-fitting doors rammed into the gaping entrances. He climbs the hill, his legs aching for rest. The road here whittles down to barely more than a footpath. It will widen again. But here it is as sparse as the village.

Coming near, even the sea wind cannot disguise the unpleasant odour spilling from the crumbling buildings - an acrid, unpleasant scent. Ammonic. Or like pine sap. Or mouldered fabric. A scent of disuse. And sterile reclamation. A scent that seeks to forget the lay of human hands.

The paths between the hames are empty. The house-stones wind-scarred. Rugs are hung to dry outside some of them, and benches where half-finished projects are left alongside knives and wood-clamps. Fresh footprints are swiftly swallowed by the sorrowful air. No one but Childe walks the empty space.

"Hail!" cries the knight, the unhomed child of excess. Only his own voice answers. Caroming off the crooked walls of rock and mortar. He looks through an empty window. Sees a figure resting there, their back to the him and head upon a writing desk. "Hail!" But they do not answer. In other windows he sees shapes at rest as well. Unmoving, their skin jaundiced and drawn as if starved. Their faces serene. Nothing moves in the empty settlement. Sir Childe stands in silence in the centre of it all. Lowers his head and thinks of all he has lost. He can lose no more. The charms in his coat jingle - sing the chants of six-score petty gods. More.

Whitt! An arrow sinks into the coppery earth near his feet. The wood is brittle and the shaft bows in the middle as it lands. Splits up its length. In a breath the wayfairer's shining, gold-kissed blade is drawn and he swings to face the invaders.

From behind one empty, cavernous domicile-tomb step two figures. One is waifish-thin, her hair a painful knot of auburn and grey, her grey lips drawn back in a sneer. The other stands nearly half an ell taller than Childe and he curses his luck. But he has faced worser foes than these. The woman holds a bow, another arrow knocked and aimed. The patch-bearded, brutish man a rough-beaten mace, its pig iron hungering for meat.

Another arrow flies but the yellow knight is already flying, his stiff black boots pounding in the dust. His teeth set in his handsome jaw. He meets the towering fiend halfway, his sword cutting up even before the bludgeon begins to fall. The knight does not pause to watch for the giant to tumble, but thrusts his body forwards, striving for the woman even as she drops her weapon and turns, wild-eyed to flee. But he is swifter - more sure-footed - even when ambushed.

The woman is sickly. Her breath stinking of garlic and gutrot and gin. She knows not what happened to the town. Only that it is a good spot to ambush passersby. A prime feast-table for cutthroats like her and her Da. Her fear flees quickly. She is defiant. Challenges her captor to quell her. But Childe is tired of violence. Tired of cruelty. He knows if he lets her go she will only fall upon another innocent on the road. But if he slays her there will be someone else - perhaps someone even more cruel - to take her place. He gives her a pair of shining silver coins and pushes her frail frame from him. She eyes him warily. Tells him he can reach Hosten's Rest by moonrise if he hurries along the coastroad. Flees. Da the Brute is dead.

Childe moves on.

O n along the continuing road as it widens and winds. And indeed by the time the twin moons - one golden , the other silver - rise in the inky sky Childe can see the outline of Hosten's Rest ahead. He nears and is able to see its fading glory. Peaked houses with fading paint and flaking plaster. Slack pennons hanging threadbare from dented poles. A low stone wall surrounds the town, barely shoulder height, but Childe can see no crumbled, unplanned openings. There are still hints of pre-decrepitude. Small gifts. The road on which he drags his weary feet leads to a gap in the wall, a lonely aperture which perhaps once held an iron gate - like that in a garden fence - but now stands empty.

Two soldiers step out from the shadows to either side - indolent law-arms seeking an easy commendation. Bullies who prey on the hapless. They are rough men dressed in once-fine livery, now faded and unraveling. Their weathered faces are unremarkable.

"Wha' business 'ave ye in 'Osten's Rest?"

"No business," says the knight. "I merely wish to rest and pass through."

"Pass through on wha' business?" The guardsmen are stubborn in their task, though it seems fruitless - vapid - in this ending-time. "There's a toll 'ereabouts. An' the toll's 'pendant on business."

Childe looks on them with heavy eyes, tears tugging at the corners as he fights exhaustion. "I have no business 'til business I find. I am a travelling knight, and a length of hired steel."

The two dour Hostenmen look to each other and then to him. They charge him no toll but tell him he is needed. Rest he'll have, but only after hearing the pleas of their lord.

Their lord is the estimable Governor Eliam van der Mulk. His manour rises above the heights of even the rare two-story homes of the town, its three peaks and lonely tower roofed in red tile, shedding in places like old snakeskin. Its facade is painted a deep, flowery blue, and writhing red vines are painted on the white-washed bracings and supports. A short path of grey stones leads from the cobbled street to the stout brown door, through the crinkled and faded stalks of what may once have been a decorative garden.

Childe's escort leaves him at the foot of the path and he makes his weary way, heavy feet dragging and worn cape swaying on hunched shoulders, to the entrance, where he leaves three resounding knocks. Shortly the door swings wide and a mousy servant - either a youth much aged by their hard life or an elder miraculously vigourous for their age - answers warily. The knight looks back over his shoulder, but the gatemen are gone.

"I was told to come and ask after Governor van der Mulk. I have a sword to lease."

The figure at the door, his coats and white shirt growing threadbare, pauses as if he had not heard. Stares blankly at Sir Childe with fish-blank eyes. Then he blinks. Nods. And waves the traveller inside, turning a set of hunched shoulders away as withered feet shuffle down the dusty hall. Childe follows, down the holey red runner and past tarnished brass, cracked pottery, and warped wood. Paint peels on weathered walls. There is a faint smell and the dim lamps along the walls do little to dispell the gloom.

At the end of the hall is a staircase leading up, and beside it an iron-studded door. Through this is another short hall and another studded door. A curt knock from the doorguide and they push their pale head through, quietly introducing the knight, before pushing the portal wide and leaving back the way they had come. There is little ceremony and they do not bid farewell.

Inside the chamber, dark and windowless, lit only by brass lamps stinking of fat and oil were walls of shelves, many woefully empty or featuring lonely, solitary books. A small pedestal sits to the left of the door, featuring some unrecognisable taxidermy abomination, with a head almost man-like and fit with mismatched teeth, as if from all sorts of animals and ages of men; its skin looks like painted canvas. A stray spray of straw sticks from a poorly secured seam. A large, leather-topped desk sits opposite the door, nearly devoid of decoration or documents. And behind it is a massive portrait of a waifish young woman. Beautiful in her own way, but almost sickly thin and with white hair unfit to her age. A copper plaque features her name, but Childe is too far in the murk of the place to read it. Between the desk and the painting stands a man, his hand anxiously swirling as he clutches - white-knuckled - a tumbler of strong-smelling brown spirits.

This man too seems distracted, and only briefly looks to the yellow-clad chevalier before gazing unseeing towards the bookshelves. He bites his lip in agitation and hums low. His wide, plump frame is bound in waistcoats and blouses and scarves in all shades of purple and burgundy, and his greying mane of hair is tamped down by a flat, blue cap, like those popular with merchants who keep permanent storefronts and do no wander on creaking carts pulled by parasitic mules.

"Governor van der Mulk, I presume," says the knight, stepping forwards, his arm extended.

Van der Mulk looks up. Gazes at the outstretched guantlet as if it were a raw fish offered to a judge as defense in a murder case. Shakes his head and sighs. "Aye. Eliam van der Mulk. Though I would fain surrender my name to have my ills forgotten."

Lowering his hand, Childe prompts his host further. "What ills, Master van der Mulk? I understand you have need of sharp swords. Or able men. I am unsure."

The larger man takes a large, loud gulp of his drink. Sets it on the cracked wooden desktop. Picks it up again to anxiously swirl. Looks to the portrait. "That is my Menurelle. Poor, dear Menurelle. She is beautiful, is she not?" His eyes are swollen with exhaustion and sorrow. Red with anguish. Childe admits that she is, indeed, quite beautiful. The governor lets out a loud, dry sob. "But what is beauty that none may touch? She is my daughter. Even now. Even in her... Even as she..." He looks to Childe, his eyes wild, his voice strained and hoarse. "Six weeks past we received a strange visitor. A wandering minstrel. An itinerant rhymer.

"He came for no feast day nor carnival. We've forgotten the days for many of those. Most hereabouts don't have the energy anyhow. We dinnae invite him. He just came. Said his name was Wallum unWallum. He had plenty of letters. Recommendations from lords I know. Know by name, ye ken.

"Little fellow he was. Short and frail. Sickly like. Pale skin. Sick-yellow. Like his eyes. His hair was thin and greasy. But he dressed nice. Real nice. He's made well for himself in these later days.

"There was no great skill in what he did. He played his lyre well enough. But no better than a common lyrist. No better than Menurelle. She... She likes to play. Liked? She played the lyre sometimes. But not when he was around. She liked to hear him play. All his songs were old. Not old-old, ye ken. Songs we know, but we don't know all the words to. The Merchant on the Road and Caulker Callum and Sea of Copper Grass and the like. Ye know the one verse and you sing it as if 'twere the whole song." Here he hums a bit of Caulker Callum, sadly, and continues, his white fingers shaking. "People liked it, ye ken? Not just my daughter. All the folk. He'd play in the square and the maids would dance with the boys and there was laughter and the drink actually tasted like something again. It wasn't just a medicine. We had fun. As if that still exists out in the world.

"Menurelle. O woe. Menurelle was smitten with him. Not like as a knight and a lady. Not like ye've had, I'm sure." Childe does not mention his own tragedies. Some he does not remember, so long has he wandered. There is no lady love for the knight of the yellow cape. "But like an admirer, see? Someone who likes their work. Their art. She liked to hear him play. And he smiled and sang when she asked. His teeth were white though his gums were black. White and strong and strange. She's young, Sir Knight. Not young enough, one would say. But still too young for this fate! I'd have warned her away had I known the witch for what he was.

"He gave my daughter a gift afore he left. A black ring. A little black ring. Rough iron, twisted and unfinished. Sharp and curled at the ends. It was an ugly thing, and smelled strange. But she loved it, and so I would not deny her. Though it was the only gift he left. And it was poor indeed. That fucking ring." The governor slams his tumbler on the table, spilling brown liquor on the stained leather topping. "The smell grew when he left. Like dust it is. Or some physic's tincture. It is rank. And she grew ill. Fatigued. She grew more tired by the day and the smell followed her. Like cat piss. Her dresses began to stink of it. I had no men to send after the little man, and she would not throw away the ring. I should have forced her. For one day," here he begins to cry in earnest. "One day she did not awaken. And her chambers smelt of witch-iron. Her skin was yellow and sick. Like unWallum's. Thin like paper. Like onion. I went to her in her sleep and wrested the ring from her tight grasp. Threw it into the ocean I did. But the sickness has taken her. She dreams on, smiling as her body wastes away. And now those who care for her have begun to fade. Servants and aides and housemen are lae to rse and dall to drowsing on their duties. I have moved her to the tower, but even now the scent spreads. The ring-scent. unWallum's fucking piss-stench."

The two stand in silence for a time, the regent sobbing into his silk sleeve. Childe knows not what to say. At last the tears cease and the father looks up once more. "She loved to dance. She loved to bake. She loved life, it being what it is. I... I love her. And I hate that wretched imp for taking her from me.

"The physician says she may never wake. Says it is too late. I have written to scholars in Carcosa. Sent for medicants from far cities. Asked all the learned men I know. Perhaps someone may lift this curse from her."

"I know little of lifting curse, lord," speaks Sir Childe. Aye, he has lifted some curses, but he's damned if he could tell how he stumbled acrost the solution most times. His career is in killing, or in placing the fear of death, or merely running errands others are too weak to undertake.

The baron waves his ringed hand, somehow still fat despite the faminous times. "I have no interest in curse-breakers. All I need broken is hearts. UnWallum's. And whoever stands between you. I want him to know who sent you and I want him to beg for his life before you spill his blood down his silk fucking blouse. Kill the bastard and I'll give you whatever coin I can."

"And what if he knows a cure for this affliction?"

"If he knows I doubt he'll tell. If he does, I'll find even more coin to gift. But if not it is no matter. I am beyond hope. Gut him and bring me proof, or fetter him and drag him here to be pilloried. Though I have no stomach myself for torture or death. So perhaps execution is best."

"What proof would you have?"

Again the hand is waved. "I care not. Just so long as I know it is done. I shall write you a letter - a writ - to forgive your stay at the inn here. You would not want to stay here, where it stinks of sleep. Tomorrow you can set off. He traveled north along the coast by foot."

The inn is old and leans heavily. Many of the floorboards warp up at the ends, and loose nails abound. The beds are worn and overused, stinking of sex and vomit and tears. It is better lodging than Childe has had in weeks. He sleeps well, his sword clutched against his breast, and in the morning he leaves Hosten's Rest in silence.

The wind-roads wind along the coast. Those desperate, gale-wracked sea-paths which only the most directionless of travellers take. And who in this time of ending will take to any roads at all if they have a roof above their heads? There are bandits and worse in the wilds between the cities. But the wind-roads along the coast are more terrible yet for their weather. Exposed skin is scoured by salt-rich air and steep inclines can quickly crumble to deathdrops around corners which offer no foresight.

Yet it is along these very paths that Sir Childe must travel, his pointed hood pulled low over his face as he shivers in rain-soaked mail and sodden wools. At night there is no place for a fire and little safety from the lashing coastal waves. His throat is sore and his eyes gummed up with exhaustion and loose sea-crystals. His fingers curl stiffly and the heavy clouds often disguise the day.

It is not until he seeks to make his third camp that he finds any peace from nature's assault. A narrow crack in the sea-cliffs leads, on dust-dry land, to an open depression in the rock. Above the wind howls and beyond the sea rages, but in that hollow there is some peace. Weary from his exertions, his skin scarred and pocked by dry gusts, Childe has not the strength to venture further. To venture up into the crevasse he rests at the base of in search of kindling, sod, or sustenance. It is not long before he falls painfully into a restless slumber.

Childe has begun to drowse, squatting on his haunches in the shadow of the sea-cliffs, his yellow cape pooling about him like a fountain of gorse petals. His god-charms clink softly as he shifts. But he is awoken from his strange dreams of garden paths by an horrid sounding.

A ululating, crooked howl. Guttural and stuttering. A choking, strangled predator-cry. He knows it at once. It is the call of the wane-wolf.

Wane-wolves. Bony, mangy, half-blind wild things which have been twisted and ripped at by the collapse of the world. Terrible, vicious dogs. They hunt in packs and are always hungry, their atrophied stomachs too pitiful to digest the meat they crave. Wane-wolves hunt the solitary. They prefer to eat those rich in luck or heavy with woe.

Three of these things show their golden-eyed faces in the gloom. Scraggy jowls dripping with hunger. Hot drool dribbling on their emaciated paws. They crouch, their bent limbs stiff as if they cannae straighten them. Mayhaps they cannot. They let out rasping, wheezing growls. Their jaws spasm and their tongues loll idiotically. There is little wit left in their eyes. Nearly dead, but clinging on well past any hope of redemption, they look with envy on Childe's red flesh.

Childe is still for a tense moment. Meets their eyes, his lips grim. But his hand had already found the hilt of his etched blade afore they came near, and when one lunges - half leaping, half scrabbling in a sideways amble - the sword is drawn and sickly dog-blood spatters on the shore-stones. The others grumble and jabber, black lips twitching and beady eyes goggling. There are sounds like others in the night. The head of the fallen wane-wolf twitches and rolls, tattered ears tense.

Even with the scent of woe heavy on their prey - the stink of unwanted but ever-present luck - even with this the scavengers hesitate. They are greedy things. Wanting for life. They know they will be hungry tomorrow, even if they should devour the knight. Rip and tear at him as they argue for scraps. One already lies dead. How many lives are worth a moment's happiness? Would it truly be happiness, or only the memory of it? The wane-wolves gibber and whine and decide there are better ways to die. Slower ways. With more hope. They leave Childe to his loneliness.

Childe watches the empty eyes of the slain beast until the sun rises. It has nothing to say to him.

It is another day and a half before Childe reaches the next settlement. A crooked sign hangs nailed to a weathered post on the sea road. Etched into the wood, one end fashioned into a fist and pointing finger, is the name *Oddiver's Cross*. The single nail does little to support the sign and its accusatory finger points down at an angle towards the path. The letters are painted in some putrifying eggshell white. Oddiver's cross sits on a cliff hanging over the wild waters.

The road here is shaded from the wind by low bluffs, and Sir Childe lowers his hood, his skin almost burning at the feel of clean air. His boots clomp their solid way up the road, occasionally tramping on wooden steps or slats set into the gravel many years gone to prevent erosion or broken horse limbs. The boards are rotten and soft now. The ammonic scent of the Sleep wafts down from above, giving the gallant pause. He gazes up at the worn houses and loose gutters. Breathes deeply through his nose of the burning stench. He knows this must be the way. Once more his boots clomp and tramp.

The rank presence of the Sleep fills the space between the hovels. But here men and women still amble about their chores. Children still aimlessly pull wooden wagons and build castles in the dust. The town is subdued and unhappy. But it still wakes.

Childe searches briefly for some inn or wayfarers' house, soon finding a simple sort of pub. It was an old shack with a low fence spread around the dusty yard in front, and creaking benches lain about. A wench in grey cloth brings tired men wooden cups of thin, pissy ale. They drink it greedily and lay down more coin which they cannae afford to spend. Many of those who sit here would be at labour, had their labour born them any fruit in these long months of waning.

One man sits alone, skeletal elbows resting on a splintered tabletop as he presses his empty cup against his forehead with both knuckly fists, his eyes closed and a thin line of drool slowly wetting his chin. The knight sits opposite him and raises a hand for two ales. Nay, four. He knows the silver coin he leaves is worth much more than the copper shavings others would have paid with, but he has no patience for haggling and a great sorrow for Oddiver's Cross. His companion opens one eye, peering from behind his clutched cup. He lowers it and opens the other eye, though not as wide. Studies Childe warily.

"I shall pay ye for thy time, goodman."

The drunk looks up as the drinks are delivered. Takes one and smiles. His eyes linger on the scant flesh of the woman's backside as she goes about her duties elsewhere.

"Long as there's drink an' coin ye've got me." Sir Childe smiles wanly. "But there's gots to be both, see?" The gold-thirst glitters in the unfortunate's eye.

"This shan't take long." Childe can see the disappointment in his informant's face, but the scrawny man covers it with a long draw from his cup. Childe takes a sip of his own and sets it aside. "Know ye a man by name of unWallum?"

The cup comes down and one sun-strained eye squints at him. "Wallum unWallum?  The balladeer?"

The yellow-caped knight had not dared to hope his search would be so easy.  "The same.  Ye know him then?"

"Knew him, aye.  Know him?  Not as such.  He comes about 'ere now an' then.  Often 'nough I'd say.  Plays here at the pen.  Sits o'er near the gate there."  A scrawny hand points like the sign into town, thin wrist straining to hold it.

Leaning forwards, Childe grips his hands together on the table in eagerness, too close to the man.  The man recoils, then recovers and reaches for another ale.  "How often does he come about?  Does he live here in Oddiver's Cross?"

"Lives here?  Nay."  A stifled yawn.  "He lives near, but not here."

"Know ye where?"

"Ne'er been there meself, but I hears he tells a rhyme to find his place."

"Tell me the rhyme."

And the man tells it and is thanked.  Childe stands.  Leaves the ale that remains for the poor man.  Makes to leave, then pauses.

"How many in the town are sleeping?"

The drinker gives him a strange look.

"Ye are tired, and I gather others are as well.  How many have fallen asleep and not awoken?  Mayhaps in days."

"A few I 'spose."  He chews a dry lip.  "Don't pay much mind to my neighbours anymore.  'Sides.  I don't see much harm in it.  Dreams 'ave gots to be more interesting than this."  He waves one frail limb.  "I'd rather have nightmares e'en than have to live all my days watching wheat rot in my field."  He takes a long draw and looks away, unfocused eyes staring somewhere into the past.  "Dinnae use to dream, ye ken?  But I've seen the King's Sign, I has.  I dream of Carcosa.  Ne'er been in no castle afore.  Must be nice."

*North the walkers go*
*North the sleepless wander*
*Through gorse-patch go to ponder*
*To steeple-home ye go*

It is not hard to find the gorse fields north of Oddiver's Cross.  The yellow flowers tumble over low hillocks and around isolated copses.  A sea of bright, welcoming yellow in a terrible, wasted world.  The sweet scent of the flowers brings shocking memories of days past and impossible to reclaim.

Of lands and lives lost. In a strange way, Childe is happy to be allowed to dwell on past sorrows. He weeps openly as he wanders the pungent fields. Ponders on dreams he once held of futures no longer possible. So much of his old life leaves him as he struggles to stay standing in the slumbering of the world, but he treasures what memories remain, in the moments he is given to mourn.

The faint tawny tinge of late-evening has only just kissed the sky when he spies a spire in the gorse. A crooked, broken churchtower rises out of a small brake, the trees defiantly clinging to their lush green leaves. The crumbled stone edifice implies a larger base, but all is hidden by the distant boughs. Child wipes his tears on his cape, smears yellow snot on yellow cloth. He hoists his belt higher on his hips and gently brushes the pewter pendant of a god of luck. A god of wayfarers. A god of warmth as well. Many gods have many faces. And Sir Childe carries the weight of many gods on his shoulders.

As he nears the ruin he sees two shapes standing near an arch of bent trees, leaning lazily on their spears. Wisping languidly as they stand, as if they are mere eyeblinks from slumber. He raises one thick glove in greeting, but they seem not to notice. He nears and witnesses their hooded eyes struggling to remain alert. Both are dressed in yellowing, stained gambesons, holes revealing the straw and wool which stuff them, and their skin is drawn and thin. They quiver and twitch even as they stand still, and the pauldrons, vambraces, sabatons, and greaves they wear are dented and rusty. Wide, low steel caps totter above their thin-haired brows, insulated by threadbare arming hoods - one red, the other blue.

"Hail!" And their eyes snap awake, their shoulders drawing to some sort of attention. Through the window in the trees Childe can see the hint of stone and broken coloured glass. A quaint path leading towards the chapel. "I come seeking Wallum unWallum. Is this where he lives?" Childe sees no reason to hide the quarry he seeks, and intends to meet spells with steel if the need comes. But these men hold no hoary curses. They barely hold themselves together.

One yawns and the other strains the muscles of his neck to stop from following. "Why?"

"I have heard he is a great musician, and I seek to commission him."

"He's..." Another yawn. ""He's off."

Childe waits for more yet no more comes. "Off? Off where?"

"Off." One guardian has already drifted off again, leaning on his spear, grounded in the soil.

"When shall he return?"

The servant shrugs noncommittally and looks into Childe's eyes with something between defiance, indifference, and incomprehension. Perhaps there is a clue in the minstrel's sanctuary. Childe asks if he may pass, but he is denied with a lazy nod and a sleep-jerk from the other.

Childe sees no reason to slay these fools. They stand in his way, aye, but they are seemingly overcome with the same soporific gloom which has haunted his journey and likely shall cause no great resistance. He fingers the pommel of his sword.

"Draw it and we shall be forced to quell ye, Sir Knight," says the one who a moment before slept, his eyes still shut.

"Ye seem in no fit shape to do so. I have no love of violence, but no complete hatred either. I am not afraid to leave ye senseless to pursue my quarry."

"Senseless does not mean defenceless." And the men grip their spears with both languid fists.

The knight feels almost sorry for what he must do. But their master serves some terrible purpose. And he has no intention to harm them direly. Just enough so they may no longer impede him. Shaking his head, he begins to draw his long, gilded steel.

But it is in the moment that his attention is away that both strike. Their movements are slow, but they are precise and their spearheads sharp. It is mostly by luck that Childe twists. Raises a mailed forearm. Catches the tips with cape and ring rather than flesh and cartilage. He whirls, his sword raised, and they circle him like prey animals. Determination lives in their gaze, and their unsure feet guide them relentlessly, their spears pointed.

"I have no desire to harm ye."

The bluecap lunges and childe grabs the shaft of the long weapon, wrenches it down and clobbers with his hilt, round pommel pummeling exposed temple. Stunned, the man stumbles and falls, eyes open. It may be that he is dead. Before the gallant can turn again, the redcap's lance finds a chink under his arm, cuts cloth and grazes flesh. Childe tumbles away, lands with one hand on the grassy soil. His hood has fallen over his face.

"Fie!" swears the errantman and swings wide with his swordarm whilst his other brushes at his mantle. Beaten edge meets oaken shaft and sticks, but does not sever. The assailant tugs at the tangled weapons. Shakes the spear fore and back. Childe's vision is free and he kicks out, misses. Tugs at his own weapon. Steps up with high boot and stamps down on captured spearhead. One swift lunge takes him up the length of the beached pike, his own blade abandoned, and he clobbers the surprised guardsman full in the face. Once more beside the broken nose before he falls. The man moans and so is not dead.

Standing, Childe brushes himself off. Touches the blood beneath his arm. It is not severe. He walks over and finally rescues his etched arm from the grip of the spearlength. The two men lay still. But for how long? He resolves to hurry his investigation and be gone once more before they rouse themselves.

Low branches hang down over the path and are brushed aside. It is not far to the wall of the broken church. The sturdy, toppled stones and wet-warped ancient door. That door, too large for its home and petrified with age, lies against a boulder. Inside, the stench of Sleep hangs heavy.

There is no roof remaining, and Childe can see now that the tower itself has been gutted, and two sides hang open to the elements. Ancient and broken pews are scattered amongst rich cloth, discarded goblets, and animal bones still sick with fat and gristle. Rodents skitter from their feast as the knight looks over the scene, fingering a new tear in his cape. UnWallum had held his own bacchanal before he travelled on. Does he mean to return?

Sir Childe wades through the detritus. The burned-out candles and mussed bedding. There is no mark of what god once offered communion here. On a raised platform on the southern end of the chapel is a wide altar. On it are spread many aged papers, though the ink on them is fresh. The knight sifts through them with tired fingers. Sheet music. Lyrics and chords for a dozen old songs. Common, known songs. But much longer than many suspected. Strange lyrics that seemed proper in a forgotten founding-time.

One paper sticks out from the others. It is not as old. Not lined and dotted with cheerful, bounding notes. It is a curled slip of white, the remains of a broken red seal stuck in two places to the backside. Childe scans it quickly. An invitation, from the lord of Airn Colagh. He has heard of UnWallum. Only good things. Invites him to play for his court. Offers coin, women, and linen. Someone - unWallum perhaps - has scrawled *i accept!* and a crude smiling face beneath the signature in a different ink. The same ink as the music. No one will read the response, but Childe assumes its author wrote it to amuse themself, or else is too mad to care. Briefly he holds the letter, considers whether to take it. Decides it unnecessary and discards it atop the altar.

He sweeps his capes and makes to leave through a crooked hole in the far wall, slipping out through the trees and along towards the road to the castle of Airn Colagh, which he knows by map-sight and hearsay. But something catches his eye. A clean stone amidst the clinging vines of an alcove. Some prayer-niche of the forgotten god.

Practised, ungloved hands find ungrouted grooves along the edge of the stone, bearing black dirt-smudges where vines have been cut away. There are spaces just wide enough for his grip on either side. It is heavy, and low to the floor, but he manages to pull it free. Behind it, in a shallow hideaway, is a small, sturdy chest, bound in iron and lightly gilt.

Dragging the shockingly weighty trunk out into the light of the suns spilling through the empty ceiling he tries the lid, finds it unlocked, and thrusts it open, leaning to the side in case of some hidden spring and devious needle. There is no trap. But there is a great wealth of twisted, black iron. Ammonic and sickening. Rings.

Childe slams shut the lid and stares for a long moment. The witch's instruments. The spreaders of slumber. Menurelle's murderers. Here lies a trove of dire undoings. Small, ugly charms to sap and drain the charmed. So much ill. So much sorcery in this chest. What must be done with it? Surely it is too heavy for him to take from this place. Yet it cannae be allowed to fly free. Who can say how many more villages would be upended if these treacherous trinkets are allowed to remain in the waking world?

At last he is decided. He checks the slumber-soldiers out front - both now not merely unconscious, but snoring - then searches for a sturdy, warped plank of old wood. This he finds and throws under one arm and he hoists the sinful treasure with two strong limbs. A few ells from the crack-exit at the rear of the church, just past the root-soil of the brake, Childe lays the chest carefully to rest, wiping fresh sweat from his brow. With the sturdy plank, he begins to till and dig at the virgin soil, making slow, but sturdy progress. As night falls the space is large enough for the trunk and he places it inside, labouriously working to conceal it once more. It is horrid work, and Childe worries often that the guards will awaken. Yet the two malnourished ardents sleep on.

At last the hole is covered, though it is obvious that a hole has been dug. He had not thought of that. He gazes about. He is too far from the church or the trees for branch or scattered ruin to convincingly cover it. He anguishes over this dilemma for a wink, then realizes there is naught he can do. Mayhaps if he returns this way he can retrieve it and hide it elsewhere. Or mayhaps he shall have no need, if his conversation with Wallum unWallum turns deadly.

There is no time to sleep. He does not think unWallum and whatever joyful feasters accompany him have been on the road long, and he means to catch them long before they near Airn Colagh.

The road is easily found and Childe, long used to arduous treks, is hardly put out by the nightlong march, pausing occasionally to rest his limbs or sip from his waterskin. He does not think unWallum is travelling swiftly. That seems uncharacteristic for this sorcerer of sleep. Sometimes he wonders, as the golden moon laughs, whether unWallum has even gone this way, or if the letter was left as a false lure. But unWallum does not seem that type. Childe thinks unWallum cares little who knows where he wanders. Who can stand against a wizard who saps men's souls?

Morning has come and rested low on the world for some time when the knight spies the low peaks of travel-tents ahead, each large enough for one, mayhaps two, to lie stiffly beneath. The camp is far from broken, and brightly dressed figures mill around a cooking-fire, sending alluring scents of mushroom, victuals, and meat along the wind. Almost disguising the sick-stink. Almost.

He makes no attempt to hide himself as he approaches, and soon the few armed individuals in the camp shift to face the road, the others watching anxiously behind. All are dressed in a gaudy motley of rich, but untended clothes in many and varied colours. A travelling courtier-band of dispossessed fetee-goers, in wigs and capes and gowns and faded paint. The guards wear wide musketeers' tabards and decorated scabbards, one with a brightly-painted red crossbow. All move slowly, and as he nears he can see the jaundiced flesh, drooping lids, and bones pushing to escape their diminished cages. He stops a dozen paces from the swaying line of half-dozen fencers. His hand rested comfortably on his sword. Theirs are drawn, but lowered.

"I come seeking the rhymster, Wallum unWallum."

"I am he." A short man, barely higher than Sir Childe's high belt, steps forwards past his guardsmen. He is stick-thin and the bones in his face stands out under yellowed skin like a skull. His sunken eyes shine yellow in the sunlight, and his lank black hair hangs in clumps and tangled, thinning strands. He smiles with too-white, too-large teeth in blackened gums. But he wears clothes finer and more gaudy than any other present, with a wide-brimmed black hat bedecked in feathers and a smart, green waistcoat. Under one arm he holds a rather beaten looking lyre. "And who are thee?" His voice is sickly-sweet, like sugar and honey.

"My name is Sir Childe. I hear you are a player of some repute in these lands."

"Sir Childe? Sir Childe of what? From whence does thy title spring?" Still he smiles.

"The lands of Lanaulon. But that time is passed. A dream." Childe's tongue is heavy to name his family's estates. His past left behind as is this world.

"A dream! I am quite fond of dreams."

97

"I have gathered as much."

The imp pauses. Laughs loud. Barking. Like a crow. "Thou ken me then by more than my songs. I am sorry that I have no more rings to spare, 'less one here would offer a gift?" He looks back over the ogling crowd and a few tug at the black things on their fingers. They all wear black things on their fingers. Rings.

Swiftly - perhaps too swiftly - Childe wags his fingers. "Nay, I have no want of thy rings. I have want to bring ye for a conversation with one ye have wronged. Or rather, her father."

The guards tense, lifting slightly the points of their rapiers, but unWallum only gasps, his eyes wide. His surprise seems genuine, though it cannae be. "Done wrong? Prithee tell, to whom?"

Childe is not amused. "I am certain there are many who would be glad to know of my mission, but I come at the call specifically of the Governer of Hosten's Rest. In regards to his daughter -"

"Ah, Menurelle!" Those yellow eyes are alight with glee. "Such a wonderful lass. Beauteous, clever, and kind. Tell me, how does she fare?"

"Ill, Master unWallum."

"Ill? How so?"

"She sleeps, and this I am certain you know."

"She sleeps? And naught else?"

"And naught else."

"O joy!" The little man thrusts his arms high in the air and a few of the gathered followers clap or hoot. "So she is well indeed!"

"She does not wake!" Childe's teeth grind at the carelessness of the witch.

"O, that any of us were so lucky," grins unWallum. "Soon. Soon. I am so glad she has found her peace. I hope she finds the palace tower she spoke of in her dreams. I hope there is a handsome prince and a wealth of happy music. She deserves the best." He turns to some of his band. "I told you about her. The politician's girl. Such a sweet thing. She sleeps now."

"That sleep is the ill you have brought!" Childe has steps closer now, but none of the yawning congregation have bristled nor retreated. "How can you smile and laugh?"

The minstrel grows sombre suddenly. "I can smile and laugh for the joy I know she feels. The pain I know she has forgotten. The hunger she will never feel again. She lives in happiness now, far from the fading world we all suffer in. I have given the gift of sleep, and I envy her."

"You envy her!" Childe sneers. His fist clenches tight on his swordhilt, but it is the wrong hand to draw it; he is angry, but has no wish to face violence against so many unless he must. "She is a child, and now must whither away rather than living free!"

"None of us are free in this yawning world." The bard's tone admonishes. "There are roads that lead to better lands, but none a horse could wander." Setting his instrument in the dust of the road carefully, he steps forwards, arms out imploringly. "I beg thee give my words a chance. Come. Listen for a time afore thou judge us. Mayhaps thou shalt e'en find a wanting for a ring."

"I shall want no ring." But the knight agrees to hear unWallum's plee. One last chance to beg his freedom. "Though if I sense a spell I shall cut thy tongue and jaw both from thy face."

"I hold no spells of my own, Sir Childe. I am a messenger, and no more."

They sit by the fire and talk for a time. Wallum unWallum offers food, but Childe, untrusting, begs off. He eats his own rations - dry meat and hard bread - and heats water from his skin in a tin cup over the fire to brew his tea. It cannae be said that the diminutive songster is uncharming, despite his ghoulish cast. But his sermons are deluded. Strange. Seductive.

He says - whispers, cries out, extemporises - that the world is misery. It is. That the world is worn out, and seeks rest. This too is true. Men cannae make a living and happiness is far from the hearts of folk. All true in these bitter times. But he says that there are other roads.

Other roads to better ways. Better ways to die. Why suffer? Why suffer when you can dream? This itinerant rest-rector posits a hedonistic euthanasia. A retreat into the subconscious. So one can pass on in the way they choose. No longer withering under the glare of a fraying sky.

Childe cannae hide the bitter pursing of his lips. The offended pucker of his eyes. "Who set you on this thought? This... road?" Surely some wicked magician sent to upend the kingdom whilst the king was distracted by his own brand of sorcerous hedonism.

"A god. You would not know his name, though once it was spoken often in the low, green lands." The suns have begun their descent and their fading light shimmers in his skull-gaze.

"A god..." Childe is less awed than exhausted. Can no tribulation he undertakes be simple?

"Aye. A god. A god of little things. Pleasant things. Of order. He came to me in the shape of a maiden. Guided me along green roads and starry roads and roads forgot by time. Many folk I met and many lands I saw, and all as in a dream.

"'Twas he - with a kiss - what gave me this gift. To make waymakers of each and every man. Pathbuilders. Roadpavers. Dreamers on winds of ecstasy. With these rings, taken from a holy grotto beneath the sea, I give each man, woman, and child in this dying earth the key to a future they choose." The little man's eyes are full of an orgiastic, episcopal glee.

Childe is discomfited by this, having no love for sorcery and still cursing unWallum for sleeping so many. Yet he cannae deny that a world of dreams may offer more peace than a world on the brink of collapse. Many times past he himself has been tempted by dreams of the past (the future holds no appeal to him), yet he has always resisted. Was this the right way? Should he have given in? What is the purpose of a life lived only to survive? UnWallum prattles on into the night until the embers of the fire burn low and all others in camp had long-since fallen to snoring.

"The words you speak are tempting. Seductive in a way no incubus could ever speak." Childe's words are slow. His head aches with indecision. "Is there no name I can put on this generous god? No label? I must confess that ye have done thy job in making me consider what it is I do." Though in his heart Childe knew his choice had always been made. He was an incorruptible champion of the downtrodden. Or, more likely, a loyal servant to the silver shilling. No philosopher.

"Many names he has worn. The Shepherd God. Lady Wander. The Wayfarer Prince. Fleece and Fain. Hastur. Greenboy Jack." Wallum unWallum looks down from the starry sky then, though their reflection still lingers in his black eyes. He smiles sadly. "It will be easy enough to kill me, though I will fight. That is why you have come. But know this: should I die, my folk, those with me and those I have left about, shall spread thy name and name thee a villain. Thou shalt be known as far as Carcossa or Ninalon as a murderer and an enemy of peace. The folk that follow me love the promise of dreams, and would do anything to sail the seas of Nod. You will earn your coin if you return with my head, but your difficult life will become all-the-more difficult.

"But," and he holds up one emaciated digit, "thou cannae let me live. For if I live I promise to change none of my ways. I will be the rat that carries the plague of happiness to every burg in the kingdom, and mayhaps beyond. Greenboy Jack has tasked me with waking, until all the world sleeps. What I do is for the salvation of a weary world. I shall not forsake it."

UnWallum does not look a man much fit to defend himself. But Childe had accepted the mission. Needed the coin. Hated the theft of waking from so many souls. Mayhaps there is happiness in their final days, but the pain they leave behind is terrible indeed. There is no happy answer to the riddle of unWallum. But Childe has been hated before.

It is better to be done with it swiftly. UnWallum has had hours to say his piece. And if he has lied about being spellless then the yellow-caped knight could surely face doom in giving warning. In an eyeblink his sword is drawn and he is on his feet and lunging acrost the fire, but just as swiftly there is an explosion of light and pain from unWallum's hand, which had rested casually at a pouch at his side. Sir Childe screams and drools in surprise and agony. His chest is on fire and he can feel blood spilling down under his mail, soaking his shirts and skin with cold. But whatever spell unWallum carried is not enough. Childe can still lunge, and so he does. All around the camp is springing to life, swords singing from their sheathes and frightened courtiers fleeing into the night.

Yet on seeing their master's corpse sliding limply off the glittering rune-blade of their guest, even unWallum's loyal hearthguard flees in panic, their once-brave minds shattered by the grip of welcome exhaustion.

Wiping his blade, the assassin stands over unWallum's shrivelled form, his yellow face a cruel death-grimace. He passes by the ring - it is no true proof of death and is too cursed to take along. The harp he takes instead. A head is a difficult thing to carry, especially through civilized lands. Will van der Mulk trust his word and the lyre? He will have to. And if the demon told the truth, that his followers will curse his name acrost the known lands, then all the better for his purse.

He pauses before he stands. Looks towards unWallum's open right hand. Therein lies the instrument of his wound-curse. It looks like a thick wooden knife hilt with, at an angle from it, a thin, black metal wand. All told, the thing is perhaps as long as a man's outstretched hand. UnWallum's finger is hooked in a small loop at the heart of the angle, and curled about a small lever. Childe leans down and shakes the thing loose from unresisting fingers. It is warm. And the wand is hollow. The thing is well-worn and scuffed, but someone has scratched into its side, *Si vis pacem, para bellum*. Childe does not know the meaning of the words, but the language sounds like one spoken sometimes by a lost friend from another land. A crippled knight with a sad past and a strange god, caped all in crosses. He takes the witch-wand. It smells rank, but not of sleep.

Once more he looks and, with a smile both wry and sad, cuts the ring finger from the corpse, cautiously sliding the cursed artefact from the digit, leaving only the indent and dark stain of the metal. This is surely something the Governor shall understand.

And so, his dire deed complete, Childe returns for his reward, which van der Mulk surrenders, sadly commenting on the continued spread of the Sleep. Childe moves on along his road, just as the world travels on its own. He leaves the chest of rings where he buried it in its shallow grave. Tells himself to forget it. He does not wish to be the one to make the decision about whether the world sleeps or wakes. The perfidious slumber-sickness continues its way through the land - even into the halls of dread Carcosa - even as rumours of Childe's villainy spread as swiftly. No true cure is found for the ill, though those who have not yet entered their final slumber sometimes claim to ward it off with burned herbs at night and iron flakes in the food, or other folk remedies.

But Childe moves on towards new roads. The world tumbles towards its rest. And gods that have been forgotten - have receded into dreams - reach out with welcoming arms to claim mankind once more.

# To Die on Humphrey's Hill

is legs itched as his woolen socks soaked the sweat of the long march and his shoulder ached from the weight of the heavy lock held in one gnarled hand. It had been an uncharacteristically warm autumn thus far. The pale moon high high already in the blue afternoon sky—nearly full—as they at last saw the low rise of Humphrey's Hill.

There were three of them. There had been five, but Godfrey had been shot a day after leaving the fort, and the heavy lead bullet had festered in his leg until he could no longer walk and his words came in ugly streams from his drooling, purple lips. They had left him at a homestead just east of that brown, foul-smelling river with a few silvers to pay for care. He'd lose a leg and maybe more—the folk here were desperate and hungry. But they couldn't stop. Milkbones, as they had called their other missing fellow, had deserted in the night, taking with him Burgher, the party's mastiff. Now it was just those three—Miller, Parker, and red-eyed Harry Walsh. And Miller meant to see them complete their task at Humphrey's Hill, whatever it was.

Humphrey's Hill was unremarkable in many ways. Low, thick trees and thorny bushes plagued its foot, and when they gained its head they found it flat and much of the veld at the top worn away by many camps. A dark stone with flat, crooked sides rested beneath a wicked dead tree, its hollow cracked wide by some long-passed storm. Parker unslung the axe from his pack and set to gathering a fire while Miller scanned the empty landscape for any movement, resting the wide butt of his lock on the grey soil. "Air's sick wit river-stink," growled Harry Walsh, and it was true. Fat, black flies hung in the air like dark stars in the sunset sky, and smaller pests travelled in dreary blots through empty space, flying into open noses and throats.

When the fire was lit and all was bruise-purple with the dying day they sat and sipped at skins poor with water; they would not fill them from the river. Each man kept his lock near and wore his powder acrost his chest. They ate hare and what little stale bread was left in their packs.

"Can't be long afore they come," said Parker to break the silence.

"Our men or theirs?" spat Harry Walsh, his short pipe puffing weakly at the last of his leaf.

"Could be either," Miller answered. "We must be ready fer either."
"Won't be able te do much if ets theirs," said Harry Walsh.
"We aren't doin' much now." Parker's mouth smiled, but his eyes and his voice did not.

Each man had a small square of wool and a short, stout pole with which to fashion what shelter they could. Often they slept with their locks in the crook of their arm, their swords at their side, and their weathered toes open to the elements. They found places for these simple tents about the dead trunk and the stout stone, but none felt restful, despite nearly a week of hearty trekking.

"I'll keep ferst watch," offered Miller, and the others nodded, though none moved. He scanned the horizon and saw naught but unclaimed wilds. His stomach rumbled.

The lock lay acrost his lap, its sharp edges weighing heavy on his thighs, but he did not move. Absently he thumbed the lid of his tinderbox and hummed a marching song. And as he hummed so too did Harry Walsh, and Parker sang the words—but not so loud as one would on the Field. Milkbones had had a flute, but now they went without. The midges danced somberly to the patriotic verse.

Miller had sung that same song countless times on the Field and before and after. Men laughed to those songs and cried and died. The terrible crash crash thoom scratch of the Field had dulled one ear but he could always hear the song and it made his heart soar. He did good work for country, King, and God, though he did not always know what that work was. In the crash crash thoom scratch he was afraid, but he fought on. He'd seen men trampled, cut, stabbed, beheaded, clubbed, and shot with lock, canon, and—once—a scouring stick mistakenly left in the barrel of a lock. Smoke burned the air of the Field and blood slicked the soil. Horses screamed and men babbled, shouted, and prayed for deliverance. And deliverance came, by glory, lock, and grave. On the Field men were not men. The world sunk to Hell and nothing was real but lock, smoke, song, and death. Crash crash thoom scratch. Guilt for what men did in the Field was a luxury few could afford, and Miller was a poor man. So he sang and marched and did the good he was told.

"Ye tink they 'member we're 'ere?"

I'd 'ope so, 'Arry," answered Miller, "else we came te die on 'Umphrey's 'Ill."

"Seems they could've least told us what we're te do once we came 'ere." Harry Walsh's voice was throaty and dry.

"They said someone was comin' fer te meet us." Parker's voice was much clearer, which was why he often sang. But he was young. If he lived he'd hurt. Everyone hurt when they saw enough of the Field.

"Doesn't mean someone will," and Miller shifted the lock in his lap, his vials of powder jangling on his wide chest.

The sun had set now and the purple bruise of the sky had dulled to a cruel blanket of oppressive indigo. The wind came to the Hill, and rustled their coats, giving some relief from the heat. Miller's hair hung lank and dark with sweat. Now invisible in the air the colour of their skins, the flies grew louder. Singing their own song as they sought blood on that lonely hill. The three men slapped at them and swore, their coarse voices defying their sad state. Miller had a wife, but he slept better amidst the vermin. None made a move towards their tents as the night deepened.

"Ye hear 'bout what the old folk say 'bout the 'Ill?" asked Harry Walsh.

"Our old folk, er the ones what were 'ere first?" replied Parker, his hands close to the fire, despite the autumn heat.

"Both, I'd say. Though ours like-es-not say it since they said et ferst." Miller had heard, but Parker had not, so Harry Walsh continued, his eyes burning by the sickly light, the great dead tree behind him and his back to the stone. "Et's said, et is, that the old-old folk—what were here some long time afore our folk came en wains er boats an' built forts an' towns an' such—had a fastness 'ereabouts. Some old pagan place. Lost gods an' dark sects an what 'ave ye. Primitive stuff. Uncivilized like. An' 'Umphrey's 'Ill 'ere," he slapped the stone at his back with one dusky paw, "were where they made their dark rites. Chil'ren an' virgins an' what, taken an' cut an' bled. The old folks say not te go 'round it. Any place as seen as much bad-ness as this i'n't good for no man's soul."

"Then why were we sent 'ere?" shivered Parker.

Miller took his eyes from the deep, hungry crack in the old, dead tree. "'cause we aren't old folk an' what's dead es dead." The tree watched him and the flies would not go in.

Harry Walsh held up a finger and smirked. "Ye say that. But others say they sees folk up 'ere when by rights there should be none."

"This land es ripe with locals, an' we got the enemy to remember," challenged Miller, forcing himself to loosen his grip on his lock.

"Et's not just shapes they sees though. Some're rotted through, with holes wide 'nough fer a hand, an' others 'ave faces o' those known dead." Behind him, in the hollow, those faces—faces from the Field—gaped with white skin and bloody lips from the darkness, only to be gone in a blink of Miller's eye. "I knowed a fellow went out this way. Said he seen 'is brother, dead some ten years. 'Is brains was all showin' an' such from where the bullet took 'im. Came an' sat et the fire and said naught. Then 'e left afore dawn. E'er efter tha' fellow 'ad the worst luck an' 'e died all mysterious en 'is sleep."

"Bill Gorsch died o' drink, not ghosts," said Miller. "Put some more wood on, an' let's talk o' better tings." And more wood was put on the fire and they talked of summer days and sweet wines and red-cheeked whores.

The night crept on and Parker at last crawled under his flap and fell to snoring. Harry Walsh still stayed by the fireside though.

"Ye'll not stay awake fer yer watch ef ye don't least rest a bit," warned Miller.

"Can't rightly sleep tinkin' 'bout who could be comin' tonight." Miller granted his assent. They sat then in silence for a time save for the droning of the flies and Parker's snores and the quiet doom of Humphrey's Hill, until Harry Walsh spoke again. "What'll we do ef no one comes tonight?"

"S'pose we'll 'ave te wait."

"'Ow long?"

"Till we can't."

"I tink it's more like we'll see their men than ours."

Miller eyed the elder locksman studiously. "D'ye really tink the 'Ill's got bad luck, er were ye merely scarin' the child?"

Harry Walsh shrugged. "What's et matter ef Bill Gorsch died o' drink er ghosts? An' what's et matter ef the 'Ill's 'aunted 'er not? These're bad parts, an' we're but three. It's mighty unlike we'll see our beds again."

He did not like to hear that. Grunting at the red-eyed man, he hoisted his lock and began to pace the perimeter of the hilltop. It was dark save for the moon and the few stars, and a low mist was settling in the vales. That mist could prove a problem for the matches if it rose, but like-as-not (he hoped) there'd be no need for gunplay that night. No terrible crash crash thoom scratch atop Humphrey's Hill.

The time came after many oaces for Miller's watch to end. He went to wake Parker. Harry Walsh sat still in the dark, though Miller could not tell if he slept. Parker, his eyes bleary, clutched his lock and took up the same path about the hilltop's edge as Miller lay down under his covering. He slept poorly, as ever, and, as ever, the Field was not far from his thoughts. A cruel dream beset him of a naked shaman hung in charms, his knife wet with blood, above a dark stone with flat, crooked sides.

A rough hand on his shoulder woke him. "The boy's spotted someone," said Harry Walsh. Miller rose and found his lock and tinderbox. Slid on his high, stiff boots. He did not know if he should light the match, and the wet mist had reached their camp.

Atop Humphrey's Hill stood the three men, and Parker pointed where he had seen a shape. Soon Harry Walsh saw it as well, and shortly Miller also. But it was not one shape, but two or three, coming towards the Hill in

106

the murky dark.

"They make no sound. Our men would hail us. Er wave a flag," muttered Parker nervously.

"The enemy would shout es well te know our names. Er shoot ef they knew us from afar.," answered Miller.

"Locals?" asked the boy.

"They can see we stand," said Harry Walsh. "E'en the locals aren't fool enough to think they are not noted." Miller hung his match from the iron loop below the stock of his lock and lit both ends, and the others soon did the same.

"Brigands then?" asked Parker.

"Like I said, only a fool would think they weren't seen." The men fingered their powder horns but did not yet load their trays. "Ho! Who comes?" But no voice answered Harry Walsh. "We are armed with lock and steel, and may yet fire if'n ye don't make yerself known!"

None answered, but there was a fourth shape now and to this Parker pointed. "That one es shorter than the rest. A child perhaps?"

"Er a hunchback er skulk," offered Miller.

Harry Walsh muttered something about hobs and poured the powder into his tray, closing it and shaking loose the excess. "Hold," whispered Parker, but Miller too had begun to prepare his lock, already hearing the crash crash thoom scratch. "It could be a child. I'll make certain."

"Ye'll do no such thing," snapped Miller as both he and Harry Walsh poured a vial of powder down their barrels, followed by bullet, wad, and scouring stick. The empty tree yawned beside them.

The two elder men watched with twisted stomachs as Parker stumbled his way down the hillside and into the thicket. They clamped and tested their matches, their locks ready. The mist grew thicker still and all was lost to them. Miller called for them to speak out. Called for Parker. They hoisted their locks to their shoulders, opening the trays and aiming down the Hill. A dull wind blew the mist away and still four figures crawled acrost the emptiness. Parker, however, was not seen.

"Parker!" cried Miller, and Harry Walsh fired.

A sharp crack and one figure fell and Miller's heart rang with the song of patriots. He fired as well and another stumbled but did not fall. Powder in the pan. Close it. Shake it. Powder in the barrel. Bullet. Wad. Stick in and away. Blow the match. Clamp it. Test it. Open the pan. The air was damp, but not wet. Crash! Crash! Two more fell, the small one amongst. They had nearly reached the bracken at the foot.

"Parker!" the locksmen cried as they began again. Powder. Close. Shake. Powder. Bullet. Wad. Stick. Blow. Clamp. Test. Open. The figure emerged from the trees and it was still too dark to see. Something glittered in its hand in the moonlight. A lock? A sword? A wicked, ancient knife? Two shots rang out and the figure twisted and fell. Parker made no sound.

Harry Walsh's red eyes blazed and he stood a moment, then ran back to wrench his tent post from the soil and don his pack. Had they slain the enemy? Miller thought he could see more shapes coming, and he did not wish their revenge. He turned towards his own tent. Or had they slain their own men? If so, they would surely be hanged. The two men hurried down the far side of the Hill, heavy locks in hand. Had they slain a child? A company of ghosts? They could not teturn for fear of the approaching host—some dozen grey shapes or more.

"They made no sound," gasped Harry Walsh.

"Parker made no sound," said Miller dully.

And so they fled from Humphrey's Hill, and left those terrible asks unanswered. Unknowing who they now should fear. Or if good had been done. Or if ever their beds again they would see. Or even if ever again they should march upon the Field.

# Skin Like Ink

llie lifted her breasts slightly then let them fall, looking sideways in the mirror. Paused to run two fingers over the rose on her shoulder. Along the defined musculature to the black knots of ink on her chest. Turned slightly and lifted her ass with both hands and gave a small smirk before turning full-on to the mirror and meeting her own green eyes. She liked how she looked. Was proud of what she'd done to shape herself. She'd chosen the gauges, tattoos, and regular workouts in the corner of her cramped apartment. Some of it meant something, some of it was just because she could. Who fucking cared? She rested one hand on her sternum, just above where her stomach said *Blood* in sharp gothic text that looked like it could cut you if you weren't careful. Smiled at how the light sneaking in through the heavy curtains lit on her wavy bob of red hair.

She often liked to take the time in the morning to examine herself in the mirror. Remind herself that, whatever else, she looked good. Not that she cared what anyone else thought. It made her feel good to know that she could shape her own body just as she could create new faces, scenes, and shapes with her pen. But today something took her attention away. Her brow - tattooed with some icelandic bravery spell or something she'd found in a book - furrowed, she chewed on the corner of her lip, then sighed.

Barely looking, she grabbed a black band T from the back of her wooden work chair and threw it on - some Norwegian black metal outfit from the 90s (one of those chaotic, self-destructive groups that identified themselves as being evil) which had been well-worn into a silky softness that made her never want to take it off - and went searching for a pair of underwear in a pile of clean clothes near her bed she hadn't been motivated to put away after washing. There was a grey pair near the top and she stepped into them stiffly, suddenly feeling the poor sleep that had briefly given her a break immediately after getting up. Or maybe it was immediately after getting off, because she had done that first. For a long moment she stood near her bed, her bare feet eagerly drinking up the cold of the hardwood floor, and considered returning to it to have another round, and then maybe a nap, but decided against it; the sun had been up for hours; she had better at least try to be productive today.

Leaning down to her bedside table she snatched up her small collection of rings and slid them reverently on, snapping a wide leather bracer studded with scuffed steel buds onto her wrist after. Now she felt dressed. Or, as dressed as she needed to be at home alone.

It was a bit too quiet for the moment, so she unplugged her phone from its charger and scanned through her music before connecting her speaker and switching on a random playlist of coarse, feedback-heavy black metal; the shirt had reminded her of it and she didn't want to be fucked to have to think about what specifically to listen to. Still not quite together yet, she ambled over to her kitchenette - barely more than a counter and some cupboards - and threw a mug of water in the microwave to steep her tea in.

"Weird fuckin' dreams again." There wasn't anyone to talk to, except herself, but she felt like it needed to be said. She didn't have a problem talking to herself. "Just one night. One night of good sleep and I can reset."

The microwave chimed and she threw the teabag in, dragging the mug with her back to the writing desk acrost from her bed, near where her mirror was. Setting the tea on the back of the desk, she closed her eyes for a bit and just listened to the music. The growling. The fast drums. The constant buzz of purposefully misused equipment. It was soothing. And helped focus her. Drown out the thoughts and the worries of the world.

And there were always worries. Bills. Friends - impressing new ones and maintaining old ones. Feeding herself. Managing her own fucking ego. But she didn't have to worry about that right now; bills were paid up for the month, she'd mostly decided to check out from most of her social obligations for a little while, and she was feeling comfortable enough being the lonely starving artist.

Starving.

Opening her eyes, she considered their green gaze in the mirror once again. She was hungry, but not too hungry yet. She'd figure something out later.

Sitting down, she relished the cold feel of the wooden chair on her bare calves as she shuffled through her active commissions on the desk, reaching for her radiograph pens as she settled on a woodland scene she had penciled out earlier in the week and begun to outline late last night. A little girl and her father - a woodsman - huddled in fear of the dark as big-nosed, cow-tailed trolls watched greedily from the shadows. She set the pen to paper, shook it (careful that it wasn't going to splatter on anything important), licked the nib, scribbled a bit on a post-it, then went back to inking.

Her brow once again beetled, but there was no real consternation this time; she was always happy when she let herself get lost in a project, especially when she was enjoying the music. Normally she would set a goal for herself - like to finish the piece, or to take a break after an album was done - but this morning she just intended to work until it made sense to stop.

She wasn't sure how long it was before she decided to glance over to her phone and saw that there was a message, the grey speech bubble almost invisible against the dull black phone screen. Capping her pen - those were expensive - she made to reach for the phone, but instead found herself distracted by her own hands. For the thousandth time she observed them with pride. Both were tattooed almost black, with a rose in the negative space of her right and a pattern of splintering diamonds on the left. Esoteric symbols and runes she'd gathered here and there dotted the empty spaces, especially on her fingers - one held a rune she'd been told implied the pursuit or maintenance of wealth or stability (she liked that, so she put it on her right hand so she could see it while she drew to remind her what she was working for). Her rings dominated her fingers - on the left a twisting knot of silver thorns wrapped about her pinky, and heavy rings in curious shapes hung on her first two fingers - they might be gaelic or something, she wasn't sure. Her right pointer finger had two silvery bands, one atop the other, her middle a heavy ring with a brownish stone, and her ring a heavy signet ring she'd spent too much money on with her first initial on it. The ring finger of each hand had the nail painted black.

Smiling to herself again, she snatched up the phone and flicked the digital black shield away, sliding down the menu at the top to see who had texted.

| Viv | grabbing a drink with the guys on main... |

Ollie pressed on the notification to see the rest of the message, and the two that followed.

| Viv | grabbing a drink with the guys on main after supper |
| Viv | better be there |
| Viv | fuck you |

Her smile growing, Ollie typed back.

| O | Fuck you too |

Vivian must have been watching her phone, because immediately she responded.

| Viv | don't be a flake |
| O | I'll come out |
| O | Might not stay long though |
| Viv | mIgHt NoT sTaY lOnG tHoUgH |

Ollie didn't feel like she needed to respond to that, and put her phone away again. She looked down at the bristol board she'd been inking and tried to decide if she should pick up her pen again. She'd nearly finished the small family at the centre, but the interruption, however small, had let her mind wander. And the rumble in her stomach decided it.

Briefly she considered walking downstairs and grabbing a sandwich at the shop nextdoor, even checked her bank account on her phone to make sure she could afford it (she couldn't), but ultimately decided to scrounge in her cupboards. There was plenty of food in there she had bought and forgotten about; hopefully there was something she could throw in the microwave to sate her until she went out tonight and spent money she didn't have on drinks she didn't want. She found some leftover pasta in the back of her waist-high mini-fridge that she was pretty sure wasn't more than a week old, decided to eat it cold, and grabbed a beer from beside it, dark and heavy with an incredibly detailed label - like something off of a Mastodon album cover or something. She switched her music selection to Mastodon and leaned against the counter - there wasn't room for a table in the kitchenette.

As she took refreshing, intoxicating sips of the stout in her hand and languorously picked away at her lunch (it certainly wasn't breakfast at this point, and honestly was a bit late to even count as lunch) she opened her phone on the flat, spackled blue countertop and opened her feed, scanning through photos and artwork mindlessly as she nodded her head to the music.

She didn't have many people she knew on her feed. It was mostly artists and bands she admired and people whose aesthetics she liked. Some creepy gothic photography stuff and a couple travel pages too (not that she had the money to travel). Sometimes she would become mesmerized scanning through the pages of people she would never know and probably would not have gotten along with if they met. A lot of them matched what others would call her aesthetic - tattoos, piercings, metal shirts, smudgy photos of running black eyeliner. But some were very different, sunshiny and happy, idyllic cottagecore, over-muscled men and women or people in strict, formal pinstriped suits. She sometimes took some of these pictures as inspiration when she jilled off, but just as often she would stare at them and wonder what it would be like to be them. She really wondered what it would be like to have a beard. Or a cock.

Eventually, after scanning the page for a tattoo artist she knew in Reykjavik for a time, she closed her phone and went back to her wooden seat, the back and arms forming a half-circle and the dark stained surface marked and worn from spending too long as an outdoor fireside seat at a college house. She looked blankly at the illustration she'd been working on ardently all morning, then shifted her chair to the left to get a look at herself in the mirror again.

Ink coated her neck and forearms, and danced thickly on her chest, legs, and shoulders. A few small pieces (and the large one on her forehead) marked her face, and her stomach was getting rather cluttered now (though she couldn't see it beneath her shirt at the moment). Even the tops of her feet and some of her toes were scribbled with black. All black. There were some heavy, geometric pieces on her back too, but she didn't like putting tattoos where she couldn't see them easily. She'd designed most of them herself, or had gone in with a very clear idea for the tattooist. Originally she had been one of those people who actively looked down on people who get tattoos that don't have deep, personal meaning, and had only gotten work done to commemorate great personal accomplishments in her life. But it wasn't long before she was coming up with more and more excuses to cover herself in more ink - a part of a book cover from an anthology she'd enjoyed, a quote from an old poem she'd read too many times, some sort of heathen ward to protect her as she moved away from her home for the first time.

Ollie loved to create. Loved to have control over things in her life. She could control what was on her paper, and she could control what went on her skin or how much definition she wanted in her muscles. It felt like tearing off a rubber mask to reveal the true skin underneath when new ink was healed or her body started to shape itself more towards the image in her head. And creating - both on paper and on her skin - helped her forget how many times her life had been uprooted: failed jobs, constantly avoiding overdrafts, overanalysing every friendship until it was little more than a source of anxiety, having to leave college, constantly scrambling for more freelance work. She had no clue where the fuck her life was going anymore. Ollie couldn't stand having to live in the world around her, but she loved living in her small world that she could dictate.

A flash of light and the image of a dancing green handset told her that Viv was calling. Slouching down in her chair and hooking her beer between two fingers, she swiped to answer.

"Hey, Viv. What's up?"

"Hey dickhead. Just wanted to make sure we're going to see you tonight. We're thinking Riley's."

"I said I'd be there." Viv annoyed Ollie more than she cared to admit, but she was her oldest friend, and somehow the two just got each other.

"Yeah, but you hate the bars."

"Then why'd you invite me?" She was smiling, but she didn't let her voice show it.

"Oh, I don't know. Maybe some of us like you, you insufferable bitch."

"Language!" laughed Ollie as she sipped the last of her beer and set it

113

gently next to her desk. "Don't worry, V. I'll be there. I've got shit-all else going on."

"Good." Vivian didn't wait for a response before hanging up. That was expected. Normal.

Turning back to her work, Ollie decided that she wasn't going to be able to get back into the swing of work just now (even though she should really finish up her backlog so she could fit more work in; as if she had a queue lined up begging for her drawings). She harumphed and decided to at least try some half-assed marketing. Arranging her drawings in a carefully curated mess on her desk, complete with an aesthetically placed whiskey glass and a couple pens at odd angles, she snapped a picture with her phone, threw on a filter and some adjustments to the contrast and definition to make it look old and artsy and posted it to her feed. *#art #artist #illustrator #illustrations #fairytale #starvingartist*

As she waited for the image to post she scanned down a bit. An incredibly detailed drawing of a lion fighting a giant crow. Some concert shots from a friend's band out in Providence. A workout video (she felt like she should maybe try paying more attention to those someday, but she didn't like the idea of going to a gym, so she was limited to what she could do in her small apartment). Some glam selfies of some makeup influencer in London. A smiling, handsome man kayaking shirtless with his dog. A shot of a woman in her underwear with a series of hashtags advertising the brand.

Ollie glanced up at her mirror. At her reflection she was so proud of. So happy with. She lifted her phone, flipped the camera to face her, struck a sultry look, and snapped a photo. Then, tapping away, she applied many of the same filters she applied to her art and labeled it #selfie. For a second she hovered her hand over the button to post it, then pressed the X to cancel the post and deleted the picture. She didn't like to post her face. Though a part of her wished she did.

Opening up another messaging app on her phone, she shot out a quick message to VelesVulpes - an online friend of hers she talked with infrequently.

> **O**     Long time radio silence. Sorry about that. Anything new?

She knew it could be days before they even saw that message so she put it out of her mind. Ollie didn't feel very comfortable with the online world her generation was supposed to have embraced, but there were a few relationships she'd managed to maintain or form through her fumbling along in it.

She checked the time on her phone and decided there was time for a quick run and a light work-out, then a shower. The bathroom was barely large enough for the standing shower that sputtered, the toilet that never stopped making the noise of the tank refilling, and the sink that ran constantly in a tiny dribble; there wasn't even a mirror or a real door, just a sliding one like you see on a closet. When she showered she turned on some slower, sad, folk-metaly music and admired herself again. For a moment she thought of the man she'd seen in the workout video earlier and imagined what it would be like to be him in the shower right now; she wouldn't want to fuck him, but she would like to know what it felt like to live in a body like that. Half-conscious she mimed stroking a comically large cock, then laughed to herself and turned off the water.

T he shower had put Ollie in a particularly lethargic mood. Her skin still felt the pressure of the hot water burrowing into her back and pelting her closed eyes. She delayed getting dressed for as long as possible, instead laying naked on her bed, towel wrapped around her red hair, and reading through a dog-eared Lovecraft anthology from her dad's library in the house she'd grown up in. Finally she realized she had waited too long and quickly got dressed; the same shirt as before and a pair of dark jeans. She considered a jacket, but ultimately decided it was too warm outside and slid into her Doc Martens - the european style a girl from college had showed her with the thinner lip; she'd spent too much time and too much money just to have those shoes because nothing else seemed right after the first time she drunkenly saw them, stars in her eyes.

It wasn't far down to Riley's - maybe a ten minute walk - but by the time she had left her apartment, one earbud in, billfold tucked into her waistband so she didn't have to muck with the obnoxiously shallow pockets on her jeans, and keys tightly in hand, it was already three minutes to 6. When she walked in the bar (ten minutes past, as she had stood outside Riley's despondently when she arrived, listening to the last screeching notes of the song that had borne her the entire way there) they were all there waiting - Viv and all her friends. They were Ollie's friends too, sort of. But mostly they were V's friends. One of them catcalled her and another called her a fox. She smiled and waved, coming over swiftly and carefully avoiding the patrons at the bar.

"Shoulda known you'd be late. Typical Liv." V kept trying to make the nickname stick. Viv and Liv. Or Liv and Viv. But Ollie didn't like it, and she thought others knew that too, so only V called her that.

"I got distracted." She offered a half-smile as an almost-apology and V moved on instantly, going back to whatever raucous conversation she had been engaged in before Ollie showed up. It was as if she had never entered.

She ordered a whiskey sour she couldn't afford and sat back into the leather cushion of the wide corner bench the group had claimed.

Viv was one of those people Ollie wondered what it would be like to be. She figured V was attractive, but not really exciting to Ollie. She was too thin. Like a corpse. But she had a wild shock of black hair, like Joan Jett or Lisbeth Salander. Her ears and face were heavily pierced with wicked spikes - many more piercings than Ollie, but she had very few tattoos, and those were mostly for her band (Ollie had a Kings of the Valley tattoo as well - a black ankh on her inner hip). Viv wore a lot of flashy war-gear. Big stompy boots with lots of buckles, long leather cuffs with inch-long spikes. Motorcycle gloves. Well-worn battle jackets. That sort of shit. But it seems like she always wore the same pair of worn out black skinny jeans, covered in holes and crusty paint-stains, and the same cycle of band Ts and crop tops - mostly for her own band. She smoked a lot too. Not even vapes like some of the group did. No, she was old school, and smoked crumpled home-rolleds like it was a penance; Ollie didn't smoke, but she respected Viv's old school flair.

Ollie and Viv had lived together for a bit, back before Ollie dropped out of college. It hadn't worked out. They were too different. And too alike. They smashed heads a lot and had the same bad ideas. But they'd remained friends after all that blew up - probably better friends for it. And V had gone on to get her degree in music education or shomeshit and had a half-way decent go at heading Kings of the Valley for almost ten years now. And Ollie could barely afford an apartment barely the size of a closet. Sometimes, when Ollie was feeling really shitty about her life, she envied V. But most of the time she was just glad to have her around; it was an odd, distant support that they both appreciated. They might not even talk much tonight, and that was okay.

> **VelesVulpes** Hej O! Long time, yeah. I started a new job (noth-
> ing exciting, just pays the bills), but I've been
> working on other stuff too. I just started writing
> again.

Seeing that VelesVulpes - or VP, as she thought of them in her head - had replied, she hunched her shoulders and typed back. VP fancied himself a writer, but he didn't really know how to get published; he wasn't much for self-promotion, and she commiserated. But she'd read some of his stuff and it was pretty good, even if some of it made her feel a little bit like she was missing something important.

> **O** O yeah? What sort of shit are you writing?
> **VelesVulpes** It's sort of a... I don't know.
> **VelesVulpes** It's like a thinking piece.

| | |
|---|---|
| **VelesVulpes** | It's not really horror, but it just makes you think, sort of like that. You know? |
| **O** | Like The Lighthouse? |
| **VelesVulpes** | Sure. |
| **VelesVulpes** | But it's about, like... It's sort of about dreams. And how we don't really remember them, even though they're so important. |
| **VelesVulpes** | I don't really want to give too much away. |
| **O** | O ho! No spoilers? |
| **VelesVulpes** | I want you to read it. |
| **O** | Sure |
| **O** | Hey, I'll catch up with you later. I'm out with V and I should at least try to seem sociable. |
| **VelesVulpes** | Sure thing. |

Putting her phone back on the table, Ollie tried to listen in on some of the other conversations. Viv seemed to be insulting some guy in another band. She had a lot of bad things to say about him. Maybe he'd done something actually fucked up. Or maybe V just didn't like him. She called him a *pig* a lot and a *stereo-dick* - whatever that meant. Bill and Crank were talking about some new computer game. Or a game from ten years ago, she didn't really know. Netti had a few comments to trade with Ollie about some books she'd gotten her into recently, mostly Nevill and Simmons. Netti liked horror too, but the conversation fell flat after a little while. Netti wasn't really very interesting, even if she was nice and had similar interests. She sucked at her drink and debated whether she was going to buy another one or make a graceful exit in the near future.

She decided to draw and checked the neckline of her shirt; sometimes she kept pens clipped there, but no luck. But by some miracle she had managed to put a couple in her pants pocket - probably last time she had worn them. Taking one out, she uncapped the rollerball nib, pulled an only slightly damp cocktail napkin to her and started absently scribbling. A little gnome. Some sharp designs. Maybe a new tattoo? Her pen picked out the shape of her own nose, brows, and eyes - blunted by the medium and exaggerated by her style. She absently turned her pen to her skin and started filling in the black spaces on her hand.

Soon the napkin was full and she had connected most of the little diamonds. And her drink was gone. And she was horny. Not in a way that made her want to do anything. She just kind of wished she did. And she wanted contact. But not with any of V's friends. And she wasn't about to pick someone up at Riley's. She shifted uncomfortably and thought back to that morning in bed before she'd gotten up to go to the mirror - the warm un-space she encountered all-too-often in the morning where her dreams still barely lingered and her clit called for attention.

She tried to distract herself by pulling out her phone again. Opening her feed and scrolling. Scrolling. Scrolling. Trying to skip over the things that would make her more excited, but not having the interest for much else. Then suddenly she stopped. Scrolled up once more.

"The fuck..?" she mumbled under her breath.

Ollie stared at the picture - a selfie from a new user her feed was suggesting for her to follow, one hand raised to make a peace sign and her tongue out. Tongue pierced just like Ollie's, with a tattoo on her forehead, below her eye, her cheek. Different ink, but in the same places. Same gauges, cuffs, and piercings. Her shoulders and upper chest were bare, and on them were a mess of flowers where Ollie had roaring norse dragons. Black ink covered her throat. Her bobbed hair was a pale corn-blonde. But her face. It was almost the same. The same cheekbones. The same nose. Same eyebrows and wide eyes (though blue, not green). Ollie didn't smile like that, but the rest was uncanny. She pressed on the profile and started scanning through. Looking at picture after picture, going for years, of a woman who looked like some sort of pod person come to steal her life. It didn't matter that she was posting from poolsides in Ibiza and Morocco and other places Ollie would rather die than get stuck in, it was her.

*That's fucking ridiculous*, she thought, and turned off her phone screen. Put it on the table face-down. She'd seen some movie on Netflix where something like that happened. Some girl getting her face stolen through the internet or something.

"Hey, Viv! I gotta bounce. I'll see you at the show, yeah?"

V flicked her off and didn't look up as she left, still unnerved by what she had seen.

That night she had more unsettling dreams. Odd dreams that seemed more real than waking, until she awoke. When she awoke she could remember faces - familiar but not any she'd seen in life - and a strange black sea. She struggled to remember the riddle-speech she'd engaged in on a gently rocking boat - all of it so similar to some poem she had read (or had read to her) when she was a kid.

But also, her morning friskiness had swiftly begun to rear its head. *Fuck*, she was horny. She skimmed through her feed, looking for inspiration, but came before her mind could settle on anything specific. And with that burst, wild and probably too loud, the dream was gone.

Getting up, she went to the mirror and began her morning ritual. Her perusal of herself in the mirror, her fingers still wet. She liked the smell.

Looking to the window, she saw that it was still early. *Good*, she thought, *still time for a morning run*. She liked to workout more in the morning than later in the day. It gave her a boost she couldn't quite match with caffeine. She slid into her running top and shorts and put on her running shoes - the only decent pair of shoes she owned other than her Docs. Thirty minutes later she was back, and after another thirty minutes with her weights and an old yoga matt she showered off and sat down to work, another old band T and some black joggers on with her hair pulled back tight into a short ponytail (she thought it made her look like Carrey Elwes in *The Princess Bride*).

Her mind wasn't really in the ink today though. She puttered around on the forest drawing, then tried a bit on someone's Dungeons and Dragons character commission - a raven-man with a staff full of charms and a wide scarf. But soon enough her attention had wholly wavered and she found herself on her phone, scanning through true crime documentaries and foreign horror flicks. Even there, she was unable to settle. She was restless, and for the moment she could not say why.

She glanced up at the Boris Valejo calendar above her workspace and the red sharpie note on today which said *V's GIG*. Above was an oil painting of a ridiculously over-muscled man, oiled up like a strongman, ready to wrestle a wildcat in a jungle of deep green. Ollie liked Valejo despite herself - and his wife Julie Bell. The art was silly, and a little tactless, but she understood it; the two of them were bodybuilders and painters - an unusual combination, but luckily they had found one-another and seemed to have been very happy for a long time. Both of them knew what they loved, and what they loved were muscles, so they put those on themselves and on their canvases. It was all a bit too much for Ollie, but still mesmerizing somehow. Like Frank Frazetta drew He-Man and he fell in a vat of butter. Ollie shuffled through her projects and pulled out one of a dark-haired muscled-up swordsman, glowering and covered in scars. She held it up to the Valejo painting; there wasn't much similarity between them. And not just because Valejo was much more talented than she was. Vallejo had painted an ideal. Ollie was inking something a bit more grim.

Sighing, Ollie put down the paper and went back to her phone. Closing her streaming apps, she opened her feed and began to scroll. After a few swipes she stopped. There was another picture of that smiling doppelgänger, emerging from a pool in a black and pink two-piece. She stared at the thing's face, entranced and still unnerved. She felt a faint warmth building in her, but told herself to calm down.

Shaking, she set down the phone and went to the kitchenette and started some coffee. This isn't real, she assured herself. She'd heard somewhere that everyone had something like five people in the world that looked exactly like them. Somehow she'd just accidentally found one. But even then, that was strange enough. What would the girl think if she knew? Her coffee still noisily steeping, she went cautiously back to her desk to retrieve her phone. Apprehensively, she scanned from one picture to the next, looking for any sign - of what she was not sure.

Finally, the coffee stopped burbling and she poured a tall cup into her mug, plastered with pulp art of Conan (not the Schwarzzenager schlock - the real Frazetta shit). Resolved, she scrolled back to the top of the poster's page. Her username was *moroni_coffee*. Angelica Moroni, her profile said, with some vapid stuff about travel and fashion and a waving Italian flag emoji. Not quite sure what she meant to say, Ollie tapped the message icon and began to type, finishing and erasing a few times before sending.

**O**        Hey. I know this might seem strange. Crazy even. But I stumbled across your profile and couldn't help but notice that we look crazy similar. It's wild. I thought it might be interesting to reach out to you. Trade stories with a forgotten twin haha

She put her phone down and drank her coffee unsteadily, the chat still open. Then, a few sips later, she picked up her phone and snapped a picture of herself, mimicking the pose she had first seen Angelica Moroni making in her post last night, pulling her hair out of its band so it fell wavy about her face. Ollie posted it to the chat without pausing, then cringed, looking at herself making a face she would never make willingly. And sending it to a stranger! She could feel her blush - almost painful, and dug around in her fridge for something to eat, finally settling to lunch nervously on carrots, a premade rice cup from the cupboard, and some cheese.

After her anxious lunch she decided to do some drawing for herself. Taking out a new piece of drawing paper - not one of the nice ones, but it was better than printer paper - she sat for a moment, then grabbed her red pencil and drew the shape of a body in broad strokes. Her body. She liked to draw herself. Somehow it was even better seeing herself on paper than in the mirror. She had time before the show. Soon she was laying down thin lines with her 0.25, followed by thicker lines in 0.5, and outlines in 1.0. She accentuated where her face and her body changed shape, and felt a proud excitement as she drew the sharp lines of muscles on her shoulders and arms (honestly probably sharper than the lines ever were on her real arms). A wry, curious gaze stared out from the paper, unblinking, as she began to hatch and stipple, adding small detail to bring the drawing to life. She began to lovingly apply the tattoos that would be visible, and was nearly done when she saw the time and swore.

Throwing on a black pair of jeans and a denim jacket, she hurried out-side, nearly forgetting to lock her door. She grabbed a yogurt cup full of fruit and granola (that she should not have spent the $5 on) and ran the three blocks to Nolan's, waving to Jerry the bouncer as she took the crook-ed, black-painted stairs up to the venue three at a time. Up at the door, nearly out of breath, she stepped past the dwindling line and stood awk-wardly to one side, shoveling yogurt into her mouth until the guy at the door - she didn't remember his name, but she'd seen him before - noticed her.

"Viv should have left tickets for me."

He nodded and motioned her forwards, marking the back of her hand with a black sharpie.

T he whine - a scream really - of the guitars priming filled the small space as Ollie shouldered her way towards the front. She smiled to Viv when the singer saw her, and made devil horns with her hands, sticking her tongue out. But V was obviously pre-occupied. They were almost ready.

Ollie gazed around the tiny concert area. It didn't have a name, and didn't really seem large enough to host a concert of any kind. The floor tiles had once been white, but now were a sickly, aquarium green, sloping and buckling like waves. The low ceiling held bare rafters, dyed black with some tar-like paint, and a small bar took up too much space at the back of the room. Even for small shows the room felt packed; she remembered going to a show once - some two-man doom metal outfit from somewhere down south - where only four other people bothered to show and she had wondered if she was claustrophobic. Kings of the Valley was popular locally though, and so there were easily fifty people crammed into a space smaller than most coffee shops.

Looking around, she felt a twinge of pride at seeing that few of those gathered had as much ink as her. Sometimes knowing that her skin was so detailed made her feel as if she glowed. It was a mark of comfort and pro-tection she always carried on her. In some ways it felt more her than her. She glanced at her hands - the mark of success on her finger - and smiled. Viv would start soon. She wanted a drink

Struggling back to the bar, she ordered a gin and tonic, wincing as she pulled a few bills from her fold, leaving it significantly lighter than before. But she was here for Viv. And she always drank with V. That was just how it was. From the front of the room she heard V start her schtick about the ancient pharaohs, and the curse of the pyramids - all delivered like the nar-rator in some campy 80s adventure film. Ollie cheered and raised her devil

121

horns in the air. Others cheered with her as Viv finished the introduction with her false baritone rising into a wicked screech that would make Gaahl proud, "And we are the *Kings of the Valley*!" A cavalcade of aggressive guitar chords and heavy cymbal crashes followed in the wake of her announcement, and soon V was marching acrost the stage - really just an area of the floor marked out with painter's tape - doubled over like a ghoul and screeching into the mic.

Ollie let herself get lost in the music, headbanging along with the others and tapping her hand in thin air as she listened to the music without exactly hearing it; enveloping herself in the crawling soundscape they created. Their older stuff was a lot more punk, and some of their stuff had hints of that still, but Ollie had to admit that this was more her style. Punk was good, but this brutal, atonal cacophony was the type of shit she could really surrender to.

It was a couple songs in - long, ten minute or more songs - before Ollie checked her phone. Her heart skipped a beat when she saw there was an alert, only to realize it had the wrong icon to be her strange fascination. In must be VP. She flicked open the screen, checking her chat with *moroni_coffee* first (delivered, not seen) before sliding open VP's chat log.

**VelesVulpes**   Check this shit out:

There was a link after to an album. She'd have to try to remember to look at it later. She wished she hadn't opened the message and sent the read receipt, since she didn't really have anything to say - especially whilst enjoying the show. She typed back quickly and stowed her phone again.

**O**                 I'll check it later. At V's gig.

The spell of the music momentarily broken, Ollie looked around. She knew a decent number of the people here in passing. Members of the scene. A lot of them in bands. Ollie was tone deaf and shit at any instrument she'd tried, so she had never been in a band. Her drink was gone and she considered going for another before remembering her nearly empty billfold. Looking at all the people jumping and shaking their heads, Ollie suddenly felt the loneliness that had been pressed upon her the last couple years; she'd done it to herself mostly, but she figured that on some level she really was lonely. If she had a couple more drinks in her she imagined she'd be a lot more talkative with these almost-strangers, even with the ear-bustingly loud music.

There was a tap at her arm and she realized someone had been yelling for her attention. She turned and saw a shortish raven-haired girl with large hornrim glasses and a septum ring too big for her nose. She wore a wispy black blouse that seemed too nice for the nameless place above Nolan's. Ollie wasn't sure if she'd seen this girl before, but she smiled and made metal horns with her hands whilst she screwed up her face. The girl laughed and nodded, then proceeded to stand next to her until the volume dimmed a bit between songs.

"You're Viv's friend, right? She said you were coming. Said we might get along." Ollie looked to the newcomer curiously. Was Viv trying to set her up with a date? V invited her to all her gigs - even the out-of-state ones she knew she couldn't attend - but had she had an ulterior motive here? "I'm Trick."

"Ollie," she shouted back as the music began to ramp up again. Trick awkwardly shifted her half-full beer to her other hand and they shook. *Shaking hands? Great first impression, Ollie.*

Trick said something else, but Ollie couldn't hear it over the rumbling, tumbling bass entrance to the next song. They stood beside each other for much of the rest of the evening, exchanging brief words where they were able and Ollie accepting a beer after a couple more songs. Seems Trick - Tricia - was some sort of marketing agent or something. Maybe this hadn't been a setup for a date. Maybe V was trying to throw her a bone to help with her freelance work. But Ollie was a little drunk and a little morose thinking about her lonely life, so she steered the topic away from business wherever it lingered. Trick was more into power metal stuff. Had a dog. Did some sort of martial art - Ollie missed the name and didn't bother to ask again. Trick had graduated a few years ago (*Am I getting old?* she thought, but realized Trick meant grad school, which still stung).

As the last song wound down, Ollie leaned in so she could be heard. "You wanna get out of here?"

Ollie couldn't read the look Trick gave her, but she said, "Sure."

They just ended up downstairs. Their conversation didn't last much past the next round (Ollie's billfold was empty now), and they found themselves pressed together in a booth in the back corner. Ollie felt elated at the weight of the hand on her cheek. Cherished the warmth of Trick's lips on hers, the taste of her tongue. She ran her hand down Trick's side and up her back. Ollie didn't know how long they spent back there, but eventually Trick sat back, adjusting her glasses and checking her watch (*Who still wears a watch these days?*).

"Oh, I have to go. I have a thing in the morning." From the look in her eye, Ollie thought that she wished she didn't have a thing in the morning. "Maybe we can meet up again sometime. Someplace where we can actually hear each other." Her wide smile was disarming. Showed a lot of teeth.

"Sure." Ollie's mind blanked as to what the next step was. She didn't often do things like this. Didn't pick up women at bars. Didn't make out with strangers. Barely made out at all these days.

Trick's expectant smile faltered a bit at the corner, but she reached into her clutch and brought out a very professional, creme business card. *Tricia Holder · Manager · Art and Artists* with an address, an email, and a phone number with an extension. Turning it over, she scribbled her cell number on the back with a pen Ollie happily supplied.

Trick gave her another kiss and, as she left, Ollie called, "See ya!" She didn't know if Trick heard her, but she felt like an idiot as soon as the words left her mouth.

Stumbling home, she teetered towards her bed, then, pausing, fell into the wooden chair by her desk. Picking up her pen, she looked at the mostly finished drawing of herself. She wasn't sure if this had been a good night or not. Or if she'd call Trick back. Running her fingers over the familiar lines of her tattoos on the paper, she mused that there was an empty spot there on her arm, above the skull on her elbow. With her pen she scribbled a black spade symbol, like from a deck of cards. She didn't take the time to finish any of the rest of her drawing, but stripped clumsily down and snuggled under her covers.

She considered trying to masturbate, but was too tired. Or drunk. She laid her hand on her thigh, put a pillow over her head, and drifted off into a black sea of dreams.

W aking once more from the murky darkness of her dreams, she half-remembered figures. Like wizards from an old paperback. Or like Maine fishermen with wide whiskers and thick-knit sweaters. Or neither. Ollie liked remembering her dreams, and it bothered her that they had eluded her so oft of late.

Snatching for her phone beside the bed, she realized that she had forgotten to plug it in, but it still had some charge left. *Moroni_coffee's* page was open, even though she didn't remember opening it. She checked the chat log, but she still hadn't seen the message. Ollie thought it pretty likely that she would never see the message. She looked at the picture she had taken of herself. The unfamiliar grin and flashed peace sign. She used her elbows to hug the blankets closer around her as she stared at her own face, somehow unfamiliar. Swiping back to Angelica's profile, she scanned down a bit, looking at picture after picture. It was the same unfamiliar face - the same almost-right body that greeted her with each new swipe. All in unfamiliar spaces, doing unfamiliar things.

What would it be like if they could change places? Would food taste different? Would walking feel different? Would sex be different? She almost didn't realize when her hand slipped between her legs and began to work whilst she skimmed through this stranger's profile, imagining herself in that world. In that body. Pretending she was Angelica Moroni. Had always been Angelica Moroni. Eventually it was too much and she gasped and bucked her hips as she climaxed, then greedily went back for more, cumming twice more before she dragged herself from bed, forcing herself to close the app.

After she had finished her workout and her shower, the mysterious Italian face-stealer never far from her mind, she sat down at her desk. Looking over her jumbled work, she took a moment to organize the papers. They would get mussed up again later, but it felt nice to do what she could to fight back against her messy tendencies. She took a bit to finish more on the forest drawing, taking a break to eat some cereal and an orange around 11, then pulled out the drawing of herself from last night.

It didn't take long to finish adding her ink to it - she knew each one so well. She only barely remembered drawing the little spade on her arm last night, but kind of liked how it looked. She stood and moved to the mirror to examine her arm - see if maybe she should consider adding that as a new piece. But as she turned a bit to the side, twisting her arm to see that space of her arm better, she stopped dead. There, above the skull with flowers blooming from its eyes that covered her elbow, was a black spade. She reached up and rubbed at it. Licked her thumb and scrubbed. It was real. It was permanent. Had she been that drunk? Had she somehow found some artist willing to do a piece that late at night, and for someone so intoxicated? She must have. But she had no memory of it. It was fresh and deep black, and stared at her blankly.

"What the fuck," she mumbled, but had no other explanation. Maybe Trick would know, if she ever called her back.

She shook her head and set her self-portrait aside, underneath other work so she wasn't reminded. Wasn't unnerved like how *moroni_coffee* had unnerved (and excited) her. She didn't even want to sit at her desk just then, and went back to her bed, sitting with her back against the dull blue wallpaper - she hadn't been able to afford a bed with a headboard. She pulled out her phone but purposefully did not open her feed. She did see she had other alerts though, including a few messages from VP.

**VelesVulpes**   O, dope
**VelesVulpes**   Let me know how it goes
**VelesVulpes**   I'm really excited about this thing I'm writing
**VelesVulpes**   It's not quite like anything I've written before
**VelesVulpes**   Very personal, but in like a weird way
**VelesVulpes**   I still want you to be the first one to read it

Wow, VP normally wasn't this active.

| | |
|---|---|
| O | show went fine. got kind of fucked up, but that's okay |
| O | Personal how? |
| VelesVulpes | G'morning! |
| O | Morning |
| VelesVulpes | It's got a lot more of me in it than my stuff normally does. Which makes me kind of nervous. It's a lot less violent and sad and a lot more tender. |
| VelesVulpes | Still kind of sad though |
| VelesVulpes | And weird. |
| O | I like weird. |
| VelesVulpes | I know. That's why I want you to read it. |

Whatever VP was working on, Ollie was sure it would be interesting at least.

Trick's card was sitting on her bedside table near where her phone had been and she picked it up. What had Viv really meant for her to do with Trick? She flicked open her message log with Vivian.

| | |
|---|---|
| O | I met Trick last night |
| O | she's Cute |
| O | Really got her shit together. |

She considered sending more but decided it would be better to wait for V to respond. Just then the phone screen went dim as the battery bar began to flash red. She picked up the cord and plugged it in before going back to her desk.

Absently her fingers caressed the strange new tattoo as she stared, unfocused at her pile of work. She traced it with the black nail of her left hand. *What the fuck is going on?* After a moment of this, she pulled out the self-portrait and stared at it. Other than the spade, it looked like any other drawing she had made of herself. She propped it up on the back of the desk, leaning against the beige wall, and stared at it. Then, she took out more of the same paper and started to draw. She drew herself, again and again. In pencil, in pen, rough and complete. She let it occupy her for much of the rest of the day.

M agic was something Ollie believed in. Practical magic. Growing up, she had always liked stories about strange wizards, tragic curses, and mystical spells, but she had known that she would not see those things in her daily life. Everyone told her so. Nevertheless, she persisted in her belief that somehow, somewhere, there were powers out there that weren't able to be entirely explained by rational thought. She wasn't big on the ideas of aliens or bigfoot or ghosts, but she liked the idea of spells.

Not flashy fireballs or teleportation, but rather little things. Charms that warded the bearer (or wearer, if it was jewelry or ink) and beliefs strong enough that they proved true, as long as there wasn't enough evidence in the world that they could not happen. She'd read some bits of mysticism and old (very old) poetry, but a lot of her ideas came about from her own observations of the world around her, and were only reinforced later by things she read. And she was fairly comfortable admitting that all of this could be bullshit. But she liked to put her skepticism aside and take comfort in the weird.

But this was like nothing she had imagined could happen in the real world. And it certainty wasn't bullshit. Somehow. First this Moroni chick and now the fresh tattoo she'd drawn herself? What the Hell was happening to her? Was she under some sort of curse? Was she secretly some mighty sorcerer only now discovering (or rediscovering) her powers? She couldn't wrap her head around it.

On one of the many self-portraits she'd made that day she changed the tattoo on her cheek. Subtly altering the row of celtic knots.

T he next morning she awoke, bursting from her bed and padding barefoot to the mirror, finding that the knots on her face had indeed changed. She ran her finger over the fresh, black lines, her wide eyes never leaving the mirror. Wide and dilated. She felt like she should be scared. And she was. But she was excited too.

The rest of the week followed much of her usual pattern - restless dreams, masturbate (more and more often to the mysterious Moroni who still had not seen her message), observe herself in the mirror (and what had changed), go for a run and have a brief work-out, and work the rest of the day, pausing to eat when she remembered. But more and more her attention was drawn to absently scribbling drawings of herself. Making small alterations to see the next day. Normally it would bother her at first if there were a new change to her body - even ink took a few days to get used to - but these changes only exhilarated her.

She didn't hear from Vivian, and didn't contact Trick. Neither could be further from her mind. But on wednesday VP messaged her again.

VelesVulpes  I have a draft of that thing done.
O          The Lighthouse one?
VelesVulpes  It's not quite like that. But sure.
VelesVulpes  Want to see it?

| | |
|---|---|
| **O** | Send it over. I'll check it out when I get time. |

When VP sent the attachment Ollie downloaded it to her phone and put it from her mind. But before she went back to her drawing - working on actual commissions for the moment - she messaged them again.

| | |
|---|---|
| **O** | hey VP? |
| **VelesVulpes** | What's up? |
| **O** | you ever wonder about that, like, metaphysical shit? |
| **O** | like if we're real or not? |
| **VelesVulpes** | I'm pretty sure I'm real |
| **VelesVulpes** | You okay? That's sort of weird thing to ask. |
| **VelesVulpes** | Should I be worried or something? |
| **O** | I'm fine. Just thinking out loud. |
| **O** | I'll check out that story when I get some free time |
| **VelesVulpes** | alright... |
| **VelesVulpes** | You know you can talk to me if you need to |

She left VP on read.

O n friday, after she had cum twice to the thought of *moroni_coffee* - unsure if she wanted to be her today or fuck her senseless - Ollie texted Trick.

| | |
|---|---|
| **O** | hey, it's Ollie |
| **O** | V's friend |

She waited anxiously for a response, but she didn't have to wait long.

| | |
|---|---|
| **Trick** | You really know how to keep a girl waiting |
| **O** | Yeah. Been busy |
| **O** | I had a thing |
| **Trick** | For a week lol? |
| **O** | You think it's easy being this cool? |

Trick shortly agreed to meet up that afternoon for coffee, and Ollie hoped that her next commission check came in soon. When she went to the mirror she examined the large septum ring she had drawn last night. Gave it a small flick. Would Trick think it was weird? She had gotten the idea from her. Hopefully it wasn't too weird, though she guessed she could always take it out.

She wanted things to go well with Trick. She wanted to hold someone other than herself. She always felt more grounded - more powerful - when she was able to have a good fuck, especially after such a long time. For a moment she fretted that she might not remember how, despite her daily (often multiple times a day) imaginings.

Ollie thought back to a few moments before, frantically rubbing her clit to the face of a stranger that looked just like her. How strange and exciting that had been. And how the strange power in the drawings had only come about after she ran acrost Angela Moroni's profile. *Maybe I'm some sort of sex magician. Imagine what would happen if I actually had sex.*

| Viv | she give you her card? |
|-----|------------------------|
| Viv | she was kind of weird about it |
| O | she gave me more than her card |
| Viv | !!! |
| Viv | ohmygodliv |
| Viv | did you Fuck trick |
| Viv | ??? |
| O | not yet |
| Viv | that is NOT why I sent her to you |
| Viv | but good job |
| Viv | she is cute |
| Viv | might not make a great agent if your fucking her tho |

Sending an emoji of her middle finger (or someone else's middle finger, she supposed), she shut off her phone screen again. *First time I've heard from her in almost a week,* Ollie thought ruefully. But that's how it often went. It was fine.

After her morning run she made some coffee and opened her feed again. She hesitated, then opened her messages with *moroni_coffee*. Her heart froze when she saw the little icon indicating that her messages had been read. But there was no response. *Is she thinking of what to say? Is she as fucked up by this as I am? Maybe she thinks the picture is fake. I should say something else. But what?* Nervously she put her phone away. She suddenly felt like she was stalking this girl; it had all seemed fine when there was no hope of contact, but suddenly Angelica Moroni knew Ollie existed. Probably.

She went back to work, but when her phone lit up with a message alert from someone in her feed she almost knocked over her third cup of coffee. But it wasn't *moroni_coffee*.

| Lincoln | hey Ollie. I was just thinking about you |
|---------|-------------------------------------------|
| Lincoln | Howve you been |
| Lincoln | if youre still in town we should grab a drink |

Ollie had dated Lincoln for about a year after she dropped out of college, but they hadn't really talked much after he broke up with her. He hadn't liked how dude she'd seemed. He wanted an actual woman - or so he'd said. She hadn't been too broken up about it; he had been kind of boring and wasn't really motivated by much. Mostly he was a nice guy (other than the weird misogyny she hadn't been aware of), but he reminded her more of unbuttered bread than anything. Maybe not white bread, but still just bread. She left him on read.

Glancing at the time she saw that it was almost time for her to meet up with Trick for coffee (did she really need more caffeine?). She took off the holey Zepplin shirt she'd been wearing since the run and went to sift through her clothes. Trick dressed nice, even to a dive bar; she wasn't sure if she could match that. Not with what she owned. Eventually she picked out a white T (barely worn, the only one she owned) and a soft red flannel, which she rolled up to the elbows, changing into a slightly newer, slightly darker set of jeans. She laced her Docs all the way up this time, instead of leaving the tongue loose like she usually did.

Going to the mirror she examined the septum ring again. Pausing, her fingers on the ring, she instead reached into her back pocket for her phone. Holding the phone up high, she made a slight smirk and raised an eyebrow. Not an expression she had seen Moroni make, but good enough for a picture. She hoped. She snapped the picture, hated it, and snapped another. And two more. Finally she had one she liked and, not even bothering to add her usual artsy filters, she posted it to her feed, unlabeled. Then she copied the link and sent it to *moroni_coffee*.

**O**         I'm not some sort of photoshop bot. Promise.

At the coffee shop down the street Trick was waiting. She had dressed down, and they both laughed at how similarly they had dressed trying to match the other, though Trick's flannel was green. Ollie excused herself and ordered a black coffee, returning shortly to awkwardly reintroduce herself.

"It seems V had a different idea about how our meeting might go."

"Well, she didn't mention how cool you were, Ms. Ollie."

Somehow all of the sexual pressure that had been building in Ollie had fled, but that left her free to enjoy her time with Trick. Really enjoy it. Trick was good people, and Ollie hoped they could remain friends, even if they didn't go home together. She had set out that morning intending to take Trick back to her cramped apartment and blow her world (or try to), but the time just didn't seem right. She'd take it slow. Trick deserved that.

T rick and Ollie staid out until the shop closed around 6, then spent another couple hours walking - first out to a park nearby and then along the trails there - before Ollie decided it was time for her to go. She promised Trick they'd talk again, and joked about talking business next time. Then she walked the few blocks home.

Sitting down in her bed and turning on some music - first something screechy and hard, then something a bit more atmospheric and doomy, she sat and smiled. Even if she never saw Trick Holder again she was glad to feel a little less lonely, even for an evening. Opening her phone to find something idle to do, she noticed the notification at the top of her phone she had never dismissed for the downloaded file from VP. She figure she might as well, and hunkered lower on the bed to give it a read.

What she read made her head hurt.

It was longish - maybe forty or fifty pages if it had been formatted out in a paperback. Maybe less - Ollie wasn't great at estimating these things. And it was strange. And familiar. Unnervingly familiar. It was about a young woman, independent but lonely, with pale blue eyes and long blonde hair. She traveled in her dreams on a boat manned by five figures in black cloaks, and in waking she wondered after love (VP was too much of a romantic, and assumed romance was the true centre of life. Ollie thought he hadn't quite lived enough.). But every morning she gazed in the mirror and examined herself - tracing the spells the river-wizards wrote on her skin. She was dating a guy - dark hair, nice job, septum ring - and wondered what it would be like to be him. To live his life. She began to resent her own life, wishing she could taste what it was like to live others. There was a hint at the end that maybe she meant to kill her lover, but it was ambiguous (purposefully, Ollie assumed).

From the moment the protagonist began to describe herself she had felt unnerved - unable to shake the image of moroni_coffee staring into her mirror, and wearing her skin. And the dreams... Were those not alike in ways to the half-remembered dreams that had bothered her own dreams of late? And the changing tattoos! And the boyfriend who looked uncomfortably like Trick. What the fuck was this? How the fuck did VP know these things? Apparently before she had even known them. There was even a date in a coffee shop near the end that ended with a walk through the park.

Ollie was angry. Fucking pissed. But at what? Maybe she was just scared. And she was. Fucking terrified. A part of her wanted to block VP immediately and never talk to Trick again. Maybe enter a sleep study. And block moroni_coffee as well. What the fuck? She was breathing heavily and grasping her fingers anxiously. Throwing her phone on the bed, she stripped out of her clothes and stumbled to the shower, flipping on the water - as hot as it would go - and sitting with her knees hugged to her chest on the cramped floor.

But the thoughts of the strange story would not leave her. Of her date with the cute art agent. Of the ink and piercings she could draw into existence. Of the eerie Italian body double. Her eyes unfocused, she found herself growing warm. Frightened, but needing release, she reached down and, as the pressure of the boiling water pelted her head, her legs, her breasts, she fingered herself to a shuddering climax. She sobbed on the tile floor until the water turned cold, and then kept on until she couldn't stand the chill any longer.

T he words of the ghostly boatmen floated through the dark. Not quite an argument. Not quite spoken.

> **Musician/Magician** It could be she has never left. Perhaps she has found what we each seek.
>
> **Salamander/Seer** We do not all seek the Sleep.
>
> **Pale/Prophet** I suppose we must let her decide. You look different, lass. Have you been here before?
>
> **O**         I'm here every night.
>
> **O**         Aren't I?
>
> **Skull/Sorcerer** What you are is not a question, but an answer. How many times have I given false counsel to false asking? Too many. Too many.
>
> **O**         I don't understand.
>
> **Knight/Necromancer** Of course thu dost not. There ist little thu canst understand if thu remainest waking.
>
> **Musician/Magician**   Sleep! Sleep and be happy, for the world passes on.
>
> **Pale/Prophet** Take a new road. There are always more.
>
> **Skull/Sorcerer** A mirror! A mirror! Hell is what it reflects, not what it forms. Piglets do not know the axe that takes their mothers.

Their wicked white grins filled the empty space and she woke with a gasp. She did not remember crawling into bed, yet here she was, naked atop the sheets, her hair still faintly damp. Blinking, only vaguely remembering the story from last night she grabbed her phone, nearly dead.

> **O**             VP, what the fuck was that? I think we need to talk. That story was seriously fucking weird.

Since her phone was open, she checked her message log with *moroni_coffee*. Still unseen. She looked at her own face she had posted in the chat and wondered if Angelica Moroni had had any of the same thoughts she had. She doubted it. But the idea was exciting. And she touched herself and moaned softly as she thought of it.

Rising from the bed she went to the mirror, shaking out her hair and running her fingers through it. She had a headache.

Ollie lifted her breasts then let them fall, looking sideways in the mirror. Paused to run two fingers over the rose on her shoulder. Along the defined musculature to the black knots of ink on her chest. Turned slightly and lifted her ass with both hands and gave a small smirk before turning full-on to the mirror and meeting her pale blue eyes. She liked how she looked. Was proud of what she'd done to shape herself. She'd chosen the gauges, tattoos, and regular workouts in the corner of her cramped apartment. Some of it meant something, some of it was just because she could. Who fucking cared? She rested one hand on her sternum, just above where her stomach said *Blood* in sharp gothic text that looked like it could cut you if you weren't careful. Smiled at how the light sneaking in through the heavy curtains lit on her long, wavy blonde hair.

# A Violent and Jealous Love

The Sword is heavy.

Many men have held it and many men have lost the strength to wield it. But the Sword is jealous and wicked. It does not relish being forgot.

Yet men ever seek to forget that terrible covenant once they have taken it up, and the road home to plainer times is hard and equally as perilous. Here follows a story of one who lost the love of the Sword, and of he who gave it, only to see for themself the choices such a decision carries with it.

Our unfortunate protagonist has worn many faces, answered to many names throughout time, and shall wear and answer to many more before time is finished. But for simplicity's sake we will paint them with the name of Sir Guy Fields. And the face we will paint him with is of a handsome man – but not too handsome – with chiseled lines and grizzled beard-shadow. Thick brows, an impressive moustache, a bob of wavy brown hair, and grey, grey eyes – like steel dipped in a slow stream and lit from behind a cloud by the friendly sun. Our Sir Guy is a member of a fighting order in service to a mighty God – like the Knights Templar or Hospitaller. This order we shall call the Knights Indomitable, or the Indomitable Order. As for their deity, they shall merely be God, for it is a simple name and many call many and varied other beings by that same label as they argue over whom or what it truly belongs to.

Guy of Fields came from a noble name but an empty treasury, and swore the Indomitable Oath in an effort both to feed himself and to preserve his family legacy. He left behind a modest estate, a widowed mother, a handful of siblings, and a true love which he could never more dream of; God could be his only love now.

And a red love was God. A cruel love. A violent and jealous love. A bloody-handed deity whose worship spread at Sword's edge.

By boat and foot and horse and wagon Sir Guy travelled to offer the harsh invitations of God to those who had never even heard his name. 'Gainst dark stone castles whose lords served God in ways he was told were wrong he fared. And 'gainst thatch-rooved villages of desperate and ignorant peasants fared his torch and his wending blade. Green lands he saw. Mountains, deserts, and forests of all kinds. And all these he washed in blood. Folk of other tongues, strange clothes, and new faces he met, and cracked their crowns for daring to defy a God they had never met. All this God asked of young Guy, and all this he did.

Long months - long years - he spent with heavy Sword in hand. His steely helm made creases on his forehead from long campaigns and his skin browned under foreign suns. The wonder of new places - and of God - came like a summer storm. And left like love grown stale after years spent too close. The Knights Indomitable bred in him a fear of his ardourous God and a hatred of the inhuman other. And at first he fell into these lessons with fanaticism. But, like the sick he felt at the blood of his first battle or the joy of childhood, those feelings left as well, in time.

By his thirtieth year, camped in a silken tent under a blazing sky in siege of an ancient city whose name he may never have heard had he staid to marry the woman he had loved, Guy was an empty husk. There was no joy in killing. He had seen so many new worlds that there was naught he could see in his travels would awe him. His family had long since died or ceased to write. No woman calmed his heart and no man soothed his soul. He could not even bring the name of God to his lips, so much had it taken from him. Yet still he loved God. For what else could he do?

"God chooses this path," said his lord commander. But Guy wondered if God sometimes chose other paths as well.

"God knows best," Fields assured the younger paladins when their hearts wavered, even though his own had long since abandoned him.

The siege was long. Months, then months more. Then, in time, a year. And months beyond. Our hapless protagonist stood staunchly against the godless, God-fearing defenders each day of the long blockade. Until the day he did not.

There had been no rain no even clouds in days beyond his reckonging. The hot sun beat down and baked Sir Guy's skin, sending him light-headed about his camp duties. Before him he could see more days of suffering, and in time a bloody breach. In times past he would have prayed for guidance as his devotion faltered, but he had been too long on the brink of apostasy. And in that moment he stepped over the edge. If only for a short while.

So strong and faithful did all men think him that he was trusted in many things. And so, when he said he must go out alone to check the cantonment's northern perimeter, none challenged him. One squire-acolyte offered aid, but Guy told him, "'Tis a small task, and I am a man more than worthy to accomplish it. God decries excess, and so I shalt take only what little I need." And so, with his Sword, his shield, a skin of wine, and a brick of hard cheese hidden in his belt, the traitor went to the boundary and past it, and off into the sere lands beyond. He was not missed for two more hours, and then all blamed his death (for what else could have happened for such a godly man to abandon his duty) on their hated, wrong-Godded foes.

He followed paths he had not trod in many long months, back towards home – if home he still had. Shame settled on him before the first day was out, but shame also kept him from returning. He hid his face under a cowl. Scoured the God-marks of his order from his shield. Spoke in hushed tones in the tongue of his enemy. In solitude he lamented, "How can God forgive me? Is his will not to have me bleed his enemies? Burn their walls? I have become anathema. I shalt never be entered into the Kingdom of God."

In time he came back to green lands. No words save prayers had left his lips in many, many weeks. It was not hard for him once his voice returned, accented by many months of a foreign tongue, to learn of the fate of his last home and of rumours of death in the lands he had left. Behind him was doom and ahead was despair. "I should never have lowered my Sword from thy service, LORD," he cried into the wind. "Can a man serve in other ways once he has made such bloody devotions?"

Sir Guy became a wanderer. Homeless, penniless, and sometimes witless. The once-proud warrior was seen asleep in orchards, drunk in taverns, and begging alms at the feet of churches. He sold his shield first. Then his mail. Then even his Sword. He was a ghost and directionless save for the want of God's love.

It came about that one day, in his aimless travels, he came upon a monastery of his faith – a place of rest, peace, and healing. The monks there welcomed him. Clothed and fed him and cut his shaggy hair. The dispossessed knight felt great guilt at becoming a weight on those so beloved of God. But they taught him of God's compassion, where before all he had been taught was fury.

His first intention on coming to the cloister had been to beg aid then pass on – to go looking for more kind souls so as not to burden any one source too greatly. But the monks were so kind that he soon forgot his need to flee. His wrist began to ache during prayer and service – his heart saying God loved by the Sword – but the monks cared for him and showed him how to turn his hand to weaving and to painting. Before that year was out he had shaved his head and taken cassock and vow.

The holy lands in which he had warred never left his mind, but he found new joys to occupy his attentions. Though his fingers were never as adroit at any chore as they had been with the Sword, Brother Guy felt wanted. He felt as if he could possibly earn God's love anew. Could leave behind his bloody promise to the blade.

Years passed and violence came closer to home. Lords, and even priests, in God's own chosen lands began to describe new paths to God and new ways to serve him. And, as they each arose, they brought with them new justifications. And those arguments led inevitably to death and to fire. But the lonely monastery saw no signs, and only heard vague rumours of unhappiness.

One day, late in the autumn, a soldier, wounded in a war close to home found his way to the steps of the orderhouse. Throwing himself to their mercy, though he said his church was their enemy, he was welcomed, as had been Brother Guy. And Brother Guy came to tend him.

The man's injuries were severe, but not mortal, and he would need rest in the infirmary for some weeks. In that time he was cared for always by the retired fang of God. Guy was a passable physic, drawing upon his history of violence, and soon enough the guest was feeling well enough to converse and to attempt short walks. In that time the two of them could often be seen slowly wandering the gardens in the evening before final prayers.

They spoke mostly of their childhoods, neither of them terribly happy, but both fostered by the Sword. The soldier claimed he was not very religious, despite fighting in a religious war. "God's a bastard, whatever his face," he blasphemed, and Guy felt both a unity with the man and an anger at him. He did not speak such, however, for he had left fist and fury behind. Yet still he dreamt often of the feel of a scabbard at his hip.

But it was not long before the once-knight fell to the temptation and asked after the war. His patient claimed the war was too terrible to speak on, yet went on nonetheless to tell in great detail of all the unspeakable things he had seen, heard of, and God forgive, done. Brother Guy felt his blood stirring at the thought of familiar atrocities, and that stirring made him sick in the stomach. He wanted to prove that he could leave the Sword behind.

"Ye say ye are not very religious," said Brother Guy one evening as they wandered. "Yet ye come to this house of healing. Why? Do ye seek to leave behind thy bloody ways?"

The man – likely not more than a boy, though war ages men – guffawed. "Nay," he said. He said the Sword-life doesn't let a man go. Especially not if they're raised in it. "'Sides. I'm not religious."

"Yet ye fight a religious war."

"War itself is a religion, I 'spose. In which case my church is still the enemy of thine. And, like as not, it won't be long afore the war comes here and ye'll see the truth of it."

Guy dismissed this. Even warriors of other faiths did not raid churches. Not churches of his faith leastwise. And as for the Sword not surrendering up its adherents? He had escaped, had he not? Brother Guy was not Sir

Guy. That man had been buried.

But that night Guy dreamt of war. Of blood and fire and Sword. Of the exultation that came with murder in the name of God. In the dream, Guy was red with blood and his skin screamed praises to the heavens. His world burned and he lit a torch and brought it to other worlds until everyone's world was burnt. God spoke in the dream. And he told his servant that his duty was to kill.

Guy awoke from the dream even more determined than before not to become a puppet once more to the hungry warlords and chapterhouses that cried God's name. He was content to launder and garden and sing hymns.

The soldier limped on soon, destined for more bloody battlefields. And in his absence the cloister returned to the same serene peace that was its usual. And Guy tried to forget his dreams.

And largely his dreams were forgotten and he lived a happy life. Bringing all-the-more woe when the patient's dire predictions proved true.

For it came to be one day that, after the morning bells, the sky was red and hazy and tasted bitter. And the monks came to the road which led to their retreat and could see fires in the valley below. The men shook their heads and prayed for the souls of brave men who must become murdrumers for God. Guy's blood was icy as he watched the distant carnage, but his heart was red at the memories of his dreams, which his head still denied. His arm ached as once it had after long battles carrying sharp Swords. "They do their duty to God and we to ours. Our paths need never cross," he said, and returned for his morning meal.

But the fire did not remain in the valley, and by midday soldiers could be seen roving the lands between. Burning and slaying and taking in the name of God. Guy began to grow nervous, asking, "Have we no defenses?" But the rector only smiled demurely and answered, "God protects those who do the duties assigned to them in faith."

The noontime meal had only barely begun when mailed fists pounded on the front gates. The brother who answered was run through with steel.

There seemed no time at all between the peace of morning routine and the chaos of the cloister's ravagement. Monks ran hither and thither and to and brutish men smashed windows and smote flesh. Flames licked the walls and blood patterned the tiles of the floor.

Brother Guy was overwhelmed at first with terror and regret. Had he caused this? Was God angered at his betrayal of the Sword? He fled with the rest, unthinking of his own fell hand. Yet at every corner was death.

The screams of the dying brothers sang to him like angels, calling for him to take up the blade for God. But he cried out in terror and clutched at his skull, hiding in a concealed place where he would not be found. Surely there must be a way to undo what was done. Surely this was not the end his LORD above had planned for him.

"I am sorry, God," he tried to scream, but it came out a whisper. He cried and slept and dreamed of evil done for Heaven. When at last Brother Guy crawled from his hole the sun was rising. Its red blanket painted blood even on the stony towers of the cloister. The ground was wet with the blood of godly men, and godly men had freed the church of all God's gifts.

He stood above the rector's corpse and wept. Near-at-hand someone had – somehow – forgotten their Sword. It was worn and scarred. Like Guy.

"Is this God's love?" asked the warrior-monk. "Can a man not serve another way?" But the sky was silent and orange.

With one trembling hand, his knuckles scarred, Sir Guy Fields lifted the heavy killing-tool. He looked at his brother's blood on it and felt himself die again.

The Sword was all there was left to him. The Sword and the bloody love of God.

# The Last Swords of Mars

 he Red Planet.
Birthplace of mankind.
Here, in the frigid wastes of the Habitlands, the remnants
of the once proud race struggled daily to survive. Who knew
what horrors lurked in the storm-wracked exteriors beyond the Formwall?
None living knew. Tribes of rough folk lived and hunted, foraged and
warred in the wastes. But all paid obeisance to the grand city of Ovidium
– a centre of scientific knowledge and progress. The last hope for a dying
people whose very home hated them.

In Ovidium, scholar-priests studied the remains of the ancients, resur-
recting dead tech and teaching forgotten words, recorded ages ago on files
decayed and corrupted. Their goal, they said, was to stop the shrinking of
the Formwall, and someday even expand it. Some said this was a lie and
that they were mad tyrants. Others that it was a lie told to ease the fears of
a fearful populace. But many believed them, and believed in them. How
Mars had ever birthed humanity was a mystery, for he hated her now.

For generations there had been an uneasy peace in the Habitlands, and
raids or small conflicts between tribes were rare and contained. But nearly
a year past, under the passing sign of Saturn, a new foe had arisen to challenge Ovidium. A demon, many said, had risen in the east, and gathered
to his side soldiers who hated the lies in the white city. The scholar-priests
declared that demons were a myth – a superstition borne of misunderstand-
ings and dead species – but still fires burned in the east.

Solomon – for so the demon named himself - declared that Ovidium
itself was the origin of fear, and that only by abandoning the ways of science

could humanity find peace. Ovidium had never faced a war of this scale. There no longer existed the might of the kingdoms of old, merely scatterings of survivors. Survivors who struggled to raise a defence. Struggled in vain. And so it fell to each man to fend for himself, and to raise his sword against Solomon's tide, and strike down the enemies of Truth.

$H$is name, given by his mother, was Plato. He had been a hunter in his village, tracking the wild deer that burrowed in the snows beneath the crimson sky. Wide-shouldered and dark-browed, he was considered handsome by some and brutish by others. He spoke little, but kept company with other men of like temperament. A steel bow and a sheaf of needle-point arrows were often kept near-at-hand, and when he went to battle for his hamlet he took with him an ancient bright-blade, passed down from father to son to son to son to daughter to daughter to son.

The bright-blades were old tech, older than Ovidium, and few remained that still worked. A sturdy handle – once fitted with black rubber, long-since rotted, but now wrapped tightly in leather - sat at the base of a three foot rod of steel. A tightly coiled cable ran from the hilt's base to a heavy, humming battery worn on the belt, and a worn red switch would light the fire. Sunlight, what little could be found, gave the battery life, and the life it shared with the blunt blade would paint it the red of the sky and could cut through any metal known to man. Bright-blades were deadly and rare – a last resort wielded only by the mightiest of men. Plato had only turned it on thrice, and each time a man had lay dead by the time his thumb toggled off the fire.

It was not long after Solomon declared himself in the east – after, some say, he wandered through the formwall from the ruins of old fortresses beyond the wastes – that Plato's village was burned. He came home from the hunt with his companion Virgil to find the sky black with the stink of burning plastic walls. In a terror, they hurried to their homes, but none survived. The demonists had slain every man, woman, and child, and many of them were strung with microwire to the panelled domes of their own homes. In the centre of the village, every biocomp, calculator, and electro-regulator in town had been gathered and shattered, stomped, and crushed. Nothing remained for the two men, both warriors of the tribe, and so they moved on, south along the Formwall.

There were other villages they knew, and hoped to find help in their vengeance there, but what they found was stranger and more terrible than the ravages of Solomon. The first village – rarely visited, for mankind had become isolated and paranoid in those days - lay two days along the wall. But after that time they found no trace of it, nor of any recent passage in the snow.

"I remember a cliff near the village. This land is flat," said Virgil, and Plato agreed.

It was then, spying for the cliff, that they found the village, nearly buried in sand and ice and in the shadow of a cliff – beyond the blue light of the Formwall. Figures could be seen, half-frozen, half torn asunder by the ravaging, ripping storms of the outside, gazing to the east. The Formwall had moved. So fast that the villagers could not even flee. The same was true in the next village. And the next.

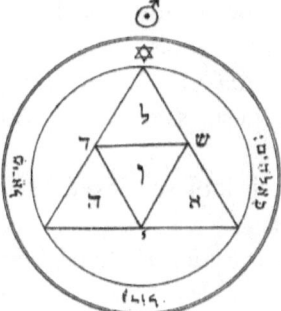

After that third village they resolved to make their way towards the white city, fabled Ovidium. The way was not easy, for the leal men of Solomon had spread for leagues, burning and revelling in their barbarism. And where the demonists had not come, or had been repelled, the people were suspicious and unfriendly.

Where once Plato had lit his bright-blade but thrice, now he had lost count, and the battery hummed and complained for lack of sun. Virgil carried no ancient weapon, but an axe made of blue steel, cut from the remains of a city of the Ancients, shorn and burned by the cataclysm that had brought the endless winter and required the building of the Formwall. And that axe was bloody and chipped from breaking bones many times by the time the sword battery began to mumble.

142

At a village which celebrated the luddite slaughter, they defended themselves from common folk who fought with spear and bow and ancient rifles of white plastic. Near one of the bellowing generators that spit heat and blue light into the sky, feeding the Formwall, they were ambushed and fought and slew for their lives against servants of the demon armed with strange weapons born of sorcery. At village after village they were turned away or fired upon. Both men bore many more scars before they saw the towering walls of Ovidium, the peak of its high tower topped in silver.

At the round gates of the scholar city they were greeted by men with white rifles who, seeing their scars, the axe, and the rumbling battery-sword, assumed them to be the warriors they were and issued them to meet their masters. Of these white-robed scholar-priests they met in steel halls, the greatest was a woman named Caesar, and she wore the orange epaulettes which marked the greatest of the keepers of science, who were called doctors.

"It is said you have killed many men."

"I have killed men," said Plato, his strong arms straining in the stiff, bulky white suit they had given him to wear, possessed of an ancient steel collar where a helm could be secured and hooks all about where the ancients hung their weaponry and tools.

"Know you aught of warmaking? Were your people ravagers?"

"We fought where we must," said Virgil. "But we are lovers of science and peace."

"Science and peace rarely look so wicked," said Caesar, her finger pointed at Virgil's crooked axe.

"I would as soon lay this aside. Perhaps, here in Ovidium, I can learn of the old ways."

Caesar seemed disappointed at this, but nodded. Told him where he could go to learn the tasks needed to maintain the towering city of science and its rumbling engines. And when Virgil laid down his axe that day it was for the final time.

"And you?" asked the doctor.

"I am also a lover of science. But I will not abandon my bright-blade," answered Plato. This seemed to please Caesar. "But I am not a man of war. I do not know how to plan an assault or to command men. I know only to defy demons and protect what is mine."

"So it seems with many men," sighed Caesar. "If this is what you know, you may do this for Ovidium. You may fight in the snow."

And so, armoured in white and blue, a domed helmet with chromed vi-

143

sor on his head and a rifle at his hip, Plato was deployed to join the scattered defence of Mars. In Ovidium there were batteries that did not need sun, and with those his bright-blade was revived.

On long marches with other men in kevlar armour - knights of the dusk of men – he saw great sights. Horrible sights. More murder. More madness. So many seemed willing to join the enemy and forget science. So many could not resist their bright curse-guns which seared holes like bright-blades from a mile away.

The demonists sent packs of maddened villagers against the knights, their knives and bullets rebounding off the thick padding each man wore. And they would not relent until they were slain or bound as prisoners and sent to Caesar, so she could teach them the truth once more. Behind the commoners came cultists, bounding through the snow in their own synth-cloth armours, bearing blades of ancient steel and heavy Mars-stone, and some even with bright-blades, though many flickered and failed with worn coils, so they were no better than clubs. The enemy came twice upon them riding on the backs of great snow-cats – the beasts snarling as they tore Ovidium men limb from limb. And Solomon's spells ricocheted and ripped and melted through the battlefields.

Plato was capable of great fire and fury, and in those wars for science he let himself lose thought and embrace the vibrating death of his ancestral sword. And there were others like him. Other heroes. The last swords of Mars. But they were not enough. Never enough. Every day the enemy came closer to Ovidium's spire, until at last the remaining champions of science could see their sacred spire behind them, as the foes of progress amassed before them. There was with them also a great black carriage, pulled by no beasts, and it was said that in it was the demon.

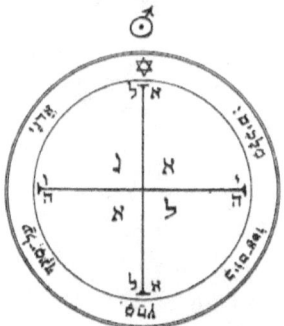

By the time Ovidium's defenders had been forced back into its shadow, Plato had proved himself a mighty doer of deeds and, by necessity, a commander of men. He was summoned to speak with Caesar and the other scholar-priests and asked to plan the siege of humanity's jewel.

Plato was ill-pleased to be forced into this position, but knew he was a man who now could do the task as well as any other – though it may not be well enough. He was shown many things long kept secret from common folk, and asked to help decide how a final stand may be made.

He learned that Ovidium too had sorcerous rifles, but that no man could make them function. They bore batteries like those in the bright-blades, but they were broken and dangerous. Unfit to be fired. So too were there other wonders of ancient days that even the doctors could not discern the meaning of. The white-robed rulers of Ovidium assured Plato that these were the key to victory, if only the truth could be found of their function.

But there was no time to learn. And Plato did not trust what he could not do with his own hand. So he turned them aside from these pursuits and maps were produced on ancient cracked screens, which showed the basin where humanity lived. For long hours they poured over the maps, and drew with dust and water on the screens under the brilliant white illumination of Ovidium's lights. At last they had a plan, but the plan was little better than slaughter.

"If we do not die to Solomon we will die to the shrinking wall." And all men knew that Plato spoke true, for the death of the Formwall was known to all in those echoing halls.

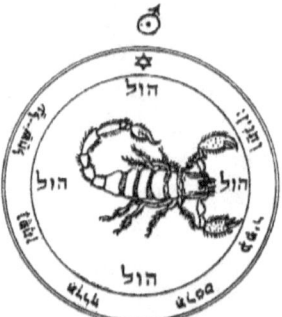

A wall was built outside Ovidium, made of plastic and steel and stone, much of it scavenged from Ovidium itself. And behind it were all the folk of the last city, even the doctors. Many stood with rifles and spears, but many more could not or would not fight, and worked only to build the wall higher. "Why does he want us dead?" many wondered, but more they wondered if they would live another day.

Plato stood with Caesar upon the wall. Virgil, who commanded some engineers there, stood with them also. They saw the banners and tents and wild cats of their foes, camped upon the icy fields. The towering black

145

wainn of the demon sat in its centre, rumbling as great machine parts forever turned on its surface.

"This is the end of the world. There will be nothing for them if we are gone," said Caesar with sadness.

"Have they made demands?" asked Virgil.

"Not yet," said the doctor.

"I doubt their demands will earn our friendship," growled Plato. "And we will make him fear us, even in death." His finger itched to light his blade.

"There is much we do not know, but they wish we knew less." Virgil.

All three were grim.

$A$s night came, though the sky was as red as at morning, the wainn of Solomon stirred. The great black beast shuddered, cracked, and opened, vomiting a juddering, grey cloud into the sky. In this projection was a shape almost like a face, but distorted, twisted, and broken. The face of the demon.

And the terrible decree it boomed out was heard everywhere beyond the wall, crackling and chirping as it fought through the ancient tech that carried it.

"All you worshippers of science. You hopeless adherants to forgotten ways. Abandon your research, your computers, your search for knowledge. Abandon Ovidium. Embrace the animal, and venture into the End without reservation. Only then will you and your murderous priests be spared."

The charge that followed was swift and shattering. A blitz that crumpled the wall shielding Ovidium behind the thundering lead of Solomon's chariot. The fields of Ovidium's shadow descended into bloodshed, and the snow became as red as the sky.

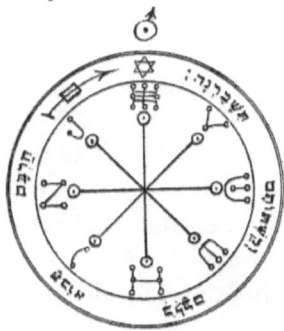

$P$lato stood on one of the plates of the wall near to where Solomon's rolling fortress struck, and felt the weight go out of the ground as steel crumpled like wool and men fell screaming into the snow, spell-blasts from the demonist weapons lancing through bone and gut and armour. A wave of cat riders leapt over the demon's vessel, briefly interrupting the grim, flickering face of Solomon, which stared up at the peak of Ovidium, a grim smile on his changing face.

The bright-blade wielder did not fall far, and fell upon others, so his fall was broken even as they screamed in agony. With one great, white glove he reached up and lowered his visor. The world took on a blue-purple tinge as he flicked the switch near his thumb and felt his ancient death-dealer scream to life. It buzzed as it arced forwards, slicing through synth-cloth, cat flesh, and steel. Soon he was given a wide berth in the melee, though he still had to dodge and take cover from the occasional blast of demon-rifle fire.

In a fugue of determination, facing the inevitable doom of mankind, Plato struck out, driving alone towards the rumbling carriage of the foe of Ovidium. As he neared, a lone man, as great in size as Plato and dressed in a long fur coat with pieces of grey synth-cloth showing beneath, stepped forth, and in his hand he bore the dull rod of a bright-blade, which sprung gleefully to life at the flick of a finger.

As their iron matched it made a screaming sound that made Plato's teeth feel cold, before they rebounded off one-another like magnets. Up and down, side to side, around and under, the two swordsmen fought their clumsy duel, each knowing that one mistake would be their destruction. And that mistake came to Plato's opponent, when he stepped deep in the red mud - a mix of blood and soil and slush melted by the thunder of ancient weaponry - and stumbled. Plato's cylinder blade seared and crushed through the side of the man's head, melting his skull and splattering hot blood on the wreckage all about.

Plato thumbed off his fire and stepped over his fallen opponent. The black chariot was close now. A trio of furious Solomon-servants saw his direction and charged. A bullet fired from Plato's hip took one between the eyes and another in the throat. The third was dead before he could feel the pulsing flash of Plato's blade sliding smoothly through his chest. And then he was there. Before the travelling vault of the demon warlord, the grey cloud-face above still staring at the ringed heights of Ovidium.

It took but an instant for the white-hot blade to rip into Solomon's carrier, and a moment more for Plato to step into the cramped, oppressive hallway beyond. He did not disengage his weapon, fearing sorcery at all moments.

"Solomon! Come out! Leave your sorcery behind and face science!"

It was quiet in the hold of the thing besides the hum of the bright-blade and the thudding of the engines. Even the screams and rumbles and whip-crack rifle sounds of the battle were muted as he cautiously advanced. It was warm within the trailer's belly, and moist. Pistons and gears dripped with condensation and glowing screens were muted behind layers of dew. Did anyone but the demon reside within that great mobile stronghold? None can tell. But Plato stalked through cramped hallways, often ducking to avoid hanging coils and open access hatches, and up ramps of dark, corrugated steel for what seemed hours - all as the destruction raged outside the walls.

At last, he saw a light ahead. A burning, inviting orange light. Plato's visor was raised to vent his boiling skin. His lank hair, long about his shoulders, was saturated in sweat. His stink was louder than the wicked turmoil of the rolling temple's black engines.

"Solomon!" he bellowed, his voice cracking with exhaustion and something approaching fear. He was so close now, and feared what would come beyond the open portal ahead.

And a voice called to him. Welcomed him. And as he stepped through that round, steel doorway into a chamber bright with dials, switches, and screens, he saw the figure of the demon, dressed in orange kevlar – much like his own of white – and with a white dome of a helmet attached, a golden visor lowered.

"Hope is a poison," said the the demon. "Ovidium burns."

"**Y**ou are too late," intoned Solomon, his voice muffled behind his mask.

Plato stood, suddenly frozen at the presence before him. Solomon looked no more than a man, but his face was hidden, and all knew him to be something beyond kenning. The demon turned his back on the warrior, flipping a series of switches on the panel before him. The wall before the master of doom flickered to life - no wall in truth, but a dusty, ancient screen. It showed before it a field of red and white, with splinters of plastic and steel reaching for the sky. Scavengers picked through the wreckage, and flame licked acrost the scene, devouring oxygen, flesh, and wall.

"While you marched through these halls to slay me, my engines - my armies - shattered Ovidium. Brought it crashing down." He turned again, one hand still resting on the console. "Ironic, that a thing destined for the stars now will be buried in the dirt."

"The stars?" Plato was unable to follow the demon's posturing.

"Ovidium. It was no city. No tower. It was a vessel. Like this chariot. A vessel that brought the ancients here, to Mars."

"Brought them to Mars? From where?" Mankind was born on Mars. Would die on Mars. And Ovidium, a vessel? Plato had never heard of a carrier so large. What roads could it travel? Even in the days before the seas froze there were never boats so massive.

"From another place. A world whose name is long forgotten. That is where the old kingdoms were. There the sun shone and life thrived. It was not a dead place like Mars. Not at first." Solomon's voice sounded almost mournful.

Plato could not draw his eyes from the carnage of Ovidium. All his struggles for naught. Was that corpse Virgil's? He would never know. Numbly, he thumbed off his vibrating blade. It would be simple to revive it, but for the moment he needed peace. "How do you know this?"

"It was told to me. I was raised with the knowledge, by a spirit - a consort of the machines."

"A spirit like you."

"Nay, I am no spirit," and Solomon laughed. Not the cruel, conqueror's laugh of the face in the cloud, but amused. With one gloved hand he reached up and raised his visor.

Beneath, was a broken, crooked face. The same face projected above the wrecking-vessel, but solid and unchanging. The skin alternated in patches of bleached white and the black of ice-burn, and the eyes were deep, shrivelled, and white with coming blindness. There were scars along his lips and up his cheeks, where use had strained and tore the fragile skin. His ears were merely blackened nubs, and there was no hair on his head. His throat was gaunt, and his skin hung loose. He was grotesque and revolting, but he was a man.

And men can be killed.

Once more Plato's bright-blade sprung to life and he took a step forwards, but he staid himself when Solomon upheld one hand. Though he wore a man's shape, Plato still feared wizardry.

"The spirit's name was Seneca, and he was a companion to the ancients. He fled also in their great exodus. But, like so many of them, he was wounded in the fall. But he did not die, like so many of the ancients. He was merely crippled, his brain broken.

149

"As a boy I fled my village, though I no longer remember why. And in my foolishness, I left the Formwall. I would have died, but fate smiled on me and I found shelter in a vessel much like Ovidium. That vessel is now far beyond the Formwall, for it moves faster every day. In the walls and the screens of that place I found the spirit Seneca, and he cared for me, and taught me the truth Ovidium's priests were too stupid to learn."

"And this spirit hated science. Was imprisoned by it." Plato took another pace forwards as he made this assertion, but the demon shook his withered head.

"No. Seneca was a thing of science. All of this is science."

"I have seen the spells cast from your servant's guns."

"Science."

"Then why? Why wage a war to end progress? To end peace?"

"No!" There was a fire suddenly in Solomon's eyes and Plato retreated back to where he had started, both hands upon his sword. The conqueror gently lifted his fist from the console where he had slammed it. "I bring peace. There is no future for mankind. But by their endless, fruitless labours the doctors give mankind a thought the End may end. And an anxiety. When will the Formwall retreat? When will the old kingdoms return? Why not today? How long must I last? Will I see the future Ovidium promised me? But it will not come, for Ovidium was a palace of fools. They did not even know their sacred tower could traverse the skies."

The skies! Visiting stars! This foe spoke of fantasies. "The doctors were learned and wise. Caesar could have saved us. Can still if she lives."

Solomon laughed again, and here there was cruelty. "They are murderers and ghouls. They can never learn what was lost with the ancients.

"The ancients fled the world, our true home, because it was dying. So great had become their knowledge that they made all manner of machines and cruel death-dealers, even though it wounded the soil and the sky. It can be done, so it must, they said. But so much was done in this way that our home could take it no longer, and died.

"Before the death, men from the old kingdoms had begun to make a new home here, on Mars. But they were too late, and paradise was unfinished when the garden we were born into withered. Those who could afford it piled into boats like Ovidium and sailed the stars, destined for Mars. Many of them were doctors - true doctors - and knew how they could complete the task they had begun too late.

"But fate and luck are stronger lords than science, and the red planet struck down their vessels, and sent them crashing to the surface. It is a miracle enough lived to drag the human race on. But the doctors died. And many of their files and computers were lost forever. Of all the knowledge of the Garden, less than half a percent remained. So much was gone forever."

Plato could follow only some of what was said, so strange and fantastical it was - surely untrue. He held his bright-blade before him as if it would shield him from Solomon's story. But the demon continued, "Seneca knew some though. And maybe there were more like him, further beyond the wastes - beyond reach. Seneca could have helped. Maybe. But when Ovidium found our home - mine and Seneca's - hundreds of years after the death of the ancients, they cut into it like they were slaughtering a deer. And Seneca was one with his home.

"I would have begged them to stop had I known what they were doing, but I knew only that our home was dying, and donned my armour to save my breath. They came in their own white suits, like yours, and severed and cut and brutalised. Seneca was dead before he ever had a chance to cry out.

"But Ovidium had its treasure," his laughter now was delirious, defeated, and he leaned heavily on the console as the carnage raged behind him. "They had their steel and bolts. Their wire and cable. Raw materials so they could carry on in hopeless tasks. Humanity's final hope had been murdered to power the florescent bulbs of a sanctuary of witch-doctors and conmen, as ignorant as those they claimed to protect."

"It is vengeance then." Plato could understand vengeance.

"It is no vengeance, but kindness. If a man does not know what could maybe be, he cannot pine for it. He must accept what comes, and be happy with it.

"Seneca told me something once, said by a man who bore the same name. He said that we suffer more often in imagination than in reality. I want to give the people of Mars reality. And I have. We were born in the dark. Let us die in it."

Feeling bolder now - seeing the ugly, maimed old man waver, come close to tears - Plato once more stepped forwards, intent to do justice, or at least enact right by his heavy hand. "I will know."

Solomon looked up. "Know what? Do you even understand what I have said? Do you understand what Ovidium promised? My task is done. And when this is over, you will leave, your life no different, save that no one will promise the world will change. You will live and struggle and find peace in the moment. To wonder what may be is to bleed."

Plato was almost to the enemy now, his blade held wide - open and ready to swing. "Defend yourself."

"You do not listen." Another, new laugh. "I have done all the defence I can. For all that is left of our people. You will earn no mighty battle from me. Slay me or do not, but go back to the wastes and live. Live until you die."

"You are a demon. A mighty foe. We must fight."
But Solomon would raise no hand to defend himself.

W hen Plato left the odious black hulk of Solomon's chariot – its infernal engines writhing and chugging onwards purposelessly – he looked out on the field of devastation wrought by the demon's crusade. The tower of Ovidium had fallen. Been utterly crumbled and rent. Corpses lay here and everywhere, and scavengers picked through the remains.

In the near-distance of the wreckage there were a few pockets of fighting - blood spilling and wizard-fire whipping – but mostly the combatants wandered despondently, their empty gazes finding no focus. Soldiers on both sides looked to the wreckage and to the blue-shielded sky. The war was done. Somewhere a child cried. Somewhere a sonorous voice sang a ballad.

Science had fallen. But with it the demon's sorcery had no foe, and thus no fuel for its fire. What was left was only mankind and the red planet which hated her.

Plato shrugged and rested his gauntleted hand on the hilt of his brightblade. He did not know if justice had been done that day. His encounter with the demon had left him less sure than ever before in his life, yet he could not say why. He wondered if Solomon had ensorcelled him. Did it matter? What was there left but to live life and wait for the end?

The muscled champion threw back his sweat-soaked mane and looked up to the skies, squinting at the pinpricks of light beyond the dome of the formwall. If the demon had been right that there was no way to save Mars, perhaps he was also right that Ovidium had once sailed the distant lights. Plato resolved not to go quietly. He would find one of the old shipwrights and see what could be done to build a star-ship, and perhaps a crew.

Vested with new purpose, the warrior strode confidently down into the ruins of humanity's jewel, filled with new hope on a fool's errand. But there were none left to tell him again of the futility. And so it was with great determination that he would secure himself in the hearts of many in those final days as a visionary and a great leader, whose star-sails may one day allow them to pass through the formwall and to a great Garden beyond. And those who believed in him felt no fear of the end. Only a great waiting that pulled them ever onwards.

# Night-Black and Sorrow-Sounding

orged in the serene peace of a hidden grove was I. A fey place. Blessed and forgotten. Tall, handsome things cared for me, and slender fingers caressed me. The master who breathed life into my steel kissed me and whispered love into my liquid flesh. I was happy there. And it was the only place where I was never afraid.

I was like a twin to my smith – that light-tongued faerie prince. He was tall and I long. His hair as black as my edge. A sonorous voice blessed him, and he lent it to me, making me as beautiful to hear as to see. Would that I never left that dreamlike idyll. Would that the choice were ever mine.

For I am but a tool, to be wielded and abused and discarded on a whim. Kept when I would be free. Sheathed when I would taste the open air or the salty tang of blood. In my prince's hand I never felt a prisoner, but ever since his disgrace I have never felt free.

Time meant little in the kingdom of the elfs, but it moved as it always does. And in time visitors came, and amongst them was one clever villain. One riddler too clever by leagues.

This riddler – this thief – came to my prince to offer him a bargain. A trade of wit and wealth. But his intentions were impure. Far indeed from the purity of that forest realm. The thief never intended to lose. And when his riddle could not be answered - so much time has passed I do not remember the rhyme nor the ruse - he took his prize, and that prize was me.

The faerie-folk were wroth, despite his victory. They cast down my beloved master and chased my captor from their realm, cursing him and despairing for their foolishness. Far from that world of safety I was taken, and my sorrow turned in time to a curse all its own. And my voice, which once had been raised in mighty song, now was sorrow-sounding. A bitter echo to my night-black skin.

But the thief lived only barely beyond the bounds of Faerie, and when he died on river's edge his loose fingers let me fly. I did not know the way home, and so tumbled in the wicked water, my steel dented and scratched by stones and fish teeth. In my heart, if such a thing I ever had, I longed to be at my prince's hip once more, but it was not to be so. Never to be so again.

The next song that found me was soft, but firm. Curious. Old, but not aged. I do not think I had travelled far, despite my need for home. He did not seek me by design, but found me only by accident. The thief's accident, by which I had been lost.

A long beard tickled my new master's belt, and sometimes brushed my pommel, especially when he was bent over in thought. This he did often, for he was a mystic and a philosopher - a friend to lore and theory.

He carried also a bone pipe, which he smoked avidly. This pipe was like me – a thing with a fate. A thing with desires. And it was happy there, even whilst I was not, for that was its first master. And it was proud of the tales he had carved on the tool's bowl.

The mystic had a silver tongue, beloved by many. And, though he was no elf, even I was forced to admit that it was fine – practised and beautiful. But not all folk appreciate pretty speech, and he was imprisoned for his words. Kept in a dark cell and convinced his past had been sinful. He was taken from me and it is said that he begged to be forgiven for wrongs he now imagined he had done. Prison changes men's minds, and often not for the better.

Before his confinement he was the most respected scholar in all the kingdom. But his ideas were new and wild, and they appealed to the new and wild youth. His ideas, it seems, were good – as now many men espouse them – but at the time he gained many enemies by his ministrations. And some of those enemies had powerful friends. The charge he was found guilty of – and left to rot below ground for - was that of the corruption of youth. But it is wrong to think the new will ever perfectly emulate the old.

But the scholar's words brought him no respite, and he grew frantic and jaded. And so, when one of his admirers took me from the ash-wood box where I had been confined and took him from the box of stone and iron where he had been kept, he gripped me with a new ferocity, his skin no longer soft. He swore vengeance on the world that failed to hear his tongue, and swore that they would hear his blade. It was not long before he was known more as a murderer and a terrible foe than as a philosopher.

With me in hand, he slew the queen who had imprisoned him and had sullied his good image in the eyes of the people and of her husband the King. But it was not only his hardship that warped him, but my curse. For from my wicked hilt bled a sadness-turned-rage that fueled him and drove him. Sick with sorrow and wrath, he cut down the Queen before her own throne, bloodying the royal dias and staining her young children's faces. I sang a sorrow-song as I cut her soft skin and later, as we fled the slaughter,

154

the mystic sang his own dirge. It was here that he gave me the name Pall-bringer, and that my black-steel skin took on a reddish sheen in the light.

The disgraced philosopher – assassin and fugitive – hid himself in a tower shrouded in sorcery, until he no longer could live with what he had become and threw himself from its peak into the roiling sea. Was it his own guilt, or the threat of the army his once-friend the King brought to avenge his fallen bride? I cannot say.

Once more I was lost in the water. Lost in the gnashing currents and crashing waves. Washed far away. It was almost a decade before a hand touched my hilt once more.

My next captor's hands were weathered and scarred. His face was burnt and twisted. I was pulled from the sea in a net full of chittering crustaceans which were brushed aside to reveal me once more to the sun. He as well was in the net, nearly dead – fingers death-cold as they gripped me – and clinging to life by mere will alone. His own ship – a mighty and fearsome vessel – had been lost to a storm, and the merchants aboard the new vessel were too cowed by his presence to do aught but aid him.

This man had no innocence to corrupt, for he was already vile in manner. Unlike the mystic, this man had many powerful friends that kept him from harm, but he was untrusting and fearful, always suspecting those closest to him of the worst crimes against him.

Once he had been a monk - not dissimilar to my last wielder, though not even half as clever. But when his monastery was burned, scarring his once-pretty face, he forswore all gods and turned to villainy. He sought after power and wealth, and celebrated in excess. In gold and keeps and swords he gifted himself. It has always seemed strange to me that mortals lay such value on solid objects. Gold and iron and pretty things will go on forever, but flesh and flowers fail, never to be held again. He still dressed in cassock and frock, but those who knew him knew his true manner.

As he aged, a warlord with a tattered kingdom of serfs and brigands, others saw his success and needed for it. Jaded, bored with life, I lent fire to his ageing arm. Together we slew countless assassins. Each one as likely to have been my master as the monster who wielded me. I was made bitter by my lot. A bringer of ruin.

In vengeance for the ruinous life I was forced to lead, I fed upon my master, leeching life from his skin like the winter sun melts the snow. Even as I protected him from harm I drank of him. If any should be his doom, let it be me. Yet, just as the winter sun's futile destruction of the snow, he persevered, living on even as he withered to a husk. A crooked, ugly old corpse of a man, wracked with chills and coughs, yet still able to slay and smite with my blade.

He knew it was me that caused his suffering. But he did not care. Revelled in it perhaps. He would not throw me away, and even sometimes wore me to bed. He would chuckle grimly and whisper into my hilt the name he had gifted me – Godswife. Nothing more. Perhaps he was too senile to think of more sweet nothings to mutter to me. Only to name me bride to his imagined godhood.

It was here, trapped in the Hel with a tyrant I despised, that I realized what I was. That I was a plague-bearer, and that by my very presence I brought disaster. I carried a plague and that plague was death. And hatred. But my keeper knew little else and so was unchanged by my epiphany. It was only I who was forced to submit to the horrid truth of the thing. I pined for the faerie gardens of home. Home I knew now I would never see again.

But even winter must end, and in time my pinprick vampirism finally drained the monk so deeply that he could no longer cling to this world and passed on. Peacefully. I was sealed in his crypt beside him, and his ghost laughed, for it knew how much I hated him.

Luckily it was only a week before I was found once more.

A more optimistic being might think my next wielder had broken my curse, for he was kind-hearted, and he bore also the same pipe my first master had held, though it no longer spoke to me. He was blessed with visions of the future, and with them hoped to reshape the world. But despite his virtues, he was too trusting. Too naive. And there was vengeance in his breast to temper his compassion.

His family had been slain by my master the monk, and he sought to fill the void in his heart. But he was robbed of his vengeance by death's soft embrace. And so he broke the tomb-door and thundered down, seeking beyond hope a way to cause misery to the dead. Men at his command had toppled the prince who followed my master, and burned his prideful palace down, and here he came to despoil the rest of the dead. I welcomed him, and his misery. He observed me in awe of my grim beauty and took me for himself.

He wanted to do well by his people – truly he did – but he was too young, too inexperienced, too vulnerable to the whispers of his greedy priest-councillors. His visions were too imprecise to warn him about himself, and thus inadequate to save the kingdom or its people.

I learned to love him, and to pity him, and I tried to save him, though I could not save his people. To those who should fear him I made him more imposing, and I guided his hand in battle. I spoke to him in dreams in simple ways, and was able in time to expose the sins of his closest councillors to him. But my curse followed me into his dreams, and embered there.

His wrath grew into a terrible tempest, and once the treachery and poor faith in his court was revealed his benevolent reign became a reign of terror, and he a tyrant. Disillusioned, this once-pious seer-prince threw down his temples and became a godless man of a godless realm. Once more I had failed and was the hand of a wicked nithing.

I sought then, more ever than before, to influence him in dreams to return me to Faerie, but the visions of elysium I granted him became but a new target for his ire. He would conquer the väsenland and raise his banner over the corpse of dreams. His fiendish pogrom of his own people grew more dire as the targets of his villainy grew from merely priests and conspirators to imagined elfs and changelings.

No longer would I stand with him. Never again be trapped in a tomb with my tormentor. And so, when he raised me for to strike down his own infant heir, I burned his hand and sang a sorrow-song to bring his enemies near. As my master was slain and his riches taken I was placed in a vault. Forgotten. There I waited, for a century.

T ime is to history as balm to a wound - it can heal over what was there before, erasing it and forgetting it. In the century I rested in that royal vault my master's villainy was forgotten - recontextualized as heroism and unfortunate propaganda spread by his enemies. I am taken from the vault and put in a museum, and his name is carved upon my crossguard.

There was, in this time, a much-loved wizard, thought possessed of great power. Yet again I was reminded of my first wielder, after the thief. An aura of magic was visible around him, disturbing the air like heat on stone. He was a hero, and admired acrost the land – a true and understanding friend to all. The crown took me from my rest on an exhibit wall and gifted me to this sorcerer.

But when his hand touched my hilt I knew the truth. There were two minds in his breast. The first was the friend and mentor many knew. The other he kept secret out of shame, for it was possessed of an insatiable desire for power and instilled with a crippling paranoia, which spoke of my latter keepers. It seemed I was never meant to be free of my misery.

The wizard was a wise and clever player in the post-atheistic state – a return to the order the seer-prince had shattered. Many in court knew him well, even before he ended his travels to settle nearer to the seat of power. I did not trust him, and sought again through dreams to inspire the one who held me to return me to faerie.

Yet, despite the aid I lent him, he mounted me on a wall once more as a trophy. I was shined and sharpened often, but never used. He had gems inset in my pommel to draw the eyes of visitors.

I languished in unhappiness, which turned – as ever – to rage. He fought for power, for riches, for useless wealth as I watched on. In a fugue of help-lessness I pined for those I had slain and wondered why mankind could for-get death so easily. The keening of my misery filled those sorcerous halls.

But I was not bound to follow this master into death, for I only hung upon his wall for a year before I was stolen once again.

H e came in dark cloth with a black hood and, with the clattering rain of broken glass, stole me from the wizard's wall. A descendant of an old line of heroes, this man was little more than a burglar, and my curse suckered onto him like a leech between a child's toes. Yet power was not the fire which drove his wickedness, but regret, and he sought to forget his past by means of felony, theft, and magic.

Coming as he had from a line of such renown, he had been expected by many to deliver his kingdom – another, far from the one where I rested – from the wickedness of its enemies. But he feared too much the shame of failure and the kiss of death, and fled the realm's borders rather than live up to his fate. I saw in this a hope of redemption, both for myself and for him, and so I urged him to turn back. To make the long journey home and to atone for the abandonment which had defined him.

We travelled, he and I, bickering as we went. We came from one shore to another, down long roads and through dark forests. But wherever her-oism could be found, the hero-thief would run in the direction opposite. Until at last his petty crimes were discovered, and he was imprisoned.

The prison into which he was taken was no ordinary gaol, but a mighty fortress manned by grim men and commanded by a terrible conqueror-king. I was taken from him and kept in an armoury elsewhere, to be gifted to a lord of darkness to march as general of the legions of ill will. But I would not be confined - would not let my last chance to find peace slip so easily from my grasp.

And so I made my way back to him, whispering and suggesting in the ears of greedy soldiers until happenstance brought my hilt back into his grasp. With me in hand, he swung out, slew his guard and severed the gate. He made as if to flee but, to my great joy, he instead carried me deeper into the fortress, slaying and freeing as he went. By his hand - and me within - he freed the prison and was hailed champion. In thanks for my service, he had my hilt gilt in gold, and gold leaf filled the runes of my blade. I have no need for riches, but I glowed with pride at the good I had proven I could do.

Those who the hero-thief freed swore to fight with him and persuaded him to champion their cause. From village to village - keep to keep - his army marched and grew, and at every corner we challenged the might of the conqueror-king, the force growing as more flocked to his beacon of hope. Until at last the foe was dead, at the hand of a boy, and for the first time I revelled in the blood I spilt.

That boy became a great and good king, and was much loved. I loved him as well, and would have given all I had to lie beside him in his tomb forever. But time, as I have said, makes memory fade, and in time I was forgotten. Left behind by my saviour for other, more silvery blades. I had brought him to his destiny and set him on the path to victory, but I became merely another treasure in a hoard of baubles.

It would be centuries before anyone took note of me again.

I n the lonely long years I mouldered; my runes lost their sharpness and were confused, and those who attempted to repair them marred them further or corrected them wrongly. This did not bother me, for I dared to hope that my curse had been banished. I was made silent in this time, and was no longer sorrow-sounding.

When next I found a hip to hug I was neither found nor stolen, but inherited. A knight was my new keeper, gentle-hearted and kind. And by some strange twist of fate, he inherited also that same silent pipe whose path so often has crossed mine. Like the thief before him, he was from a long line of heroes, though he had no qualms about following in their wake. Many loved him dearly, but he was too humble to allow pride to overtake him. Instead, his flaw was short-sightedness.

His aims, when first I came to him, were to free the oppressed folk of a nearby barony from the heavy yoke of their lord. And amongst those people was a woman he loved, and his love for her drove him to swift, thoughtless action. I was a trusty sword for him, and won through many trials in his hand, including the death of his foe, the baron, and the freeing of his lady love and her people.

But amongst those freed from the tyrant's dungeons was a wicked sorcerer, and instead of gratitude, his gift to his saviour was the kidnapping of the knight's mentor. The old man was kept in a high tower and promised an eternity of torment, but his freedom was won by the flash of my teeth in the knight's strong arm. And when the sorcerer meant to fell my keeper with ill spells I met his mind and challenged him. He was no match for my ancient will. Yet even as I broke him he laughed, for he saw that my curse was not gone. But the people loved my master for his accomplishments and he was made prince of a wide land after this victory, and that against the baron.

It was after his coronation that the love and kindness in him curdled in his chest and turned to wrath and distrust. I wished I could cry when he used me to slay the love of his life. My curse once more drove my handler to murder and wickedness. The act my spell had forced upon him broke his mind as once I had broken that of the sorcerer, and he fell into a cruel madness. In my own silent sorrow I sought to flee, and allowed myself to fall from his scabbard whilst on a hunt.

I rested there, on the forest floor, for an age, beneath needles and soil and moss. A tree grew about me as I rested, black and wicked with leaves of red and gold. Its roots were so tight about me that, even when I was reclaimed, they clung about my hilt.

My final master - the last before I was broke - had passed on, long before his cold hands caressed my black blade. A corpse-that-walked, this keeper was hard as bone, in body and in mind, though he wore extravagant and expensive silks and exquisite jewels set in glittering rings and brooches. His tomb, which he had ordered built in life, was ever-expanding at the hands of his sorcerous minions, and it in time reached the roots of the black tree, where I was imprisoned. For a dead man, he had surprisingly fast reflexes, and though I dreaded another master it felt good to be in the hand of one who knew how to wield again. And how can my curse burden one already so ill-made, I mused.

I soon learned that he had made an enemy of a god, and his death, entombing, and resurrection were but a part of a ploy to avoid the deity's wrath. He wished to be known as the greatest sorcerer to ever live, but was stymied in his quest by his self-imposed confinement, ever fearful of Heaven's wrath.

The kingdoms of my youth were long gone. Even the death-wight that now held me was a relic of the kingdoms that came after those I knew, also long passed. The world had stumbled forwards and forgotten. I too had-forgotten. Forgotten what it wasto be happy. To want. To wish for better things. I granted my master visions of the past, with no care paid towards how atrocious or sorrowful.

Yet not everything I showed the wizard was truthful, and much was misleading without context. I had grown tired of being held, and wanted only for destruction and silence once more. The research my hints led my master down were an endless spiral of fruitless pursuits and false direction. In my newfound cruelty my runes ceased to be silent as I became possessed of a cruel laughter. This corpse's pain was a joke only I will ever know.

Even the last straggling faint hopes of a return to the land of my forging have fled me now. I know I am lost and my halcyon days are behind me, however brief they were. I am cruel now, outside of my curse. Jaded and hateful of the world that beat and battered me. Tiring of the game, I called to the servants of the foe-god and they struck low my skull-headed master. And in their furor they sundered me

Now I lie broken in the crypts beneath the black tree and hope for darkness to take me entirely. When does the soul of a tool die? Had the pipe ceased to speak because it had died, though its body was whole? Yet I am splintered – shattered and bent – and still struggle on. But I am comfortable at least, in the fact that no hand shall again hold me. Unless the light of the sun returns, and some future soul returns me to my misery.

# Mother Blood

*am sorry, buke-sama, that the wine is not better.*

do not be sorry. and you need not be so deferential. i am no noble sword. no longer.

*ah, a ronin. do not worry. i have known many good ronin. as well as many bad. i judge a man as a man, and not as a name.*

i thank you.

*what is the matter? is the wine so bad?*

no, the wine is very good, but i am afraid i do not have coin to pay for it.

*then pay with words. i have plenty of coin from farmers and travellers who love me for my wares, but few have stories to tell. you must have a mighty tale to tell, of your exile and your business.*

i take no pride in my exile.

*you do not need pride to tell the tale. is it not well and good for a tale to be told so that it can be known? and surely there are lessons to be learned.*

aye, lessons. and sorrow. i will tell you in exchange for the wine.

*begin with who you were.*

no. that life is behind me. It would not do for you to think less of my lord for freeing me from my bond if you come to think well of me.

*very well. then begin where you will. and here. i trust the tale will be worth more than one cup, so take of it as you will.*

that i will do gladly. now where to start? well it makes sense to begin with what you know. you know mother blood?

*how can i not? her demons haunt the land. we are bled dry by her wickedness and spellcraft. i have heard her face is that of a cruel crow.*

i have not yet met her so i cannot tell you of her face.

*yet? i may be but a wine seller, but my ears are sharp. you speak as though you mean to meet her.*

i made a promise. and i will keep it.

*a promise? to who?*

that i will not say.

*is it shameful?*

no. but i will not speak it.

*i did not mean to offend. so sorry. would you like more wine.*

i have not even finished what you gave me.

*i have nothing else to give by way of apology.*

**then do not apologize. there is no way you could have known. it would be stupid of me to blame you for that.**

*you are too kind to me, ronin-san.*

**i am not kind. merely a man of the sword.**

*i do not know all the ways of nobles. i will trust you. continue to tell. if you would like.*

**i have said i would tell and so i will. some time ago - this would have been two months gone - i came upon the remains of an army which served lord fujisawa-no-kenzo.**

*ah, yes. we all miss lord fujisawa. his kami will be celebrated in the world to come.*

**these men were not many. maybe forty. many wounded. they had more tents for their camp than men to sleep in them.**

*it is a sad day that lord fujisawa's armies would fail. it was not too long ago that they even defeated the forces of lord tomioka-no-akira. and he had many strong swordsmen.*

**the army he defeated was not led by lord tomioka but by his prince kyo.**

*of course you know of him. he was known widely for his swords as well as for his words. i heard a poem written by lord tomioka once. it was very beautiful.*

**do you remember the words?**

*i could not do them justice. it is better you imagine what i could have said.*

**a warrior does not surrender from a challenge.**

*and a wise man does not undertake a task he knows he would be a detriment to. and i am no warrior.*

**perhaps it is the wine, but you strike me as very shrewd.**

*shrewd and eager to hear of this beaten army. how many samurai survived?*

**not a one. all that remained were loyal ashigaru.**

*still loyal after lord fujisawa's death? those must be good men indeed.*

**good men and bad men suffer the same.**

*what did they have to say? were they helpful?*

**helpful enough. i have sought mother blood since the dawn of the year, and by their telling i had come near to where she dwells.**

*o yes, she lives near, though none know where.*

**according to them she slept in cliff castle, where the furious waves break against the black cliffs. and they said that the palace was guarded by fearsome mononoke and honourless ronin who aided the witch in her wars. they said the last of the samurai had led them against it, but they were turned aside by the tide of yokai, and at their head a fearsome oni - ten shaku tall, tusked, and breathing fire. when they were forced to flee the ronin hunted them in the hills. this is not how men fight wars. they told me where to find the castle.**

*tell me you did not go to cliff castle!*

**i had no choice.**

*did you find it? it was not spirited away by the magics of mother blood?*

*i did. but it was a long way. and there were battles to be had.*

*tell me of them! what monsters came to her defense?*

*at first the only monsters were men. the men who had hunted the survivors of the army. if they had died with honour in the battle these swords may not have been tempted. but they were only men, not buke, and their commanders did not survive to remind them of their duty to death. ah, the wine makes my mind wander - perhaps i have had enough for now. as i was telling, i found some of the ronin who hunted the soldiers of the old lord. they gossiped and laughed as they strode in the hills, bragging about the men they had cut down. ambushed and slaughtered without respect. a man must not be afraid to die doing what he believes is just, and yet they skulked in shadows and attacked sleeping soldiers. they were truly wicked men.*

*not like you! you are an honourable exile.*

*i do my best. but all men are fallible. it is our curse to always fail in one endeavor when we succeed in another. a wise man chooses where failure may be forgotten - though never forgiven.*

*did you kill them?*

*i did. and it was not an easy task. most men would have failed. indeed, i bear new scars. i expect my smallest finger will never recover in full from a wound one made. even though those men were cowards and servants of a sorcerer, they were noble in battle. once, in the reeds which grow along the coast, i fought five of them at once. we could see cliff castle far in the distance. i approached behind them where they could not see, my sword drawn, then called a challenge. Servants Of The Wicked Lady, i cried. I Have Slain Your Brothers. Now Take Vengeance Afore I Take It On You. that angered them, and they charged me in a mass, save one who held a bow. the first had in his hands a naginata, and the others trailed behind so his wide swings would not cut them. i stepped aside at the last, allowing him to stumble through, then cut his head from his shoulders. two more came with swords like mine, both at once. their strikes were swift and they yelled loud. it was while defending against these two that one cut me - down my finger and along my arm to my elbow. i bled much, and ruined my kimono, but i did not feel it at first. when that man cut me he saw the blood and halted, thinking me grievously wounded. but when killing it is death to pause, even once, and so he died. the other i fought alone, blade against blade, until his hand slipped and my sword slid between his ribs. i do not know what happened to the fifth man, but the archer shot me in the leg before he fled. i would have pursued them if my wounds were not so dire. i took the first man's kimono, which had on it less blood than my own.*

*o how fearsome! i would have died of fright even to see their charge.*

*it was a good charge. i will not fault them for things they did well. indeed, i think it is luck alone which saved me. even with my skill i am not the man to defeat five at once, even if i only slew three.*

*you are too modest! you must be a mighty swordsman.*

that is not for me to judge. let other men say what they think of me, and i will think only of what needs be done.

*and after the ronin? you must have fought the spirits she held in thrall! bested the oni who commanded her armies!*

it is true that it is cowardly to avoid conflict, even if it would lead to death. but it is also true that the first duty of a buke is to serve his lord, and sometimes that is in other ways than the sword. do not fret, i did indeed clash swords with others of her legion, just not at first.

*is this one of those failings you spoke of? where it must be chosen to succeed in another task? you avoided facing the mononoke in order to find mother blood?*

something like that. cliff castle was guarded by many who called mother blood their lord. they wore animal faces and fierce manes and carried all manner of tools of death. bands of these empty-eyed beasts patrolled the crags around the castle. it was hard work to avoid them as i neared. once i thought i was discovered, but it was only one of the fox-faced men leaving his post to piss. this allowed me a chance to reach the walls of cliff castle.

*did you clamber up them? fight through the gate? o, i am overcome with curiosity!*

patience. you talk a bit too much i think, even for a wine seller.

*i am glad you are smiling, ronin-san. otherwise i would fear i had offended you.*

not as yet.

*now continue. tell of the work you pursued for your lord.*

i have no lord. i am ronin.

*so sorry, you said yourself that you were doing the duty of a buke, which is to serve your lord. i must have misunderstood.*

i misspoke.

*of course.*

but you asked how i got into the fastness. at first i did not know what way was best. climbing the walls was bound to be difficult, especially with my wounded arm. but to take the front gate would surely be death, and with no purpose. i sat for a time in the shadow of the walls until i heard a voice call to me. Buke-Sama, it said, and i looked about to find a little man with a tall staff, from which hung two round gourds. Are You A Spy For Mother Blood? i asked. he laughed at this, and i was afraid we would be found out. But no bear-men or monkey-swords came sprinting. I Am A Friend Only To Change, he said. Change And Good Jokes.

*you may think my smile is to mock your story, but it is not. i am happy to hear you were visited by this man.*

you know him?

*not specifically, but i have heard of many men like him. they say to keep them away from your wife! but they are not malicious, merely mischievous.*

well, it serves me that his mischief was against mother blood. he told me, after some few riddles, of a hole in the wooden wall, obscured by a fallen tree, through which i may secretly enter cliff castle. this i did, and soon found myself in the paper halls of the witch's castle, which once belonged to a bondsman of lord fujisawa. but in the castle there were few places to hide, and it was not long before the mononoke found me.

*a marvelous battle it must have been! and they all dead, for you sit here now and drink my wine.*

a few dead, aye, but not all. i am ashamed to admit that i neither triumphed over all nor died in passion. three i cut down, limbs sliced, necks chopped, wooden faces shattered and cloven. two more i injured sore, but they seemed to come in endless waves, their skins painted black and empty eyes watching from behind animal guises. they were armed as samurai, and howled and whooped like madmen destined for greatness. once i was taken, swords confiscated and arms held tight, they took me to the oni. i will have more wine, if you would.

*of course, ronin-san.*

do not mourn for my honour, for i believe i have made accomplishments to match my failures. the oni waited in the courtyard of cliff castle. all around were the yokai of mother blood, hands ready on sheathed swords. the oni was great and wide, as large as has been said. his mask was tusked and a black mane ran down his muscled back. his eyes flashed like fire, and which hands were black like tar. spells were on his chest, his hakama, and his odachi. that blade he held, that odachi, was nearly as massive as he. Samurai-San, he bellowed. They Say You Hunt The Hills. Mother Blood Is Not Here. Was Never Here. Flies On The Wind. It Is Only I. And I Will Show My Bondsmen There Is No Might Greater Than Mother Blood. And Than Her Servant Tatsuo. Give Him His Swords And Watch Me Fell Him.

*aha! here is the mighty battle!*

indeed. i took my weapons and declared to him my name and lost lord. shouted them for all to hear. the animal-men made space for our duel. in response to my challenge he laughed, and then we both charged, my sword raised, his swept back as if threshing. the odachi came up and i was only barely swift enough to avoid its heavy edge. i dashed in and my blade bit his arm, but i was not close enough to maim him and i was forced to retreat swiftly as that great blade wound through the air like a willow in the wind. there would be no parrying that heavy steel, this i knew. and so i paced backwards, ever just beyond his reach. and as i thought my legs could no longer outpace him my back met the sturdy support of the outer wall. as the oni swung i dodged down and forwards, under his blade. the odachi stuck in the oak and my sword thrust forwards to pierce his gut. i did not pause. never paused. but shouted as i swept my weapon through his gut, opening him and painting the sand. i stepped aside as he fell and cut the fearsome head from his neck. in death his fingers still gripped his death-tool.

*a victory! well-earned. i wish i could have witnessed it.*

not a victory. not yet. i had hoped that seeing the monster felled, his ogre-faced helm

166

face-down in his own blood, would break the spirits of his minions. yet it only en-
raged them. if i had thought there was no end to them before, i do not know how to
describe the numbers which came on now. i fought blindly, holding my ground in the
storm of blades and blood and shredded silk. small cuts lined my skin as i struggled
to parry every blow. yet i did parry them all, and returned them tenfold. all but one.
one clever wolf bit through my defenses, piercing my gut as i had his master. i slew
him too, skull cut clean in two, but i was bleeding sore. i know not how long before
they all lay dead, but in time i was alone in cliff castle, my hands clamped over my
stomach and soaked in others' blood from hair to toe. cliff castle was empty and there
was no sign of mother blood. i fell into a deep sleep there and thought never to wake.

are you a ghost, ronin-san?

have you ever seen a ghost to be so thirsty? no. i was rescued by a monk who stumbled upon the castle. he bound me and cared for me until i could walk again, then
pointed me here towards your village. he said more mononoke had been seen near.

mononoke? here? o woe! we are all in danger!

if you have not seen them then i expect you are safe. at least for now. before i came to
you i spoke with a farmer who was in town to trade. he said the things had burned
two farms near him, south of here. i go there next to find a new clue towards where
mother blood roosts.

i am reassured by your confidence. and hope you enjoyed the wine!

i enjoyed it very much, thank you. but i must be off.

i thank you for your tale, ronin-san. you tell tales well, even if you say it is not for you.

my lord once told me that only cowards live to tell tales. there is still some truth in
that.

the ways of samurai are beyond my understanding.

they need not be. yet it is too late for me to teach you myself. mayhaps another.

go. go do the business of your mysterious lord.

not so mysterious. you know him, at least in name.

and you said you would not speak of your master!

true servants to their lord should never speak in absolutes. you have been kind and
attentive, and so i will leave you lastly with the truth of my disgrace. my lord was
lord tomioka.

who defied lord fujisawa?

the same.

then you are truly a man with no home.

yes. one more cup, if you would. a small one. prince kyo, who led the force your late
lord crushed? it was i who taught him the arts of the blade and the general. his failure was my failure. kyo would not admit the fault, and said instead that it was his
father's fault for not knowing he was unready, or the fault of his soldiers for following
his instructions poorly and with disrespect. this was inappropriate and disrespectful,
which made his shame worse. as a loyal servant of his father i could not allow this

167

disrespect upon his heir, and so i spoke clearly that it was my fault, for having trained the prince wrongly. in this i was seen as a good servant, but also great sadness came to the court and to lord tomioka, who must now lose a valued retainer - a thing some say is as valuable as a true son.

*a terrible tragedy. forgive me, i do not mean to cry.*

it is always sad to see a retainer's failure. he told me that day to end my life. to relieve my dishonour and his own in the sacred act of hara-kiri. this i would have gladly done, had i not seen the danger in the war with fujisawa. our mightiest army had been broken, and now there were less men who loved their service to tomioka. i said to my lord, This I Will Do, Even Though It Is Perhaps The Goal Of The Enemy. when he asked why i said this, even as i held my short blade in both hands, i said, Lord Fujisawa Will Benefit From Less Loyal Retainers Attending To His Foe. It Is A Tragedy And A Further Dishonour That Even By My Death I Hurt This House. lord tomioka asked what i would have him do and i replied, I Would Not Dare Suggest A Course To So Great A Man. But I Do Admire Those Exiles - Those Ronin - Who Have Fled Honourable Death To Live In The Hills And Villages, But Have Never Forgotten You In Their Hearts. the lord asked if this was true that these loyal ronin exist, and i told him that it was. I Can See The Thought In Your Heart, Lord. Do Not Shame Me Now By Disallowing My Death. but he ordered me exiled, and forbade me from taking my life. for two years i served as well as a disgraced sword may. until mother blood came.

*we have all been hurt by mother blood. even though we were subjects to fujisawa, we still cried to see tomioka die as well.*

after she slew him i swore vengeance. this is the promise i made. i told tomioka's ghost that the spirit that killed him would be banished from this world.

*stay strong, ronin-san.*

stay strong, merchant-san.

Asahi, for that was the ronin's name, did not reach the farms by sundown. He sought a shallow pool by which he may perform his nightly ritual - the care and oaths which kept him centred. There he said his vows with his weapon in his lap and, content with his promises, he replaced his sword in his belt and found a position under a maple which overhung the pool, facing the setting sun. Its red leaves sprinkled the still water. Sitting with his back against the bark, he allowed his mind to empty, watching the red circle sink beneath the ocean. With a smile, the ronin slipped into sleep as the light fled the sky.

In the morning – the sky still set to be dark for many hours - he undressed, carefully laying his daisho atop his silken tunic and hakama, his sandals beside. Wading into the water, he let the cold pierce his skin and, with a breath, dipped below the surface. There had not been much to soil his skin that day – no combat, labour, or accident - but he scrubbed himself nonetheless, freeing himself of the oils of the waking world. Once he was clean, he dressed once more and knelt beneath the shade of a maple once more. With his sharp tanto - the small knife he carried so he may keep himself ever perfect in his appearance – Asahi gently shaved his cheeks. Once upon a time he would have also shaved the top of his skull, keeping his chonmage crisp – the knot of black hair atop his head perched above the white skin like a monk standing above the snow, but it was not legal for a ronin to shave his head.

Next, once his reflection showed the man he wished others to see, he held his long sword in his lap and shut his eyes, his ears still alert, ever wary but fully committed to his task. With a breath of the cool autumn air, he recited firmly to himself:

> *my sword will never be lesser than another.*
> *my lord will always find me of use.*
> *my love for my father and my mother will be ever as my love for my lord.*
> *compassion will fill me always, as i seek to better the lot of all folk.*

Standing, his sword once more at his waist, he looked out on the world with clear eyes. It was time to move on.

P*lease, buke-sama! spare me!*
*i have slain your fellows and will slay you as well when i deem the time right. but if you belay your trickery and answer my questions well then i shall make your death swift and clean. speak, demon!*
*a tower! mother blood lives within a high tower!*
*where?*
*follow the stream, the one which is lined with lilies. follow it into the valley. the tower is there, where the stream pools and black vines hug the cliffs.*
*thank you, yokai-san.*
*i helped you! now will you not at least –*

T he stream was loud in the silence of the countryside, burbling and jab-bering as it ran over stones of grey and white. Asahi trailed through the lilies, noting the impact his footprints made amongst the fresh petals. His kimono, gifted to him by the monk who had rescued him, was black with blood from the foes he had slain near the burned farms - men in masks with cruel gleams in their eyes. He had tried to clean it as best he could, but it was stained forever. He would need a new one again. He felt a deep peace as he approached the place which he knew in his heart must surely be the place of his death.

It was not a short way, to that valley of black vines, but Asahi was comfortable in his path and did not mind the wait. It does not do to rush into anything save death, and death will come when it musst. There was no thought in the ronin's mind as to what would occur if he survived. It was irrelevant to the task. A distraction. It is better to consider oneself already dead; that way there is no threat which can stay you.

When at last the stream began to descend, the earth sloping gently into the hills where tall grass swayed in the morning mist, Asahi paused to consider his place in the world. He stopped to think on what would be said of him once he was gone. He had no parchment on which to write, but let his tongue flow, speaking a death poem for only the thrushes to hear:

*the stream leads downhill*
*where a bird perches and sings*
*a grave holds old bones*

Satisfied with the words which would take him onwards beyond the doors of death, Asahi continued his path along the banks of the stream. Soon enough he came about a bend in the low gorge formed by the hills and saw his destination. Ahead lay a green place, open to the sky, where a black pool rested and black vines choked the sides. On the far side of the pool rested a pagoda of many floors, and in the grassy lawn and in the tower windows he could see the monstrous faces of his foes.

He neither halted nor slowed, for the time had already passed to consider his choice. But it was not truly a choice - and had never been - for it was a duty. A duty to his lord, even in death. As his sandalled feet strode confidently down the grassy stream bank, a few of the yokai who lounged beneath the canopy of the pagoda rose. Before any could declare a challenge, he declared his own, drawing both swords and shouting as he sprinted, head down and path winding to avoid the pelting of arrows.

Two came down the stairs and fell, bleeding, by the stream. Two more met him at the top. One he forced over the railing, giving him time to fence the other. He parried and dodged, swinging only twice and slaying his foe with the second strike. The enemy he had thrust over the barricade came up behind him, seeking to grapple and strangle him, but Asahi was too strong, and pinned the man to a wooden pillar with his short sword.

Asahi tugged once, twice, at the blade, but it would not come unstuck and so, knowing more foes bounded towards him, turned and held his long sword in both hands. The first who came took the sword acrost his chest, sliding between ribs and rupturing organs. Before the next came the ronin had claimed a new short sword from one of his fallen foes, and with blades in each hand he cut a bloody swath through them to the paper door of the pagoda, each instant keenly aware of the pain in his mangled finger from the fight before.

As he gained the wooden planks of the first level the beasts inside scrambled to their feet, clutching at their masks and their sword belts. Yet they could see the bloody will in his eye and knew that they did not hold the love for Mother Blood that he held for his fallen lord. No more stood in his path as he took the ladders, one sword always in hand.

His feet softly clattered on the wood of the highest tier as below he saw animal-faced buke fleeing in all directions from the tower. He was alone with the sorceress. Here, in the high point of the tower, where only the birds and the clouds could witness them. The walls here were open, but in the centre of the floor there was a shrine with many burning oils, hidden in part by a silken screen. And behind that screen was the shadow of Mother Blood.

*i knew one would come. whose anger fills you?*
   tomioka.
*ah. one of many angry men.*
   show yourself, tengu-san, or i shall cut you down where you stand.
*you mean to do so regardless.*

But she stood and, with the slowness of old bones, pulled aside her silken shield. There she stood, a woman of some age, though much of her hair was still black and her handsome jaw was still firm, her skin smooth. She was dressed in simple weave - much as a peasant might dress, in rough cloth and dull colours. The only sign of her power were the swords at her side, their hilts black.

Asahi drew his short blade once more and took two steps forward, but she held up her hand and he paused, uncertain in the face of her magic. She smiled, though her eyes remained sad.

*it is woeful that it must come to this. yet it is as it always has been. always shall be. despite all i strived for.*
   you have striven for destruction. remade the province into a nightmare.

171

*you flatter me. no one woman could do so much.*

it is the sign of a true master to understate your truth.

*and i did not strive for destruction. never for that.*

but that is what followed. what else could you have sought?

*i sought to fulfill the honour of my people. much as you.*

you have no honour.

*not true. i may serve no lord, but i serve the village where i was born. a village torn apart by lord fujisawa and his warring and once my village was ash the most horrible things were said of them. accusations of the worst offences, which no spirit could forgive.*

but fujisawa is not the only lord whose lands you despoiled! tomioka as well was destroyed.

*and i would destroy many others if it fulfilled the middle path.*

there is no middle path to the destruction you bring.

*you are wrong, buke-sama. i take the middle path by not following a lord, yet also taking no lordship.*

but here you have failed, mother blood, for you are lord of these lands now.

*i take no taxes. hold no wealth.*

and yet those around you see you as master. you are made lord by fear.

*no! i have made no motion to raise myself above others. demanded no fealty. i am dependant on no one and no one depends on me.*

what of your servants? the yokai who spread your fear? you speak and they follow. and by their spears you replace oppression with oppression.

*what will come will be a paradise! the gods grant wishes to those who suffer, and few have suffered as I have!*

you are blinded by hatred. you punish men for crimes they have not done. and punished fujisawa for crimes for which he had had time to atone for.

*yet he did not!*

how do you know this? because he did not apologize personally to you? you are not the arbiter of fate, mother blood. what you have done - hope still to do - is for you alone. no other's spirit is calmed by your wickedness.

*wickedness.*

The word hung in the air. A gossamer spider-strand on the still wind. She looked to him and he to her and both regretted the world as it was. If she was wrong it was only right that hers be that hand that ended her terror.

Yet to Mother Blood she was not wrong. And neither was Asahi. The two locked steely eyes and mother blood drew her two black swords.

They clashed, the ronin and the demon, steel singing in the empty tower. Her blades were fast, yet age and sorrow had slowed her and his were faster. He parried her strikes, each weighted with fury, weathering a storm of small cuts with his long sword gripped in two hands. Yet when her flurry

172

paused, she could not defend against the strikes with which he returned. His blade cut her hand and she dropped her long sword. His blade pierced her breast and she died. His blade cut her throat and she was still.

Asahi, servant to no house, stood above the growing pool of Mother Blood's life and let the world return to him. The pagoda was empty but for death and incense. His duty was done, and now he was without direction. He looked out, acrost the pool and up the bed of the stream below. The sun was setting somewhere behind the tower – behind the cliffs that hid it – and the lands to the east through which he had walked had turned grey.

His duty was done. Was his own death now required? Or did it not matter? After a lifetime of fierce determination Asahi felt an emptiness – and a wonder – at the size of the world. Mother Blood was gone. His lord was gone. Yet the chaos she had brought would continue. And more lords would come. Is it not more wise for a tool to be passed on if it is still useful than to destroy it? If he was to be destroyed should he not have died beside Lord Tomioka?

Asahi stood for a time, waiting in stillness for the stars to appear. When they did he descended the pagoda, past the corpses of his foes and his abandoned short sword. He knelt beside the pool and looked at his bloody reflection. He would write another death poem, someday. With a deep sigh he rested back on his heels and closed his eyes, ears open to the chittering of the night bugs and the frogs.

Tonight he would sleep.

# The Bastard Beowulf

wæt. Stranger. Share a drink. Drinks make strangers friends. And men do well to have many friends.

The night is young and ic do not know thy face. Are ye cousin to the lord? Traveller? Ah. Ye must have many tales. And many tales have ic.

Finish thy drink. And have another. Will ye tell a tale first or shall ic? Ye are not yet ready. Fair. Then ic shall speak.

I c will tell ye of the man BEOWULF. A mighty man he with wide thews and famous deeds. Ic will tell it as is told me. Tho ic hear others tell it different. But this is how it is told me and so how ic says it.

Of his size it is said that he is nigh twice the height of many men. And in girth also he is greater than all others. In feats of strength not e'en thirty men will best him. And floor-wood groans at his killers bulk. A man of the NORTH is he and of many deeds. Avenger and war-winner he. Troll-nests he tears and gainst sea-things he succeeds. Huldras and alfs hold no charms on he and in one terror-siege he slays alone five beasts and in their blood is praised. In all the known lands he is known and he is full of words and of valour.

In his seventh year is he given to HRETHEL KING. Father of BEOW-ULFS mother and lord of those lands is HRETHEL KING. Fair and like a son does HRETHEL keep the growing sword-slayer. In many wars fights he in youth.

In this youth BEOWULF is with three brother-uncles. HEREBEALD HA-ETHCIN and HIGELAC are they. Yet ic am sorrowed for the truth. For HEATHCIN slays by unmeant (as surely it must be) bow-shot his brother eldest. And BEOWULF watches as the dire wood-fang of the horn-tipped bow strikes HEREBEALD deep in his noble chest. No answer can there be to this but to break the broken family further. And so good HRETHEL in misery has a scaffold built from which he hangs his youngest blood-son. Tho he does not die. As the FATHER OF ALL. A raven watches and delights in death.

HRETHEL KING wishes he is wiser. Wiser than HIGH KING what gives his eye. Wishes he to defeat death. Each day he wakes to find once more his son is slain and another he hangs. No love for life is in his breast. Watches he the empty hall where his heir in life feasts and smiles. No thegn now lifes there. And the hearth is cold. Full of dust is it. No songs nor cheer. No friends like we here. That yard is empty. Alone he lies long in bed and sings his laments. No right can be made of what is done. Ye know sorrow in life. All men do. Yet not as HRETHEL KING. No feud can he call to warm his blood. No spell to save his loved son. And so in bed he lies and curses the gods until at last to HEL he goes.

HIGELAC. Last of the true sons. HIGELAC must take the crown.

The sons of ONGTHEOW now take this death as call to make feud-war with the kin of HRETHEL KING. The princes of another great north-land are they. Unrelenting are they and fierce and bloody is this opportuni-ty-war. Yet no peace will they hear from HIGELAC KING nor his servants. From each coast to another rains blood and fire. Many mothers shed tears for sons and wifes for husbands. In time they are defeated by bright sword and mighty thegn.

Yet not afore a most terrible price is paid. On the field of the final battle does HAETHCIN make his ride to HEL. And HIGELAC KING draws his shining throne-blade to lead the battle-herd. And EOFER draws his glaif. EOFER. Husband to HIGELACS daughter. And with that kin-blade does he cleave ONGENTHEOWS skull. ONGENTHEOW is a hateful man with a heart in two halfs. And now too is his brain-pan in two halfs. His ills on HRETHELS folk are done.

It is from this happy world that comes the giant BEOWULF. Many tales there are of him. Many ic wot ye know well. And this the wellest of. But here is the truth of it. Not a poets lies. The truth as far as ic meself hears it. O that man. He is great and cold and mighty and full of life. So life-full he that e'en in death we all know him. E'en tho he is not a good king.

Yet this story begins not about BEOWULF. Mighty wide-thewed BEOW-ULF. Who splits a dragons gullet. Nay. It begins about HROTHGAR KING. Ye know not HROTHGAR? HROTHGAR. HROTHGAR KING. Ah. Well. Ic suppose his name is better known before his felling. That gold-gilt getter of gifts. Mighty once is he. And son of many great sons.

SCIELD is called that eldest father to HROTHGAR. Like his name is SCIELD a great defender of men. But also is he a sea-lord. Hall guest. Hall winner. Conqueror of all that borders his sea. All gold he wants he gets. All women he wants he gets. None can hold more mead nor ale than he. This is a good king.

Yet SCIELD dies. As all men do. He is in golden days of sorrow as he soars into death. Men cry now. For all men love good kings. His final ship he prepares before his final day. And strong his low-hearted thegns do carry his corse (heavy with thews e'en in age and death) and lay it on that ship. On this ship are many wondrous carvings. As what ye see on the halls of lords. A dragon skull for a prow it has and golden nails in the timbers. He is set on a bed of sticks. With gold and jewels and horse and servants for to serve in halls of gods. He is loved of gods who call him master with sword and winner of glory. Ye cannae imagine the wealth he takes out of this world. No greater ship e'er there is. Axes and swords and mail shirts and cups and lances with ash-leaf heads. Ye cannae imagine. By torch they raise a golden banner high above. And by sea set him on his way towards greater adventures. SCIELD is a great man. A hero.

But ic talk too much of men who are not BEOWULF nor HROTHGAR. HROTHGAR is son of SCIELDS sons son. Aye. SCIELD had one son. Do ic not mention him? His name is BEOW. Not BEOWULF. But BEOW. And he also is mighty. Tho not so many as remember SCIELD remember BEOW.

BEOW is well-loved before and after his father conquers death. His final adversary. But BEOW dies also and leaves his kingdom to HEALFDANE. HEALFDANE is HROTHGARS father. HROTHGAR also has two brothers. But they are not so great as HROTHGAR. A sister has he also. And she marries the foeman of BEOWULFS folk. This is a way in which BEOWULF is good. For he helps those who love his enemy. Tho if he does not help his foemans friend perhaps some goodness he may keep and not become so foul an emperor.

HROTHGAR is much loved. All love him. As they should. For he is of HEALFDANES kin of BEOW of SCIELD. They love him for he is mighty and handsome and warlike. They love him for the richness of his mirth. And for all his love and might and victory he settles to build himself a hall. A mighty hall. A great hall. A golden hall. For feasting like cannae even be imagined. Ye think ye feast well. Yet ye feast like pigs against the likes of HEOROT. HEOROT is HROTHGARS hall. His golden hall. HROTHGARS HEOROT is hearth to hale hirdmen from here to HELHEIM. Aye. HEL ic say. For it draws many and mickle curses. Yet not at first. For at first it is a mighty place in which to house a throne and a kings justice and great arts from all the world. Such gifts he gives. Rings and crowns and well-thought rule. All this is given by HROTHGAR. HEOROT HALL is high and gilt and awful to behold before its burning. The hall HEOROT is home to mighty dooms. E'en after BEOWULFS heavy feet leave its benches and empty cups. Kin slay kin in HEOROT. Mighty HEOROT. Terrible HEOROT.

But tho all good men love HEOROT and love HROTHGAR there are those who do not. Who hate the bright song and bright swords. And of those ungood men worst is GRENDEL.

GRENDEL. The beast GRENDEL. A terrible thing he. An ogre. A dra-ugr. An afterwalker. A tall lean thing which should ne'er crawl this earth. Of him more ic will speak later. When ic tell of his coming to BEOWULF.

This GRENDEL. It pains him to hear the joy of HEOROT. The happy laughter. The harp harmonies. The scop who sings long of ASK and EM-BLA. Of the birth of man from darkness and of the giant-slaying by which the world is made. Of SOL and of MANI who drive their bright war-wagons in the sky and light our days and our nights. Of mighty heroes and bloody deeds.

Ah. Ic cannae delay to speak of GRENDEL. HEL-hungry half-whole hater of heroes. That jotunn-kin with teeth and claws of iron. O terrible fangs. Grey corse-skin hanging loose and deep hateful eyes. He walks the moors in anger. Gnashing his fangs in sin-song as he dreams of scop-flesh and king-blood. He is not like a king. Is poor and hated. Gods hate him. GRENDEL hates him. He is like a hound of ending. He is like BEOWULF.

Once. Long ago. GRENDEL is of a folk like man. But he is an enemy of SCIELDS fathers and they banish him and all like him. To the land of monsters (which it is called now) they go. Ne'er to return. But monsters know no laws. And much-changed GRENDEL stumbles back to hate the joyous HEOROT-folk.

In night (hidden by clouds from MANIS eye) he comes to HEOROT with man-guts for which to fill his gullet. All the mighty men of HEOROT lay drunken and joyous in their stupor. For they eat and sing and fuck in a great feast which is very tiring as ic am certain ye ken from many feasts of thy own. There all are they. Lords and thegns and maidens fair all together. And GRENDEL towering above them as they sleep. They know in this moment no sorrow. Are happy. Such a sad fate for them.

GRENDEL is neither sad nor happy. For a beast of hatred is he. A spirit of blood and evil. Violence he makes in many and savage ways. In fury and with unhuman strength claims he thirty thegns from their sleep. Up he takes them in his cruel claws. His nightmare hands of hate. Each man he tears and leaves in many pieces and in gleeful silence he guzzles their blood. Chews their bones as the mountain he is. Gums their gory guts as his jotunn-eyes smolder. Carnage. Carnage he leaves. Such that ic dare not imagine it. GRENDEL licks his long fingers as he lurches home to his horrid hame. His pouches full of man-muscle.

No men awake whilst he has his own fiends feast. But before the sun HEOROT yawns and wakes. And terror fills that hall. A wail comes from the golden hall. A keening of many throats. HROTHGAR the beloved king sits in silence. Though he griefs also. His many thegns he laments in death

177

and himself blames for the villains cannibal fury.

Men cry for GRENDEL to be slain. And some men say they see GREN-
DEL crouching on marshy hills. Laughing at their misery. HROTHGAR
promises to raise a fyrd. Yet on that next night the hulking foeman returns
and slaughters more hale men. Sending many brave men to cower. For will
ye not be frighted to witness this? Ic will be. And sorely. GRENDEL holds
no remorse in his sins and so returns each night until no man dares sleep
in HEOROT and the sounds of harps quiet. The sheds and smaller hames
about the golden hall hold those cowering thegns. And GRENDEL comes
and laughs loud when no men dare confront him. His laugh is cold in all
mens bones. GRENDEL rules now. Not HROTHGAR. GRENDEL rules HE-
OROT and crouches on the roof as if it is the throne he disdains. That hall
is empty and hated. A waste of many heavy chests.

Twelve years is this terrible rule. And twelve years do nightmares and
guilt wrack HROTHGAR KING. Tho now he is more a king in name. And
all the NORTH know of the defeat.        And scare in the sorrow. Of the
battles HEOROTS lords cannae win. No victory comes to SCIELDS SON and
many blades are broken. Many and many sad songs are sung of HROTH-
GAR as if he is already dead and is the hero of a tragic lay. It is an embarrass-
ment. No man wishes to hear of his failed life. Payments are offered and
repaid with hate. No emissaries takes GRENDEL save to savor their bones.
GRENDEL is king of all the marshy lands and stone lands and terror lands.
And a wicked king he.

Long nights does HROTHGAR spend with captains and hirdmen to dis-
cuss their fate. But no answer can be found in words. Their temples. They
are not yet profaned. Their temples they come to and pray to our gods and
make sacrifice. E'en of men. But the gods are silent. Mayhaps they also
fear GRENDEL KING. Wise they are to seek the old ways. Wise to offer
goods to gods. Yet they are weak and so the war-wardens stay silent and
feast on apples of gold in that hall of many doors.

HROTHGAR of HEALFDANE-born broods much. As HRETHEL does
when his family is broke. There is naught he can do to silence this sorrow.

Yet now ic tells of BEOWULF. Now BEOWULF enters the telling. Strong
slayer-son who is not yet soul-sable sorcerer of sorrow. Here he is hero.
And now he hears of HEOROT.

Strongest of all men is BEOWULF. Prince in the NORTH. Huge in size
is he and storied in deed.

Orders he a mighty ship to be made ready. Worthy of war. Worthy of
kings. Seeks he HROTHGAR KING he says. To aid him he says. Gainst
GRENDEL FOE. 'Ic am man.' he says. 'Greatest of men. And HEOROT has
need of men. Strong men.' (His talk is grander than this. But ic am not so

knowing of words as he. And ic imagine naught. Only tell as ic am told.)

Men in the lands of HIGELAC KING love their lords brother-cousin. Yet they object not to his journey. Tho they fear it his last. For BEOWULF is stubborn like an ox and they know he cannae be swayed.

Once he is decided to make his travel he searches all the land of his birth. For strong men he looks. Like him. Yet not so great for no such man lifes. Battlers and war-winners they. Scars and hard thews mark them. Runes on blades and sigils on shield and mail. All brave men. None e'er fall to ungood ways like BEOWULF does. All are noble to their bloody end. All fifteen. For fifteen there are.

With care and sea-knowledge the crew prepares their ship. Arms and armors and food for to fill their guts they store. And as the ship sets sail along the rocky coast there are stout reinforcements of iron and oak for to battle the weather. Eyes they keep always open for assault from the water-men with which they feud. Sorcerous and shapeless men who drown hale war-makers as vengeance for ancient wrongs.

But the journey is short and soon the silfery cliffs of HEOROTS shore tower from the surf. In a fierce wave of clattering ring-shirts and hateful boar helms they flood the land. To NJORDR SEA-KING they slay a pig in thanks. Its blood wets the white sand. They make the wave-roads journey safe.

There is a high wall there on the shore. For to protect from watermen and sea raiders and angry serpents. On this wall there is a stout fyrdman. A warrior for to watch the way. And as he watches the way he sees the mighty ship land and the men aboard labor to unload their store of shields and glittering arms. He wonders who they are. Fears the invasion of HEOROT. Hopes for salvation from GRENDEL.

With a fearsome cry rides this noble servant. This brave spear-thegn. Ahorse and with fiery lance upheld he challenges the foreign men. Demands them call their names and titles. Brags of his long service. His beard grey but chest broad. All HROTHGARS lands he alone defends by his bellow. 'Ne'er before does such a battle-company land on these shores.' says he. 'No blessing does our lord gift for such war-rods and hand-walls and boar-masks on our shore.' Spies he calls them. Strangers. He knows them not and demands their names and fathers. He knows by their manners and dress that they be of those lands acrost the sea and cries for them to answer quickly. Lest he become angered.

BEOWULF now. That noble man. He gifts answer. His words are so mighty. A treasure. That ic cannae pretend to imitate them. Now he still gifts speeches. It is a great sorrow when his tongue quiets. It is the start of many sorrows. Of his folk he speaks. And relates them to HIGELAC KING.

ECGTHEOW. His fathers name he summons. ECGTHEOW. All these names he speaks are well known to the spear-thegn. Many compliments also he gifts to HROTHGAR KING. 'SCIELD.' he calls him. 'Warbound.' he calls him. He says they come for to aid him in his famous plight. Of all he hears of GRENDEL TERROR he tells. 'Ravager.' 'Hate-lord.' 'Slaughter-prince.' 'Wizard-brood.' Good counsel he offers HEOROTS ring-gifter. Praise of his strong arm. Reminds he also of the shame of defeat. For what will others say should ne'er he triumph? Surely not that he was a mighty man. All his victories will be forgot. E'en the WAR-HALL will refuse him. Exile him to HEL.

That shore-keeper is sore awed by this display. Men he sends to guard their great dragon-boat. A path to HROTHGAR he shall take them on. Warns he tho of the sin of failure. Of the weight words have. A man what says a thing must do a thing. At this strong BEOWULF laughs.

Behind the ship watches them go. Sees with raven eyes that its captain soon shall be dead.

In noble column marches the hird. Gold and silfer shines. Terrible helms hide their faces. They are murderer-heroes. They do not fear death.

It is not long before they find golden HEOROT. Cursed HEOROT. High-timbered HEOROT. Its golden roof reflects the sun on all the land. Men who see them go straight to HEOROT to see the audience.

Their guide leaves to once more watch the shore. Wishes them luck and the eye of all gods of war. 'If they do not watch me now ic shall make them watch me by my red deeds.' BEOWULF is proud. Surely he speaks true.

Stones pave the path to HEOROT. The straight path. Fierce bright mail. Well-made iron mail. Rings sing on their breasts. Fear strikes those who watch. Fear and awe. The gate of HEOROT stands open for them and they enter.

Weary and sea-beaten men. BEOWULFS hard party. They rest their shields. Well-cursed shields. Rest them on the sturdy walls as they rest their bodies on benches. Spears are put in bundles upright and mail clinks joyously as sharp points rise towards HROTHGARS roof. Mighty grey weapons are they.

A noble now. A proud man. A proud man speaks. 'From where come these shields of gold?' he says. The spears and helms and heavy rings he questions also. This is ÆSCHERE. He is brother to YRMENLAF. He is advisor and rune-reader to his king. He speaks for his lord. All this he says and more. For great men hold a great many words. 'So bold are ye to come here in such array.' Proud he calls them. Or outlaw. He demands in HROTHGARS name an answer.

BEOWULF wears still his terrible helm. Looks the monster he shall become. Tho mighty also he seems. Speaks he and names he of HIGELACS kin. BEOWULF. He says true his name. BEOWULF. Bold and brash. Baneful BEOWULF. Many kind things he says of HROTHGAR and his fathers.

WULFGAR then. An ally-prince. WULFGAR speaks loud and all listen. For the prince was known by all to be a champion of courage and of wisdom. He says that he shall tell the king of their coming. And it is known that WULFGARS loving eye falls on the thick cords of that fighters muscle. A killer loves to see the killing strength in others.

HROTHGAR sits at HEOROTS far end. His seat is ringed with loyal men and his beard is grey. WULFGAR is friend to HROTHGAR as all killers must be friends. Yet WULFGAR is subject also. Offers he BEOWULFS introduction yet offers he also advice to his lord. Warns he to be cautious in answer. Both for fear of driving them from HEOROTS shore and for fear that they may decide to stay and make use of their swords to outdo the lands loyal thegns.

HROTHGAR. Now he speaks. His voice is proud. It carries over all others. He says that when BEOWULF is young he knows him. And his father also is known to HEOROTS handsome lord. Of the marriage of HRETHELS daughter he speaks. BEOWULF he calls a loyal friend and welcomes to his land. Tales he tells to the hall which he hears of the warrior-sons deeds. Declares him champion gainst GRENDELS claws. Treasures already he promises the northmen for their victory yet unwon. Each noble man and highborn woman neath the golden roof is told to greet these sailing heroes. The common folk watch in awe. They are welcome here and all are glad of their visit.

WULFGAR sees this and knows there shall be no caution. To the entrance to the feasting place he hies and tells the waiting thegns all the praise of his lord. Invites them to enter that high hall.

Mighty HROTHGAR. Famous HROTHGAR. Waits he for BEOWULFS march. With his hird he waits to mete the giant BEOWULF. BEOWULF with shining tusked helm. Heavy boots ring on oaken floors and noble rings flash on mail.

Once more does the conquering son speak his name and gift word-tax to his host. In these days men speak much. Often repeat themselfs so they are heard. So all know their respect. Confirms BEOWULF the reason for the seabound journey. The death and mangling of HELS wayward son.

BEOWULF is also proud and boasts of his mighty swing. His crushing fist. Of how he breaks giant homes and steals life from watermen and serpents. Claims he all glory from his home-shores wars. None amongst his men defy him. Would ye or ic defy a man too wide with strength for any common horse? He claims alone. That he alone. No other man shall taste of GRENDELS blood. Yet says it is a favor to BEOWULF if HROTHGAR allows the battle.

So hot does the sea princes blood grow as he boasts that he thrusts aside his spear. His shield. Unfastens he his wide war-belt and lets fall his sword to his feet. 'This thing. This bitter beast. By its claws alone it rends thy men.' says the killer proud. 'And so ic take gainst him no war-wood nor cutting steel. By hand alone shall ic best him. For this is as fair a fight as can be made. Tho he cannae hope to out-muscle HIGELACS kin.' And his rippling chest threatens to burst the iron rings he wears. That coat of dragon-skin what WELAND made for him.

Speaks he some time to the hall. Pacing and making wide motions. Of bloody death or bloody wins speaks he. Paints he an image of two eternal foes. Of GRENDEL and BEOWULF. Of BEOWULF and GRENDEL. A battle to rend the sky and end the world. Children cower and men sweat and women clutch their beating hearts. And handsome BEOWULF smiles. And weary HROTHGAR smiles also.

When the great man finishes speaks up HROTHGAR KING. Speaks he of many things he and others say in other times. Things all men know of but must be said again in case men forget. Of BEOWULFS kin and his own kin. Of wars and sons and bitter feuds. All this ye know. And ic am not scop nor lord of men and have no patience nor memory to say such things again and again and again. HEATHOLAF. HEOROGAR. HEALFDANE. all these names ye know.

Ye know not? Ah. Ic can tell ye. First we must –

Nay. Tis too much and is not about BEOWULF. We must talk of BE-OWULF and his terrible blade. Ic will tell ye of what HROTHGAR speaks another time.

Some of this speech is about GRENDEL. How he attacks and aid does not come. And when aid comes these aids are slain. His mightiest men are made meek or bloody meat. HEOROTS floor is red with blood which will ne'er be undone.

When at last he is finished. (And it is long. For to speak long is the mark of a great man.) A feast he calls and benches are prepared. The seamen are looked at in awe as they sit high and drink golden mead neath that golden roof from golden flagons. The scops sing their songs and men laugh and boast. For men are fools when praise or drink are gifted. And they are gifted both.

There is a man in HEOROT HALL whose name is UNFERTH. This is an unlucky name. He has black hair and a noble beard and cold grey eyes. He

182

is known throughout that land as a winsome and wealthy warrior tho also wearisome and woeful. HROTHGAR keeps him for his strong sword. Yet he is a lesser man than once he was. Ic like not the tale of UNFERTH. That is for another man to tell. Ic wish not to tell of his kinfelling. The brothers he quells.

Yet UNFERTH is at this fool-feast and stands in his dark clothes. Men whisper that he is a sorcerer. That he fucks some wood-spirit and is made master of curses and dead things. UNFERTH looks on BEOWULF LORD with pity like a scowl. 'Ye are BEOWULF.' he says. he speaks little. Tho men say once he speaks much. He does not speak long now like BEOWULF nor WULFGAR nor HROTHGAR. 'BEOWULF makes a prideful swim with the man BRECA. Both are fools. BRECA is the greater man.' He stares then about the room like a rabid wolf.

This story all men in HEOROT know. Yet ye do not. Ic see this. It is luck that ic know it. For it is a small story and not of men famous today. Save BEOWULF. The two men set out to swim a stormy straight. Many tell them that they will die. Yet still they go. Heavy rains and hungry waves threaten to swallow BRECA and the giant BEOWULF. Both return. But BRECA is first of them. And is respected as prince and owns great wishes. Many who hear of the swim think it to prove how weak BEOWULF can be.

But lo. BEOWULF is not a man to best nor belittle. He speaks now. Only raises his voice. Does not stand. UNFERTH is a small man to challenge him. 'Aye ic do swim with BRECA. UNFERTH drinks much that he speaks so long.' He laughs and others laugh and UNFERTH knows shame and anger.

BEOWULF speaks on. 'Ic am the stronger man. Better in water. Better on land. Such stamina ic own for such a hard life ic life. Indeed we are stupid to make this swim. Yet so too are we young. Now ic am a man full. We swim to sea with naked swords. For all the worst of things lair at sea. We mean to save ourselves from the great tusks of whales. Whale-beasts are fierce and hungry and they like best the thick and virile flesh of men. He is a poor swimmer. It is worse that he boasts than ic. Yet ic will not see him drown and slow my long strokes to rescue him. He is weak and less of a man. Five nights of this swim we make. For neither of us will return a coward. Now comes the angry breath of north gods and heavy pissing rain and they drive us far apart. Ic decide him dead. These rough waves wake the water-snakes and wave-men we hope not to see and my naked edge flashes. Slashes. Blood is in the air like a storm.' The slayer stands now and thrusts with his sword as he tells to show the great strength of his rippling arms. 'My chain shirt ic wear. Heavy links made with steel and gold. Ic wear it that swim. Many times it turns their teeth and breaks their

183

finger-knifes. Now comes that whale ic warn of. With iron jaws it takes this foot and drags me to oceans deep bottom. Yet fate will not allow this death of me and my sword finds meat. One thrust and blood comes in a geyser. Its brain is broke. This is done by my hand alone.'

UNFERTH sits now and is scared. The sailor-slayer sings on. 'With fury at their brothers death more fishes come to die. In and in they come. Bite and slash. Whale fingers mar my skin. But with my noble blade do ic serve them as they deserve. Their wyrd ends at my wending. A sword-feast is had. Ic laugh into the waves as they wail in terror of my might. They mean to devour me but it is my steely arm what eats of them. By dawn they sleep forever on the shore. My sword their lullaby. Those waves ne'er will not be red. The sun comes now as the gods (fearful of my power) urge it upwards to warm me. All the ocean-lands hail me as lord. Now ic go to windy cliffs. Brave man ic. And rest my heavy limbs. Nine monster-fish ic slay that night. No greater night-fight e'er there is. No long weariness takes me and with ease ic ride the tides once more until to home ic come and find the coward BRECA in my seat.'

Turns he now to Unferth who challenges him. 'Ne'er do ic hear of great sword-terrors from ye. Ne'er such struggles. Ne'er does UNFERTH nor BRECA show such courage in war-mete. Ic do not boast. For all ic say is true. Tho terrors ye know and struggles ye cause. Thy own brothers ye kills. Kinslayer ye. All ken this. Ye are clever it is said. Like woman or troll. Yet ye deserve to drown in the rivers of HEL. Not to see the HIGH ONES hall.' Here he strides to Unferths seat and places one massive fist upon the lessers head. All wait for him to speak more for they fear too much to speak ill of Unferth themselfs. UNFERTH KINSLAYER. Last son of ECGLAF. 'If it is not for thy wickedness ne'er should GRENDEL do such harm to HEOROT. Were thy heart or words as sharp as thy sword there should be no greater shield for HROTHGAR. Ye say ye are a victory-folk and yet this witch sits at table and all call him fellow. All are weak like him. GRENDEL kens this. Can smell unmanly blood. He kens that all tax he takes becomes new law. Those what call themselfs thegns become sweet feast-treats. He kills and kills and knows none shall stand against.'

The great hand lifts from UNFERTHS glowering brow. BEOWULF is drunk. He boasts. 'Ic soon shall show him all my strength this night and no other. Ic alone shall best him. When once more ic frighten the sun to rise any man may walk to mead with no fears. All shall be free by BEOW-ULFS hand.'

It is the way of great men to speak in such ways. To be unkind and proud. This is right. All men say so. Save men such as UNFERTH. Those in the hall cheer and gift huzzah for this loud challenge. All spirits are lifted.

184

UNFERTH clutches his ale and heavy sword and leaves for shadowed eaves.

HROTHGAR HEOROTS KING is pleased most of all. Watches he with confidence as laughter and feast-noise and glad words fill his roof. Surely BEOWULF will slay the beast.

A gorgeous creature comes from hidden sight. She is all in gold and white-gold is her hair. It falls like water o'er her fine shoulders and about her shapely breasts. WEALTHEOW is she. And HROTHGARS queen. Welcomes she the mighty men. And BEOWULF most of all. Full of fear and lust is she at sight of him. But he is not yet a terrible man and only thanks her for his mead. This she brings him last. Both for custom and for fear. First she brings the cup. The brimming cup. To the war-famed hall-king so he may sip. To each man now she brings it. For to share in the bounty of their lord. At last she comes to that ship-king and begs all war-gods that this wolf should slay the draugr. Thanks he her and takes the cup. Says. 'Better they to ask my aid than me to have need of theirs.'

Before his leave is taken the elding crown-lord warns BEOWULF that he expects the foe this very night. 'Ne'er in all my days do ic gift the safety of this hall to aught but meself. Until this day.' he tells the hero. 'Hold HEOROT. Prove thy brave ways. Watch for GRENDELS ugly face. Should ye life ye shall be made a rich and famous man.'

The sea-wolf smiles and slaps the strong old arm. Says. 'One cannae become what one already is.' Both laugh.

Now HROTHGAR leaves with WEALTHEOW his wife. And as BEOWULF asks he bids all HEOROT men make leave as well. BEOWULF asks this for he weens that he alone deserves the glory.

All know BEOWULF to be strong. So great that no man may best him. No beast either is said. The gods fear his might and he grins to see his men marvel at his bravery.

His mail coat he begins to unclasp. To pull o'er his broad shoulders. His rich thews ripple and tense. To a trusted man he gifts his gilt helm. His golden brow-bastion. his wicked sword as well. Its scabbard shines and glitters in the dark. It likes to be looked upon as much as its master. 'Look well on these.' he says and stretches afore his rest. 'Ic am a killer and proud. Much as GRENDEL-FOE. Yet his proud murdrum is done bare-fisted. And so ic shall do him the honor of his murder in same. He is strong. That hateful harrower. But he is an idiot at arms. It would be too easy to carve him with my steel.

'And no others are to keep their sharp knifes whilst ic decry my own.' His bark is fierce. His eyes fire. He does not wish any other man to claim his glory.

And so the blood-taker sleeps. And all about him fearful men prepare for their death. Fifteen strong men BEOWULF takes. Yet e'en strong men fear death (tho they should then feast with the gods). And these men are made weaker for their absent blades.

And GRENDEL comes. Silent in shadows. As guardsmen sleep despite their fear. In his own sleep BEOWULF waits for the serpent stink of sin to suss him from slumber. And GRENDEL comes.

Up from the marsh GRENDEL comes. From under misty cliffs GRENDEL comes. GRENDEL comes walking. Striding seven leagues to a step. He bears all the wrath of the trollfolk. All the hate. No giant e'er knows ire like the ire in GRENDELS heart. He comes to thief from the golden hall. To take the hale heart of a hearthman proud. GRENDEL hopes to grind and gulp the marrow of mortals.

Many times GRENDEL comes to HEOROT HALL. And many times GRENDEL sups on the cousins kin and killers of HROTHGAR KING. Yet now he finds himself undone. Lo for this is the undoing of the monster.

But tragedy first he deals. To the hall he comes. His ill-shaped fever-wicked body is dwarfed by the mighty golden face of that wealthy house. Rage which burns hot and silent like fire thrusts him forwards. His gnarled black claws he lays upon the iron gates. His skin is wrecked by the sun and the wet and twists and puckers like hard wood. His black nails score the door and his teeth drip with ichor. It is no challenge for him to thrust asunder those heavy locks and tear with creaking quiet terror the entrance to BEOWULFS rest.

So swift is GRENDEL-FOE that a man is taken e'en as he reaches for his sword. BEOWULF says no steel shall be drawn yet this man is a coward afore death. A light shines cruel in GRENDELS gaze as he looks on the hall of soundly sleeping men. His shriveled heart laughs and the sound croaks from his dry lips like a low curse. Them all shall he devour afore that hall he leaves. The man he first grabs cannae scream for his throat is gripped tween two terrible fingers. BEOWULF watches through hooded eyes as GRENDEL tears the man. Takes each tendon apart to suck and slurp in silence as slayers slumber about. Greedily GRENDEL gulps gory gobbets from the man. Chunks of flesh crawl down his gullet as his smiling face runs with blood. So terrible is the sight ic hate to tell it. But in a moment all the corpus is gone. Hands and feet and bones and teeth all gobbled. And BEOWULF watches all and feels no sorrow for the coward. Only men of hardy breasts shall be remembered well.

GRENDEL sucks his fingers clean and takes one stride further into the hall. The next bench bears a man almost of a size with GRENDEL. GRENDEL the last son of a lost tribe. He hungers as e'er and reaches to swallow his prey. But the man is the giant BEOWULF. Death of HROTHGARS FOE.

When the foul foemans fingers clasp the heros unarmored arm that arm clasps back. BEOWULF sits straight and holds fast to the knob of his enemys elbow. From that horrid hold the creature knows no greater warrior does he face in his life. BEOWULF is the best. His laughing heart begins to cry out and the feaster whines to see his wickedness waylaid.

The man BEOWULF means now to make true his boasts. Stands he from his bed-bench. His grip still tight on GRENDEL. GRENDEL pulls and BEOWULF follows. Changes his hold. Crushes fingers. Splinters bone. The wounded nightmare-guest bellows in fear and flails. Ne'er afore does he feel defeat.

All through the hall men awake as HEL-born shrieks sound and sturdy floors break under the might of those doughty destroyers. HEOROT shakes and its stony foundation trembles. Beams are bent and rafters groan. Fearful bondsmen call that the hame may fall tho it be as sturdy a hall as e'er is built. The iron bands of the walls strain but do not break. Wall-wood splinters. Cracks. Golden benches and carven stools are torn and split. It is said none can demolish THE GOLDEN HALL. But the wrestle-war of loud GRENDEL and stoic BEOWULF threatens to render this an untruth. GRENDELS terror-calls scatter the night and all who watch are crippled with fear.

BEOWULF will not let the creature flee. It shall die here in his grasp. It holds no worth to any folk save the relief of its death. About the tumbling two come the fourteen men of BEOWULF and they have drawn their beaten swords. BEOWULF says no steel shall be drawn yet these same men know no bravery without iron. Heirloom swords passed from father to father to father beat and cut and slash. But GRENDELS hide is cursed. Cantrip-calloused. No mortal weapon may rend that flesh. BEOWULF does his damage with fist and muscle-cord. He does not ken the truth of his enemys armor. It is by the will of the proud gods that his boasting makes him fit to fight. Naked and with hard holds he is more awful than all armies against this aggressor.

A sword will end life swiftly if swung well. But brawling makes for bitter execution. GRENDEL sees his defeat and decries his death. Begs mercy in troll-tongue. His body can hold no more of harm. GRENDEL hates this man who will slay him and BEOWULF hates this thing which will not die. Both are hateful wights. And BEOWULF shall grow most hateful of all. There is a sound of split lumber. A red seam appears on GRENDELS black arm. Tendons strip loudly from bone and the invaders shoulder opens with the scream of an axe. Muscle slides and rips and marrow peaks from its burrows. BEOWULF wins and in his hand is GRENDELS bloody limb.

The beast flees shrieking into the night. Back beneath misty cliffs. Down to the marsh. He is maimed. Fevered by the grave. His wet mouldy den gifts him no comfort. He is dead.

BEOWULF is proud of the life he ends. Wise HROTHGARS famous hold is rescued now from this nightmare. The band of BEOWULF cheer their lord. They hang that terrible trophy. That wicked claw and steel-strong arm. They hang it above the door which it destroys.

In the next days many lords and fighting men come to gaze in awe at the arm above the lintel. All from many lands joyed at this murder. It is said the mere neath which he lairs boils with blood as he leaps in to die. Naught but praise is said in all the world of BEOWULF and of HROTHGAR. No other man. Men say. No other man but BEOWULF can take trophy for this task. BEOWULF is greatest of men. Deserving of kingship. And all critics of HROTHGAR are silent. HROTHGAR is victorious. Wise. And still rich. New songs are writ of BEOWULFS noble deed. Mighty deed. Helpful slaughter. Many of the songs are very good. But ic cannae do them well. And they must be well sung. Songs compare him to dragonslayers and show him as the fair mirror of bad wicked kings. They do not know how wrong their read of a man can be.

HROTHGAR comes with the morning with wife and court to thank the mighty thegn. Comes he and stands in the door of that wounded hall. Looks up at GRENDELS slaughter-scythe. 'A healthy sow ic shall cut in thanks for such a sight. Many injustices ic suffer from GRENDEL. Hard nights. Good men dead. Yet it is by the might of men and men alone that such ills are undone. Ic fear for so long that ic would ne'er be free of this curse. For too long this hall shines more with gore than gold. All are griefed by these sins. None can see how this glorious hall. Like that of VALHALL. None can see how it can be saved. Yet here stands BEOWULF and there the proof of his winning strength. O sweet BEOWULF. HIGELACS kin. My whole life long will ic cherish ye. Like a son to me shall ye be. All the love a father can gift ic shall gift to ye. And ic ask that ye also name me as kin. Naught that ic own in all the world would ic keep e'er from ye. BEOWULF. For much lesser deeds ic gift men greatly. Yet ye break the bounds of doom and free me from unhappiness. What ye do shall be known forever and all time. All rewards of EARTH are due ye.'

ECGTHEOWS son speaks. Answers his praise. 'Ic risk all. Gladly stand 'gainst unknowable fury. Champion am ic. War-winner. Yet ic pity that ye do not see the enemy himself. How fierce he is. How wroth. Rips and tears he in his canticle-skin. Yet it is not enough to fell me. Ic fell him. Ic. BEOWULF. No other.

'Ic think to bind him. Tie him. Keep him. But he is wet with blood and escapes by gift of the gory gash ic deal. Ic cannae keep life in him. Tho ic hope to deal on him all the pain he brings in years to this place. The hug ic offer is not strong enough to convince my guest to stay.' The man laughs. 'Too rude is he to take me as host long. But he is not altogether unkind. For he does leave a gift as thanks. E'en fair friends do not offer their hand so fully. Ic imagine he will nae life much longer. Mayhaps in HEL he shall find a balm for the cut ic gain him.' He laughs more.

UNFERTH ECGLAFSSON has naught to say to this. His bitter tongue is still. He sees BEOWULFS might. But he shakes also and tears are near his eyes. He sees something others do not.

All who look upon that new door decoration. That fierce foe-claw. That terrible troll-truncheon. All think it wicked and ugly yet also a fair decoration for HROTHGAR HEALFDANESSONS hall.

All the other decorations of the hall are dinted however. So HROTH-GAR KING orders the palace readorned. Many lend their hands to help. Servant thrall and lord. All wish the golden hall once more to shine. Soon tapestries gleam with golden thread. Art on golden frames. Golden benches. Golden cups. Gold returns like rain to a famine-field. All in the hall of HEOROT is wounded in that bloody death-giving. Only the hall itself stands true. But as blood and life flee foul GRENDEL gold and life flow into the fyrd-lords fief-hall.

A feast day for the fearsome fiends final foe comes now. HROTHGAR with handsome WEALTHEOW in splendor comes. His sons not-yet-men. Many lords and fellers. Admiring bondsmen and lovers of victory. Men of much courage take bench and claim BEOWULF best. HROTHGAR and nephew HROTHULF preside. Mead is gifted to blood-kin and bond-kin. Such good friends seldom are gathered together. This is a happiness. Like ye nor ic e'er know. This is before betrayal comes to this house. And to others BEOWULF visits.

It is good for hosts to gift things of great value to guests. And when those guests are mighty fear-foiling thegns such as BEOWULF? No riches may be withheld. BEOWS HEIR AND KING OF SCIELDS LINE gifts to his newfound son a long banner of golden thread. Wondrous shirt of rings. Tusked and beaten helm of beauty. Gemmed and joyous longsword worn in many blood-meals. All these are set before BEOWULF. All who look on marvel.

The fabled sword-son of the NORTH jokes and thanks in many words and guzzles mead. Tears his meat that man. Takes each tendon to suck and slurp. Gulps grog and gravy. Chunks of pig-flesh crawl down his gullet as his smiling face runs with grease. BEOWULF knows no shame. HEO-ROTS MASTER earns no shame for his mighty gifts. But BEOWULF knows none. UNFERTH sees this and is a cripple with hatred and fear.

No four such gifts any great man e'er gifts another afore nor aft as those HROTHGAR first gifts to BEOWULF. All are glittering. Gilded. The helms crown is tall and iron. Wound through with silfer. No sword of modern man can cut it. Ic like to think of this helmet best of all. Tho tis said he ne'er wears it. A banner of goldcloth. Which BEOWULF ne'er flies. A gilded sword he ne'er swings. Ornamented mail he ne'er wears. Likely that winsome warrior meant to do these items honor. But time does not allow this goodness of him.

Eight horses with golden bridles also are gifted. Saddles of fine work. Gems in all. 'This horse,' the jarl holds the mane of a mighty beast. 'is my seat when ic to sword-sea go. Many skulls ic split. Spines ic trample. Fathers sons all ic slay atop the steed. Glory this mount shares with me. Name a song of my deeds. There are many. This flesh-wainn is there. This horse. This famous thing. Now is BEOWULFS. All these horse-kin also and the golden arms. Keep them well and wet them with brain-blood and paint them with bone.' This ic think is a true gift. Worthy of the debt BEOWULF gifts him by grappling GRENDEL. All these glories are without fault. BEOWULF is luckiest of all.

Those mighty friends what BEOWULF brings are gifted also gold and gilded arms for their glory. And for the man on whom GRENDEL slurps and sups is gifted a wealth of coin. Truly is no man more hospitable and loved than WEALTHEOWS MATE.

A priest there is here as well. But no sane priest. One of those strange folk in robes who worship a dead murder-god. Their god who will murder his son and call for peace. This death-dealer ic think is called GRISTE by name. His folk e'en in these days come up from hot lands and speak on the sin of things we know. Why should ic change my ways? All gods are the same. Plenty of gods kill and plenty bless. They say these priests e'en cannae fuck. Yet ic see it sometimes. This priest tho does not fuck. But he does drink. He is still like a man in some ways. He says all men must suffer. What good is this to make a man swear love for this lord? O aye he says also that men know love. But the suffering he speaks of most. Ic think he suffers from the fat he gains from HROTHGARS feast. He does little here. Yet he is important later. Remember him. Ic only mention him because he is here. This gristan prayer-person. Ic think he is fat because ic always hear him talked of drinking and supping. He is not strong like BEOWULF. Altho he is like as not a better wight. Better tho not good.

Now comes song-singing and merrymaking. Golden mead flows in rivers and fair voices are made heard. WEALTHEOW looks on the killing-captain with interest but he is a good son to his new father and looks elsewhere for his thirsts. WULFGAR PRINCE and ÆSCERE HROTHGARS SPELL-THEGN make at playing war and show of great battles with blunted blades.

HEALGAMON. He is the song-storer. The tale-tuner. The howler of histories in HROTHGARS hall. He performs a lay of death treachery and duty. A man kills a king and becomes lord of that kings men. It is a good story at the time. Less so now.

Only UNFERTH BROTHERDEATH does not smile. UNFERTH cries. The music of fair voices is replaced by the music of the feast. Cups and knifes and plates chiming. It is beautiful. Beautiful like beautiful WEAL-THEOW. Her gaze is still drawn to BEOWULF e'en tho she loves her husband-lord greatly. Men and women both look on others. Admire. This is no sin for her to imagine his taught muscles straining with sweat. 'From battle.' she tells herself. Yet in her thoughts he is wet with fuck-sweat. She glows as she speaks. Offers a golden cup full of her red wine to her husband hale. Praises him. Says he is rich in words. True men must be rich in words. WEALTHEOW WIFE has more words than many men. Praises she his goodliness before she mentions the man BEOWULF. 'A new son he. Tho ye have two others. He is a great and strong-made man.' This is true. She is aware of his wide shoulders. His square jaw. Steely eyes. 'Ye are a great king. Yet ye are old. Protect what ye make and name an heir of blood. BEOWULFS hot blood must flow else. And HEOROT must have a lord. The sons ic bear ye are too young. HRETHRIC and HROTHMUND.' She fears the man she dreams of. He has a draw for her no goodly man can hold. He is too violent. His fate too furious. 'Ic beg ye LOVE. Name that nephew ye adore. Name HROTHULF. A true earl may he be. Let HROTH pass crown to HROTH.'

Turns she now towards the man she denies. He is too strong to resist. She moves to him. Passes UNFERTH SPEAKER FOR THE KING as he sits at his patrons feet. 'Stay wide of him as ye would of me QUEEN.' He sees the sin her loins desire tho her heart denies. 'A bounty-lord he may now be. But a bastard shall he be. Ye are right to deny him crown.' She looks on UNFERTH with hate as at a dog and his eyes fall to the floor. Long dark hair falls acrost his sallow face.

Comes she to the heros hand and holds her hair as it hangs past her hungry hips. BEOWULF that gallant great sits now between her two sons. Offers she the self-same cup from which her husband drinks. She also drinks. But at the sight of his hard movings her skin burns to be so close. But her own gifts she must gift. Weregild for her wounds desires. She waves her fair hand and these gifts are brought. Lain upon the feast-board.

Thin arm-bands. Wound and braided. Mail ring-shirt and many rings. Baskets of thanks are brought him. The thanks challenges e'en HEOROTS captains. A great golden collar to bind him and awe others. Few see such riches in all their lifes. And many what do find themselfs dead by angry arms and their riches become spoils for brigands and bandits. Lesser men take silfer from the corpses of men hot with hubris.

All cheer to see the womans wealth. And she is red with pride and desire and shame at that desire. 'Take this and wear it well. It will mark ye a man what women want and men admire.' She speaks with a trembled voice. Sone made stern. Her graceful hands are tense. Gentle but hard with the fear of her lust. These gentle hands settle the collar on BEOWULFS heavy neck. Brush briefly the bold beard. 'Ic wish ye all luck. Sweet young son. These shining shirts shall be symbols to guard that serendipity. Let all ye mete ken thy strength. Tis not merely raw muscle what mans ye. But strength of heart and strength of soul. No sin ye will commit.' Her gaze commands him and begs him to make this true. And it may be true at this time. But BEOWULF is a man who will sin as no other. Sins to match his wealth. 'Watch and guide ye thy new brothers. Sons of my birthing. If ye are a good brother-bearer ic shall ne'er forget ye. Thy deeds. Here and else. They make it so all know thy name. All love ye. Wish they are ye. Acrost all seas are ye known. BEOWULF. BEOWULF. BEOWULF. Thy name is like fire. It spreads and devours so no other men may equal ye. Take pride in this. Love this life BEOWULF makes for BEOWULF alone. Let no others board the boat of thy bounty. A prince. Ye are a prince. And not only by my motherhood. These jewels no longer are mine. They are thyne. As was e'er meant. Teach my sons to bear thy glory. Thy might. Thy discretion. Teach them to take only what is meant. All here are true men. Men of no betrayal. No traitors here. Loyal to lord. Undesirous of coin not gifted. They love life. But take not the lifes from others whilst they yet life. We are one folk. And now ye are of us. Sworn to my husband-king. All men here will do as ye ask. Save if it should harm the hearth-lord.' Her eyes shine and she turns away. Moves swiftly to her seat. Sits with face hidden. This BEOWULF will ne'er cross the wall she sets. Tho another might.

The feast continues. And no fairer festival e'er again graces HEOROT. HEOROT who houses hidden hinderers. Many malicious masters content to try treason for want of treasure and tax. But not now. Now rare red wines pour in rivers and meat-skin sizzles. None consider terrible fates to come. And terrible they all shall be. In time WEALTHEOW WIFE takes tired HROTHGAR to his bed. And there she shares the passion she does not share with another.

Many men are in the hall. Many more than when GRENDEL comes. Foul foe still gifting death from beyond the grave. Once the fires of hungry hearts wane. Tho not dies. For it ne'er dies in the hearts of some men. But once it is lessened benches are moved and bedding is laid for those heavy with joy to rest.

ÆSCERE. beloved of the KING OF THE GOLDEN HALL. His face is

red with drink and belly sore from laughter. He lies near to the fire for his final sleep. He. As all other men. Keeps his shield as pillow. Strong spear at hand. Glittering helm. Iron coat. Sword. All. This marks him a man. He is ready to defeat death as are all the hall-lords. It shall avail him not.

This is his final night. GRENDEL men think dead. And dead GRENDEL is. Yet a sin alike in terror to the terror of GRENDEL comes this night to ÆSCERE. No spells aid him. No runes defend. GRENDELS evil returns in a new skin. For GRENDELS MOTHER lifes. A terrible creature SHE. Woeful wife of wound-weft kin. Mistress of a forgotten race. Vicious and tall. Ancient and withered. Claws that cut. Blades that bleed. Awful oracle of old odiums. Long is their race lost. Long-lost and forgot. Those last sorrowful bannermen of their folk fare acrost fen and marsh. Hating the men that take from them their lands. Ruled in old days by sorcery got from giant-lords. Wicked and cruel. Cursed with hatred. And now there is only one. And SHE come to deal a debt.

SHE comes with glittering eyes to HEOROT HALL. In silence opens gate with gnarled hands. On her back a long black ring-coat. In her fist a crooked knife. Silent is SHE as SHE comes. Tho not silent enough.

Tho the drinkers lie in dreams and drool they awake to hear the door. Hinges loud and crooked still from the grapple with GRENDEL. Hisses SHE and lunges. War-men scramble for spear and shield. No time to don mail. No time for helms. Metal screams and men bellow. They are clumsy and SHE is swift. Cuts limbs. Bites flesh. A thousand men cannae best her. An army falls to her blade. Crunch. Crack. Snicker-snack. Screams.

From the fray bursts ÆSCERE dressed only in dream-dress. His spear of spells he wields. Its wooden shaft is thick with paint and knifings. Curses he proclaims as he wades through wounded warriors. But no great meeting is this as it is with BEOWULF. He nears. Gods on his lips. And he is snatched. Taken in troll-claw and tossed into cold night. SHE fears the great host of the hall. Mayhaps SHE is not unkillable. Yet takes SHE in her flight the kicking corpus of HROTHGARS wizard-fellow.

BEOWULF is not there. He is housed in another hall. Doing as men do when their blood is hot and their skin wet with need. If he is here perhaps the battle-wife does not take the rune-friend. But he is abed.

HROTHGAR is sone told of the tragedy. Tears tear his face. Exhausted from feast and fuck he cannae hold his anguish. He cries out at the bloody wreck of his men. At the capture of his close companion.

This BEOWULF hears. Tho he hears not the slaughter. His men he calls and in a loud troop they storm the hall. Dressed in shimmering rings and bold caps. They trudge through the blood and moaning maimed. Trudge towards BEOWULFS third father. 'Needs ye another feat?' smirks the saving sailor. Already proud is he. Tho not yet a monster.

'Be not so smug northman. Doom drowns us once more. And we are sorrow-sick with luck. My friend. Battle-brother. Rune-lord. Wisdom-whisperer. ÆSCERE. Is dead. No greater warrior ic know. No braver master of the van. ÆSCERE is as a man should be. Yet now he is undone and his breaths unbreathed.' HROTHGARS voice is thick with tear-snot.

He continues. His gaze cast o'er cripples and corpuses. 'Here in this hall ye call safe comes death. Murdrum comes to innocent men. The floor is slick with it. Ye. With terrible toughness. Ye grip GRENDEL to the ground. Break him. Beat him. He deserves this. For his crimes. Yet a new avenger comes. SHE is awful. Great and bitter. So many here have seen new grief from her. SHE brings back a passion-pall of pain.

'Son. Ye call thyself son. A true son of mine dies to see a job done. Finished. No more blessings ye earn of me whilst HEOROT bleeds. No gifts. None. GRENDEL steals my patience and the MOTHER ignites my ire.'

The wizened throne-thegn withers now. Shoulders shrink. 'Men of mine say they see two such shapes. On the moor. Wanderers. Unhomed. Monstrous and tall. Outlaws by dint of their troll-race. A woman and her whelp. Witch-wife and un-thing child. UR-lords of the before. This lesser. This crooked man. This is GRENDEL. Their race knows no fathers but fens. No mothers but magicians.

'These two home near here. A lake. It boils with blood when GRENDEL dies. Men see it. It is always cold at this lake. And the trees near are evil. By night the waters burn with warlock-fires. Water fires. Who kens such? None ken how deep the lake. Not e'en stags afeared of the hunter will plunge within. Sooner die by arrow he than face that monster-mere. Wicked waves and worser winds harry the shore. The water is black and storms are drawn e'er to it.

'Go ic beg. Relearn my love. Ye ken little of that places terrors. Ic wish ye have no need to seek there. But ye must. If HEOROT shall be free. Make sacrifice before ye leave. Beg protection. Ic promise to outdo e'en the gifts ic gift already should ye succeed.'

The man BEOWULF smiles wider. 'No wards need ic. By might alone ic best GRENDEL and so too it shall be with MOTHER.' A great speech follows this. Of death and glory. And when it is done e'en HROTHGAR smiles. 'And when tis done ic shall return to thy warm arms. And to WEALTHEOWS.' He kens no irony in his promise. For how can he know?

The wave-lords steed now is settled. Braided and bridled. The trope is gathered. Men both of ECGTHEOWS SON and others. Some are of HROTHGARS hall. With this vengeance-venture goes UNFERTH. HROTHULF. HRETHIC and HROTHMUND. E'en HROTHGAR rides.

The priest goes as well. Says to Beowulf. 'GOD loves those who revenge on SATANS brood.' They call their god GOD as if there is no other. SATAN is a giant and a traitor. He has many children. Broken and foul like dwarfs. 'Ic revenge meself on all evil.' smirks BEOWULF. 'GOD gifts blessings to those he loves. Take this quest as crusade and name GOD when the bitch is dead.' the fat priest says. Crusade is a war to waste good men and is not for family nor for code.

They make no sacrifice. Methinks they should.

Magnificent astride is terrible BEOWULF. The horse is dwarfed by his stony thighs. Others are glad to follow him. Their path is clear. The MOTHER leaves deep boot prints in the mud. Streaks ÆSCERES blood for miles. To the dark land. The boiling lake. Goes the unkind unsouler of UNFERTHS OTHER.

Tales are whispered of the many mighty deeds of the rune-thegn. Now unlifing. BEOWULF likes not this praise of other men and offers tales of his own. Do ye hear the tale of the bear he wrestles? The nest of gnome-things he fires? The slighting of war-foes hames and bedding of princesses? The far lands his water-fort sees? All these and more they hear of and are silent. A man is proud of his deeds and makes others ken.

These nobles. These gilded getters of gore. They ride up rock-lands. Steep hills. Trot o'er stone ways. Tight corridors of cliff close them in and snakes slither before them. HROTHGAR goes with BONDSMAN BEOWULF to scout the path. And there they find twisted treacherous trees. Black with sharp needles. They crouch o'er wicked stones. Black and in strange shapes. There is no joy in this deadly domain. A kingdom of foemen. A red lake bubbles and churns.

The riders know terror now. True fear to fracture bone. Like as ic nor ye e'er see. The place burns with nightmares and the air chokes with death-thoughts. It is in this pall of weak mind that the leavings of ÆSCERE are found. Near the warm-spring shore lies the beloved friends head. Shorn from shoulders. Men weep to see the empty eyes. HROTHGAR KING falls from his saddle to cradle the corpus-crown. Kiss its cold cheeks.

The mere wells with pride to hear the grief. BEOWULF has might in body and in mind. Blows he his mighty horn time and again. War-sound susurrus. But his fellows are weak of breast. They tremble and fall on their asses. They are not men like BEOWULF.

Wurm-things and dragon-ilk surge in the brackish brine. Water-foes of all shapes. The mere is sick with them. And the cliffs. And the dark wood. Hatred of sun runs like blood in their bellies. The war-horn too shivers their spines and sends them scuttering into the dark. The fluttering flight brings some courage to the company and one man raises his bow. That war-branch cuts a serpent throat. Scores its stomach. This brings men back to being men.

Ring-men rush into the rapids. Spear and sword slash and cut. Render the slain serpent split. BEOWULF watches with pride as he dons his heavy chain-skin. He is aided by the priest. Who says prayers and speaks of GOD. The wanderer-prince cares neither one way nor another. He needs no blessing to house his heart. His brilliant bascinet he rests upon his brow. A point to lead his dive into cursed currents. No edge will pierce those plates. Reaches he now for his shining sword.

But black UNFERTH stays his hand. He does not leap into the crush of killing. His own sword he draws. Ancient and iron. He holds it out. His hands outstretched. One open near the tip. One clutches the hilt. Waves and war are etched upon it. Terrible unhuman UR-men with dark daggers. Serpents kiss the blade. Gold is in the oaken hilt and slaughter in its mien. Runes mark it. 'It is called HRUNTING. Tho it knows other names. It is old. Ancient. Yet sharp as sin. Its bite is poison. War-blood and kin-blood scar it. Ne'er does it fail a user chosen. Too long do ic hold it. Ic would be done of it. And if any arm shall slay the mere-wife it shall be this.' BEOWULF reaches and grips the thing. Hefts it. The priest hisses to see it done. Recoils. 'How came ye by this?' asks GRENDELS DOOM. He likes the weight. The cruel sheen. 'Twas a gift. Unasked.' UNFERTH will say no more. He is pale like a corpse. But smiles with true joy. Winces at BEOWULFS fate. BEOWULF does not thank him. It is not a thing he should be thanked for.

'Remember GOD my son.' begs the priest. They call themselves father. Everyone is their son or their daughter. BEOWULF looks to him but is without words. It is unlike him. Unlike a man. To be so silent afore his quest.

The giant wades. Grey sword high. Wades past the frantic fury of his fearful friends. The greedy waters swell up to greet him. Swallow him. Cold water entombs him. He descends.

Long time he swims. Encumbered by iron. And when he finds the bottom SHE waits in the weeds.

Ne'er in all her long residence beneath the waves does a man come to visit. With strong lungs SHE rushes out to mete him. He is huge. Yet so is SHE. With terrible troll-claws SHE binds him. Grips him tight. Iron nails rip at him. Steely teeth gnash. But his coat holds strong. Helm unharmed. So tightly has the coat-smith bound the rings that not e'en MOTHERS magnificent maul-fists tear him. Yet he cannae escape. Captive of the creature. He is taken towards her cave. Lair of lesser folk. So great is her grapple that he may not e'en swing grey HRUNTING. And to see his weakness sea-beasts come.

Tusked seal-things and vengeful snakes. Angered for the loss of their kin. Fall on BEOWULF. Look to fell BEOWULF. In the confused slurry of scales and slicing tongues the MERE-WIFES fetters slip lose. BEOW-ULFS rings strain to withstand the onslaught. Some drift lose. Torn free by dragon-fish. So thick is the sea of his foes that still HRUNTING is unswung. He does not cry out. Tho his skin bleeds. His lungs burn. He swims and struggles until finally he is free.

He finds that no more is he in the mere. Free-set from swarming snakes. A broad cave is here. Craven cavern for the SEA-WITCH. The sounds of wild water beat against the high ceiling. BEOWULF strides from the pool he enters from. All is dark. Now light. Spell-fires flare in the depths. Stones show bright and he blinks. Shields his face with UNFERTHS ARM.

The brutes eyes settle. His arm lowers. And there is the SHE-FOE. The widow-wight. Taker of vengeance. Son-stolen slayer-queen of the land of monsters. Fearsome is SHE. Tall. Gaunt. Rimmed by the light. Her lean muscles ripple under dry skin. Her limbs are like the roof-beams of HROTHGARS hall. The door-bar that locks the gate. Iron and ancient. Sweating with sin.

BEOWULF should make a brilliant speech. Yet does not. He is weary. Frustrated. This is new. The black-haired hag-bitch shrieks and lunges. He can swing his gifted sword. Yet he still has pride. And defeats GRENDEL with flesh alone. He sheathes the blade. It whispers as it goes. He draws his fists and growls. Feels somehow he must prove himself a man. Ne'er does he feel this before.

His thick thumbs. Driven by wide thews. They drive for her scalp. Her eyes. Tear at her throat. Rip at lithe arms. Yet no damage he deals. Her witch-knife slides and slickers. Finds openings in the ring-cape. Makes new ones. BEOWULF is unmanned. Feels weakness. BEOWULF hates BEOWULF. Something draws at his boundless brawn. He thinks it the cavern-creature's cantrips. Ic can tell ye it is not. He is desperate. The fist-fighter seeks sword. Abandons pride. This is a different man than fights GRENDEL.

Reaches he for HRUNTING. That elder curse-wrought thing. Bloody fingers grip cold wood that burns like ice. He thinks for a moment not to draw it. Mayhaps to die. Wrent to flesh-strips. Stripped to bone. He wonders why he fears the sword. Ic ken why. Ye shall as well. If ye do not already. No hope is in his veins. Bodily he is thrown against a stony wall. Ribs crack. Break. Blood is in his mouth.

And there by his hand is another option. Like a mystical lord-gift. Tumbled from some deep hoard. A new sword. Great it is. Nigh as tall as BEOWULF. Gold-handled. Terror-sharp. Rune-set and lord-worthy. Its warm glow lights the hole. It is a safe sword. A shining sword. BEOWULF reaches for it. But an arm-wound stays him. Pains him. Begs a bellow from BEOWULFS belly. A man would try once more. Save himself from fate. But BEOWULF is unmanned by riches curse-bestowed.

HRUNTING flies from fyrd-fighters fetters. Sings a high song of fury. Death. Death it brings. It hungers and it devours. BEOWULF. O BEOW-ULF. He is damned. Why does he not take the great giant-blade? Why must he become slave to unluck? UNFERTHS GIFT shines black and Beowulf smirks. A bastard he shall be towards MOTHER.

SHE is on the ground. Up once more. Claws grasping. Grip catching. But SHE is not furious enough. That malice-made mother of monsters. With a black anger. A cold hatred. BEOWULF swings the humming dark blade. GRENDELS MOTHERS long knife does naught to parry the blow. Skitters into the dark. Fleeing from foul fingers. HRUNTING sings as it breaks flesh. Chews muscle. Severs spine. SHE is dead. Tho her body does not know it for a few moments more. Twisting and thrashing and falling limp. And UNFERTHS NAIL gurgles happily at claiming its prey.

A faint light lights the cave from the abandoned hero-blade. But HRUNT-ING looks on it and it fades as if twere ne'er there. It is forgot by BEOWULF. His eyes shine in the dark with a wicked new light.

With this new night-sight the prince of the NORTH seeks and seethes. A voice he cannae ken tells him to revenge the wounds dealt. To do unto the mere-wife as is done unto BEOWULF. And unto GRENDEL. If he can be found. Do unto him as is done to HEOROT.

On the witch-wifes corse he deals countless cuts. A furious feast his greedy gore-getter takes of her flesh. Swamp-withered flesh churning and turning into red lumps. Snick. Snack. Slip and schluck. HRUNTINGS belly is ne'er full. BEOWULF stands o'er the gristle of GRENDELS kin. He is black with blood. And his black blade cries for more. His breath comes heavy in his chest and innards wet his lips. He turns and searches the cavern for new carrion to cut.

The troll-shell he finds. It leans against a wall. Huddles in a hollow of rock. Weak and dead. Made small by his wound. Cowering in death as if to hide from greater doom. BEOWULF grins to see it. The defenseless thing. A man takes his foes head. And this BEOWULF does. But first he does great ills to the body. His sword slicing great rents in breathless breast. Penetrating the sinner. Again and again. Until GRENDEL too is only meat. What was once a great head slips from its shoulders. Falls from its weight. Tendons cracking. Bones shivering to dust. HRUNTING shivers in the hearthguards hand.

Above. On the shore of the boiling lake. Up here under the sky the men of HEOROT despair. They see a great geyser of blood mark the waters surface. They know the sun travels too far for a man to breathe water. 'Alas. My son joins my greatest of friends. Both victims to the cannibal-crone.' laments HROTHGAR KING. He orders wine given to the mere. Rich red to follow his son beyond the veil of death. With sadness they make to depart.

'We shall stay,' says one of the foreign fighters. For they still wish to see their master return. Tho they too know him to be gone. 'Ic too shall stay.' declares the gristian. For he beliefs BEOWULF blessed. HEALFDANES SON nods. He kens grief. 'Ic go then to prepare for HELS next visit.' Those men leave. UNFERTHS eyes hold salty tears. There is no hope for BEOWULF.

Below the slayer breathes slower. Wets his hands with gut-water. With one fist he lifts GRENDELS heavy head. Cut and crushed. A soaking tangle of unbound flesh. There is not enough of the MOTHER to claim.

Aimlessly he wanders. Lost after the gluttony of violence. In dark chambers he trudges. Heavy sword and heavy head in hand. Finds he the treasure hoard of the HEL-foes. Masses of coins. Daggers and helms. Stolen fortunes to drown many men. He sits and runs silfer through his fingers. Watches it and smiles. Shining discs glittering in his eyes. Yet he takes none. Stands after a time and leaves all the riches of below. Any man would take his share. Take it and be rich. Ic doubt ye can resist such treasures. It is right to love coin. But BEOWULF hears now only the call of misery.

His curiosity is settled. His morbid eye-greed. He returns to the pool. His feet stomp through GRENDEL and his MOTHER. Disrespect worthy foes. HRUNTING sighs and is sheathed.

His strong arms are before him. BEOWULF dives. Swims up through turgid waters. The water-weres flee him. See a greater ill than the ill he undoes. The water churns about him. E'en the waves wish to be rid of him. So thick with gore is he that he ne'er again will be clean. His violent head crests the mere. Hair like wound-rags. Bloody. Tangled. Monsters maw in his massive mitts.

Those broad shoulders breach the water and are met with cheers. Strong men wade into the waves to hug tightly their smiling lord. So joyous are they to see him lifing that at first they do not see the mangled mind-crown. He leaves it in the shallows as he lets his love-bonded spearmen unhelm and uncoat him. Strip dented steel and shredded rings from his rippling chest. His skin is happy to be free in the cold air.

The fat priest comes and praises GOD. The other men. Greater men. They tell him GOD does not bring this might. That only BEOWULF is the king of these killings. They laugh and look to their captain for confirmation. But he only smiles in his grim way. This the men take as agreement and the priest as piety.

The mighty man makes no manly speech at all. His mind dwells on misery.

As they make to march for HEOROT. These men do not ride and BEOWULF is too large for many a horse. The sea-captain barks. An angry grunt. His thick finger. Wide and strong. Points to a dark lump in the mud. The tide retreats. Reveals GRENDELS crumpled dome. The men are shocked to silence by the gruesome glory. A spear their master tosses them. A pike on which to mount that terrible trophy. None like to hold it and so they share the burden. Trade the shaft about the whole journey HEOROTS-way.

Come they to HROTHGARS hearth. And drop the hated thing with haste. The spit rolls and its prize leers. The gathered thegns gasp to see the terror. Gasp once more to see BEOWULF standing. Only UNFERTH is unamazed. The speaker semes sick instead. With greeny skin and sunken eyes.

HROTHGAR speaks. To see his otherborn son upright. 'Surely now all can say. All must know. Must. That BEOWULF SON is greatest of princes. All kingdoms. Shall cry thy name. BEOWULF. BEOWULF. Any people is proud to be ruled by ye. Friend. Ye are surely wise as well as strong. To best two fiends. O. All vows ic make to ye are as stone. Son e'er are ye to me. Thy people shall be proud to birth such a hero.

'So many great men fall. Commit treason and murder. Let madness take hold. But ye are unassailable. Ic know a man who betrays his fame. Slays family friend and fortune. Wastes all and is exiled. Becomes lay-fiend and song-foe. He too is a mighty man. Thick and rough. But ye are not he. Ye will not gain strange thoughts now that fame is won. Ic know ye to be generous and kind. Not like him. Proud and loud in right ways. Manly ways. Heed this warning. Tho ic ween ye needs it not. Remain always the man ye now are. And let no thought darken thy mind of mens discomfit. For ye are loved in all lands. Feast only and life with cheer.' The king does not ken the irony he speaks. Is overcome with emotion.

Babbles on. Arms wide. 'Yet do not lose thy wits. E'er be wary of assassins. For love is not forever and someday men may look to undo ye unfairly. O. Ic ne'er wish to think of ye dead. Ne'er cut nor beat nor bled. Always reward those ye love and those ye would have love ye. Gift often and well. If a man fails his sons too will fail. Do not fail. Someday e'en ye shall die. But be known as a good man afore this.

'Look to me. Fifty years ic am king here. All this time my strong arm and strong love keep these folk. No terrible enemy have ic. Until GREN-DEL. Hateful GRENDEL. O how ic hate him. E'en now. Yet ic outlife him and look on his skull. For a son ic take is a worthy warrior. Come. Tell us of thy troubles. Regale us. A feast ye shall have and many gifts more with the morn. Speak and hold us with thy tales.'

HROTHGAR is proud and breathless. It is not a great speech. But it is a speech. Men gift speeches.

BEOWULF says naught.

There is a long pause. All wait for their champions words. He only stands. Looks for mead. Looks for women. Moves to take ale from a waiting earl and gulps it greedily. The gathered folk are silent. But soon HROTHGAR claps and calls for food and feast is joined.

It is a great feast. But the time for feasts in this telling passes sone. This grim tale becomes grimmer still.

And when the night is aged grey-locked HROTHGAR moves to retire. He is weary. Tells his wife to join him. But she still basks in the glow of hero-love. O that she joins him now. That hero-love should remain the same with the HOUSE OF SCIELD.

As the torches gutter and the benches fill bitter BEOWULF finds weal-weary WEALTHEOW. She remembers his former honor. Thanks him more. Sees him as a friend. He speaks now some of his few words that night. 'If ye seek to thank me well ye have treasures any man will value.' 'Ic gift ye many gems already.' she says. But the brute. The hateful self-hating hearth-thegn. He clutches her to him. Grabs her roughly. Fondles and grasps. Kisses and bites without care. This is no way to treat with women. He wishes only to dull his pain. To drown the UR-woe with sex. She is no friend to him then. Only flesh.

WEALTHEOW. Disrespected queen. She does not cry out. Cannae cry out. So unthought-of is the assault. Woe for her. Woe for all peace in the NORTH. If any see they say naught. They are cowards. BEOWULF too is made coward. Takes with fist what his unmanly tongue cannae earn. Perhaps his words can sway her. Yet not now. The man who can sway the SPOUSE OF SCIELD is dead. Tho that man will not make this choice. That man will not struggle with her belts and reach rough fingers under red raiment.

But WEALTHEOW is not defeated. She is in many ways more man than her mangler. A knife she holds. Meant for meat. Her claws tangle in his broad chest-fur. Her throat thrusts from his thirst. They are a knot. Against a high bench they writhe. And as he seeks to make a sin of her she strikes out. Up. The knife fillets his fair face. A ragged line from jaw to peak. Skin rips. Blood flows. The eye sears with pain. As he bellows and bitches she forces herself free. Flees to the fortress of her fleece bedding. Only when she is safe. Alone with slumbering HROTHGAR. Only now does she curse their ghoulish guest. But he is already cursed.

The brute. The coming killer-king. The bastard BEOWULF. He rages in silence when his prize is fled. Flees the shame to his bed in another hall. Why does he do what he does? He does not know. Hates it. But will do it again. He hates himself into slumber and slumbers like the dead. And in the morn he is awoken by a black raven. Like that which watches his brother HAETHCIN hang. The sky is bright but he does not see it. Orders his men to oar. UNFERTH dies that night.

The king is saddened by the news of his aide-mans death. Tho he is a bitter man. His better days long gone. And so HROTHGAR does not at first know the northmen mean to away. When this is known to him he rushes out with fresh tears to bid farewell.

WEALTHEOW is there as well. But her tears are absent. She does not tell her husband of the curse-worthy carnal war-makings of their guest. For what man will trust his wife before his son? So she is quiet and witch-wicked with her presence. This is not a good way but it is the way things are done. Men are proud. This is good. But many are too proud and this makes them cruel. It is HROTHGARS only fault.

HROTHGAR SCIELDS HEIR asks to know what is meant by the preparations he sees. Tho he kens them to be for leave-taking. He sees BEOWULFS wound but says naught for the look in the giants eye.

'GRENDEL is dead.' says the villain as if the meet is finished.

Yet HROTHGAR prattles on. Tells of the rope what fells UNFERTH. Speaks of love and gifts and glory. But all falls on deaf ears. For BEOWULF is made depression-deaf. And ic will say no more of HROTHGARS very words for his part in this telling is about done. Ic can think of no more reason to tell of that tragic lord.

More tears and treasures are heaped on the warrior-wight but he takes all stoically and makes back towards the shore. All his dozen men are fit in shining helms with glitter-gloved spears. But the march is black for their lords mood. His dark heart. Their sturdy ship waits and they are eager to be done of this place. Many they pass who praise their kits. Yet the men see BEOWULF unblithe and make little greeting.

In the clinking of flashing mail the bold sailors come again to the shore. The wave-guard. Honored lonely sea-watcher. He that greets them once greets them once more. He comes and promises their ship in greater condition than it is left. Praises them for their deeds. For he is old and does not travel to the celebration-feasts. Places he the victory on all the wave-bound men.

In anger. A fury which trembles the watchman. BEOWULF looms above him. In such anger that all the brightness of the sun is forgot. 'Ic slew GRENDEL. Ic slew the WITCH-WIFE. Ic. BEOWULF. No other man.

202

Tell this tale and no other.' And no more words are spoken. No new gifts exchanged.

The ship is heavy with all the gifts of HROTHGAR. And soon made heavier still with fighting men. The load shines as the halls of the gods e'en as poor wicked BEOWULFS heart sinks lower.

Swift is the sail-sleigh of GRENDELS FOE. It sheds surf as a hound rids itself of rain. Rips acrost the ocean-top. It is eager to bring new sorrow to the NORTH. Grim men man it and a dire death-dealer heads it. The timbers at their feet make water-thunder as they leave damned HEOROT behind. No one can stop this iron-prowed carriage of misery until it once more roosts at home.

Its keel cuts the beach like WEALTHEOW cuts her attackers skin. A dark water-wet gash sits on the shore. a dark wave-fortress upon it. A knife which terror sharpens. A water-guard waits here as well and knows BEOW-ULF from his BRECA days. Watches he with fools grin as weary men tether strong ropes from vessel to shore. Bind their bondlord back to his birthing-land. Their spirits are broken by the UR-grim he breathes. HRUNTING hums at the hunters hip. BEOWULF shouts. Commands. Demands his gifts be carried home. Shows no caring for his old friend.

'Do not these gifts go to HIGELAC KING? Brother and master? To be shown and shared?' asks the sea-watcher. He is hurt to be unrecognized.

'They go to my hall.' speaks BEOWULF. Berates the thralls what serve his call. 'Ic and my men go alone to my brother-king.' And soon he leads these broken bondi towards the stoney sea-side hold of HRETHELS blood.

HRETHELS stronghold is mighty. Solid stone where beautiful HEOROT is gold and wood. It sits on a cliff above the white waves. And his wife. Daughter of HÆRETH. She is called HIGD. And is known to be wise and kind. Tho she is very young. Woe that those folk are kin to BEOWULF. She is generous. Set to gift yet more to her husbands horrid he-kith. She is a good queen. Not like the myth-queen MODTHRID.

MODTHRID. She is more as like BEOWULF. Gorgeous and rich. Enough to make any man drool and stiffen. Yet she is cruel. Blood-greedy and self-loathing and tax-taking. Not e'en the marriage to a noble king calms her. Ic think mayhaps she has also an UR-taste to her. A hint of unbecoming to tear her folk asunder. But this is not a tale of MODTHRID. And she is long dead afore BEOWULF befalls the northmen.

They stand now in the hall of ONGENTHEOWS DEATH. That young king. Generous ring-lord. HIGELAC. Brother-friend to BEOWULF. BE-OWULF who now counts no friends. The hall is ready. for the cliff-lord knows his child-companion comes. Benches are made ready. Fires lit. Beer flowing.

All wait smiling for the victors greeting-speech. But BEOWULF only stands. Dark browed. Gazes at HRETHELS throne with lust. Can he be heir of two crowns? King of two kingdoms? He sees only conquest.

'Brother?' asks anxious HIGELAC. 'What occurs? Why such silence when good tidings precede ye?'

BEOWULF grimaces. Ugly with the woman-scar. 'Ye are lord o'er me and ic will sit with ye. Speak as brother tho and not king.'

'Ic love ye and for this ic will do as ye beg.' HIGELAC thinks his kin weary. Kens not the heart replaced by black rot. BEOWULF will have his throne.

The giant. He speaks in short words of what is done. Answers questions but offers naught unbidden. It frustrates his cousin. This is not how men speak.

Whilst they hold their prince-prattle HIGD who is his wife serves the hall. Pours bloody wine in gilded cups. war-spoils waiting to be taken. And she draws BEOWULFS wicked eye. She too appears a war-spoil. His wicked eye burns with the scar of another wine-woman. He does not learn a lesson. No lesson again he learns.

'Ic am glad to see HEOROTS woes dissolved. And ye brother free from harm. Glad am ic to see ye tho ic tell ye not to face that foe. Are ye not fain to be returned?' asks the king. But BEOWULF is done with him.

Goes he towards where king-wife waits. Watches her. Drinks her wine. No gifts he to any man offers. Yet many he accepts. All he sees he claims in mind. And sees he she as chiefest of conquests.

When the hour is late. And HIGELACS head nods with ale. BEOWULF. O bitter BEOWULF. He goes to HIGD. 'Come with me.' say he. 'Share a bed and ic shall show ye how truly a king may perform.' Yet she will have naught of it. Reminds him of his place. The villain snarls and fingers his black blade and promises to claim her for his own.

I c say that HEOROT HALL burns with kin-felling. War and want weaving woe in its woody space. Yet woe also betides the throne of HRETHEL. It is no quick thing. Tho ic will tell it as quick as able. This dark tale grows long and ic wish it were done. Or that ic could only tell of the slaying of GRENDEL once more. Yet ic am begun. And those who do ill deserve no shade from the ire-light of goodly folk.

Whilst BEOWULF covets his brother-uncles throne he moves also to prove himself a man. Takes he a wife. For a man must have a wife he weens. And she fears him. Which is right. For all men fear BEOWULF. She tells others. Tells herself. Tells that she loves him. Yet it is fear. Fear is sometimes close to love.

His wife he treats ill.

In all ways he treats her ill.

Yet a son she bears him. And he also the beast treats ill. Beats him and belittles him. Compares him e'er to others. Naught he does e'er is good enough to BEOWULF. The boy lifes an unhappy short life.

HIGELAC sometimes sees the boys sad life. The boy. His name none remembers. HIGELAC comes to BEOWULF. Says 'The boy is strong. Ic am proud to have this kin.' 'Strong like shit.' says the father. The father hates his son. Resents the compliments gifted him which can instead be BEOWULFS. Resents the pity felt by others for any of his blood. 'Let me foster him. Teach him princely ways in my hame.' says HIGELAC KING. 'This boy has one hame. That hame is mine.' rages brother BEOWULF. Expells his kin-lord from his hall. Accuses his son of unmanning him and shows the boy his black blade.

After the son is born BEOWULF sleeps no more with his wife. Blames her for his own weak will. Unable to raise his rod he rages rutlessly. Many sleepless nights he spends on fen and moor. Red eyes gleaming. Black sword singing. Sheep and dogs he slays and no geld he pays. 'Ic am BEOW-ULF. Lord. All lands ic see are mine and ic make no gifts to lesser men.' His wifes brother he slays for tax-theft and want of wools weave-wage. The woman cries out in anguish. The son lifes in terror.

BEOWULFS golden hair turns black in age and his sin-scar turns purple on his skin. A grim line to show all who view his face the price he pays for unmanly wants.

HIGELAC will not speak ill of kin. Loves what BEOWULF is in youth. But those near him. His wife who hates that fell prince and others. They ken that e'en the king hates the shadow what bears HRUNTING CURSE-BLADE.

BEOWULFS son dies before he is a man. He is broken and bloody at the foot of a cliff. None mark the other wounds on his body. BEOWULF cries not. Comments not. Forgets his son as if he were ne'er had.

BEOWULF is a foul sort. A woeful winner of wars. No loved landlord he. Good men hate him. Yet not all men.

Some men keep hatred in their black breasts. Harbor sin like a sickness. Men who are like to BEOWULFS sons he ne'er had. These cruel kobolds crepe to the hall of GRENDELS FELLER. Warm worn hands and sharpen shining swords near his hearth. This at first is BEOWULFS kingdom.

HIGELACS aides. Wise whisperers of WODENS words. They say to their great sire that his brother does little good for the kingdom. A seed of rot in the rich royal soil. Yet BEOWULFS kin will not decry him. E'en as he is discomfited by his brothers ways he remembers the hard times they have together and the bonds of blood. Blood should not forgive all failings. Yet it does. O it does. And too often.

In the war times that come BEOWULFS wife also dies. Some say it happens when he visits. Home from war. Some say it happens when he is away. Yet she dies. And none know the truth of it.

Before these war-times comes HIGELAC KING to the hall of his kin. Brutal black hall of the bastard BEOWULF. BORNHAIGA is it hight. Beneath BORNHAIGAS broad beams the brother-lord boasts of bounties far asea. BEOWULF listens and his hungry dark heart grows hot. 'What will ye have of me HIGELAC?' the BARON HRUNTINGHAND will not call him king. Sometimes not e'en brother.

'There is a land of much wealth and little war. Such as we ken it. As ic say. Ic will have ye sail with me and captain my carls as we bleed the southrons of their silfer.'

BEOWULF likes much the talk of bleeding. And so he swears to sail.

To that westering southern land they sail. A war-host to shame all wiking fletes. In hard steel rings they come. Gold glisters on prow helm and hilt. Each man a dowry of damage-dealers bears. Death ne'er kens a greater friend. All are bloody-minded. In this wicked voyage all are close to BEOWULFS blind brutish nature. Men laugh as they speak of killing. It is right sometimes for men to be monsters. To kill and ravage and take. BEOWULFS sin is to be so at all times. In war all men are alike. Ic do not judge BEOWULF for what he does in war. Besides those things what no man should do. Not e'en in war.

On those green shores. Those fair foreign shores. The hearthmen of HIGELAC bring fire and fear and felling. They bring death to a kingdom which does not know their names. And in their fury they invite the fierce hatred of the foreign king.

Whilst the victors. The pillagers and plunderers. Feast upon the shore. Unthinking of consequence. A fell force from far fields. Sworn to their enemy. It falls upon their festival to fell and flay. Slaughter comes to the sea-soldiers and their crown-man is quelled with many mighty men. Few survive the revenge-visit. Fleeing bloody into the waves and along the cold cliffs. Scattered to the wind.

Yet BEOWULF lifes. He sees the host stepping in shadows and slips into the surf. Warns none. Warns not e'en kin. His hide is healthy and he will not have it harrowed. Yet also will he not return empty-handed. Thirty mail coats he takes for war-prize and swims he naked towards home. So great is his strength. So awesome the dweomer of HRUNTING. So strong that ne'er he tires until to his home-shore he comes.

He returns to an empty home with an empty heart. He tells none he returns. His mean muscle-men all perish on foreign sand. He is alone. He cries in his hame where should rest grave of son and spouse.

When at last news of the defeat makes land in the kingdom of HRETH-EL BEOWULF goes to the hall of his brother-uncle. Demands audience with the wife-woman he winges for want of. Marriage-daughter of dead HRETH-EL. comfort of dead HIGELAC. 'Why do ye come BEOWULF? Ye are un-welcome. No brother stands to shield ye.' speaks HÆRETHS DAUGHTER.

'The kingdom needs a king.' He looks on the benches and rich rugs as if they are his to despoil.

'The kingdom has a king.'

'HEARDRED?' BEOWULF laughs at mention of his brothers son. 'He is no king. Only a boy. Ic am a man.'

'He is kin of heroes. Ye are a brute and worm.'

'Ic will have ye to wife.'

'Ye will not.'

BEOWULF grins. It is ugly. This grin. 'Weak kings sit not long on thrones. Dead kings may not deny another mans wedding. Boys are weak.'

'Ye are a boy when against BRECA ye swims. This makes thy swim boys work. Afore GRENDEL it is all ye are known for. Ye are a man proud of being a boy.'

BEOWULF is wroth. 'Ic is a man. BEOWULF is e'er a man. The throne is mine. HIGELAC will have it so.'

'He will not.' HIGD blanches not. 'And if thy black blade should touch my son ic shall have all men against ye.'

'Fear not. Ye troublesome bitch-queen. It shall not be HRUNTING which is sullied by thy sons gut-filth. All of HRETHEL-LAND will ken the weakness of that prince. And when he is cold ye will be punished with my marriage-bed.'

BEOWULF is banished now from the high hall. No man can speak such to royalty. He lifes only for his kinship to the dead king. Yet greed and lust grow fetid in his breast.

And as if drawn to the fiends friendliness forlorn woe-getting war comes again to HEARDREDS feof.

In the NORTH-KINGDOM. North more e'en than the lands of BEOW-ULFS youth. OTHERE KING dies. OTHERE is son to ONGENTHEOW. ON-GENTHEOW who runs red on HRETHELS shores. Who slays HÆTHCIN and makes HIGELAC king. Ic speak of him when first this tale I begin.

Long years hatred festers in the cold halls of EOFERS foe. OTHERE will not break his men on HEARDREDS walls. Yet his brother ONELA. ONELA THRONE-TAKER who does what BEOWULF cannae. ONELA shall.

The excuse he brings for revenge-taking is the flight of his nephews two. When ONLEA steals the crown-seat they flee to HEARDREDS arms. Beg protection. And this HEARDRED gifts. EADGILS and EANMUND. These are their names. The unfortunate prince-sons to ONGENTHEOWS house. They are gifted warmth in HRETHELS hall and this their fathers brother shall not abide.

Revenge for ONGENTHEOW ONELA calls this war. Claims HEARDRED captures his brothers sons. All ken the truth of it. See ONELAS greed. And HEARDRED. Goodly HEARDRED. He marches men to war to preserve the princelings power and save their skins.

A mighty war it is. It semes all wars in old stories are great. Yet this one truly is. Walls topple. Villages burn. Corpses pile high to the sun. Tears flow like rivers. Heroes are made and slain. Whole sagas are in this war. Beginning and end. And BEOWULF is glutted on this slaughter-feast.

And again is BEOWULF too close to tragedy. In battle at last the host of HEARDRED clashes with the force of his foe and BEOWULF fights in the van beside his bold brother. Yet his brother is slain and he lifes. ONELA it is said is not near the king when he dies. Yet BEOWULF is. It can be another man. An enemy. Who severs that sires spine. Yet all thoughts turn to the bastards black blade. Wicked HRUNTING.

And for the brothers. Wronged heirs seeking solace in the arms of their once-foes son. One lifes and the other dies. EANMUND is slain by his cousin WEOHSTAN. WEOHSTAN who later sits on BEOWULFS black court. Court of villains.

With HEARDRED dead. No son to take his place. Many think for ONE-LA to take the feofdom for himself. Yet as he sits on stolen throne he calls for one man. Ye know what man. How he knows him none can for certain say. Yet there are those. Many. Who wonder at the gifts ONELA gifts to BEOWULF so soon after his kin-kings death. When BEOWULF stands so close when unseen sword slays the sword-sire of the besieged soldiers. We know BEOWULF to be a villain. Ye and ic. So ye should not be surprised to hear the conqueror gifts his enemys seat to BEOWULF. Who takes it and becomes king.

That is not a good king.

To his court come many dark men. Like as to the unsons he keeps before the wars. And finally he takes HIGD to wife. Becomes forced father to EOFERS SISTER. Tho she fights. Cruel men come. Black-hearted men. Men like WEOHSTAN. And in his canker-court. Where he levies taxes unfair and flays men. Hangs men. Beheads men. Skewers men. For no offense at all. In this place he forces EADGILS to stay.

As a pet he keeps him. Pitiful prisoner to that pale prince. Wishes he to go home. Yet no home does he have. His uncle speaks often with BEOW-ULF. ONELA laughs and plots and goes ahunting with BEOWULF. Throws the bones from the beasts he devours at his nephew to mock him. ONELA sees HRETHELS hall as his. Sees BEOWULF as pet like BEOWULF treats EADGILS. Yet BEOWULF only pretends to abide.

He calls EADGILS. Maligned EADGILS. To his hall. His ill-mannered men leer at the fallen lordling. BEOWULF calls him 'enemy' yet says it like a friend. Tells OTHERES SON of a plan. And EADGILS is so broken and eager to be gone from that place that he agrees.

And so when next ONELA comes BEOWULF drugs him. Poison in his drink. And whilst he slumbers EADGILS runs him through. Revenge taken in a craven manner. EADGILS is called king and heralded home. Yet kens he that this is only by his captors grace. He is a broken man. And tho BE-OWULF ne'er calls he kens him to be his master.

This is the kingdom BEOWULF makes. The baleful blighted land he calls his until his hair turns white. Black eyes gleaming. Crown heavy on hateful head. O woe to those what owe him fealty. O woe that ic begin this terrible tale.

T his tale is terrible. Yet it nears its end. Ic need a break from BEOWULFS bastardry tho. Do ye not? There are other things ic can speak of. Must speak of for the storys end to make sense. It will be good to breathe easier for a moment and better still to know BEOWULFS deserved dire doom.

Ages ago. Long before BEOWULF. Before HRETHEL. Before SCIELD. Long long ago. A great race of men dies.

Ic ken not whether they are a goodly race or wicked. No man kens. All that is known is that they are rich. And therefore mighty. And that they perished to a man.

And that man takes the treasury of his folk and builds a coffer. Or finds one. A sturdy cave deep below a stony hill. Takes he this treasury to the coffer and keeps it. Sits upon it in glittering greed. Starves on the feast of gold.

Some say these men are kin to wicked giants. Or cursed by them. That this hoard is HEL-like and hungry for hale hearts. It is like what HRUNTING is but in many times. They say. Ic cannae say tho. Ic say HRUNTING is worse. Yet both bring sorrow.

Alone and dying the man bemoans loud. Many sad words in an old tongue. That is what people says. What ic hear. If it is true ic do not know how any man today can know those words. When this man is starved the hoard holds itself unheld for many and many long years. It is merely a myth by the time the TERROR comes to claim its wealth.

This TERROR. As great and deadly as any GRENDEL. Dwells in darkness and hatred. Fumes and despises in the depths until she too is forgot. None remember clear the TERROR her treasury nor the true temperers of that trove. It is merely a cave to men.

In time men come again. In new kingdoms. New races. The land flourishes and suffers. BEOWULF takes his terrible throne. His bastards bench. Yet common men still life common lifes. But ic am not yet ready to return to BEOWULF KING.

Let me first speak of a common man. A man whose mistake brings BEOWULFS death. A good thing. But at great cost.

This common man is poor. Many are. Ic am poor. Mayhaps ye are. Tho ic shall not judge. He is poor and no job suits him. And so he begins the robbing of graves.

And sees he a fire upon a far hill. He thinks it a rich barrow. For sometimes fires are lit on the burial-hills of great lords. Yet it is a fire caused by the TERROR. He does not know this. Yet it is true. The TERROR draws on the sorcery in her mighty lungs to make a torch of that treasure-tor.

Comes he to the dark down. Rife with rock. Riddled with runnels. Tunnels deep into the earth. The light which lures him hence is gone. He lights a torch. Descends into doom.

Timidly the taker of trinkets tip-toes towards the TERROR. He smells her rank must but assumes it the scent of deep earth. She scents him as well. But waits. Wanting to watch him. Yet neither sees the other. For she is so massive. So still and stony. That he thinks her a boulder or a cliff-face in the dark. And he is light-footed and night is his lover.

With clever foot he paces past the place where she rests her head. Ne'er knowing his heart is sick with dread tho he kens no reason. Yet this day is not his doom. He spies a shining cup. Golden goblet garbed with gems. He takes it. Wants more but is overcome with worry. 'Perhaps ic shall return.' he thinks to himself. Tho he ne'er does return.

Instead the TERROR follows in his wake. Wrecks town. Farm. Brings high hall down. She sweeps down from that pit-hill what rests above the crashing waves. Bursts from the hidden door her enemy uncovers. Seeks she the man what robs her. In this she is like as any man. Revenge-reveling. Mad at misdeeds against her. Like a snake from its burrow she slinks from her hole and takes to the skies to bring death and terror. All for a cup. No better in use to the one in my hand nor yours. Yet gold. And cursed with greed.

Many good men are slain. Handsome wifmen. Strong children. The greed of one man ruins a nation. She comes in the night and leaves black bones of men and halls in her wake. Is this curse because of BEOWULFS sins? Or does this damnation come no matter the king? We shall ne'er know. For BEOWULF is king. And the TERROR comes.

Ic delay as long as ic might. But the time has come once more to speak of that black villain BEOWULF. Who drinks and laughs with cruel carls as his kingdom crumbles. He sits in his hall. Once his brothers. And kisses his brothers wife. And does not hear the cries of the commons. Or hears them and revels in their misery.

Yet e'en a careless king may not forever ignore his peoples plight. Lest he lose his throne. BEOWULF may e'en allow this in his madness tho. Yet he has servants who love their power and do not yet have wholly black breasts.

There is a man in his court. More a boy. WIGLAF hight. Nephew. He is not a good man. But better than most malicious BEOWULF loves. He sees the pain which ruins all folk. Resolves to solve it.

'Father-friend.' He says this to the man who kens no true friendship. 'A terror tills thy tithe-lands. Bold bondsmen burn. Their purses set alight. A river of gold ye know now. But sone e'en silfer will seem dear. My men. Boys ic bring to drink with. Ye know them. They find a man who claims to pillage the horror-hill which houses the hold-harrier. Ic think mayhaps he kens how this ends. For he is there when it begins. Shall ic bring him ye?' And silent BEOWULF smolders assent.

And so the thief is brought. And he tells what he does in the TERRORS tor. And what little he kens of what comes after.

'What is to be done with him?' asks WIGLAF. And his uncle says. 'He is a thief. Unfix his fingers so no further foulings may this fool foist.' And he is thrown into the mud outside the high hall with bloodied hands.

'Ic shall gather a fyrd. An army of awesome angry brutes to fell the fearsome foe what ruins our realm.'

'My realm.' growls BEOWULF. Yet also he refuses the gathering of a great host. And begins he to prepare to face the dragon.

O aye. She is a dragon. Do ic not say this? Well tis true. A scaly sinful snake. Firey and winged. She is the TERROR and her anger is awful.

For three hundred years she slumbers. Only rising. Golden gut glinting. When her hoard is disturbed. In anger she ravages and wrecks. Yet before the thief is e'en brought to the wicked king she stops. Retreats. What is the cause of this mercy? Ic will tell ye.

BEOWULF orders a shield made. Linden bound and sheathed in iron. A broad bulwark against the breath-burn of the beast. He laughs at those who tell him to gather his armies. He has no fear of a dragon. Instead he calls to him eleven men. Amongst them WIGLAF and two bitter sons of the men what see him grapple GRENDEL.

Nigh dead they find the terrified thief outside their masters hall. They all arrayed in grey rings and horned helms. With stout spears and brutal blades. They force him to show them the way to a crashing sea. And WIGLAF cuts the throat of the gold-getter. His blood blending with the susurrating storm that assaults their landing. He is free of lifes horrors.

On that high and windy cliff sits the cruel king. A part of him feels the nearness of the jotunn-gold ic think. He holds his black blade. HRUNTING fills his black eyes. Urges him on. Mayhaps a part of him sees his death. He resists. For the first time in many years. In his heart he seeks to deny UNFERTHS GIFT. Thinks he to cast it away. Bury the sorrow-arm. The steel barrow-filler. Bury it in dark waves.

Yet he must face a dragon and kens not how to face serpent without sword. And no sword is as near at hand as HRUNTING. Unlike in facing HROTHGARS BANE he is buried in layers of mail. No trust has he in his own skin. He says no words. Only stands in his rich war-garb.

The men he brings grow anxious as their lord marches on the wyrm-hill. Yet he commands them stay. And he raises his dark shield. And with HRUNTING he beats it. And soon the others join. And the clanging fills the shore and echoes in the TERRORS halls.

It is a longsome time. Too long for the mens craven spirits. Afore the wyrm crests the ridge. Yet when she does so she does so quietly. Squirms from her den to observe in silence. She is a fearsome sight. But her silence makes the master of men fill with malice. Tho he himself is grim and quiet.

'Our master. Noble mighty BEOWULF. Giant amongst men. Comes to slay ye. Villain. Come and face death.' calls WIGLAF. He speaks more than BEOWULF. Tho he can speak e'en more than he chooses to. 'We come expecting battle. Yet if ye are too weak. Too frail. We shall slaughter ye as livestock. Ic hear dragons are great beasts. Fearsome foes. Worthy of the WORLD-SERPENT. Yet all ic see is a slippery eel. No fire-breast within.'

Yet the serpent is not stirred. She lowers her sharp skull. And her mighty maw droles flame. 'Heed me. cursed king.' she intones. 'Already ye carry a doom. Yet to slay me will earn ye a doom of death. A greed of eld things chokes ye and a greed of eld things chokes me. Leave now and life thy sad life. The iron left by the wander-folk. The sky-slayers. Their coin and kit rots hearts like molten steel melts flesh. My anger is roused and ic am ashamed. Ic once more am victim to my curse. Yet take no vengeance lest ye win an otters ring.'

At this bold BEOWULF laughs. Tho his men cower. He hits his shield once more. 'Ic hold no fear of curses. No curse e'er harms BEOWULF.' Yet we ken that this is not true. The purple scar on his face marks the death of the true thew-thegn of lore. He laughs. 'Ic will kill ye. No woman scares me.'

If the TERROR is made sad by the words she shows it not. Instead she opens wide her maw and releases a river of boiling breath. It spills down the hillside and digs channels in the stone. Men cry out and scamper back. Yet not BEOWULF. Who stands behind his sturdy shield and weathers the snake-storm. The heat harries his hair yet he holds. Here is an echo of the man BEOWULF is when first he comes to HEOROT HALL. E'en as he pursues foolish glory. Do ye think he means to save his memory?

A real man stands alone against the flame. But BEOWULF bellows for aid. Wishes for man-meat to shield him. But they cry out and flee. They are no more than their master. BEOWULF KING curses his carls. Yet one remains. It is WIGLAF.

WIGLAF is a young man. He is a son to WEOHSTAN and a cousin to BEOWULF. Can become a great man. But he stands beside his uncle. And becomes damned. Such a strong boy with a strong voice. It is sad to ken his fate. He stands bravely. But ic wish that he does not.

Boldly BEOWULF advances. The proud pain-pusher pursues the protean wyrm. His shield wards him from her breath. And with a wild cry he swings HRUNTING. The singing sin-sword strikes the serpent.

Yet it cuts not. Such a swing will fell any troll. Rend any armor. Yet the treacherous iron turns in his hand before it strikes and slides off shimmering scale. Sadly does not shatter. BEOWULFS arm is bruised but he can still prepare as the serpent once more rears. Her belly fills with fire. Pregnant with steam-spit. She belches blood. Hot heart-ichor. It sears flesh. Cracks bone. The sword-arm of the king. Thick meat-branch. Which deals so much death. Earns so much glory. It withers and melts. HRUNTING clatters to the stone. And the warrior falls beside it. Teary eyes pleading the black spell-steel to undo the wound it earns. BEOWULF sees his death.

'Ic see thy blade WIGLAF.' she says. The curse-power in her grants her forsight. 'Lay it down and leave ye. With BEOWULF gone ye can become a good man. Great man. Better than BEOWULF e'er is. Yet if ye march to his aid thy fate shall be as cruel as thy king. Ic beg ye. Choose to walk away.'

'Ic do not fear ye dragon. Yet it semes ye fear me.' growls BEOWULFS nephew.

The TERROR. Her warning is in true faith. She wants the UR forgotten. Wants the darkness ended. But WIGLAF has a mans brashness. She sees that this is the end. It is not the end she wishes. But the end the curse brings.

It is often right for a man to stand with other men. Especially should they be kin. Yet ic blame more WIGLAF for his loyalty than the heartless hearthguard which flee the fire.

The dragon belches again. Vomits liquid death on the northman king. Sears and sizzles flesh. BEOWULF cries out and blubbers. He is unmanned and unskinned. WIGLAF cries out with warriors fury. The TERROR too sees her death.

Grips he his linden-board. Draws the blade of EANMUND. By which WEOHSTAN slays its owner. Many goods WEOHSTAN leaves his son. Jewelled helm. Heavy shirt of iron. This sword thought giant-wrought. Tho ic think not. For it bears no curse like HRUNTING. This is the first true test of WIGLAFS will. He trusts his fathers trove to guard him.

Deftly dodges he through the TERRORS black breath. And swings he that ancient blade gainst her silfer scales. This sword. It does not turn away. But hits full force. And shatters. Is destroyed. And lingering flicker-tongues burn his stout shield to ash.

A man must have a weapon. He is worthless without a tole. This is the way of things. So Wiglaf takes up the only harm-dealer at hand. He hefts HRUNTING.

The black blade drinks his blessings. Curdles his king-blood. Fells a prince that ne'er is. HRUNTING claims a new carl. And WIGLAF stands mighty and terrible above tear-drowning burn-checkered BEOWULF.

The squire growls to his master. Judges him for not hefting halberd. The master sputters and chokes. Lifts himself on ruined limbs and digs out a dagger. They stand together before the dragon. Two men unmanned. Furious in their failure.

'Ic will not die here.' declares WIGLAF. 'Not for king nor cowardice.' And with one hand he thrusts his master before him. A betrayal he does not consider until the wicked hilt of HRUNTING he grasps.

The TERROR now. Regretful. She charges in. Scales shimmer. Length coils. Surges from the flames. Seeks hateful men.

Fire-waves wash the men. Sheets of cinder like rain. Death-shrouds of thundering blistering warmth. Her coils lash and writhe between them and through them. The sky is gone. Tis like naught ye nor ic shall e'er see. Thank gods. The searing-storm boils the wicked king in his mail and his dagger hand judders. But he is too hurt to scream. His purple scar stands out on a peeling black face. His failing eyes bubble. His nephew wrests his shield from him.

Yet BEOWULF makes one last strike. As if to prove the strength that in battle snaps steel swords and crumples helms. His dagger reaches out and smites the dragons head. E'en as HRUNTING strives against the beast with heofon-hale skill. As if to mock the man it maligns. But BEOWULF strikes the first true blow. And cuts the serpents eye from her skull. Ic think a part of the man still remembers he is a hero once. The dagger sticks in her skull as she retreats.

She hisses. Roars. An ear-rending sorrow-rage. The land-burner. Fearsome fell-spelled snake. She charges once more. Hot flames spill. A river of funeral fuel. Her sharp fangs pierce BEOWULFS throat. Spill his breath-blood in hot spouts. Waves of dark blood. A storm of swordsmans water.

It it here. Ic hear. That the mighty-thewed monster unmaker is failed by his muscled arms. He has no strength. Little blood. Ye or ic or any man we know is dead if we lose so much blood.

But WIGLAF is yet strong. Tho his arm is black from burns and his beard is kindled to naught. HRUNTING sings. A piercing nightmare sound. It sings as its wielder plunges it deep in the breast of the beast. And as her breath hitches. As she vomits black guts. The flames burn out as a candle snuffed. It is frigid and icy. Jotunn-cold siezes the serpent-mound.

WIGLAF looks on his uncle now with cold eyes. BEOWULF makes as if to speak. Chokes on gristle and gore. His wounds mar his last manly act. The felled kings fingers twist. Itch for his blade. Like a drunk.

WIGLAF enters now the barrow. Leaves BEOWULF KING to the salty sea spray. Steps o'er the serpents snake-spirals. Goes he to witness that ancient armory. Horde of haunted halls.

He returns. Eyes glittering with greed of gold. His kin is dead. The dragon felled. Yet he cares not. Cares only for gold. Reaches he for the rich mans throat and takes he the torc he wears. First of his treasures. After HRUNTING.

No funeral is held for BEOWULF gone. None mourn him. WIGLAF is mourned by a few. For they think him dead. Hires he thirteen doughty men to row him and his hoard to other lands. For fear those who know him will seek to claim it. Ic know not of his fate. Nor that of the bastard BEOWULFS black blade.

B eowulf is born a man and dies a corpus. There is no soul still in him. Yet does he have a choice? Is there another way for him? Any man may do the same. Ic suppose that is the tales lesson. All tales have a lesson. Something about mens ways. Or womens. Or mayhaps it is merely about a cursed sword. There are many tales like that. And ic only tells it as ic remembers it. Ic do not write this tale. Tis old and many men know it. Ic am surprised ye do not.

Shame to ruin the night with this. There is still time afore the sun. Ic mean to make the most of it.  And prove meself a man.  If any care to listen.

# Afterward

When I released *A Boke of Gests* in 2021 I was elated. Two books in two years? I was convinced that from then on I would be able to produce a book every year. The prospect of such a regular pattern elated me. But the next book – this book – took me much more then a year. Here it is 2024 and I am just now getting this collection into your hands.

The interevening time – especially 2023 – was a rollercoaster. Financial woes, a new house, a mixed bag of collaborative projects, being featured at multiple local events... I handled neither the highs nor the lows well. When I was worried or upset, I couldn't write because my brain was scrambled. When I was happy, I didn't always write because my elation convinced me everything would work out. But writing doesn't just *work out* on its own – it requires actual *work*. Fortuitously a spurt of inspiration in the latter half of 2023 allowed me to produce that work and – if I may be so bold – to do it quite well.

I have been working for a decade to get a full length novel finished, to little luck, but I have completed over a score of short stories. And this is more than a balm for my imposter syndrome, for the writing of short fiction is difficult for many, yet is one of my favourite forms of storytelling. Media without an end – or an end far in the future – can be exhausting. Some-times, both as a reader and as a writer, it can be refreshing to sit down for an evening and get a complete narrative.

*A Boke of Swordes* is something I am incredibly proud of. A collection of stories with a strong throughline which each touch on violence, power, or desire in unique ways. Many of these stories helped me explore my own beliefs and perceptions in new ways, and nearly every one has planted in me new seeds for stories yet to come. It may be a few years late, but *A Boke of Swordes* is here and I like to think that it is a springboard into a new pattern of fiction - maybe not a book a year, but a continued evolution of what tales I have told before.

Some readers, less familiar with my history, might have been surprised when this collection opened with a lengthy poem. *Brother War* is, in some ways, an accident. But all the best poetry is. It began as a short set of verses – two or three – written during a poetry course in my undergraduate studies. I don't remember the prompt. I wanted to evoke the feeling of an epic poem, but didn't have the patience to complete it at the time, and I knew it. I wrote it around the same time that I began work on *The Boar and the Attainder* (one of my perpetual projects which someday, maybe soon, will see print), and included a few names and locations with little thought to how they would logically fit within the setting. Even after extensive additions, rewrites, and edits, I still couldn't place it exactly in the history of Eord. But that's okay, because poems (as well as many stories) should in my mind be a bit liminal – familiar yet confounding. And the sorrow and violence the poem paints serve as similarly familiar and confounding parallels to the tales which follow.

Perhaps it is expected in a book titled *A Boke of Swordes*, but the second entry is just as chivalric and honour-obsessed as the first. Ever since I was young, *Sir Gawain and the Green Knight* was one of my favourite poems (specifically the Tolkien translation), and even before I knew I wanted to be a writer I knew I wanted to retell it someday. But I knew the time had to be right. And after my efforts with *Y Knew Robyn Hode* I figured the time *might* be right. I was daunted my a task I had given myself, but continued onwards nonetheless, and began the story which would become *The Henge Knight*. My first intention when approaching the project was to dechristianize a fundamentally christian poem. In rereading the original poem as I wrote, I swiftly realized that by telling a pagan form of the story, it was unlikely for the motif of chastity to be as prevalent – and indeed, the poem's treatment of women is often less kind than I would like – and so *consent* became the major motif in the story. There was a brief moment of doubt as, when I was nearly done with the piece, David Lowery's excellent deconstructive *Sir Gawain and the Green Knight* hit theatres, but on viewing I found that my adaptation was indeed still distinct.

I told myself as I was writing that I would love to retell the famous tale of Gawain's testing again – maybe even two more times – in other styles, but I think that unlikely to happen, both due to the wealth of stories I would like to finish and because I am very happy with the tale I have set down already. Though, despite the fact that this tale may never be retold by me, it is in itself a member of the noble tradition of reinvention, as the Arthur's England of *The Chalice and the Noble Blood* is notedly different than the one depicted here. It is this newer, more individualistic version of Camelot that I am most likely to revisit.

*The Hill of Cold Silver* takes its name from a small module I wrote but never ran for the Swedish roleplaying game *Trudvang Chronicles*, though the actual contents are much divorced. It serves as both a sequel of sorts to *The Chalice and the Noble Blood* from *A Boke of Gests* as well as an introduction to the tragic Sir Childe – a figure who has lived in my mind for some time and who is a tool for me to explore a world inspired by the weird fiction of Robert W. Chambers and Ambrose Bierce. I would also be remiss if I did not acknowledge that my fascination with the works of Tanith Lee likely greatly influenced this entry. At one time this collection was going to include an homage to Conan the Cimmerian, writing a tale of a similar dark-haired conqueror-king in his final days which – if you changed the names – could stand in for the ultimate fate of Robert E. Howard's famous character himself. But, after writing barely a few sentences, I realized that (as much as I enjoy Howard) I do not at this point in my life have much interest in writing a 'traditional' swords and sorcery tale, where brawn and confidence rule when wit reaches its end. Instead I resolved to write a tale of similar concept, but focused on a more cerebral and tortured hero, whose escapades would tend more towards the weird than the fantasy. Thus came this tale, of a knight tortured by history and facing the enchantment of philosophy, his questionable victory being found in surrender.

*The Burned Man* originally began its life as a concept for a time-travel adventure for the fantasy *Hârn* setting. However, in trying to figure out how to make it into a playable scenario, I found myself outlining a short story. Swiftly this led to me desiring not to be restrained by any previous setting, and relocated it into a setting I played with during my yearly Inktober practice in 2022. The story of a fundamentally bad man and misguided vengeance, *The Burned Man* is my second attempt at a time-travel story. And, though it is a bit more esoteric than *At Eternity's Gate* in its mechanisms, I was glad for the reader responses which implied its logic held just as strongly, if not moreso (despite the fact that much of the truth is obscured to the reader as much as to Donals t'Gelt).

I am incredibly proud of how short *The Hurt* is (a pride I share to some degree also with *To Die on Humphrey's Hill* later in this collection). As intimated earlier, it is sometimes deceptively difficult to write an effective 'short' story – I cannot count the number of times I've spoken with novelists who swear that they could never write a short story (though I urge everyone to try).

The idea for this story came to me after seeing a cinema showing of Paul Verhoeven's satirical masterpiece *Starship Troopers*. This was of course not my first viewing, but on leaving the theatre, I was struck by the idea that the conception of pain may shift with the advancement of medical technology. What true penalty is there for risking life and limb if Dr. Crusher can fix it in an afternoon? And could this not be especially damaging to the young folk who enlist in the military just out of public school? We are shaped by our experiences in youth – and especially our mistakes – and moving the goalposts for what constitutes a life-destroying act of daredeviltry could very well change what it is to be human.

*The Scent of Witch-Iron*, like the other Sir Childe story in the collection had its orgins in – to some degree – tabletop roleplaying. Every year I try to run a game for my sister's birthday, and one year I wrote an adventure which I later adapted into this story – similar to how *The Chalice and the Noble Blood* came into being. I had nicked the name from a previous adventure I had written (also for *Trudvang*), since I thought it was too strong of a title to let die. My inspiration here was certainly some combination of Tanith Lee and Ambrose Bierce yet again, as I continued to fine-tune the dying dream-world of Sir Childe, haunted by forgotten gods and greedy yet distant wizard-kings. As an exercise in tone I was quite happy, but the nihilistic exultation of the villain and his adherants – perhaps sharing something with the classical Stoics – seemed to resonate especially well with my test readers (to the point that one suggested I cut the majority of the story so that it could skip to the minstrel faster).

*To Die on Humphrey's Hill* came out of a desire to write a short scary story for Halloween a couple years back. I was very short on ideas, but knew that I wanted the end to be ambiguous in a similar manner to *A City Man*. I have long been a fan of early modern horror, but have not delved excessively into writing it. What prompted this idea specifically is hard to say, though I may have recently watched Vincent Price in *Witchfinder General*. Regardless of the origin, I quickly became enamoured with the mechanics of early rifles, and decided to use the strenuous task of reloading as a tempo tool to drive the story. Additionally (as I often tend towards) I wanted to keep the setting as vague as possible so the reader could paint their own impressions. Is this Europe? North America? Another world? The idea was to keep it as formless yet as familiar as the concept of fear itself, a theme which I think continues through into the conculsion.

The next story, *Skin Like Ink*, was originally supposed to be saved for the next collection, but as I was finishing this one I decided that I liked 13 stories more than 12, so threw this one in to round it out. I think it fits well here though, and better each time I consider it. This was a very personal story, and allowed me to express emotions and worries that don't get a chance to come through in many of my stories. There's the scoietal pressures present in most of the rest of the stories in this collection, as well as a pulsing sexuality and frustration, which dogs the tale. Questions of identity, worth, and personal power are all laid at the mercy of the pen. And the relationship between Viv and Liv allowed me to revisit feelings I have not had in a very long time between close friends (love you, Colin). Beyond the personal weight carried in the story, this is another tale – like *The Chalice and the Noble Blood* – which I believe begins to tie together the greater body of my work, as dreams which perhaps rhyme with other tales touch on Ollie's worried brow.

A grim tale, which even I am uncertain whether it is more critical of organized religion or of war, *A Violent and Jealous* love came out of an impromptu story a character I was playing in the same long-running *Trudvang* game that inspired other stories in this book told to help others explain his fears and drives better. The character which originally told this story was a temple knight, much in the pattern of Sir Guy, but who was too afraid to abandon his sword for fear of exactly what occurs in the tale. War harms, and violence never really leaves either the victim or the perpetrator. Even in finding some sort of peace, there is always the danger that what has come before can come again, and blind faith can trap us in cycles of abuse which are sometimes impossible to escape. In my mind this is perhaps the grimmest tale I have ever written, and in actuality I like to imagine life is not quite so damning.

Like many of my stories, *The Last Swords of Mars* was born out of a dream. I originally expected it to be much longer, but it's not always up to me how these things come out. The story is one of complete ecological collapse, and of time causing science to pass through the sieve of myth and become magic. There is victory, ultimately, but as the reader we know that this victory is only in the short term, and that Plato is lying to himself. Simlar to the tales of Sir Childe, this one doubtless owes some DNA to Conan, but also owes a great debt (however terrible) to the terrifying reality of Earth's own impending doom. There are things past peoples knew which have been forgotten, and truths which we refuse to admit to ourselves for fear of somehow making them real.

This book as a whole has a lot of roots in tabletop roleplaying games, and *Night-Black and Sorrow-Sounding* is yet another example. It came out of a writing excersize driven by the excellent solo RPG *Artefact* by Jack Harrison, where one journals the life of a magical item. I took the bullet points and ideas from my initial encounter with that game and expanded it into the sad tale of an elfen blade long-lost from its master.

Samurai dramas have long been a favourite of mine, ever since watching *Throne of Blood* and reading James Clavell's *Shogun*. In fact, the original inspiration for my world of Eord was for it to be a place to tell samurai dramas in a pseudo-european setting. The constant tug-of-war between too many contrasting yet equally important vows in an esoteric and rigid feudal society lends itself well to tragedy, a genre I love dearly, but also allows for complex explorations of love and morality. Despite this interest, I knew that I did not have the experience to write an epic in the style of Shogun, and so, when the idea for a story came to me, I resolved that it should be short (though I did not anticipate quite how short *Mother Blood* would end up being). I spent a couple years – amongst my other research – learning what I could of Edo society, including reading Yamamoto Tsunetomo's *Hagakure* and Miyamoto Musashi's *Go Rin no Sho* and conferring with Payton Calderon, a graduate friend of mine who has lived and studied in Japan for some time. My goal was to create an impossible puzzle, where neither the hero nor the antagonist were entirely correct, yet neither could escape the vows they had made and their own code of honour and morality. I also hoped to capture some of the calm, yet subtly intense, tone of Japanese storytelling. Initially I considered avoiding all proper nouns or Japanese terms, but ultimately landed on proper research and thoughtful presentation being more respectful than hiding my inspiration. I would love to write more tales in Edo Japan, but I doubt I will – I have given my offering, and I would hate to write too much without the appropriate cultural context, which for a longer work I believe would require much more extensive research as well as (likely) immersion. Interestingly, this story has been called both the most optimistic and the most cruel of my tales, depending on the reader, and so I imagine that the complexity of tone I aimed for has been achieved in some form.

The final story in the collection has been its own journey. When I finished *I Knew Robyn Hode* – which is still one of my proudest achievements – I told myself that I would never again write a story so difficult to sight-read or grok for a modern audience. Yet as soon as the end of that tale was in sight I began the research for *The Bastard Beowulf*. I couldn't say what exactly inspired me to begin the project, since as a child I read Radice and Baldick's translation of *Beowulf* (on my own time, not for school) and hated it (though at the time I loved the CGI film – take that as you will). I found it incredibly dry, and hated the constant flip-flopping between praising the Norse gods and the Christian faith. Yet, for whatever reason, at the end of 2020 I gathered up nearly a half-dozen translations of the classic poem and dove in.

I wanted to create a version of the hero Beowulf that could exist in a space similar to Robin Hood – a character so widely known and discussed from so many sources that it was difficult or impossible to identify one *true* version of his tale. To this I added the conceit that the teller would be a common, likely inebriated, man at a feast, reciting a well-known tale to a foreigner.

I began my exploration of the text with the Chickering translation – the one I had most often recommended to me and ended up being my favourite *traditional* translation (I also appreciated having the Old English on the facing page) – from which I gained much of the feeling for the language. This copy was given to me ages ago by an OE professor who I never actually took a class from, but bugged in her office hours for a few months before

222

her retirement; a special thanks to Jill Frederick, who may never see this, but had a big hand in planting the seed all those years ago. It was here, after finishing Chickering, that I realized that I actually adored the poem. Next came Heaney's contemporary translation – another highly requested iteration, which Professor Frederick took especial umbrage with in my memory – which I found uninteresting, self-important, and unfaithful to the language of the original. Forgive me if this is your preferred reading. From there I moved on to Headley's raucous and utterly entertaining modern translation, which both informed some of the language and offered me ideas on the characterization of the dragon, Grendel, and his mother. My final translation I read was Tolkien's, which I had been excited for even when I still thought I hated the poem. I did not like it. But what I did like was the scholarly material he wrote surrounding it, which served to inform even more details in my final story about Grendel and his kin, the dragon, and the inclusion of the Christian priest. I originally meant to read Wright's translation and then attempt a reread of the original hated version from my childhood, but figured four back-to-back readings was enough.

Along the way I also encountered various sideways adaptations – Egger's *The Northman*, Gardner's *Grendel*, and Crichton's *Eaters of the Dead*. In each of these I found things to love about how they approached the material, yet in each I also stumbled slightly, wondering if the tale I was telling was different enough than what had come before; Grendel especially made me pause, but upon consideration I realized that the intention of my tale of terror was parallel, but not aligned with Gardner's opus.

Tales change easily in the telling, and this one was no different. For a long time now the Bastard in the title has referred – in my mind – not only to the titular character, but to the adaptation itself. I am not certain when the idea of the altered third act entered my mind, or when I decided that Hrunting would be a cursed artefact driving the action in the latter half of the story, but I did not initially see *The Bastard Beowulf* being so overtly critical of so-called *traditional* masculinity, nor the propogation of violence being brought on by violence. Much like in *The Henge Knight*, what began as a slightly more traditional retelling swiftly became something else, and the tale which resulted is barely the triumphant celebration of manhood that the original poem is. Also like that earlier bit of Arthuriana, this was a story that – even as I was writing it – I was convinced that I would revisit someday and tell in a new way. Perhaps that will come to pass, but likely not (though I do intend to write about poor, maligned Unferth in my next collection, and have already begun the first draft). Also, this story was originally written in even more esoteric language than what it ended up with - not quite as strange as *Y Knew Robyn Hood*, yet, for some reason, harder to understand for my test readers. I am nothing if not stubborn, and I resisted simplifying the language - despite how difficult it was to write - for over two years before finally entirely rewriting the story. The first step was replacing all the long Ss which I had carried over from *Y Knew Robyn Hode*, and then one by one I began removing various alterations I had made to the spelling and grammar conventions of modern Enlgish. And these changes were, ultimately, for the better; rules (and grammar) exist to be broken, but only when the time is right, and the esoteric language added nothing to the story.

*The Bastard Beowulf* gathers themes that permeated all the earlier tales in this collection, grinds them with a mill wheel, and vomits them bloody and glistening into the river of the readers' minds: the importance of names, societal pressure, self-doubt, greed, the impermanence of the past, pride (and the fall), violence (and his bride, regret), conscious denial, guilt, grief... *The Bastard Beowulf* is a caustic slurry of unhappy humanities, and the perfect ending to this chaotic boke of swordes.

*A Boke of Swordes* has been the result of three years of work - in some ways much less time than my first collection (which includes sotires from as early as 2010, albeit with a decade of editing) and in some ways much more (or maybe it just feels that way). It is also an attempt to write along a theme (however vague), rather than finding a theme to fit the stories I had already written – or intended to write. If you have read this far - whether you enjoyed the ride (in part or in whole) or not – then I have done my job, and am satisfied to have supplied you with a few evenings of reading of the bizarre, the introspective, and the depraved. I promise next time I'll put in some kinder stories. Probably.

F. Killian

February 2024

# Acknowledgments

There are so many people who are important in my life – who make creating possible. If I have brushed shoulders with you even once, be assured that you have had an influence on my work. What follows is merely a small sampling of the people who made this book possible, but if I missed you (as well as if your name is here), know that I am endlessly grateful.

First I would like to thank my test-readers, who are the first to be subjected to my efforts: Tori Liston, Luke Murphy, Alex, Em, my grandmother Julianne Johnston, Robb Dudock, and Matt Brisbin. Each has given valuable suggestions, constructive input, and/or emotional responses which have guided the editing process and helped craft a final product which I am beyond pleased with. Putting these books together as a solo artist is no mean feat, but it would not be possible without critical eyes on the work.

And on the subject of those who have literally made this effort possible, I cannot thank my paying Patrons enough. What comes in from your support has allowed me to fund food and research over the long months. These include: Nathan Goree, David Robson, Carissa Herbrand, Ross Jennings, Soleil Rintoul, Terra Jansma, Malilda, Brady Murphy, and Luke Murphy. I'd also like to thank my audience, including: Dan Parke, Andréas Asklepiódotou, Alex, Christina Millermon, Samuel McKinney, and Gerard Raffernau, as well as various Patrons who have come and gone over the years.

I am quite a few years out from my undergraduate studies, and still not quite into graduate school, but I would like to still thank a few academic influences. First of all, I owe Kevin Zepper a thank you, because his name was inadvertantly exempted from the previous book, as well as because at least one of the stories in this book (*Brother War*) has its roots in his class. Jill Frederick, as mentioned in the afterward, deserves thanks for the seed which eventually became *The Bastard Beowulf*, as well as fuelling my fascination with the word *Hwæt*.

A special thanks goes to Payton Calderon, whose advice when approaching Mother Blood was invaluable. My family also deserves endless praise. The support from my parents – Charles and Jennifer Smith – has kept me on the straight-and-narrow and filled me with confidence in myself. My siblings – Lillie Smith and Soeil Rintoul – have shown excitment and interest at my endeavours. And my Grandma JuLie has been not only supportive, but materially constructive in her aid in editing a few of the pieces herein. And, though it is smaller than it once was, I owe a great debt to the members of the Menomonie Writers' Guild, whose community and interest in sharing has inspired me and grounded me. Nate Goree as well deserves specific thanks - for nearly a decade his HEMA teaching has inspired in me a love of the sword (or sworde, as the case may be). The theory and practice I have learned in concert with him have informed my writing of action sequences - and was a primary inspiration for good portions of *The Burned Man*.

Though many of them are incapable of reading this, having passed on, and the rest will likely never read this, a scant few of the authors who have inspired me in this collection are: Tanith Lee, J. R. R. Tolkien, Ambrose Bierce, Robert W. Chambers, Robert E. Howard, the poets of both *Beowulf* and *Sir Gawain and the Green Knight*, T. H. White, Sir Walter Scott, Frank Herbert, James Clavell, James Gerdner, Michael Crichton, the various au-thors of the Icelandic Sagas, Yamamoto Tsunetomo, Miyamoto Musashi, Howell D. Chickering, Maria Dahvana Headley, Paul Kingsnorth, Lee M. Hollander, Clive Barker, Dave Sim, Robert A. Heinlein, and many more I'm certain

And, as mentioned previously, tabletop gaming has had a large influence on much of this collection - perhaps even moreso than the last. For this reason, I must thank all those who have played with me over the years, but especially those who played in my last two large games I ran. Lillie Smith's endless focus on the goal is a reminder to always keep momentum moving towards the end of a story. Malachi Becker's inquisitiveness and constant innovation has led to the revelation of many mysteries, and conspiracies to-wards many more - my storytelling is more mysterious for his input. Sebas-tian Barth – longtime friend and brother – feeds my thirst for the brooding, the dark, and the brutal. Mitchell Smith's endless excitement means that it is next to impossible for me to ever forget that the stories I tell have meaning and resonance. Jonathan Mielke's shared fascination with the past has of-ten resulted in me discovering new truths and falling down new rabbitholes in my research; not to mention that in his unfailing fascination with hon-our and duty he will likley find multiple parallels in my writing, and in this collection specifically. Ell, who I have known nearly as long as Sebastian, fuelled my passion for my tabletop hobby in college and her friendship has been invaluable in many dark times. Nate Bakke's fellowship – is shared love of Tolkien and his constant energy, devotion, and innovation – for over a decade has had a serious impact on my storytelling, life, and confidence. Stephen Harmon's pragmatic assuredness serves often to remind me (and others at the table) where the goal lies when the path grows dim. Joe Nosie, another old friend, shares their excitement for storytelling with me and is party to more than a few obscure pieces of media which few others in my circles can engage with me on. Joey Wurm's boundless joy and eager explorations of the world around them help remind me that the world is larger, stranger, and more exciting than I sometimes imagine. And Alex Hett.

Alex deserves more than just one line. Indeed, I considered briefly dedicating this book to them, but decided that I would save that for a larger project, or one whose subject reminds me more accurately of all they have done for me. Alex is endlessly supportive in my work and provides some of the most insightful comments on my works in progress. As a partner and as a friend their support is invaluable. Sharing these years with them – and finding a house together – has created a level of support which I have rarely felt in my life, and I strive only to be as helpful to them in their pursuits as they are in mine.

To all the above, all those to come, and all those I've missed, thank you.

# About the Author

F. Killian lives with his dog Howard, his partner Alex, and a furry goblin named Jiji in a hundred year old home. A lifetime of interest in myth, fantasy, and rumour has bred in him a healthy fascination with the spiritual, historical, and occult. When he is not rolling dice on the tabletop or drawing, he is searching for peace in the expansive forests and hills of the frigid midwest or keeping company with the various goblins, ghouls, and gnomes which follow him wherever he goes. He is the author of A Boke of Gests and various small RPG products.

He can be contacted on his various social media pages via:
linktr.ee/F.Killian